D0765502

DISCARDED

Also by Steven Barnes

Great Sky Woman

Dream Park
with Larry Niven

The Descent of Anansi
with Larry Niven

The Kundalini Equation

The Legacy of Heorot
with Larry Niven and Jerry Pournelle

The Barsoom Project

Gorgon Child

Achilles' Choice
with Larry Niven

The California Voodoo Game
with Larry Niven

Firedance

Beowulf's Children
with Larry Niven and Jerry Pournelle

Blood Brothers

Iron Shadows

Far Beyond the Stars

Saturn's Race
with Larry Niven

Charisma

Lion's Blood

Zulu Heart

Star Wars: The Cestus Deception

Shadow Valley

Shadow Valley
Steven Barnes

Ballantine Books
New York

Prescott Valley Public Library

Shadow Valley is a work of fiction. Names, characters, places, and incidents are the products of the author's imagination or are used fictitiously. Any resemblance to actual events, locales, or persons, living or dead, is entirely coincidental.

Copyright © 2009 by Steven Barnes

Maps © by Toni Young

All rights reserved.

Published in the United States by Del Rey, an imprint of The Random House Publishing Group, a division of Random House, Inc., New York.

DEL REY is a registered trademark and the Del Rey colophon is a trademark of Random House, Inc.

Library of Congress Cataloging-in-Publication Data
Barnes, Steven.
Shadow Valley / Steven Barnes.
p. cm.
Sequel to: Great Sky Woman.
ISBN 978–0–345–45903–9 (alk. paper)
1. Prehistoric peoples—Tanzania—Fiction. I. Title.
PS3552.A6954S47 2009
813'.54—dc22
2009006474

Printed in the United States of America on acid-free paper

www.delreybooks.com

2 4 6 8 9 7 5 3 1

First Edition

Book design by Laurie Jewell

For Octavia Estelle Butler
(1947–2006)

Many dream of better worlds.
Few help create them.

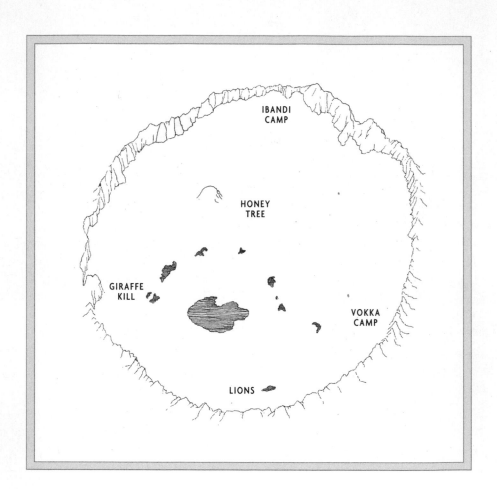

IBANDI
CAMP

HONEY
TREE

GIRAFFE
KILL

VOKKA
CAMP

LIONS

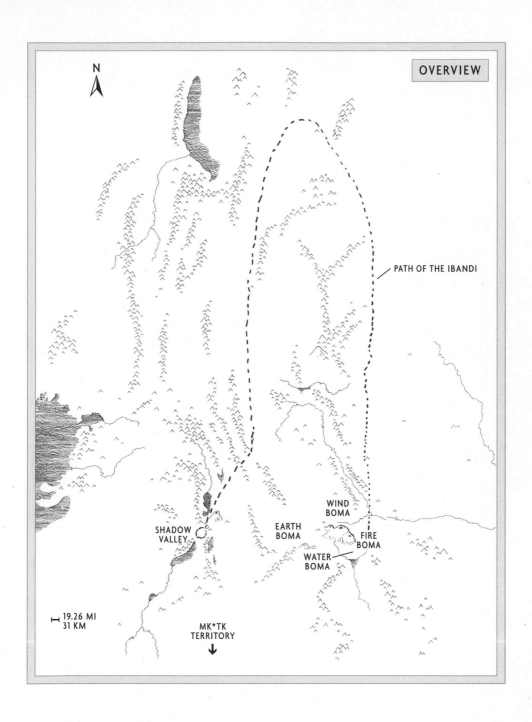

N

OVERVIEW

PATH OF THE IBANDI

WIND
BOMA

EARTH
BOMA

FIRE
BOMA

SHADOW
VALLEY

WATER
BOMA

19.26 MI
31 KM

MK*TK
TERRITORY

Who is more wretched than he who has
no gods, yet dreams of demons?

—MOTHER STILLSHADOW

On the first day there was Kori, nothing.

Out of Kori came num, and num birthed the jowk, the lake of fire, in whose depths dwelled a butterfly and a spider. The spider wove num into fibers, making himself a dream world. The butterfly wove num into a glowing egg cocoon bright enough to shame the stars. The spider wove bones for the egg, and thus the first man was born. The spider and the butterfly were pleased, and let the man play in the dream. And then made other men, other creatures, and let them play as well. Because it was his nature, the spider gave them Hunt, the game of life and death.

The spider thought the game so grand that he wove Great Sky into being and lived there and named himself Father Mountain.

The butterfly loved her children also and wove Great Earth and lived there as Great Mother. She thought the spider's game cruel and gave her children Love, the game of male and female, so that through sex they could free a little num and awaken from the dream, if only for a moment.

In the fullness of time, Father Mountain calls for their bones. The egg cracks, the cocoon unravels, and the num returns to the jowk. The young and the sleeping are told that "You die, and then Father Mountain gives you new bones!"

The truth is that there is no "you" to give them to. There is only jowk.

Jowk *is what looks out through your eyes, and back at you through the eyes of another.*

The egg thinks it is you. Most eggs fear the day Father Mountain returns their fragments to the earth. Most will struggle against death and would struggle even if struggling were the only sin. But then, the door opens. There are no words for that knowing.

Most think this First Way is the only path through the darkness.

But there is the Second Way: to awaken within the dream. It is not easy or even possible for any but dream dancers and hunt chiefs. And most of them will never awaken fully. But those few . . .

As you know the taste of your own mouth, they know that we come from Kori, *and to Kori, the nothing, we return.*

They also know that the Nothing is everything.

—IBANDI SECRET TEACHING

Shadow Valley

Chapter One

Summer's warm rains had long since riven the earth, then dried again to dust. Three moons would wax and wane before the winter rivers swelled within their graveled banks.

Hot Tree had lived most of her adult life in Fire boma, the bamboo-walled cluster of huts a day's walk southeast of Great Sky. Now her hair was streaked with white, her brown skin deeply wrinkled, her breasts empty sacks. Years had cooled the fire in her dancing feet. She felt both hollow and heavy, and knew it would not be long before Father Mountain summoned her bones.

So much had changed in the past few moons.

For generations unknown the Ibandi had lived within the sheltering shadows of the mountains called Great Sky and Great Earth. The peaks were home to Father Mountain and Great Mother, whose timeless passion had birthed the world.

Three moons ago, Great Sky had exploded, the cataclysm wreathing the sky in stinking smoke and spewing rivers of boiling mud down its verdant slopes. Trees had been wrenched up by the roots, tumbling like dead brush. The Ibandi hunt chiefs had died. Some believed the god Himself had perished, but Hot Tree did not, though she well believed that the explosion was a sign of His displeasure with their wickedness.

Whatever the truth might be, a second disaster soon struck. From the south came the Mk*tk, brutal men who killed many and even stole three of the sacred dream dancers. The bloody war had almost undone the Ibandi.

If Hot Tree's daughter had not brought her here to Water boma, Tree did not know what might have become of her.

Much had changed since then. Sky Woman, the girl who had earned her name by climbing Great Sky, had fled north with half the tribe, accompanied by her lover, Frog Hopping, who had climbed Great Sky with her in search of wisdom. Some said he was a mighty hunter, but Tree had never been impressed by Frog. Both his elder brothers, greater providers by far, had died on the great mountain, but their widows, Ember and Flamingo, had traveled north with Frog.

Hot Tree inhaled deeply. The afternoon air reeked of burnt grass. She stood just outside the boma's bamboo gate at the edge of the wide blackened zone singed every moon to deny hiding space to leopards. Beyond that dark space, grass grew knee-high, and beyond that the plain was broken by round and flat-topped trees and dusky scrub ranging out to a thinly ridged northern horizon. The air smelled of dust and burnt thornbush.

Her old eyes could just barely distinguish a hyena's brownish-gray pelt, lurking a spear's throw from the edge of the blackened zone.

Another four or five spear casts distant loped three giraffes, two adults and one calf half the height of its parents. Even as she watched, they dissolved into the shimmering air, much like the cloud creatures the strange boy Frog had so often babbled of.

Night Song approached from behind. Hot Tree would have known that tread among tens of others: Song's rotten left knee caused her to drag that leg a bit. No hunter's accident or thieving disease had caused this, only that great hyena, time itself.

"I wonder where they are?" she said, not realizing she had spoken aloud.

"Stillshadow?" Night Song's hair had faded to gray stubble. At times it was difficult to see the nimble young dancer trapped within her twisted, heavy frame. Despite her age, Song's voice was still honey, and her dark eyes brimmed with curiosity. Song was Hot Tree's sister-in-law, an old and valued friend. "Gazelle? Sky Woman?"

"Yes. And Snake," she said. "Sweet Snake. When he was young, and I was not yet old . . ." Her smile was both bitter and sweet. Despite the intervening years, the memory remained a deep, swift ache.

"Do you wish you had gone with them?" Song asked.

Hot Tree sighed. "It is strange. Fire boma seemed so hollow. Then, I thought I was too old to go along. Now I fear I was not young enough to stay." The old ways were shattered. If . . . *if* the Ibandi could rebuild, that new world belonged to young skin, not old bones, even such sacred bones as Mother Stillshadow's.

"Perhaps they will return," Night Song ventured. "They will learn it is safe and come back to us."

Hot Tree made a clucking sound. "And how will they learn that?"

"What?"

"How will they see that it is safe? Are we to send runners? We do not know where they are."

Song shivered. "I made a song," she said. Many of their people forged habits that complemented their birth names. "I sing it to my daughters, and as I go to sleep . . ." She described it, sang a bit. It spoke of the old woman who had birthed so many of them, named most of them, and whose acolytes sung the sun to life each dawn. "Perhaps she will hear my song," she concluded, "and they will return. . . ." Her voice trailed off, as if unable to convince even herself.

In the eyes of the Ibandi, Stillshadow was Great Mother incarnate. The old woman's voice held the songs, her feet taught the dances. In former days she had walked the Circle once a year, bringing medicines and knowledge, knitting Earth, Wind, Fire and Water bomas together. She healed, dreamed names for their children and in the ripeness of time brought talented girl children into the ranks of the dream dancers.

Hot Tree cupped a handful of soil in her hands. "Things are not as they were before Great Sky died." The earth trickled out between her fingers. "Heaven and earth are far apart. It is said that in the last days, old bones will dance again. Boar Tracks says the hunters have seen . . . *things* on Great Sky."

Night Song asked, "What manner of things?"

"Thorn Cloud told me that a ghost roams the slopes." Once, such a thing would have been unthinkable. But that was another time, before so much death and fear. Before the shape of the world had changed. Surely, power great enough to reshape a mountain could split the thorn walls separating life and death. "Perhaps it is a hunt chief's spirit."

"Then heaven's gates have opened," Night Song said.

The air seemed to take on a deeper chill. If heaven's walls were breeched, might not hell's gape as well? Good men went to Great Sky. But beneath the earth, locked behind Great Mother's protective arms, demons raged, devouring the souls of evil men.

Chapter Two

Through tufted grass, across soil not much richer than sand, a hand of Ibandi walked single file toward the horizon. Far to their left, the sun was dying.

Three walked with the grace and confidence of hunters. Leopard Eye and Leopard Paw were tall, lean young men who shared the same face, twins who had been raised together in Water boma. The third, Rock Knife, had come to manhood in Earth boma. The Leopard twins were the only surviving sons of Stillshadow, the head dream dancer. For two moons they had been their mother's primary guardians. Walking by her side was Sky Woman, the girl some still called T'Cori—a name that was actually no name at all. The root word, *Kori,* meant a void, an empty space.

The old woman called Stillshadow leaned upon a bamboo spear haft and stepped as if her hips were as fragile as eggshells. She raised her withered hand, a sign for stillness and silence. She squatted, her dusty heels raised high. Stillshadow stirred around in the dirt with her fingertips, and closed her eyes.

For many breaths the three hunters watched the dream dancer. They slowed their breathing, pulling it down to their stones to cool their impatient blood. At long last, the gray-hair stirred from her trance.

"What did you see?" Leopard Eye asked. His hands were knobby, his mouth broad and smiling even in repose. Quick to laughter and slow to rage, he was generally thought the best hunter of the men who had followed Frog Hopping and Great Sky Woman on their trek north. Most of them were now to the northeast, traveling toward their next resting place.

Stillshadow, Sky Woman and their escorts had gone to the west, seeking visions. They would catch up with their people tomorrow night perhaps. Or the day after. The walking families would find a camping ground, then wait for them. Two tens of tens of families left a very clear trail.

Neither brother had been raised by their flesh mother or father. As with all dancers' male offspring, they had been raised by Stillshadow's cousins and siblings.

"What do you see?" echoed Rock Knife, shortest of the three.

"Thirst," Stillshadow groaned, eyes still closed tightly.

"You see what I feel." Leopard Paw scratched his side, plucking out a little purple itch-thorn between the thick nails of his thumb and first finger. "Is there water? Plants to draw the leaf-eaters? My belly wants meat." He slapped his stomach. For the last two moons they had traveled endlessly, never spending more than a few days in any one place. Stillshadow said the ancestors demanded this sacrifice in exchange for future happiness.

"Quiet, now." T'Cori sniffed the air. She stood, spread her arms wide and turned in a slow circle. Her eyes, ears and nose absorbed hands of hands of scents and sights and sounds. The breeze swam with mint and fire cactus. Click beetles mated in the tall grass, burring with pleasure as their love made new life. The air chilled as clouds shaded the sun.

T'Cori crouched on her hands and knees, hovering in trance, a gift of the plant children and her endless years of breath control, prayer and sacred dance. With their help, she could see through the world of men into that of dream, and perhaps even into the *jowk* itself.

Her gaze shifted to her mentor, lost in her own visions. Her *num*, the field of living light surrounding Stillshadow's body, flared. For one brief moment it seemed bright and clear enough to transform night into day.

"There," the old woman said at last, pointing to the east. "I will find my answer there."

They walked a time, until after a quarter-day they heard hiccoughs of baboon laughter floating through the yellow grass. Stillshadow stood, one hand pressed to the small of her back. Her face flattened with pain but then regained a dignified calm as she walked toward the chuckles.

"Careful!" Leopard Eye called. "There is much danger."

"For you, my son. But then," she reminded him, "baboons do not like leopards."

T'Cori shook her head. "Mother . . ."

The great dreamer grinned. "It will be good. Look." Stillshadow knelt and brushed the earth with her fingertips. The soil was torn, speckled with blood and bits of bone. "Something bad happened here. What do you see?"

"I don't know. . . ."

"This is not a *knowing* thing," the old woman replied. "It is a thing to *see*."

T'Cori closed her eyes. Freed from vision, her mind caught memories like fish in a net. At such times it seemed that she could touch yesterday, and the yesterdays before that.

And then she saw.

The baboon troop had spent a long, lazy day eating dates and lean dry-season grasshoppers. As the wind shifted, three brown-backed males at the outskirts caught a strong sour meat-eater scent. They growled and barked. The rest of the troop crouched low, submitting to them completely. The females grabbed their young and fled to the circle's center. The younger bucks gathered around the females and their pups and bared their teeth, snarling.

The leopard's belly had sharp teeth. The rains had not fallen in moons, and as the water holes dried, the flesh she so desperately needed had wandered far.

The two or three big bucks moved around the outer edge of the troop, pacing back and forth, eyes fixed on the starving cat. The troop did not panic or run away. In other days, the leopard might have avoided baboons, but this was not one of those days. Baboon was juicy and delicious. Emboldened by hunger the leopard was at the height of her strength and power and aggression.

She advanced. The three big bucks, followed by several younger shaggy brown males, scrambled to meet her.

T'Cori blinked as she finished her dream of torn branches, footprints, and bloody soil. "I have seen this before," she said. "Baboons are smaller than leopards, but . . . they are many and the leopard is only one. They come from all directions. Look! Only scratched earth and blood remain. Just scraps of bone and fur, flung in all directions. Baboons frighten me. No other monkey acts so."

Stillshadow stood ten paces from the troop's edge, not close enough to alarm them. Three males shambled toward her. The old woman stood as motionless as a tree, even when the apes bared their fangs and barked in chorus. She closed her eyes.

The baboons circled her, barked a few more times and then retreated. The troop watched her as she opened her eyes and backed away, watching them the entire time.

"Mother," T'Cori said when the old woman returned. "Did they . . . speak to you?" The four-legged made signs any hunter could read. But speech? This would be marvelous beyond even Frog's imagination.

"I heard them," Stillshadow replied. "There is game and water—" she pointed north "—beyond the horizon. There. Now come. We will find our people."

Chapter Three

Beneath a swollen skin of deep blue clouds, two tens of tens of Ibandi wandered north. For two moons now, most had looked to their trek father, Frog Hopping, for wisdom. Although he had lived only two tens of summers, they believed his climb up Great Father's treacherous south face had conferred wisdom beyond mortal years.

Frog was the height of the average Ibandi male but a bit thinner. His head sometimes balanced uneasily on his slender neck. His eyes were exceedingly bright, his hands nimble. Despite his slightness he was an expert climber and hunter. His hair was a mass of tight black coils and a thin thorny beard speckled his narrow cheeks.

Only he and Sky Woman had survived the climb of Great Sky—although to save his honor they had lied and said Uncle Snake had completed it as well. Now Sky Woman shared his hut, and together they led twice ten tens of Ibandi northward to a new life in new lands.

By twos and fives the Ibandi walked behind them, through drought-stunted acacia trees and across cracked riverbeds littered with dead branches and bleached bones.

Once those bones had held flesh, enough flesh to feed their grumbling stomachs.

Bones that had once been living creatures, and that now pointed the way to the death awaiting all men.

"Come!" Frog called over his shoulder. "We shelter before the sun dies."

A small boy walked near him. The boy was thin, with a bald spot on the right side of his head and bright, questing eyes. Frog knew him as Bat Wing.

The boy and his mother were from the Wind boma. As they walked, the boy studied every bush, every stone, every dung beetle and mantis, his moon face seldom less than merry and inquisitive.

Frog had rarely seen the boy without a smile of welcome or curiosity. Had he himself ever been so light of spirit? Could he ever be again?

Bat Wing glanced back over his shoulder at the ten or so family groups in easy sight. Others were straggling along farther back. "Will we wait for Sky Woman?"

Frog forced himself to shrug. "She will find us."

Before the sun had moved a finger toward the horizon, they came upon the sparsely grassed banks of a trickling stream. A weeping wattle tree's spreading branches webbed the ground with shade. Careful to avoid ant nests and sharp rocks, they set their lean-tos and skin rolls for the night.

During rest times, food was shared within and between families. Whether the wanderers originated in Fire or Earth or Wind bomas, all now stood within the same circle, walking toward unknown horizons.

Just before the sun touched the western horizon, Frog went to find his mother, Gazelle Tears. She and his younger brother were on the far side of the shallow bowl chosen for the night's camping, near a tumble of fallen trees. He had just greeted her when a boisterous shout reverberated through the hills. "*Stillshadow!*" came the cry. "They are back! The dream dancers have returned!"

Worry flew from his heart. "At last."

His mother squatted at the side of their new fire, feeding it twigs. "You were afraid?" she asked. Time had sharpened his mother's shoulders and cheekbones. Her hair was streaked with gray but not yet white. Nor had she clipped that hair short as many other Ibandi women do when the loss of their moon-blood signaled entrance to the elders' circle.

"Of course not." The lie slipped from his tongue so quickly that he barely tasted it. It would not do to have his people know how heavy his heart grew whenever his love left his sight.

He was soon directed to the stream just south of the camp, where it burbled across mossy green rocks. There he found T'Cori and Stillshadow, filling gourds with fresh water. Game tracks dappled the ground around them. Perhaps this was the place they had sought?

T'Cori smiled up at him, but continued to busy herself with some little game that she and her teacher had been playing. To Frog, that smile had always been like the birth of a new sun.

To some, T'Cori seemed a sparrow. But Frog was not deceived by the long fine bones in her forearms and thighs. She was stronger than any hunter, any champion of the wrestling circle. Her strength, not his, had carried them to the top of Great Sky.

Her gleaming hair cascaded to her shoulders in tightly woven braids. Her hairline descended slightly at the center of her forehead. Like most dream dancers, she wore a deerskin covering both her breasts and her sexual organs.

All human beings had seven eyes: two on the face, two in the palms, one in each foot, and one in the the sexual organs—the seventh eye, the most powerful and precious. A dream dancer's sexuality was for her to gift and for no man to steal with hands or eyes or root.

T'Cori's eyes were the most remarkable thing about her: they were the color of yam skin, brown with greenish tints and speckles of yellow as bright as sunflowers. They were soft but piercing. He often wondered if they could see past his skin to the blood and marrow beneath.

Stillshadow cupped water from the stream with her hands, raising them and offering her apprentice a sip. Every time T'Cori bent, the old woman let it run out between her fingers. They laughed heartily, and then the game was repeated. He drew close enough to hear Stillshadow's whispers.

"Listen," Stillshadow said. "Whether flowing from the ground, touching your lips or cooling in your gourd all are water, yes?"

T'Cori nodded.

"How did you see water on Great Sky? Steam? Rain? Streams?"

"And there was more," T'Cori said. "Hard, clear water. There are no words to describe how cold it was. Even more, pieces of the cold hard water fell from the sky."

Frog cleared his throat, announcing his presence. "Old one," he said, "did Great Mother give you a vision?"

"Yes," Stillshadow said. "Soon. There." She pointed at the northern horizon, as she had countless times before. Then, as if her strength was spent, the crone's shoulders sagged, and she seemed to collapse. "I must rest." She shuffled off to find shade.

Frog scanned the shallow brown rise of the distant hills, their straggly thornbushes breaking a monotonous horizon.

A dust-colored hawk bent the branches of a bush only a spear's throw away. Its head rotated almost like an owl's, gazed at him and T'Cori.

"Blessings, winged sister," she said.

The hawk skawed, flapped its wings and climbed steeply into the sky.

"I wonder," Frog said, "if she knows something we don't."

"We have horizons to cross," T'Cori said, "but we *will* find it."

Frog wondered. "You are sure?"

"Very sure."

"I was worried about you," Frog said.

She trailed her fingers softly along his arm, sending sparks. "It was only three days. I was safe with Leopard. You know that."

"There are many kinds of danger."

T'Cori frowned. "What are you saying?"

"He has no wife," Frog said. "His root swells when he dreams of you."

"Ah. You see these things? You dance in the other world now?"

"No, but a man knows these things."

"So does a woman," she answered. "And no matter what he dreams, I am yours. Unless, of course, he needs me to make medicine with him." The corners of her mouth turned upward, hinting at mischief.

Frog made a clucking sound. "If you are to be his medicine, he had best be very, very sick. Sick enough to wilt his root." Could he demand that Leopard meet him in the wrestling circle? Certainly. And one day he might do that, if he wanted to eat dust a few times.

She rubbed cheeks with him, smooth against rough. "You have nothing to worry about."

Frog laughed. "I will be back to eat soon. We have yams and spring hare for dinner."

Her eyes sparkled. "A feast."

Frog headed off toward a circle of men, who were sharpening spears and knives. They waved as he approached.

Uncle Snake stood quiet and alone at the circle's edge. After the death of Frog's father, Baobab, Snake had hunted for food for his brother's family and cared for them. After his first wife's death, Snake had married Frog's mother and raised Frog. His left eye had been torn away by a lion many years before. A pale web of scars masked the left side of his face. His uncle's good right eye blinked as Frog approached. "I will go and see if the women need anything," he said.

"Uncle!" Frog protested. "Wait. Please. Sit with me." They squatted together, away from the others. The wind rustled around their ankles, rippling the grass.

"It is worst with the children," Snake said.

"What?" Frog asked.

"Their eyes are so bright," the old man whispered. "The young ones believe in this great man, this hero named Snake." His thin shoulders rounded forward. "Why would Father Mountain not give me a stronger heart?"

Frog knew his uncle's pain but could not ease it. After the Mk*tk war, the holy women had decided to climb Great Sky to ask Father Mountain and Great Mother for advice and aid. Seven had begun the climb, two had completed it. Four had died and one, Snake, had given up. But Frog and Sky Woman had lied to protect Snake, had made him a hero of the climb.

What a wonderful, blessed lie it had been. In that lie, Hawk Shadow had died on his feet instead of his knees, crawling away from the wolves. Fire Ant had died defending Sky Woman instead of trying to kill her. Snake had driven them on with the supernatural strength of his *num* instead of turning back like a coward.

His uncle, whose strength and courage had failed him, had been transformed by Frog into the strongest of them all. Was it wrong to protect the man who had fed and raised him?

He considered, then asked the question that itched at him. "When was the last time you took pleasure with my mother? She loves you, and you do not touch her."

Snake's lips twisted in annoyance. "Why do you say this?"

"I know my mother," Frog said. "When she is loved, she dances through her day." He paused. "She has not danced in moons."

"I am old," Snake said, "and my root-fire is low." Snake seemed unable to meet Frog's eyes. "I should steal *num* from Gazelle?"

Frog shook his head. "You cannot steal what is given freely. And I do not believe your root has wilted. Just a year ago, around the fire you bragged of how you made her sing in the tall grass." A hummingbird-swift shift of Snake's eyes told him his arrow had struck home. It was Snake's spirit that failed, not his flesh. "You have loved little since we came from the mountain. Since we began our journey. Is she so ugly to you now?"

Snake winced. "Do not say such things!"

"Are her breasts empty?" Frog bore in, deliberately provoking. Anger was better than self-pity. "Perhaps her eyes were brighter when she'd danced fewer winters. Has she lost a girl's easy step?"

Snake growled and raised his hand as if to strike his adopted son. He hesitated and lowered it again. "Do not speak of your mother so."

"Why don't you go to her?"

Snake's nostrils flared, but his tongue found no words.

"Uncle," Frog said, "as men, we think that all our strength comes from our muscle, our bones, our *num*. I think that is wrong. I think that a man is strong when his soul vine binds him to his woman."

"What of the hunt chiefs?" Snake retorted. "They lived without women, and were they not strongest of all?"

A good question. All had died, save the coward Boar Tracks, who had refused to attempt the climb of Great Sky.

Could the dead ones have been strongest of them all? When he, Frog, had done what they could not? All his life he had believed the songs and stories, but now he was not certain. "Were they? Did they? Uncle, they *all* had Ibandi women. Whenever a hunt chief's root hungered, he needed only walk down from the mountain and display it. You suffer no weakness. You believe you are no longer worthy."

Was that a *smile* tugging at Snake's lips? "Perhaps."

"Uncle . . . I was strong because I had the Nameless One, she we now call Sky Woman. You walked alone."

"And your brother Fire Ant?"

Frog flinched as if Snake had thrust a stick at his eye. "I do not speak of him."

Snake frowned. "Frog, he is dead. He died trying to save his people. There is nothing you could have done."

"Perhaps." Frog ground the ball of his foot into the dirt. When he finally replied, his voice was flat and harsh. "And if you could have been braver, stronger, you would have been. And can be now, if you will forget the past and look to our future. Your future. With Gazelle."

Snake found Gazelle Tears with her younger son, Wasp, and Fire Ant's plump widow, Ember, and her baby. All crouched near the stream's trickle. As their campfire burned to glowing coals, they busied themselves with preparations for the evening meal. Ember held her infant girl to her breast with her left arm, as she and Wasp pounded seeds against rock, splitting the husks and shaking out the meat to make mush balls. "I bring impala," Snake said, and dropped the carcass on the ground before Gazelle.

"It looks scrawny. Not juicy at all." Her eyes twinkled. "But I will cook, and we will eat together. Wasp," she said, "clean this." If they found a home . . . *when* they found a home, the boy would begin his run with the hunters. For now, he remained close to his mother.

"We need to speak," Snake said quietly.

Her pounding slowed. She moved a bit farther away from her son and daughter-in-law. "You need to ask? When have I refused you anything?"

He looked south, toward Great Sky. For the first moon of their travels, the sacred mountain had wavered behind them in the distance. Then only when the air and heat and light were *just so* did it appear, as if floating above the horizon. And then one day . . . it was gone. "Perhaps because we are distant from our home."

"Sky Woman says that home is where we build our fire. Where we feed our families. Where we hold each other."

He looked at her, curious. "You've heard stories of what happened on the mountain?"

"Yes," she said.

"Everyone loves a hero," Snake said. "They make dances and sing songs for the hero. I do not know who this 'hero' is. Is it this 'hero' you love?"

Gazelle Tears laughed.

Wasp grunted, sawing at the web of muscle between the deer's ribs. The boy was a smaller, younger version of his brother, Frog. Grunting, he ripped a section of ribs free and handed it to Ember for approval. She nodded and passed it to Gazelle Tears.

She selected herbs from a leather pouch, and crumbled a healthy pinch onto the meat, then began kneading the seasoning in with a smooth, clean rock. "I brought our sons, Frog and Wasp, our daughter, Little Brook, into the world through my body. Each was born wet and wrinkled. Brook cried as if she were the first lonely soul in all creation. I helped Frog take his first steps, and now people speak about my son as if he is no longer a two-legged. It makes me laugh." Her eyes crinkled at the corners. "I don't know what my son felt and saw on the mountain . . . but he is still my son, as much as he was before he could wipe his own bottom."

"And what of me?" Snake asked.

"I don't know what happened to you on Great Sky," she said, "but you are still my husband. When you rub your hips against me, my body opens to you. It is no *hero* I pull inside me. It is the man who fed my children when their flesh father died. The man who taught little Frog to wrestle and hunt."

"You will still cook my meat?"

She pressed her palm against his forehead, and gave him a little push. "Always."

She plucked a pair of tubers from the pile beside her, rolled them in green leaves and handed them to Wasp, who slipped them into the coals. "Do you remember our first night together?"

The very memory sweetened the moist, warm air. "Of course."

She touched his arm. "Tell me what you were thinking."

Snake nodded. "When my wife died, I mourned and thought my heart had dried. You made me food and made me laugh and made me come."

"These are all good things." Gazelle Tears chuckled.

"I needed these things," Snake said. "And you needed a man to hunt for you."

"Even before your wife died, you hunted for me," she reminded him.

"Yes. But after she returned to the mountain, I hoped you would see me with warm eyes."

In that moment, Gazelle Tears seemed a young girl once again. "All my eyes are warm to you, Snake. All are open now: two hands, two feet, two face-eyes."

"And the seventh eye?" he asked.

In answer, she rubbed her rump against his. The smoothness soothed one ache but intensified another. If the sudden, delicious heaviness in his root was any measure, he was not quite as old as he feared. Snake smiled. "Perhaps tonight . . ."

"Yes." As she pounded the seeds, her tempo quickened.

"A walk in the brush . . ."

She sighed as if he had entered her already. "I will roll my hide. It might be nice to have a place to sit."

"Or lie."

Gazelle's shyness had vanished, replaced by something with sharp, friendly teeth. "Yes. It might."

Snake crouched between his wife and Ember. Ember's man, Fire Ant, was gone, dead on the holy mountain. Since his death Ember had been closer to Gazelle Tears than ever. She had chosen to travel with Frog rather than return to her own boma.

Here, Ember was a legend's widow. She seemed to take some comfort in that, at least enough to get on with her life.

Could a legend's widow be stronger than a legend? This was not a question Snake could answer. Instead of trying, he busied himself pounding leaves and herbs and ground seeds into the slab of deer ribs. In every way, tonight would be a feast.

The sun was a thumbnail-sized spark, sinking toward its grave below the western horizon. To T'Cori the clouds seemed layered there, dark orange at the bottom and edges, darkening in the middle as the sky sighed and prepared for sleep.

She and the other women tended to gather at their own fire, a few paces from the men's. A world away. Out here on the unknown northern savannah, where their former lives had blown away like cobwebs in the wind, the informally drawn boundaries seemed more important than ever.

Tonight, six women crouched around the blaze, its living shadows painting their faces. Hearts open, they awaited morsels of wisdom or comfort from Stillshadow. Perhaps they would be called to sing. Song and dance could transform a dreary night into a celebration. T'Cori had brought along her drum in hopeful anticipation.

The lead dream dancer sat at the edge of a log, her elbows resting upon her knees, her weathered face tilted up to the darkening clouds. Stillshadow rested her hand over her heart. "I die soon."

Fear tightened T'Cori's throat. "Mother! Do not say such a thing." Then she paused. "When?"

"Not today or tomorrow," the old woman promised, "but there is much to teach and little time to share it."

Relief flooded T'Cori's heart. She could lead, alone, if she must. *But please, Great Mother, not yet.*

"Where do we begin?" Sing Sun asked.

"When we find our new place," Stillshadow said. "We must make a new drum."

"What is wrong with this one?" T'Cori asked. She reached down and ran her hands along its worn sides. The drum was as tall as her forearm, as broad as a large man's hand. It was formed from a hollowed willow log, with deerskin pegged with bone splinters stretched around the rim. T'Cori had owned it since childhood, and she slapped her palm against the drumhead to make a high, mellow thump.

"It is a fine drum," her teacher said, "but a new land needs new music. We make it from the trees, from the animals. In that way, when we play, we speak to the land itself. We will walk on. We need to be swift but careful."

Her brow wrinkled. "I feel that in a new land, we need a dance as quick and light as rabbits. Bring the drum, and we will teach our men the rabbit rhythm."

"Yes, Mother," T'Cori said.

"Sky Woman, tell them the story of Zomo the rabbit drummer," Stillshadow said. "Hunters use Rabbit when they must run fast and quiet for a short time. This is Zomo's rhythm."

T'Cori's hand fluttered on her drum, tapping out a song. As the thumps triggered memories of dance and song and mushrooms, she searched her memory, hoping to earn a smile, or an affirming nod, from her mentor. . . .

Zomo was not very big or strong, but he was a very clever rabbit. But Zomo was greedy and wanted something more than cleverness. He wished for wisdom. Father Mountain told Zomo that in order to earn such a boon, he would have to do three things.

First, he would have to bring the scales of Big Fish to Great Sky. Second, he would have to bring the milk of Buffalo to Great Sky. And third, he would have to bring the tooth of Leopard to Great Sky.

Zomo promised Father Mountain to do exactly these things.

First, he traveled to the edge of the sea seeking Big Fish. There he sat and began to play his drum. He played so loudly that Big Fish heard the music and swam up to dance upon the sand. Zomo beat his drum faster and faster. Excited, Big Fish danced so fast that all his scales fell off. Naked and embarrassed, Big Fish leapt back into the sea.

Zomo scooped up all the scales in his sack, wiggled his tail and hopped off into the forest. While hopping through the trees, he saw Buffalo. He insulted Buffalo by telling her she wasn't big or strong. Zomo dared Buffalo to knock down the little palm tree.

The little rabbit made Buffalo so angry she ran to tear the tree up by its roots. But because the bark was soft, her horns got stuck fast.

While Buffalo struggled, Zomo slid down, reached under her and filled his drum with milk.

Then Zomo went to the top of BreakClaw hill, a place where Leopard was known to hunt. He tipped his sack and sprinkled scales on the path, and then tipped his drum and spilled a few drops of milk into the dust.

Zomo went to the bottom of BreakClaw and hid behind a big rock. Soon Leopard came walking over the hill, where he lost his footing on the slippery scales and the milk. Leopard slid all the way down the hill. His face hit a rock, and a tooth popped out of his mouth. Zomo grabbed that tooth and ran away just as fast as he could.

So he took the three things back to Great Sky and climbed it, and at the top he found Father Mountain. "See?" he said. "See! I did what you asked me to do." The little rabbit stood proud and tall. "Give me wisdom!"

But despite all he had done, Father Mountain just laughed at Rabbit. "You are clever enough to do what cannot be done," Father Mountain said. "So now I will give you wisdom. Three things are worth having in this world. Courage, good sense and caution. Little rabbit, you have much courage, a bit of quickness and no sense at all. So the next time you see Big Fish, Buffalo or Leopard—you'd better run!"

And that is why to this day we sing: Rabbit is not big. Rabbit is not strong. But Rabbit has wisdom, so he runs very, very swiftly.

At the same moment T'Cori finished singing her story, her fingers fluttered to a rest.

The six women around the fire had been joined by others, including men and children, come to hear the tale. They smiled and clapped along, and laughed with pleasure as she came to a close.

While warming, their praise skimmed the surface of her heart. Only Stillshadow's approving nod warmed her to the core.

T'Cori, Sky Woman, had done well.

T'Cori lay on her back beneath their lean-to, her stepson Medicine Mouse sleeping at her side, his wet nurse's milk moistening his breath.

Throughout the rest of the camp soft burring snores replaced conversation and laughter. The twin fires burned low.

For a time she thought that Frog lay sound asleep at her side, then felt him nudge her ribs. The shadowed darkness barely revealed his form, but she felt him jerk his head toward the lean-to's open side.

Taking care not to awaken his son, T'Cori followed Frog out.

Their tens of families had clustered their skins and lean-tos around the fires. With the exception of a pipe-smoking shadow to the south, all seemed quiet and still.

They moved around to the other side of the acacia's trunk, sitting close enough for thigh to brush warm thigh. "What is it?" she asked.

"I have thought long about this, and come to a decision." He paused, as if gathering strength. "I want you as my woman."

She stared at him for a moment, and then struggled not to laugh. "I cook your food, I share your roof. I spank your son when he is bad and kiss him when he is good. What more remains?"

"My tongue tripped. I want you to be my *wife*," he said. "For us to make ceremony before the tribe, before Father Mountain and Great Mother. I want us to own each other and proclaim that bond before all: to the sky, the mountain and the earth."

She sighed, mirth gone. "Great Mother's children have needs. And those she provides. We do not get everything we want."

He smacked the flat of his hand against the ground. "Why not! So many things in the world have changed. Why not this?"

She waved her hand at the lean-tos and twin campfires. Peaceful now. Tomorrow, they would rise and walk another day. And a few days after that, another walk. And on and on, until Stillshadow and Sky Woman told them they had found a home. "Look upon them, Frog."

"Upon who?"

"Our children," she said.

"Children?" He rested his hand on her rounded belly. "Do you see the future now?"

T'Cori laughed. "No, fool. I mean our people. The ones who follow us. They trust us. Need us, like children do. Hands of hands of families."

"I see them," Frog said.

She leaned her cheek against his shoulder. "Just as you see the faces in the clouds. Watch them. They watch us. They try to laugh, to sing, to dance. They try to be brave . . . but they are afraid. Too many things have changed. If all things change, they will have nothing to hold on to. We must wait."

"Wait?"

"Yes," T'Cori said. "Yes. In seasons, all things come. You and I can love, because more and more every day our people see you as our great hunt chief. But if I became your wife too soon, they would say you had taken Great Sky's woman. Then, what if the *jowk* makes evil play with us? If a hunter is gored or if plague falls? If a baby is born with six toes, they will say our union is cursed. Please, my love. We must be strong."

"But . . . you will still share my hut?" he asked, irritated by the pout in his own voice.

She nodded. "Only as long as you will have me."

"Then you are mine forever."

T'Cori sighed, and nestled closer. "We have lost so many things."

"My father," Frog said. "Three brothers." Scorpion and Fire Ant, dead in fire. Hawk Shadow, torn by wolves.

"And I, four sisters." Small Raven, dead of cold. Fawn Blossom, killed by a crocodile. Dove and Sister Quiet Water, lost to the Mk*tk.

Could such tragedy be overcome? Dared they even to hope?

"Can we hold on to each other?" His voice was a little strained. Anxious.

"Of course, big ears." She laughed. "Who else would have either of us?"

Chapter Four

In girlhood, Hot Tree had danced from dusk until dawn, but those days were now gray ghosts. Muscles once tireless now felt like rotted string.

"My bones are heavy," she said more to herself than anyone else. In still water, when the sun was just so, her grandmother smiled back at her. So strange. How could this be? Where had this old woman come from? Deep within the cocoon of fatigue, Hot Tree still felt like a girl.

A boy with a round head and a huge nose tugged at her arm. "Gramma? Is there something you need?"

She shook her head. "No, Snail. Just gather the firewood. Pick up branches in the firebreak. Be a good boy."

"Always," Snail said.

Imitating his full name, Snail Crawling Backward dropped to his hands and knees and scurried away giggling, toward the boma's walls and safety. She barely noticed, looking off toward the south, her brow furrowed.

Something was wrong. She could not *see* it. Could not *hear* it. But whatever the danger, Great Mother would protect them. She knew it.

Ibandi men had beaten the Mk*tk. Surely now their gods would smile upon them and protect them.

Surely, the Mk*tk would not dare strike their hallowed ground.

That evening, Hot Tree served her family yams and monkey meat on a bed of crossed broadleaf. Most of those remaining in her daughter's boma were old men and children—barely enough hunters to provide flesh.

There was rarely as much meat to share as there had been before Great Sky had died.

Nor were there enough men to protect them. Something tickled at her nose, a scent . . . sweat? Perhaps—if that sweat mingled the musk of man and lion.

"The wind stinks," Hot Tree said.

Snail hugged her leg with all the strength in his small arms. "I smell nothing, Gramma."

"Go to your mother," Hot Tree said.

"Nana," Snail Crawling Backward begged, "come with me."

"Never you mind," the old woman said. "Just go."

Hot Tree shuffled to the gap in the boma's bamboo wall. It was a man and a half tall, its poles sharpened at the top and lashed together with vines and leather strips. Its door of woven thorn branches was open during the day and closed at night. Although dusk had descended, the door had yet to be lashed shut. She squinted toward the east. Nothing but dried grasses and flat-topped acacia trees, dappling the plain as far as the eye could see. She started to turn and then changed her mind. If there was nothing out there, why did her spit curdle in her mouth?

Then as she turned, she used a hunter's trick: from the sides of her eyes she caught something she could not see straight on. Men thought this secret belonged to them, but women could use it as well.

Every moon, hunters set fire to the brush around her daughter's boma, to deny cover to lions and leopards. The edge of the blackened zone snarled with dense brush. Her tired old eyes detected one shadow oddly . . . *different* within that tangle of moonlit thorns and stalks. Larger than a man, but smaller than a lion. It was darker, *harder* than the other night shapes. Motionless as a cactus, it crouched.

Then it began to move.

Stealthy as a spider, the shadow crawled toward the boma.

Her muscles became bones. *Now* she detected other forms, humping across the burnt grass, blending with the shadows as clouds throttled the half-moon. Hot Tree might have been in the dream world, her arms and shoulders struggling to run, her feet rooted to the earth, stuck as fast as her namesake.

Thick, twisted silhouettes stood erect, shadows casting shadows. Stillness. Apish faces stared through her, past her, intent upon the boma walls to her rear. *One. Two. Three. Another. A hand. Two hands of two-legged shadows.* Spears and clubs bristled. As yet unmoving, they regarded the woman standing in the gap in the boma's thorn walls.

She backed away, at first unable to speak, then suddenly unable to stop screaming, "*MK*TK! MK*TK!*"

Fighting panic, Tree barely dragged the thorn wall halfway closed before the first wave of attackers fell upon her. Agony drove thought from her mind as a spear point pierced her belly. She fell back, blood clotting the breath in her throat. The Mk*tk stomped on her chest and wrenched his weapon free, then leaped toward the huts.

Inside the boma, her people screamed and ran, trying to claw their way through the thorn walls. There they were caught by the Mk*tk, trapped by the very walls that had once sheltered them.

Curled onto her side, blood-slimed fingers clutching her belly, Hot Tree's dying eyes reflected the flame from the huts and boma walls. She heard Snail Crawling Backward scream for his father. His mother. Anyone.

No one.

She closed her eyes, praying as her grandson's howls dissolved into grunts of pain and terror.

Pleading for Father Mountain to take her, Hot Tree lived to hear her sisters, wrists lashed together, wail as the Mk*tk's flaked rock knives stripped meat from their men's bones.

She lived to see the Mk*tk leader, a blunt-faced giant with two finger stumps marring his left hand, raise his bloodstained arms to the moon. She lived to hear her people's thick, wet sobs die to silence.

Only then, after everything she loved had turned to dust, did her broken heart end its dance.

The sky swam with stinking black smoke, Flat-Nose's solemn tribute to God Blood. As leader of his clan it was his responsibility to see that his people's every action, every deed was right in the eyes of He who had vomited forth the world.

Their deeds would be woven into Flat-Nose's death song, the tale he had composed his entire life. It was a bleeding tattoo etched into his victims' bruised skins, designed to carry their souls to God Blood. If the forces of night found a man's story to be good, then the terrible one might choose Flat-Nose's flesh as a special, succulent meal at the end of days.

Surely, God Blood would approve of this: slaughtered weaklings, sobbing females taken for pleasure and work. Young grubs peeled and staked for the vultures.

The hot air reeked of flesh and flies. Jackals and crows circled as the Mk*tk departed, driving the howling women before them. The Ibandi women's anguish was a beautiful thing, but he did not want them to lose all hope. A single woman might even be allowed to escape, to give the others spirit, spirit that Flat-Nose and his men might then relish shattering. Thin boned and small they were, but if they were like his third wife, Dove, they were ready and eager to learn what a true male demanded of a female. And, in time, their supple backs and buttocks would yield all that was required. *That* was the true nature of the female, something these weaklings seemed not to understand.

They would find Flat-Nose an excellent instructor.

Not one Mk*tk dared looked back. Although brave beyond the ability of an Ibandi to conceive, there were limits: it could blast the body and soul for mere mortals to watch God Blood at feast.

Chapter Five

In T'Cori's dream, a green creeper vine as long as the horizon stretched between the peaks of Great Earth and Great Sky. She was a ring-tailed monkey climbing hand over hand across that divide. But when only halfway across, arms rose up, like the arms of beast-men who had clutched at her in the sacred caves. They pulled her down, and as they pulled, she changed from a monkey to a woman once again, and the beast-men transformed into Mk*tk.

And they did to her what they had done in hands of hands of other dreams, on ten tens of other nights.

T'Cori blinked her eyes open and was born into darkness.

Medicine Mouse had rolled against her hard, restless in his sleeping space between her and Frog. His soft, warm mouth sought her nipple in vain. Her milk had not yet come down. Today she would have to take the boy to her adopted sister Ember, who produced milk enough for Fire Ant's daughter and Mouse as well.

But for now, the tiny slack body, eyes closed, mouth open, smelled of last night's liquid supper. And T'Cori reassured herself that the perils of the dream world did not always follow men and women into the world of flesh.

"*Whaaat?*" Frog's voice was groggy as he pushed himself up.

"Dreams."

Frog nodded. "I know. Every night I see death."

"Mk*tk?"

He nodded.

"Every night," she said, "I dream they push at my body. They take what is not mine to give."

He pressed his lips to her forehead. "What you have, no one can steal." He rose, grasping his spear near the point.

She did not have the heart to protest his blasphemy or mourn his blindness. Whatever he was not, whoever he was not, she needed him and so did her people.

"Train hard," she said. "When I close my eyes, I see blood."

By the time most hunters crawled out of their lean-tos, Frog had already painted a human outline upon a tree trunk. Before others had wiped the sleep from their eyes, the calluses on his palms were already hot and raw.

He thrust, changed positions and poked again with a twisting of wrist and arm, imagining the spear tip digging its way through muscle.

As the others prepared themselves for the day's walk, they scratched their heads as he thrust and gouged his spear into the pitted wood until his hands bled and his strong young body gleamed with sweat. Frog shut the gawkers out of his mind. He did not see the surrounding termite mud hills, or a berry juice outline on the tree trunk. His eyes saw only snarling horror and the death of hope.

"What are you doing?" Leopard Paw asked from a few safe paces distance.

Frog's tree was a spear's throw away from where most Ibandi were encamped, near the forest of chest-tall, orange-brown termite mounds. When his foot brushed one of the insect trails, he paused to shake a few six-leggeds off his heel.

"Practicing," Frog said.

"Why?"

"A dream."

"Well," Leopard said, "the tree looks very fierce." The hunters laughed.

Frog did not let their mockery touch him. One day they would understand. That day of truth terrified him as no previous imagining ever had, but he could not shut the fear away. Not this time. That had been his tactic through much of his life. This time, he would turn fear into skill.

When the other hunters drifted away, Snake remained, watching, fingers twisting his thin beard. "I watch you train. You were not seeing boars or lions in your mind. You saw men."

"If Mk*tk *are* men," Frog replied. He stepped sideways, then stabbed and slashed the tree from a new angle as if it had threatened Medicine Mouse.

He dreamed of Mk*tk. T'Cori dreamed of Mk*tk. When two dreamed as one . . . only a fool could deny that tomorrow and today were bleeding into each other. "Are they?" he asked. "Are they men?"

"Whether or not they are men, they are horizons behind us." Snake seemed genuinely confused. "We walk *away* from them!"

"Perhaps," Frog said, "they run to meet us. What then?"

"I don't know," Snake said.

"I do," Frog said. "And I have thought about this." His voice dropped to a whisper. "Snake, in your days with the hunt chiefs, what secrets did you learn?"

"Many dances," he said, "and ceremonies. I remember so little."

"Try harder." Frog leaned on his spear. Sweat dripped from his forehead and puddled in the dirt like summer's first raindrops. "I say we talk to Still-shadow, ask if she remembers the hunt chief's dances. Or anything we might use against the Mk*tk. If we don't know more than we did, and we meet them in years to come . . ."

Snake shook his head. "But they are *behind* us!"

Frog gazed up at the clouds. Shapes. Faces. Still. Moving. At one time or another, he had seen everything he had ever known in the sky . . . and some sky forms he had never seen in the real world at all. For instance, the face of his father—said to be broad and strong like Fire Ant's but with wider eyes. Frog wished he could have seen his father's face, felt his kiss, just once.

Snake had tried to fill that void, and could not. Perhaps his flesh father would not have been able to see the faces and creatures in the clouds, either, or known the voices of the fire people.

In Frog's dreams, his lost father could do those things and more.

This was not fair. Snake was all he had, and Snake wanted to follow Frog. Snake, his elder, should have dispensed wisdom. Frog had never wanted any of this.

All he had wanted was family, water, a warm fire, a good hunt and a safe night's sleep.

Frustrated, Frog screamed his reply. "How can we know what is out there, waiting for us? We cannot. And so we must be ready, or they will eat our children."

Snake's single good eye squinted. "You really believe this?"

"Yes," Frog said, "I do. Sky Woman says that there will be blood."

Snake bowed his head. Then he lifted his chin, opened his eyes and looked up. "I think the Mk*tk are far behind us, but I trust you, my son, and will prepare for what lies ahead."

"I know you will," Frog replied. "We will all do what we can."

And his greatest fear was that, in the end, it wouldn't be enough.

From day to day, no one knew what meat the hunters might bring. The women had to be prepared for anything. Today, gathering was more successful than hunting: finding a trove of yams and tubers with a thick, fine yellow flesh.

Using a flattened rock, T'Cori scraped out a hole as deep as her forearm. She crosshatched brush carefully, struck sparks into kindling and nursed her fire to life, rolling stones into the pit while the flames still crackled. After they died down she laid leaves and grass on the stones, sprinkled some water, then laid down the yams. On top of them she lay more grass, sprinkled more water, then more grass and a thick coating of earth, leaving the yams to cook.

As a dream dancer, she was more familiar with the medicinal qualities of plants and animals than their value as food. But all Ibandi women knew how to convert any edible living thing into a nourishing meal, if not a feast. She missed the easy comfort of her days walking Great Earth's slopes, plucking thistle top, boar weed, and crowfoot. Those spices were good to chew raw or add twisty flavor to a stew.

Blossom had taught her the best way to prepare wildebeest: singe them, gut and scrape them, then stuff the carcass with hot stones. The carcasses would then be rolled atop a burnt-down fire and sizzling ashes heaped on top. *Great Mother!* Her mouth watered at the memory.

Dear lost Small Raven had loved ostrich. They had been in conflict over many things but had shared happy days preparing the great birds for feast— plucking and filling them with smoking stones, leaves and even their own feathers—laughing and singing as they alternated layers of leaves and feathers and ashes atop a stuffed bird so that it roasted from within and without. The aromatic smoke rose all the way to Great Mother's peak, carrying their spirits.

Creatures eaten with love surely rose to the top of the mountain, to play the games of love and hunt again and again through all the seasons to come.

These days, T'Cori usually made do with a few yams and an occasional bird. Her hands shook as she prepared a scanty meal, and it was impossible for her not to think of smoked porcupines and opossums, ducks roasted in mud balls, strips of iguana meat roasted or stretched in the sun, mussels and crayfish and ostrich eggs cooked in glowing coals or hot ashes.

T'Cori remembered the splash of cold stream water against her thighs as she and her sisters beat the river with hides, driving fish toward the nets. Hearing the water-children squeal and cry with fear like scaly birds.

What wonderful times those had been!

She smeared tears away with the back of her hand. *No.* Such memories would break her, and she had no right to break. She must be strong. More than strong. To be anything less than Great Sky Woman, the hope of her people, would be a complete betrayal.

T'Cori was so absorbed in her work that when a gray-haired man touched her shoulder, she hadn't even realized he had been waiting behind her. Her visitor was stooped now. Her medicine woman's eyes told her his bones ached, but she knew he never complained, and he never walked in the rear.

He was Water Chant, her father, the man who had abandoned her as a child. The coarsely knotted hair above his narrow face had faded to white. She had heard that he had once been the strongest, fastest hunter in Water boma. She had never known him, had not even suspected that he still lived, until he came to her just before the Ibandi left the shadow of Great Sky, pleading for her forgiveness.

Forgiveness she had given happily.

"I would have words," he said.

"Of course," T'Cori answered. For a moment she considered adding *father,* but in the time it took for the thought to form, the moment flew.

"In days past," Water Chant said, "our speaking shamed my heart. Once upon a time I feared my daughter's blindness, blindness I now know was a sight beyond my own. I know my sin cost your mother her life in childbirth. Great Mother has never let me love again."

T'Cori did not want him to say these things, did not want to open that pathway. She knew that lurking at its end was the lonely girl she had once been. Like the kernel of an ancient baobab, that child would always live within her. That girl had often dreamed that somewhere, someone loved her as a father or mother loved a child, and would hold her close and call her precious.

With nothing and no one to fill that void in her life, only Great Mother and Father Mountain offered solace.

She honored Water Chant but could not love him, and she hoped he would never ask if she did.

T'Cori took his hand. "I believe you are my father. If that is true, and you are a good man, then I am sure that you did only what Great Mother told your heart to do. Because of you, Stillshadow found and taught me—"

He blinked, holding back tears. "I don't know why Father Mountain or Great Mother gave you to me. But even if you could not call me father, I think you should know your sisters."

"Sisters?" She blinked in shock. In all these moons, she had not gone to him and asked if there were brothers or sisters who might have accompanied him. Had she been afraid to ask? To *hope*? Had that been another piece of herself she had abandoned to be Sky Woman?

Just twice ten tens of Ibandi, walking for moons now, and she had not known that her sisters walked among them. What mists had wreathed her mind? What manner of leader was she?

She turned just in time to see two girls approaching along the shallow streambed leading from the camp. From glimpses of her own reflection, she knew they resembled her. Two or three years older, perhaps, with the same high cheekbones, beautiful dark-clay skin. Their hair hung in ringlets instead of braids, but was the same brown as hers, a few shades darker than their eyes. They had slender bodies, with full breasts. Unlike T'Cori, those breasts were exposed: a dream dancer's sexuality was reserved for Father Mountain's chosen hunters.

Her sisters could have been her, living different but very familiar lives. Strange. She knew them to be lovely but had never thought of herself in such a way. A clutch of children dangled from their arms and followed at their backs.

Both women noticed her swollen belly, touching it and clucking approval.

"Sisters?" T'Cori repeated, stunned.

Water Chant pointed. "This is Flower, and this—" he said, pointing to the shorter of the two "—is Morning Thunder."

"Such a strong name," T'Cori said.

Flower smiled. "She was a very loud baby."

"Louder than me?" T'Cori asked.

"I think so, yes," her father said.

The two girls were her people's future. Great Mother . . . if her people had any future at all. She could not allow her private terrors to intrude. Had Water Chant waited for her to come to him? She had never done it, nor reached out. Now, Chant had risked his heart to present his daughters, her *sisters,* whom she had never known.

Their eyes welled with wonder and with hope.

Morning Thunder was the first to lose her shyness. "Is it true you are our sister? Could our greatest dancer share our blood?"

Be what they need. "We all share blood," T'Cori said.

Disappointment clouded their faces. Swiftly, T'Cori added, "but I think that we three may be closer than any. We can make our own small circle within the greater one. Bring your food to my fire tonight. We will eat and then walk together."

And for those words, they gifted her with eager smiles.

By the time Frog returned from his morning exercises, T'Cori and her sisters were laughing and talking like childhood friends.

She met him before he reached their fire, taking his warm, strong hand in hers. "Come," T'Cori said. "Meet my other family."

"Family?" Frog protested. "What is this? *I* am your family. The dreamers are your family." At first she feared he was serious, then saw the mischief a-dance in his eyes.

Ah. *That* was her dear Frog.

"There is more." She smiled.

"Then let us celebrate more fully," he said and thumped his spear butt against the ground. "Another miracle!" he called. "Let me bring Little Brook and Wasp and Mouse and call my mother and Ember and Flamingo. It is a good night: our circle has grown again."

Chapter Six

Frog, Uncle Snake and Leopard Eye crouched at the watering hole's edge. The afternoon sun peeled Frog's back, the sharp, spiky grass cut his skin and tiny, black gnats sipped the tears from his eyes. Half a moon had passed since T'Cori's father had revealed her sisters and Stillshadow had declared the reunion a good omen, one promising happy days to come.

In truth, it seemed to Frog that the old woman used *any* opportunity to tell them good days were soon to come. But for once, he wondered if she might be right.

Because here, right before his eyes, was a miracle.

Hands of hands of leopards, lions, ibyx and warthogs lazed sleepily as if all one happy winged, hooved and clawed family. With glazed and groggy eyes they stared at one another, as if barely aware that some were fang and the others flesh.

The pond was the largest they had seen since leaving Great Sky. It might have been fed by rains or perhaps an underground spring. Although there was no sign of a stream leading into it, the waters were deep and clear. Slender trees with broad-leaved branches lined its banks, offering shade. But the water's source was not what puzzled Frog.

The meat-eaters and the leaf-eaters barely noticed one another, too fascinated by the flies buzzing around their snouts. What matter of dream was *this*? "They lay side by side," he said. "I do not understand why the lion does not kill the antelope. Are they too tired even to eat?"

Beside him, Uncle Snake had ceased peering stealthily through the grass and was sitting cross-legged in plain sight, scratching the dead skin on the left side of his face. "I have heard," Snake said, "that only the hungry lion frightens the antelope."

"And how does the antelope know the difference?"

"For that—" Snake grinned "—we must ask an old antelope."

They crept closer. Frog's belly gnawed at him. For far too long, he had eaten little, save tubers and jerky. Slings had killed birds, and traps had netted moles and monkeys, but it had been moons since a real meat gorging, when sated hunters and their families groaned with bursting bellies, rolling onto their backs to belch and fart thanks to Father Mountain.

And now, as in a starving man's final dream, meat beyond reason lay within arm's reach. "What are they doing?"

"Drinking," Frog said, "and sleeping. Strange, but they seem *happy.*"

"Happy?" Snake was dubious. "Perhaps it is not water for men or animals. Perhaps it belongs to the gods, and they will be angry with us."

Magic. There, that word. Frog had stood atop Great Sky and had seen nothing. The world he knew contained many things, things that he could not explain, but no gods. And he had been to their home.

Even if he was the only one who knew it, who could or would speak such truth, truth it remained. "We should be careful, I think. Perhaps it takes away the hunger. I have never seen this. It is . . . a new thing."

"Like fill grass?" Snake asked. "Is this what you think?"

Frog felt certain. Dark fruit twice as thick as his thumb clustered on the branches and scattered on the ground near the water. "Perhaps. I have never seen that fruit. Perhaps it is like fill grass. It falls in the water, they drink . . . and their hunger goes." Hunters used fill grass to kill hunger pangs on long hunts. Not magic, just a gift of the plant people. If this oasis was such a gift, his mind could grasp it eagerly.

The water flowed from his mouth. *Father Mountain,* if this was not a wondrous feast, such a thing had never existed at all!

They crept closer to the tree, spears tilted at the ready. He had never been so close to a lion before, barely three paces from the tip of the killer's languidly lashing tail. Its sleepy yellow-green eyes blinked at him, but it didn't move. Hunger, fear and curiosity all battled in Frog's mind, and curiosity won.

The greenish brown fruit was clustered in bunches along the branches. They plucked several up from the ground, then crept back away while keeping an eye on the drowsy cats.

Once he and his men had retreated to safety, Frog bit through the skin, exposing sweet, pulpy flesh. He nibbled, then gobbled.

"Are you still hungry?" Snake asked after they had waited awhile.

The very word turned his belly into a fist. A sour belch affirmed its emptiness.

"I smelled that," Snake said. "A good answer. But very bad fill grass."

"Maybe it is the water."

Again, they crept up to the pond's edge and sipped. The taste was a blend of sweet and spoiled, a bit like figs rotting on the ground. Frog wrinkled his nose.

Beside him, Leopard Eye sipped. "It is not good," he said. Another sip. "But not bad either."

He lapped some more. Two other hunters crept up next to him and sipped, keeping their eyes on the lions, who merely watched them woozily.

Frog's head felt hollow, his belly snarled and sour. He rolled onto his back and closed his eyes. In the darkness, his heartbeat seemed to slow and deepen. Around him, sounds seemed both muffled and intensified.

Around him, his fellows were drinking the water, laughing, joking, as if casting aside moons of worry and woe. Laughter bubbled up from deep within him, and he could not stop it. The world behind his closed eyes began to whirl. He remembered being a boy, spreading his arms and spinning around and around until he tumbled to the ground, the world atilt, nothing in all creation save giggles and soft grass.

He was that child again. He felt . . . *good.*

"I am a great hunter!" Leopard Eye called. Frog opened his eyes to see his friend slapping both broad hands on his muscular chest. "Yowwww!"

A spotted gazelle lurched clumsily to its feet, staggering a few steps before its front legs folded. It collapsed onto its side, thick saliva bubbles welling from the corner of its mouth.

The hunters roared with laughter and beat on their chests. They ran and fumbled and tumbled as if their legs had fallen asleep.

Leopard thumped down beside Frog, his face alight with a huge and foolish grin. "I must tell them!" Leopard Eye said, his voice slurred. "I will run and tell them all of this great thing. This great, sacred, wonderful thing."

Leopard Eye pushed himself up and stumbled off toward the east. Frog smiled. A miracle indeed.

Now *this* was a new thing!

By the time that others arrived, dragging Stillshadow on her sled, T'Cori at her side, most of the animals had wobbled away, annoyed if not alarmed by the raucous humans.

Stillshadow sipped and wrinkled her nose. Then she drank more greedily. After a while, she was heel walking in slow circles, chanting and singing to herself. She raised her wrinkled arms. "I foresaw this place," she declared. "This is the place of my vision."

"We have meat!" Snake crowed. An ibyx hung loosely across his shoulder, its slashed throat drooling blood onto the ground. "We have meat! It did not even try to run!"

Stillshadow raised her hands to the clouds, the loose flesh sagging from her arms' undersides. Her eyes were as bright as a child's. "Of all signs that you might have given us, this is the strangest and surest."

The people ate and drank and danced, shouting up at the half-moon. Those with no partners pranced with their shadows. "This place could be our new home." Frog said, watching as they hooted and pranced.

"Let us make camp," Stillshadow said. "Perhaps Great Mother will give us signs."

"There is meat here," Frog said, "and the magical water. What greater sign could there be?" *Oh,* he thought, *why not call it magic?* If anything had ever deserved the name, this was it. And if it was not magic, if it was some wonderful gift of earth or sky, where was the harm in letting the others believe it divine?

T'Cori pointed northwest. "I saw that ridge in my vision. Beyond it grazed antelope and warthogs."

Frog closed his eyes and whirled off into a private world. Three human figures congealed out of the chaos. His heart leaped and his eyes burned with tears. This day, this precise *moment,* was the very best of his life.

"Brothers," Frog said, gazing out over the cactus trees, the sand and brush and heat shimmer from which the flesh of his flesh and heart had emerged. *Scorpion. Hawk Shadow.* "Fire Ant. Do you see me? Am I what our people need me to be?"

For a moment his brothers' ghosts danced over the sand. That vision dissolved into heat mirage and then condensed into new dark forms as nine men approached in three lines of three.

Frog squinted. Who could these be? He could not trust his eyes but thought that it might be the dead hunters from the Mk*tk wars, from the time of Great Sky's climbing. Perhaps the gates of heaven had opened. Perhaps their loved ones were returning from the place beyond death. Would not such a miracle signal that this was their promised land, a home in which their people would not merely rest but root, grow and bear new fruit?

What would he say to Hawk Shadow, who had been exhausted in the climb, remaining behind as others had scaled the peak? How could Frog ever explain that they had tried to return in time, only to find Hawk's wolf-ravaged body?

And what would he say to Fire Ant? Would words ever hold what his heart needed to say? Could Fire Ant forgive him for choosing Sky Woman over his own flesh? The tears flowed more rapidly now. Everything had seemed so clear on Great Sky. T'Cori had received her vision, a message that the Ibandi would have to leave the mountain's shadow if they wished to survive.

Fire Ant would not countenance it. Demanded that she change her story, that she not tell the people what she claimed the gods had told her.

Ant thought that all the Ibandi might rally around the heroes who had climbed Great Sky. That those heroes would lead the Ibandi and become great hunt chiefs.

But T'Cori would not yield. Crazed by his own visions, Fire Ant had threatened to kill her. Frog stood between them, playing the protector. Struck his brother in the head with a rock to slow him. What foolishness, to think Sky Woman needed protection. She had lured Ant onto a thin sheet of frozen water, through which he had plunged into a searing death below.

Many times, Frog had dreamed of that horror. He would have given his life for a chance to relive it. Surely there had to have been another way, something other than death and betrayal and shame.

Frog shook himself out of his fantasies, blurred vision falling away as he realized that the newcomers were not a dream, but not his brothers either.

Not kinsmen. Not bhan. Not Ibandi at all.

Curiosity warred with alarm as Frog crawled sluggishly to his feet.

Their dusty calves were too thick. Their lips and ears were pierced in clustered rows. "Who are you?" the first asked Frog. His words were so thick Frog barely understood them.

A keloid spider crouched from brow to chin and across the stranger's cheeks. A bleached splinter of bone pierced his upper lip. While no larger than Ibandi, their bodies were nettled with old scars. Their cold eyes held no compromise. These men had seen death in endless waves, were more comfortable with war than peace.

A gravelly taste coated Frog's mouth, as if he had licked a rock. Leopard Paw and Snake were suddenly, quietly, behind him. From the corners of his eyes, Frog saw that they gripped their spears almost as tightly as they had a quarter ago, when facing lions.

"We come from Great Sky," T'Cori said.

"We speak to your *men*," the stranger said, refusing to meet her eyes.

She raised her shoulders proudly. "I am Sky Woman, and I speak for the Ibandi."

Spider Face stared down at her. "Since before our grandfathers, we have come here every year, to drink from the sacred waters. This is *our* place. These waters are the gift of *our* god. You must leave." It was not said as a threat but as simple fact.

"We mean no harm," Frog said, dismayed by the desperation in his voice. "We want to share and rest."

"You must go," Spider Face said. The eight men behind him stood impassively, no overt threat about them. They were above such things. These men had seen and done much killing and were now merely waiting to see if the time of red spears had come once again.

"When people travel through our land, we offer them food. Shelter. Water." Frog fought to keep his voice steady. "Whatever they need."

"This is not your land," Spider Face said. His voice was flat and dead.

T'Cori's hands shook, but then she calmed them again. "I know you are a great people," she said. "We mean you no harm. Tell us what we must do to be guests in your land."

Spider Face's hooded gaze was pitiless. "You did not ask. Must . . . ask." His gaze was like fire.

"I ask now. We did not know. We did not see your sign—your hunters are too clever. Our children are tired. We beg your pardon."

A hawk skawed above them, its gliding wings silhouetted against a blue-white cloud. Frog tried to find Hawk Shadow's face in that cloud: a chin? A cheek?

Nothing. He shivered, alone.

Hawk Shadow would have known how to talk to these men. Or Fire Ant.

The spider tattoo seemed to swell. "You stay tonight. Leave before sun high tomorrow, or we wash our spears."

Frog tried again. "Please. This is a place of plenty. We are few."

"You must go," Spider Face said.

"I think I remember you," T'Cori said. "Didn't you trade at Spring Gathering, in the shadow of Great Sky?"

"Not so great, now," Spider Face sneered. "The sky crawled with smoke. Ash in our mouths for a moon." He peered south. "I cannot see your god. Can you?"

She ignored the question. "Trade with us now. What can we give you in exchange for a moon of rest?"

"You have nothing we want," the tribesman said.

"We will share our hunts with you." Desperation had crept into her voice. "We have medicines. Songs."

Spider Face's pierced fleshy lips did not change. "You have nothing we want. Go. Or die." His voice was as cold as the wind atop Great Sky.

These were not Ibandi. Nor were they Mk*tk. They were something else. Their words were not cruel, merely blunt. These men were fearsome, but not because they were strong or fast or vicious. What was it, then?

And then Frog looked at their scars, remembered their limps, and knew. These men had fought for their water hole, for their land, many, many times. Those struggles had changed them in some way he hoped never to be changed. It was not that they were eager to kill. It was that they were ready to die.

He snuck a quick glance at his own men. Although still woozy from the miracle water, their shoulders were tense, nostrils flared, jaws jutted forward. Ready to fight at a word.

He lowered his left hand, showed them the pale flesh of his palm. *Do nothing.*

Did T'Cori see what he saw? He was not sure, but from the way she plunged onward, without changing her plea, he doubted it.

"Great Mother and Father Mountain ask that you let us stay," she tried.

"Your mouth moved, but I heard nothing. We are not of the mountain. We do not live in the shadow. They are not our gods." He regarded Frog with distaste. "She is your woman?"

"Yes," Frog said.

Spider Face hawked and spit into the ground between Frog's legs. "If the mouth between her legs is the size of the one in her face, you must be a great man."

The spider tribesmen turned and left. Frog started after them. Surely there was something he could say or do.

Fingers as hard as bare bone gripped his arm: Uncle Snake, pulling him back. "Begging will only anger them," Snake said. "They are not evil men. But they will not be pushed. We will find another place."

Something inside Frog gave thanks that Snake had spoken. His father still had wisdom to share: the truth of his words rang in Frog's bones.

Stillshadow sighed. "Unless we are going to fight, I suppose it's best these old feet walk another horizon or two. Help me up."

Frog felt lost. "What do we do?"

"We rest," Stillshadow said. "We watch. And tomorrow morning . . . we move on."

"The mountain is gone," Snake said. "His shadow no longer shelters us from the fire."

Stillshadow shook her gray head. "The night is His shadow."

"He is everywhere," T'Cori whispered.

"I do not feel Him."

T'Cori gripped Frog's hands, suddenly a woman of stone. When he looked into her face, frozen wind shrieked in his ears, memories of the mountain. "You can say this?" she asked. "You stood in His presence. How could one who has done such a thing ever doubt Him again?"

All around them were open ears, shining eyes. The young ones watched Frog, hoping that one day they might be the smallest finger of his mighty fist.

Frog saw them. Where they saw strength, he felt only weakness, but he heard the meaning behind T'Cori words. Now was not the time for pale words. His people could not afford doubt.

"Yes," he lied. "You are right. I feel Him now."

By the time the morning sun had climbed above the horizon, the Ibandi were again on the move. Their hunters had easily caught enough of the drowsy animals to fill their cook fires. Tired they might be, but T'Cori gave thanks that her people would not walk in hunger. "Mother," T'Cori asked, "who leads now?"

"I don't understand the question," Stillshadow said. She had awakened that morning feeling strong enough to walk a bit. To T'Cori it seemed that her teacher needed all her magic merely to place one foot before the other.

"In the mountain's shadow," T'Cori said, "we knew our roles. They were rules that our mothers and fathers had followed since the beginning. The men hunted. The women healed and sang the sun to life each dawn."

"And you think this changes?"

T'Cori searched inside herself before replying. "Yes. The men cannot lead now, because they rely upon us to tell them where to go. They meet new people and cannot speak to them. What happens if this goes on—if women lead and men follow?"

Stillshadow shrugged. "Then women lead and men follow. You think this has not happened before? And will not again? Girl, I thought you knew better than this."

T'Cori flinched, fighting to tamp down her shame. "I was so full of pride. I . . . erred with Spider Face. Everything I said was wrong."

Stillshadow clucked. "Better to blame me for drinking the magic water. I had never seen or heard of such wonder."

T'Cori chuckled. "Never," T'Cori said. "As Frog says: It was a new thing."

Stillshadow cackled, still enjoying the memory. Then her face grew serious. "What you speak of now is a deeper thing. We need you, and you are afraid."

"You see much, Mother." Too much. Did she really want anyone peering that deeply inside her? "There is one thing I fear."

"And what is that?"

As they walked, T'Cori kicked at a rock. It bounced a few paces, then rattled into a bush. "Our people do not know what happened to me. Don't know that the Mk*tk took what was mine to protect."

At last, the old woman understood. "You fear they poisoned your *num*. Cracked your egg."

T'Cori trembled. The violation was more bleeding wound than mere memory. No ceremony or song or dance could staunch it. "I cannot see my own *num*-fire. You can see me. Look at me. Tell me." She straightened her spine, lifted her chin with challenge. "Have I changed?"

"I see more deeply into you than into any of my other daughters," Stillshadow said. "I see more pain and fear than damage."

"But there *is* damage."

"Our scars can make us strong."

"I am not worthy," T'Cori said.

"So you say. But do you think I feel no pain? No fear?"

"What do you fear?" T'Cori asked.

The old woman's eyes narrowed. "Dying before my work with you is complete. Before I teach what you must know."

"As you taught your daughter?"

"As I taught Small Raven, the daughter of my womb. You, girl, are my heart's child. Always, I knew you would be stronger than Raven. Despite that, I could not place the Circle in your hands."

She was stronger than Raven? Madness. True, Raven had perished climbing Great Sky, but T'Cori had had Frog and Raven had not. "Why not?"

"Child, Raven was my daughter and was greatly loved by her sisters. A war between you would have torn our people apart. But now . . ."

Stillshadow did not need to continue.

T'Cori nodded. "And now, I must hold everything together."

"Yes. Now you must. For whatever days I still may dance, I must give you songs and medicines and ways of seeing."

T'Cori squeezed her mentor's shoulder. It felt like squeezing dry sticks. "I am a slow learner. You must live many, many summers, that I may learn all you have to give."

The old woman clucked her tongue. "Don't be too clever, girl. Our peo-

ple need you to be strong and wise, not clever. However many seasons remain for Sky Woman and Stillshadow, one day only Sky Woman's bones
will remain above the earth. I have to know that you are learning as fast as
you can. I make you a trade: you give me your whole heart, and I will try to
live a few moons more."

The gray, clustered boulders crouched on the open plain like stone lions.
That night, beneath their passive paws, the tribe pitched their lean-tos and
spread their skins. At the northernmost edge, Frog and T'Cori assembled
their simple shelter's sticks and brush, put a well-nursed Medicine Mouse to
sleep, and rolled into each other's arms.

That night both T'Cori and Frog dreamed of four-legged beasts with
men's eyes. Beasts who raped and killed. Who felt no remorse or fear or
compassion, because they had never dreamed their own deaths. Death was
something that happened to other beings.

Beneath their lean-to's folded branches the two young Ibandi tossed
awake. They went from sleeping to staring into each other's eyes in a single
moment, uncertain either then and later exactly whose dream, or startled
breath, was whose.

Chapter Seven

Within a snarl of dry brown baobab branches, the speckled gray warthog lay on its side. White specks of dried foam lathered its snout. Its scarred flanks were torn and bloody. Terrified and exhausted now, its leathery lids blinked as its killers approached.

These were the two-legged creatures with hurting sticks. The warthog had seen two-legged before, but those had been smaller, easier to evade.

These were larger, stronger, faster.

The warthog was too weak to move. With each breath it felt colder.

Its fading eyes watched the gnarled two-legged striding through the brush and saw it raise its stick.

Pain flooded the hog's body as the stick pierced its side. Then . . . numbness. It was dead before the stick was wrenched out.

"Praise God Blood," its killer said. "We eat."

The Mk*tk were poor gatherers. They knew little of netting trout or stickleback or trapping rabbits as did the weaklings to the north. A Mk*tk preferred to fill his belly by hunting and raiding. In truth, raiding *was* hunting. Humans of other tribes were merely prey—not to be eaten, of course. Human flesh was for God Blood's teeth alone. But their bodies might be used in any other way. The Mk*tk used human skin for leather, their bones for spears and decorations.

"What happened to Fire Gut?" Flat-Nose asked, pointing at the wounded man on the ground.

Hard Tongue shrugged. "We chased a wildebeest and stirred a one-horn with her calf. She chased us."

Now they had caught his curiosity. "And Fire Gut was caught?"

"He took the horn because he was shitting behind a bush. He was running and shitting at the same time. Even the one horn laughed!"

The Mk*tk roared with mirth. Even Fire Gut tried to laugh with them. Then blood gushed from between his lips, ending his ghastly spate of mirth.

"I am sorry," Fire Gut said. "It hurts."

"Soon," Flat-Nose said.

Hard Tongue ignored his cousin's agony. To acknowledge it would shame Fire Gut, encourage him to beg for mercy, which would deny him entrance to the next world. "How went the hunt?"

His brother Rain Hand shrugged. "Our spears are strong but cannot kill what does not live."

Flat-Nose shifted his balance. He felt something hard beneath his bare heel and ground down until it cracked. "I know where better hunting can be found."

"North?" Hard Tongue asked.

"Yes. North. We need but take the land."

Flat-Nose hunkered down, staring off to the north. "Hate their smell," he growled, "their weakness. So many of them. But they are weak. We will break them."

"We had many wounded," Hard Tongue said. "Many killed. Must be careful."

Flat-Nose's arm blurred, knocking the other man to the ground, then stood over him with his short stabbing spear. "Careful?" he roared, spittle flying from his thick, scarred lips. "Are we women, to be *careful*? No! We are men! And God Blood gave men courage! Gave men spears and claws. We will feed our god until His belly bursts."

At night, when Flat-Nose lay his head down, God Blood sent him visions of his children and grandchildren hunting in the northlands, eating their fill, slaughtering their enemies, plundering the women on the bloody ground.

He shook the pleasant images from his mind. "It is time."

Fire Gut spit blood and raised his chin. "I am ready."

Flat-Nose gazed toward Great Sky. The gigantic god mountain was invisible beyond the horizon, but sometimes, on some days, it seemed to waver mistily in the heat, floating above the horizon. "Tell God Blood to make us strong. Soon, we give him new land." Starting with the boma the Ibandi monkeys called Rock.

Flat-Nose plunged his spear into Fire Gut's wound.

Fire Gut bit through his thick lower lip, struggling not to cry out. If Fire Gut's screams were silent, God Blood might answer his prayers. Despite his wish to die with courage, at last both flesh and spirit failed. Fire Gut shrieked, his body curling back away from the shaft.

Flat-Nose wrenched the spear back and forth. As the light in Fire Gut's eyes disappeared, Flat-Nose leaned over and whispered to him. "Your children will sing your death song. God Blood will savor your flesh."

Then he wrenched the spear free.

Chapter Eight

Through a forest of dung-colored anthills, one slow, heavy step at a time, Leopard Eye and Leopard Paw dragged Stillshadow's sled toward the horizon. They each had one leather strap hitched over their right shoulders. They relied upon elephant breathing's slow, powerful strokes to postpone fatigue. "*Huh! huh! huh!*" they grunted, one exhalation timed to each drive of their right legs.

Stillshadow felt every season she had walked, which she now reckoned as six tens of winters. Perhaps more. Her memory was not what it once was, even if her old heart still felt strong.

It brought her pleasure to watch her boys pulling the sled. It was a shame that neither of them had been chosen for hunt chiefs, but that had been Cloud Stalker's decision, and she had often wondered at it. Now she wondered if some part of her lover had known what would happen on Great Sky, known that Father Mountain would slaughter his sons in such a fashion. Could he possibly have denied Paw and Eye entrance into the brotherhood to spare their lives?

Thank Great Mother she had them now. Good boys. Good men. Either of them would have made a good husband for Sky Woman, were she not in love with Frog. She did not understand Frog, but the *num*-field about his head shimmered with a yellow-white radiance unlike that of any other man.

He was not something she understood. But she approved.

T'Cori walked at her side. As Stillshadow's twin sons labored, the girl kept one hand on her swollen belly, striving to control the ebb and flow of her own breathing. A stew of emotions simmered on her apprentice's face: *fear, fatigue, despair.* All fought for her heart, a fight she dared not allow them to win.

"I have tried," T'Cori said, "in every way I know, doing everything that you have taught me to do."

Stillshadow's wizened hand slipped into the girl's smooth strong one, a contact comforting to both.

"This last thing is not learning," Stillshadow said. "It is the opposite. It is letting go of what you think you already know."

"Of what?"

"Of life," Stillshadow said. "Of life itself."

T'Cori looked back over her shoulder, and Stillshadow glanced back as well. Behind them, tens of families followed. Most seemed merely struggling with the body strain. Some sang songs or made games to entertain their children. The young ones ran ahead of their parents or wandered behind. Stillshadow could not see Snake, but she knew he would be near the back of the line, ensuring that no stragglers were lost.

So many lives in their hands. Such gentle, loving trust. It was not enough to earn it. One had to feel *worthy* of it. And since the Mk*tk had taken Sky Woman, her greatest student had felt worthy of little save disdain. There had to be some gift to give the girl. Something. She could think of nothing.

But if Stillshadow's mind was empty, her husk almost ready to return to the earth, she might still find one last miracle. "I know what must be done and how to do this thing that must be done. One closer to death than life sees these things more clearly. I go now."

"Paw. Eye. *Stop,*" Stillshadow said. Her order obeyed, the old woman levered herself up off the sled.

Stillshadow's legs wobbled, and T'Cori caught her arm.

"Where do you go?" T'Cori asked.

"I need my vision," Stillshadow said. "There is truth, and I cannot see it."

"What will you do?"

"It is a secret thing," the old woman said, "one that I may show you when I return. Perhaps."

"And what will this thing help you to do?" T'Cori asked.

"I must dig deep," Stillshadow said. "Find the heart of the world, its drumbeat. Do not fear."

"Mother," T'Cori said, "there is a thing that I have not spoken of before. I think that you already know what I must say."

"Perhaps," Stillshadow said. "Perhaps. Regardless, speak as you will."

"There is so much you do for us, more than I think I even dream. Mother, if anything happens to you . . ." She dropped her eyes.

Darling child. You think you are the only one who doubts? "And you fear you cannot?"

T'Cori turned her eyes away, but not before Stillshadow glimpsed the fear within.

"You climbed Great Sky!" the old woman said. Her deeply wrinkled hands cupped the girl's chin. "Listen to me. When I think you are ready, you *will* be ready. Today is not the day. This is not the time. This is the time for me to go, alone, to do what must be done."

"But you might die!" T'Cori protested.

Stillshadow smiled, her deepest, softest smile. "And you will not?"

As Father Mountain's countless eyes emerged from a darkening sky, the people prepared evening meals, lashing branches and hides together to make their simple shelters.

As Frog's sister, Little Brook, brought Mouse to him, Bat Wing wandered near. In better days Bat Wing would have spent more and more time with his father or uncles. They would have taken him away from the boma on their hunting trips, teaching him the twists of strange streams and the rise of untrod hillocks. Now, each day brought new horizons, new lessons, lessons passing too swiftly for even the keenest mind to absorb them all.

"This is your son?" the boy asked.

"Yes," Frog said. "He is Medicine Mouse."

"A fine boy." Bat Wing prodded at the infant. Mouse clamped his tiny soft fingers over the tip of Bat's finger as he waggled it gently. "He has strong hands and feet. He will walk far and kill many zebra."

Bat Wing pulled back on his hand, teasing, and seemed genuinely delighted as Mouse gurgled and held on more tightly.

"Where is your father?" Frog asked.

Pain flashed across Bat's face. "He died fighting the Mk*tk."

A flash of shared pain, like dry lightning in a summer sky. The boy's grief ripped open the memory of the war, of that terrible night of blood and blindness, when men struggled with monsters for the land they loved and the families they cherished.

So many had died that night. More Mk*tk than Ibandi had died, to be certain. Frog felt a fierce surge of pride: that night men had broken beasts!

True, Ibandi had outnumbered the giants three to one, but they had triumphed. Didn't that count? Didn't that mean anything at all?

If the death of this young boy's father could hold some small meaning, the world itself might not seem so empty and cold.

Frog clasped Bat's shoulder. "Then he is atop Great Sky." What harm in such a small lie?

Bat Wing scratched at the bald spot over his right ear, as if deciding whether or not to answer. "Yes. I know. Sometimes I see his face in the clouds."

Frog's ears tingled with disbelief. "What did you say?"

Bat Wing poked at the dust with his toes. "I am sorry." He started to turn away. "I am a fool."

"No!" Frog said. "Tell me what you said."

The boy stared at the ground as if searching for a lost toy. "I should not have said it."

"Listen to me," Frog said. "I want to hear you. Your words were good." He cupped the boy's chin in his hand. "Never be ashamed of your thoughts. I spent too many winters fearing what I heard in my head—" he tapped his temple with a finger "—what I saw in my dreams. Tell me."

Within a heartbeat, the boy's face melted from doubt to cautious optimism. "I . . . it is just that when I look at the clouds in a certain way . . ." He trailed off, perhaps still doubting Frog's sincerity. "I can see an ear *there*—" he pointed at a rounded, fluffy edge "—and the shape of an eye."

Of all the strange things that Frog might have seen or heard that day, this was the very last he might have expected. "Have you always seen this?"

Bat nodded and then drew back. "Am I bad?"

Frog seized Bat Wing under the armpits and lifted him up to the sky. For as long as he had drawn breath, he had been the only one who saw the faces in the clouds or heard songs in the wind. Frog felt as if a stone had been rolled from his heart. "No! This is very, *very* good. Now tell me . . . what else can you see?"

"There—" Bat Wing pointed at a cloud squatting near the horizon "—a mountain." His finger shifted toward one that nearly eclipsed the sun. "A deer."

"Yes," Frog said, his heart full and warm. "Yes, I can see it."

"You can?" The boy squinted doubtfully. "You're laughing at me."

"No," Frog said. "I laugh because my heart is happy. You have no father. Do you have an uncle?"

"Two. But both remained in the shadow. Only my mother walks with me," Bat said.

Frog hugged the boy, felt Bat Wing's strong young heart dancing against his own. "Then if you will have me, you are now my nephew." He rubbed the tips of their noses together. "Those who see strange things should be family together. From now on, you will walk with me, if you wish. Would you have me?"

The boy's eyes gleamed. "Uncle" was the only word he could say.

Chapter Nine

The evening shadows had merged into a dusky mask. The air had cooled, and the dry, sharp tang of hot sand yielded to the whispered perfume of night-blooming cactus. Quietly, without drawing any attention to herself, Stillshadow hobbled out to the camp's edge and then beyond. She did not seek to meet or hold the eyes of any that she passed, nor did they seek to meet or hold hers.

Her people pretended not to see her or to comprehend the risks entailed by such a brittle-bone traveling alone into the night. She did not need their doubts and fears added to the chorus echoing between her own ears.

Her old hips and knees were slow fires. The bamboo crutch beneath her right armpit carried enough of her weight to walk, but every halting step groaned of flesh's frailty.

Certainly, some must have worried. Such an old woman alone? And at night—when human sight failed, and the powers of fang and claw were at their height?

But she was Stillshadow, and as such could not be questioned. Even to doubt her actions would be wrong. As it would be wrong to add their fears to her own.

She walked and hummed prayers to the *jowk* as the ground crunched beneath her sandaled feet. For a quarter of the night the old woman walked. Her senses were open, seeking a sign. In the whisper of flowing water or a hyena's distant call. Or a fruited scent, floating on the wind. There was no way for her waking mind to know where she might find a sign.

A plant. A berry. A mushroom. A venomous snake or scorpion. Any or all of these could be her doorway into the dream world. All she needed to do was be ready and watchful.

Before the moon had risen fully, she glimpsed a thing of interest and turned from her path to investigate.

There, revealed by the cloud-shrouded moonlight, sparkled a spiderweb's jeweled rungs. She leaned down, close enough for her old eyes to detect the clustered knot of legs and swollen belly crouched in ambush at the web's upper corner. This brown striped eight-legged was known to her: the black head was unmistakable. "Grass spider," she whispered, drawing closer. "So long has it been since last we spoke. Within you dwells the spirit of all eight-legged. I ask that spirit to restrain her anger. I must kill this one sister. I need her blood in my veins."

She reached down into the web. As she spoke, the brown and black spider crawled over and over her hand. As it crossed her palm she made a fist, then winced with the sharp, sudden pain.

Stillshadow lowered herself to her knees. She chanted, twitching and wincing.

A wall of poison fire, the spider venom leapfrogged toward her aged heart. *Frogs. A wall of fire. What?*

Then conscious thought faded, and she slipped into the place behind her dreams.

A place of trees and shadows, of game and clouds and plants. An endless stream of human faces capered behind her eyes. She saw . . .

Mk*tk leeched of color. Men with the fangs and fur of wolves. Spotted yellow women with long necks. A great green circle . . .

Mortal terror hammered at the walls of discipline. She shuddered, trembled. Stillshadow tried to walk and could not. Tried to crawl and toppled onto her side.

"Great Mother, help me," Stillshadow whispered. "I have the sight but not the strength. Give me your power. . . ."

Her muscles knotted. Her breath contracted to a low rattle in her aged throat. "Help me, Great Mother," she said softly. "All my days, I have served you. I thought my flesh would follow me, but Small Raven fell. So it seems the foundling was your chosen. Did I somehow fail you?"

Now the tears flowed without end. All questions vanished, like winter leaves drifting into a pond. The world flew apart, and the emptiness behind it crawled out to engulf her.

Stillshadow turned to face the dark eastern horizon. For the very last time in her long and honored life, she sang to the sun.

"Great Mother," she whispered against the wind. "All my days, I have breathed for no one but you. And yet, we lost our land. The ground wept with our blood. And now, when my people need me most, my inner eye sees nothing. Is this right? Have I not served you?" She listened for an answer that did not come. "I beg you to tell me: Is this right?"

In the wind's cold cry there were no words, no answer. Her fingers gouged grooves in the rough, sandy soil. "Help me."

Stillshadow stared and wept and sang. And in answer to her final call the sun struggled to be born, wet and red from its celestial womb.

Before she reached the edge of the camp, T'Cori heard Frog's "*Huh! Huh!*" exhalations from around the cairn of weathered, sand-colored rocks marking his practice site.

She watched as he turned this way and that, jabbing and cutting. It was almost like a dance, really. The body flow was the same, but Frog was concentrating on something outside himself, a target. Dream dancers focused within.

When Frog paused to hawk out some of the dust gumming his throat, she went to him. "I was told to be silent, but I worry."

He wiped away a thread of sweat dripping from his lashes. "What is this worry?"

"Mother Stillshadow went out last night," she said. "She did not return."

His hand froze. "Where did she go?"

"She said she needed to find our dream."

He stuck the tip of his spear into the ground. The gesture was so familiar to her now, and so dear. He reminded her of a brown flamingo. "We will find her," he said, "or leave our bones in the sand."

For half a quarter, Frog, Uncle Snake, and the Leopard twins had tracked Stillshadow through the mud flats and brittle grass. If Frog had believed in gods, he might have offered a prayer for her delivery. Any other Ibandi might have made such a prayer, but other Ibandi had not climbed Great Sky or gazed into the icy silence at its peak. This knowledge, more than his worries for Stillshadow, dogged his every step.

"This is good," Snake said.

"Wait," Frog said. He dropped to one knee and turned an ear into the wind. He heard a single distant howl, followed a few breaths later by two more. "Do you hear?"

"Baboons," Leopard Eye said.

"Hyenas, also," Frog said. "Come."

As morning shadows drifted across a wide and fire-scarred plain they ran. Across grass and through scrub they ran, across tumbled rocks and through scratching stands of cactus. Their sprint slowed to a trot and then to a halt. There just beyond the parted grass crouched four of the spotted, heavy-jawed scavengers. Beyond the hyenas clustered a troop of baboons.

They were big ones, half the size of men, covered with bone-white fur. Their jaws were longer than the width of their narrow shoulders. Black lips peeled away from gleaming fangs. Their eyes, far back up on their heads beneath a sheltering shelf of brow, burned like tiny yellow fires.

Five hands of the manlike creatures were circled, the young and the old hidden behind a line of aggressively postured males.

At first Frog doubted his eyes, but there in the center of the circle, with the elders and the young, kneeling just beyond the hyena males, an ancient woman stared out into the western horizon.

"*Father Mountain*," Snake whispered.

As the Ibandi approached, the hyenas barked and fled. But the baboons merely parted their ranks, almost as if they had awaited the humans' arrival. For all the notice she gave to the scramble of furred limbs, Stillshadow might have been made of stone or wood or even been a woman of chalk, a mere silhouette scratched beneath her own sitting stone.

"Old Mother?" Frog said.

"Great Dancer?" Snake dropped to one knee. "Speak to us."

Frog came closer. "Stillshadow?"

No response. For a moment he wondered: *Could she be dead?* Panic fluttered in his chest, but then he realized: *No. There.* His newly sharpened eyes detected the rise and fall of her withered shoulders.

Stillshadow tumbled sideways into their arms, as all about them her hairy guardians danced and howled their fierce delight to the morning sun.

Beneath the slanted roof of sticks and leaves, Stillshadow lay curled on her side, muttering aloud to gods or *jowk* unknown. T'Cori had packed the old woman's eyes with mud and cactus pulp, then covered them with wet leaves.

Despite her own growing fear, T'Cori struggled to find some part of her still unshaken, unafraid, able to offer visions or leadership. As a consequence, she barely noticed when Frog approached from behind her.

"How is she?" he asked.

"I am not sure," the young medicine woman said. "Her *num* and *jowk* are weak, but her face-eyes . . . they are dead."

He shuddered. "When we found her, she was staring at the sun. She did not move. Did not even blink."

T'Cori nodded. "Why would she do such a thing?"

Frog had no answer, and closed his eyes.

T'Cori tried to imagine what he was feeling. Frog already felt unable to act or decide or do anything other than follow her lead.

Was he now imagining himself sightless? Wondering what use a blind hunter would be to his people? Did he think that if he lost his eyes it would be best for him, for her, for all of them if he walked out into the brush and kept walking until Father Mountain took his bones?

Yet somehow, Stillshadow seemed undiminished. In fact, there were ways in which the old woman now whispering to the spirits seemed more alive than she had even a moon ago.

Almost as if she heard the blasphemous thoughts, Stillshadow pushed her way up to a seated position. From behind her herbal wraps, she seemed to be gazing *through* T'Cori's flesh. The ancient eyes saw bone.

Her dust-parched throat was capable of little more than gravelly whispers. T'Cori offered her a water gourd. The medicine woman sipped and swallowed.

"Bring ten pebbles," Stillshadow said finally.

"Pebbles?" Frog asked.

"At once!" she snapped. Then Stillshadow lay back again, seemed to shrink to the size of a child.

Frog retreated from the lean-to and ran off to do as she had asked, returning swiftly with two handfuls of stones.

When he had placed them on the ground before her, Stillshadow smoothed her hands over them. She plucked up a purplish one and rolled it between her palms. Then, one stone at a time, she laid out a circle, only deigning to speak when the circle was complete. "Every year," she said, "the herds go north in spring and return in fall. They travel to Father Mountain's favorite grounds, to amuse him with their feeding and fleeing and rutting. They grow fat on Great Mother's sacred grasses, on the four-legged flesh. They go out—" her hand traced up and then cut across to the left "—and they return. To find them we must travel *west*. There, we will find hunting lands as fine as our own, where the herds travel as they return home."

"Always," Frog said, "we thought that the animals went out, and returned the way they went, in a line. You say they travel in a great circle?"

Stillshadow ran her fingers along the earth, fingers brushing the freshly grooved soil.

"What would that mean?" Leopard Paw asked.

Stillshadow tried to push herself up to her elbows. "What serves the four-legged serves the two-legged as well. Find them, and we find our way."

"It will be done," Frog said.

Chapter Ten

Bracketed between her brothers Leopard Eye and Leopard Paw, Blossom escorted their mother back to her lean-to.

Blossom's heart beat like a hummingbird's wings. She craved and cherished any moment spent with Stillshadow, struggled not to resent the fact, obvious to all, that the chief dream dancer preferred Sky Woman to her own flesh and blood.

Blossom was four hands older than the girl now called Sky Woman, and in fact had been the foundling's wet nurse. But despite her purity of heart and strength of blood, Blossom had never risen high among the dancers.

Blossom had helped her brothers build their mother's shelter, wedging it between a dead ant nest and a cactus tree. Twice the size of most Ibandi hutches, it was lined with zebra skin and roofed with branches and leaves, large enough for an audience of three or four. Rude it might have been, but Blossom was proud.

"Mother," asked Leopard Eye after they had set her comfortably on a bed of grass, "is there more we can do for you?"

"Not now," Stillshadow said. "Please go. But, Blossom, please remain with me."

As the twins left, Blossom crawled into the shadows with her mother.

The old woman stretched out her arm until Blossom reciprocated. They linked hands.

"I am happy with the others," Stillshadow said. "But I see my womb daughter is sad."

Blossom sighed, struggling to keep the fear from her voice and failing. "How can you see anything?" she asked.

"Only my face-eyes have closed. I have five more, and all speak your sadness." Stillshadow smiled. "Then again, perhaps it is Cloud Stalker who tells me your mood."

"You speak to my father?" Blossom asked. Stillshadow *umm-hmmed,* the corners of her mouth turning slightly upward. "In the dream world?"

"He says that he loves you."

"I wish," Blossom said wistfully, "to see the world you see. I will never be so strong, and I know it. And I know that as long as I help my people survive, I have purpose. All that you ask, I have done." She wiped at the corner of her eye. "You asked me to nurture Sky Woman, and I did, before she ever had a name. You asked me to step aside for her. I did. To leave the only home I have ever known and come with you." Here Blossom paused. "How could I not? You are all I know and love in this world." Tears blurred her vision as she squeezed her mother's hand. "Perhaps I am not the dancer Sky Woman has become, but I love our people and our path. When I thought we had lost you, I died."

Stillshadow sighed. "My child—"

"Please." For the first time she could remember, Blossom interrupted her mother mid-sentence. She could hardly believe her own daring and wondered at the desperation that had driven her to it. She fisted her trembling hands and thrust them against her thighs. "Let me speak. I do not know if I will be able to say it ever again." She took a deep breath and began. "I remember the days only Small Raven and I could call you mother. I was not the prettiest, or the best, but I could call you mother, and the others could not." Despite her low spirits, the memory brightened her. "Even as I suckled that little nameless child, I knew she was special. But I never dreamed that one day she would rise above me."

"Blossom," Stillshadow tried again. But Blossom's flow, once begun, would not be stemmed. If she did not spit the venom from her heart, it would destroy her. "So my suckling stands above me. Empty One climbed the mountain with Small Raven and returned alone." Her brow wrinkled. "Where was the right in that? Where?"

Her brow smoothed again. "I am told that Empty One is the holiest of women and that I should love her."

"Her name is Sky Woman," Stillshadow said.

Blossom crossed her arms, defiant and silent.

"You do not love?" Stillshadow said at last.

"I loved my *sister*," Blossom screamed. The tears burned her cheeks. "I loved *Small Raven*, the one who shared my flesh. And I love you. But I do not love *Sky Woman*." Her lips twisted as if the words burned them. "I have danced every role you asked. Lived my life as a lie. But if I had known what she would be, what price I would pay, I tell you, Mother, I would have crushed her skull as she slept."

"Blossom! Do not say such things!"

For a few breaths there was no sound in the hut. Then Blossom sighed and reached out and took Stillshadow's hand. However withered it might have become, it remained the most precious thing in all the world. "But I did not, and I do my best to honor her. Am I a bad thing?"

"None of us can tell our hearts what to feel," her mother said. "I hope I've never asked you to be anything other than what you are."

"No," Blossom said. "Never. You have been mother to all of us, but most of all to me." She leaned her head against her mother's thin shoulder. "I am not clever. My voice holds no magic. But I loved Small Raven. And I love you."

Had it really been so long since childhood? Blossom remembered so clearly when her mother could lift her with a single arm, could carry her everywhere. When had the daughter grown so large that the mother could no longer carry her? If only Blossom had known such a day would ever come, her last day cradled in Stillshadow's arms would have been more precious. More . . .

Words died before they could be fully formed.

Great Mother. What has become of the world?

"What if I cannot love her?" Blossom asked.

"It is not about you. Or Sky Woman. Or me. It is about our people and what they need. And what they need is to love Sky Woman."

Blossom felt as if she were falling, had grasped at her mother's protective hand and come achingly close to safety.

But in the end those fingers had brushed past her and moved on. Only the people mattered. And the people needed Sky Woman.

In the end, Blossom's bleeding heart did not matter at all.

Dust devils capered in the tall yellow grass as the Ibandi wound their dusty way north. As they had for four moons now, weary children held their mother's hands, dark-rimmed eyes gazing out at the horizon.

The Ibandi were stretched into a thin line, but groupings within that line changed many times a day, so that they could while away the time talking to family or friends. They shared their food and water, and what hope remained.

Blossom decided to walk with Ember and little Flamingo, sisters by marriage to Frog Hopping. They spoke of clouds and sun, their hopes for the future and other things. Then finally the conversation fixed upon past days.

"Blossom," Ember said, "you suckled Sky Woman."

"Yes," Blossom said. The memory made her nipples itch.

"I . . . it may be sin to say such a thing," Flamingo said, "but I am afraid. Stillshadow says that Sky Woman is ready to lead us. You know her better than we."

"Better than anyone," Blossom replied.

"I was sure of it." Ember seemed relieved. "Tell us, is she really ready to lead us? Should we believe?"

"She is strong," Blossom said. She weighed her words with care. "Mother Stillshadow believes it, and I believe Sky Woman to be a great dancer. Even when the Mk*tk took her seventh eye, it did not diminish her strength."

Ember gasped, stricken. "*What?* What do you say? The Mk*tk *what?*"

Blossom turned her face away. Curse herself for letting that slip out! "I . . . I say more than I should. Please. Tell no one I said this." The knowledge that Sky Woman, their savior and salvation, had been taken like any common bhan could not pass outside the ranks of the dancers.

And yet it had. The words had been an accident, of course. An accident.

Ember backed away along the dusty line, staring at Blossom in disbelief. Which had been more alarming—Blossom's words or the fact that she had spoken them?

Blossom held Medicine Mouse against her breast; the boy's small, moist mouth sucking. Despite the fact that Ibandi women often shared wet-nurse duty, Mouse fed in her arms more often than most. He was a dear child, a sweet child, but his smiles did not heal her heart. Despite his contented sounds and small, warm graspings, her tears fell.

Blossom had seen almost four tens of summers. She had given birth to only four children, and none of them had been chosen for either dream dancers or hunt chiefs. The babies had been taken away and given to women of the cardinal bomas.

But after her first child, delivered when Blossom had danced ten and five summers, her milk had continued to flow. As a consequence, she had been given a child to feed, a child chosen by Stillshadow from among all those born in the circle.

Blossom's body was strong, could feed children, and she had nursed more hungry mouths than she could remember. Some had remained within the dancers; others had found the life of service too rigorous and returned to the circle.

They came, they went, but Blossom remained. Even if her own mother, the greatest woman who had ever lived, could not see the depths of her, Blossom was special. She was blessed.

No matter what anyone said or felt or thought. Now or ever again.

Chapter Eleven

T'Cori and Frog huddled together around the fire that night, cuddling Medicine Mouse between them. The rest of their people were scattered, eating the last of the fresh meat. There was sufficient jerky to last several days, but if hunting did not improve soon, bellies would grumble.

Frog took great comfort in embracing his boy Mouse, feeling his small strong wiggles, kissing his forehead's soft, leaf-thin skin and smelling the fresh milk on his breath. Blossom had complained that her breasts were tired, had brought them another wet-nurse, begging a few days rest to let the milk rise again.

His child. His flesh, his only reminder of his lost wife, Glimmer.

Young Bat Wing ran to him, small feet kicking up the dirt.

"What?" Frog asked.

"Some families crept away in the night," Bat Wing told them.

"How many?"

"A hand of families," the boy said. "They go home?"

"I hope," Frog said, "that there is a home for them to go to." He sighed. Over the moons a few had straggled off, but never so many at once.

"And there is more," the boy said. "Stillshadow's daughter, Blossom, is gone."

T'Cori's eyes went wide and round. "No! It is not possible."

"I do not lie," Bat Wing said. "She and a few others left before dark. Should we go after them?"

Frog ground his knuckles against his eyes. What to do? What *was* there to do in such a world?

"Does Stillshadow know this?" T'Cori asked.

The old woman's lean-to was paces away, too far for hearing, but in the silence following her question, a plaintive sound rose from its depths.

At first Frog did not recognize the sound. He had never heard it before.

But it seemed that T'Cori had heard it, perhaps more often than any of them had ever suspected.

"My mother is crying," T'Cori said. "She knows."

"What do we do?" Bat Wing asked.

T'Cori closed her eyes. "Let Blossom go," she said. "Let any who would leave, follow her."

For days more they walked, past herds of elephants, too big and strong and smart to be prey. A hunter was almost always killed or crippled trying to take one of them. Reluctantly, bellies growling, they passed the great beasts and hoped for meat to come.

Occasionally they glimpsed other four-legged, usually at a distance, but they dissolved into heat dreams before the Ibandi reached them.

Some of the grasslands were brown from drought, others blackened and twisted by wildfire. There was no place that called to their hearts, that felt like a patch of sand and soil where they might set down roots.

More discouraged with each fierce new sun, they walked on. For the time being they were not sick. Their children did not starve, their ribs did not protrude through shrunken skin.

But that day might soon come.

Chapter Twelve

T'Cori found Stillshadow staring blindly up into her lean-to's thatched roof. Since Blossom's departure ten days ago, some fire in her mentor's heart seemed to have died. All day and half the night the old woman muttered endlessly, conversing with her dead lover, Cloud Stalker, with the *jowk*, perhaps with her long-dead mother and teacher, Night Bird.

Who knew such things?

"Mother," T'Cori said, "I need your wisdom."

"What can an old blind woman do for you?" Stillshadow's mouth moved, but in the deep shadow, her expression remained unchanged.

"Mother . . . the hunters grow weary and afraid. Is there a ceremony I can give them? Anything that might help?"

"In my dreams," Stillshadow said, "I still see Cloud Stalker. Often, we spoke of hunting. Of the soul vine stretching out from our men to their prey."

"The same soul vine that connects a man and woman during sex?" That was a small miracle she had experienced many, many times.

"Yes. It is a thing that connects all. It is also what connects the healer to the wound or sickness. If you can open your own senses, go more deeply within yourself, you might open the way for them as well."

"How do I do that?" the girl asked.

There seemed genuine regret in Stillshadow's reply. "I cannot give it to you. You must find it within yourself, and then give from there."

T'Cori thought hard. Medicine had been her path since childhood, one harder than an outsider could ever have believed. *First know all things. Then understand the One, from which all things arise.*

So confusing: *one and many. The living and the nonliving. The jowk: a burning lake or a spirit arising from that lake or the living spirit animating a sack of skin.* Too many truths. Some minds fought against the knowledge. Hers had surrendered, and now she saw truth everywhere, even if she could not convey that truth to others.

What their hunters needed, she thought, was a bit of magic. If she could show them more of what she saw, if only they knew what she knew, their children's bellies might not rumble.

"Once, you taught me a seventh eye dance. Shouldn't a hunter's eyes be as open as a dancer's?" Two face-eyes. One on each hand. One on either foot. And the sex organs. *Seven eyes.* The soul vine extended through the sex organs and connected human beings to one another and to all the world. They saw what came before we were born and knew what would be after we were gone. They were the straightest path to the dream world and the world beyond.

Stillshadow nodded, suddenly more engaged and animated than she had been in days. "We are speaking well together. Yes."

"Then this is what I will try."

T'Cori and two of her sisters spent the next morning gathering hands of hands of stones that looked or felt alike, that sang to her, that possessed some sacred similarity of grain or color. With those she created a small ring and around that another and beyond that another still.

They blessed their rock garden with smoke and spit, setting a fire at the very center. Then they sat, awaiting the hunters' arrival.

For almost a quarter the hunters had sat in a circle: smoking their bone pipes, speaking of sex and building huts and hunting.

Frog felt odd, and oddly sad. Accepted as a hunt chief, or the closest thing the Ibandi had to one, he had failed his people. He had not the training or skill to be a real hunt chief, and he possessed that honorary title purely because of his climb up Great Sky and the fact that he was beloved of Sky Woman.

They trusted him to guide the hunters, to read sign and smell water in the wind. More, they needed to trust *someone*—and to have someone to blame when things went poorly. At this moment, blame for the failure of their hunts sat directly on him. Now his woman was attempting to compensate for his failings. He hoped, he *prayed* that she would succeed, but he did not know what he would feel if she did.

He searched to find even one space within his heart free of guilt or fear, and he failed. If T'Cori's ceremony did not succeed, what would become of them?

Before his mind could travel further along that path, Sky Woman appeared.

Only six dream dancers had accompanied Frog and T'Cori on their travel north. All but Blossom, T'Cori and Sing Sun had turned back. Now only T'Cori and Sing Sun remained. But in the moons since their departure, Stillshadow and her apprentice had been sharing the secrets with a few of the women who had dared the walk north.

This is a great medicine journey, Stillshadow had once said. *And those who dare all, win all. The woman who follows me, follows Sky Woman, has a dancer's heart.*

And Frog thought that might have been the truth. The six women swayed toward the hunters balancing ostrich-egg water bowls in their palms, singing as they stepped. Their faces and shoulders were painted to resemble blue and yellow flowers, their hair twisted up with mud and bits of shell and bone, lips painted bright red.

Their songs were not in human tongue. They babbled bits of animal talk, their mouths formed wind and rain sounds, shifting and changing from step to step so that thought fled Frog's mind. Fled from words and toward pictures, memories, away from reason and toward sensation.

"Come, men of the Ibandi," T'Cori called, beckoning them.

The two tens of hunters knelt or sat cross-legged, forming three rows. They stared at the dream dancers, too entranced even to blink. If before, the women had seemed little more than dusty traveling companions, now they seemed to have regained a precious fragment of their former glory.

Leopard Paw's lover, Sing Sun, dipped her finger in cool water and drew a symbol on Frog's forehead. "Blessings unto you, hunter," she whispered, her mouth close, her breath warm, sweet and moist. "You are our life. It is your strength, your courage, that keep us alive. You fill our bellies, feed our children. You are the muscle, the sinew, the brain. We are your heart."

She brushed her lips against his ear, depositing upon his nervous flesh a single, precious kiss. A promise? A taste of the world unseen?

There was no other world. No gods. No *jowk.* Frog felt as if she had peeled away his skull and licked his brain.

Fire.

Flames raced through his bones, consuming his marrow as she moved on to the next hunter in line.

From the corner of his eye he saw that a different symbol had been painted on each hunter's forehead, although he could not see what the symbols had been.

"Close your eyes," T'Cori said to them. The last thing he glimpsed before he obeyed was Stillshadow, sitting behind her on a rounded, brown-speckled stone, whispering to herself, seemingly watchful despite her blindness. She nodded approval as the women passed from man to man, drawing fingers over their faces, shutting the hunters' eyes.

Finally T'Cori herself approached Frog. Her cool soft fingers against his cheek soothed him. In the last instant before darkness stole his sight, her face, wreathed in ceremonial shells and paint, was barely recognizable as the woman he cherished. He realized that the truth was as she had said: *Sky Woman was not his.* She belonged to the tribe, and, as painful as it might be to admit that, it behooved him to remember, lest she be forced to remind him herself.

He closed his eyes.

One of the women—he didn't know which one—pressed against his chest, reclined him until the sand pressed against his back. Strong, small hands uncrossed his legs and stretched them out straight.

"I need you to hear me," she said. He knew the voice: Sing Sun. "You, the men of the tribe, the hunters, must listen to a weak woman. But the hunt chiefs, who once did such things, are with Father Mountain now and cannot help us. You must listen to me, because there is no one else to hear."

Sing Sun chanted her words, and slowly they were echoed by other voices. Who was there? Judging by the footsteps tapping lightly around him, it was possible that half the tribe had gathered around.

"Your face-eyes are closed," she said, "but I want you to open your hand-and foot-eyes. They will guide the bow, the spear. They will follow the meat trail, you must find and ask your prey the great question.

"And that question is: *Will you die for us?* Are you willing to feed our women and children? Will you yield in blood, knowing that in time all things return to Father Mountain, that all souls are equal in His mighty eyes? Knowing that in the beginning, all things came from Great Mother and that they are all Her children?

"Because understand: all existence is *num,* but all life is *jowk. Num* makes *jowk. Jowk* has *num.* All *jowk* is *num,* but not all *num* is *jowk.* All life is only *jowk,* wearing uncountable skins. As water can be poured into skins and eggshells and cupped palms, *jowk* is found in many shapes. But do not mistake the skin for the *jowk.* You and your prey are the same *jowk,* wearing different skins.

"It is the nature of life to rise and fall. We ask that if this is your time, you fall for us and not for the jackal who waits in the shadows. Submit to the strength and courage of our hunters, and we will sing your praises, where the jackal only laughs as his jaws crack your bones.

"Breathe for me," she said. "Push the air out. Then relax, trust Great Mother to give you air. Just exhale and relax. Again and again.

"When you call your woman to you, do you not feel your seventh eye yearning? And when you call the antelope, is it not the same fleshly hunger?"

"See them," T'Cori said, taking Sing Sun's place. "See them. See your women in your minds. Feel their soft skin against yours. Feel your heat rise."

Nervously at first, the men grasped their roots.

"No!" T'Cori's voice rose sharply. "Do *not* touch yourself. *See* the touching, but do not touch."

Confused, Leopard called out, "What do you ask of us?"

"See it in your mind! As if you were dreaming. Before you fall asleep or just after you awaken, there is a moment when the worlds of man and dream are very close. There, I know, you have thought of hunting and sexing and other things. Use that same dream mind. See yourself. Touch yourself . . . but *only with your mind.*"

Finally grasping her meaning, the men spread their arms and gripped at the ground with their fingertips, eyes tightly closed.

Slowly at first, then with greater and greater fervor, their hips gyrated. They bucked and arched, barked and howled as if trying to mate with the clouds above them.

"Now," T'Cori said, "that same yearning, that same connection . . . extend your soul vine to the prey. In your mind, see the animal you wish to hunt, as if imagining your lover."

"Yes!" one hunter screamed. "By Father Mountain!"

They were shouting and writhing and coming now. In all his life, Frog had never heard such a thing. Had anyone?

His breath sang in his throat. As the pace quickened, his body hummed on and on with unrelieved tension. The women's clapping grew louder. They hummed and sang along with his breathing.

T'Cori's bright, quick voice winged above the others'. His mind-eye saw her clapping her hands and stamping her feet, driving them on with her *num*.

Frog's own breath somehow turned *inward*, so that he was riding a river that blazed through the darkness behind his eyes, taking him away and down and away.

Once again, Frog Hopping stood upon Great Sky, gazing down at the plain. Upon it grazed uncounted hands of impala and giraffe. He had but to climb down and claim them. A hand at his shoulder seared his skin. He turned around to see his beloved brother Fire Ant's skeletal fingers clawing at him. Ant's eyes and cheeks were hollow. At Frog's left shoulder stood Hawk Shadow, his eldest brother. Both Hawk and Ant were dead men, all maggot and shriveled flesh.

"Brother," they spoke as one, "mourn not for us. All two-legged die. And so must the four-legged. If they do not perish upon your spear, it is not because they were so swift or clever. It is because you have given your flesh, but not your bones, to the hunt. Give yourself. Give . . ."

Their bodies unraveling, they disappeared.

There were no bones beneath their flesh.

Frog saw many things then: earth and fire and water. He watched clouds melt and re-form into the faces of men and women. From their cloud sitting stones they mocked the petty affairs of men. Around him the breathing dwindled to lustful calls and groans. Sparks drifted in the wind like fireflies. Flames seared the darkness behind his closed eyes. They were like falling stars, only these flew upward from his groin, as if he was self-pleasuring. His root grew firm. With every breath those sparks grew fatter. He was no longer trying to direct his breath. The strange thing happening in his body was no longer under his control. It was like running down a hill that gradually grew steeper and steeper. At first, you control your feet. Then, the earth itself pulls you, and you can do nothing save run or tumble.

He was tumbling.

The light seared his eyes. In the midst of it stood a great antlered deer, a buck who had climbed atop a doe. He humped his hips, thrust as if burning with seed. The buck's vast dark eyes met his own.

"Mate, my brother," Frog whispered. "Make your children. And then . . . die for me."

The buck's eyes clouded, and he nodded his crowned head. Then the fire within Frog erupted, and his body was rocked with num *enough to char his hair.*

•   •   •

Frog's eyes fluttered open. All about him, the ground was littered with the hunters' curled bodies. Each had experienced his own powerful changing. Frog's hand brushed his root. His fingers came away dry: there had been fire but no spend.

Truly, this was a miracle.

Chapter Thirteen

As dust devils danced amid the thornbushes and scrub, seven hunters prowled in search of prey.

"I am strong. I am fast and brave. I hunt for my people." Uncle Snake's good right eye narrowed fiercely.

"We will kill many!" Leopard Paw said.

"Quiet," Frog said. "The prey approaches."

"Truly," Leopard Paw said, "Sky Woman is a mighty dancer."

The brush on the far side of the clearing rustled, and a hog's bristly head poked through. They froze: the pig was still beyond spear or arrow range. It sniffed the air. Would the breeze betray them? Curse it, they were upwind and had not masked their scent.

"You are thirsty, so thirsty," Frog coaxed. *"The water is cool. Come to the water . . ."*

Instead, perhaps sensing danger, the hog backed away.

The shadows lengthened and then shrank once again. Although they waited with both patience and skill, they gained nothing.

"Let's go back," Frog said. "Perhaps some of the others were more fortunate."

"If not," Leopard Paw said, "I will be eating fill grass tonight."

"If only we could *find* fill grass," Frog said.

"If not," Leopard Paw grunted, and spit toward the south, "then plain grass will have to do."

•   •   •

The hunters straggled in quietly that night. The most successful of them had been Leopard Paw: three hares swung limply from his belt.

Gazelle Tears took the fattest and hefted it by the ears, clucking with disapproval. "This won't feed many," the old woman said. "I thought you were a great hunter."

She laughed, and the old toothless ones chuckled along with her.

"A few hares change nothing. This is worse than it was before," Uncle Snake said. "We cannot live like this."

Chapter Fourteen

The afternoon sunlight glinted from the thin, oily stream running a spear's throw from their camp. Wispy black monkey thorn trees and a single stunted baobab shadowed the water, vied with the thin grass for its moisture. A few hands of Ibandi children romped in the shallows, splashing and rolling and pushing each other as their mothers filled gourds and skins.

Frog and T'Cori sat between the twin fires, watching the play with a shared wistfulness. Not so long ago, they were still children, surrounded by a world that could be brightened by a few moment's play.

Now, they knew that tomorrow would come and might not bring happiness with it.

T'Cori's face was long. "I fear it did not work the way it should have. My magic was not strong enough."

"We will hunt," Frog said. "It is not for you to say if you are strong enough. That is for Great Mother. For Father Mountain."

"I must raise my *num*," she insisted. "Weave it into a soul vine. Still-shadow was our strength, but now she is blind. There are so many things that we relied on her to do in the dream world."

"What things?" Frog asked in a quiet voice. She rarely revealed dream dancer mysteries, and he never pressed her.

"She walked the second path," T'Cori said. "She awakened within the dream. To awaken within the dream gives one the ability to awaken in this world as well."

"We are not awake . . . ?"

Her eyes went very wide. "I should not have said that. It is a great secret."

Frog's teeth toyed with his upper lip. "What manner of worlds do you see? I see this one, and it is all I know."

"As you have told me, many times."

"What is it that Stillshadow once did that she can no longer do?" he asked.

"She knows every berry, lizard or fruit. Knows every four-, six- or eight-legged." T'Cori's head swam with the memories. She remembered her first climb up the slopes of Great Earth, picking the delicate purple, black-edged morning glories. Only Stillshadow knew where the first would open, its nectar a rare medicine. Stillshadow knew the very day the green berries would turn red. She knew by touch and sight and smell when a blister or boil was ready for cutting.

"All of them have uses," she said. "Many times we would be walking, and she would suddenly find a new plant with a purple berry to our right. And then a quarter later, a dung beetle rolled away buffalo scat to our left. She knew how to mix berry and crushed beetle to heal fever."

That comment caught Frog by surprise. "The world is so large . . . how can you know enough?"

"Not knowing," T'Cori said. "*Feeling.* Her egg and its fibers embraced the *num* of things, knew how the *jowk* combined to make things useful to men. The butterfly whispers in her ear—"

"Butterfly?"

T'Cori flushed. "Oh! I keep forgetting that you do not know these things." She looked swiftly to either side, to see if they were being overheard. No one near the trees, no one near the tumbled tan rocks. Then she whispered, "Great Mother was a butterfly."

Frog sighed. "And Father Mountain is . . . what? An elephant shrew?"

"A spider." She poked him with her elbow. "The father of all spiders. Do not jest."

"I try," he said. "You do not make it easy."

She glared at him. "The butterfly teaches her to do these things. She does not speak to me as often or as clearly."

A pause, and then she added, "And when they do speak to me, they don't tell me things I want to hear." She leaned her head against his shoulder. "Thank you. I have been alone all my life, except Stillshadow. And now . . . she abandons me."

"I will not leave," he said. "T'Cori . . . forgive yourself. We cannot make the rain fall or the wind blow. Be happy with what we can do." He brightened. "See? I begin to sound like you. Does that mean that if we are together long enough, you will begin to sound like me?"

"As long as I do not *look* like you, pig face—" she rubbed her nose against his "—or *think* like you! Look!" She tucked her hands into her armpits, flapped her elbows and cawed like a crow, pointing at the sky. "I see cloud people!"

"Where?" Frog said, squinting up into the afternoon sky.

"There! Hawk and Scorpion are wrestling."

His expression flattened. "You laugh at me."

"Sometimes," she said, "laughter is all that stops the tears."

She pressed against him, tangling their arms and legs together. "You do not see what I see," T'Cori said. "The world is not rock and wood."

"What is it, then?"

She sighed. "Wind and fire and sensation. We leave scat, Frog. All men leave sign, wherever we go. All the world's creatures do this. We are netted in all our yesterdays."

"There is always tomorrow," Frog said. "Perhaps you and I will not be there, but the new sun is always born."

A pause. Over a whistling wind, a hyena's distant cough. Then: "Will I be ready?"

"Yes," Frog said.

"You are wise. It must be true."

"If Stillshadow dies?" Frog asked.

"Then I become chief dancer. It will be my place to go into the cold spaces, to speak to the *jowk*."

"It seems . . . so dangerous." He turned his head away. "You may die."

"And you will not?"

It felt good to laugh at the old, familiar joke. In times like this they were more than a man and woman bonded by family. More than the leaders of a people. They were friends, something unutterably precious. He had family, but aside from T'Cori, no friends at all. "There have not been many smiles of late." He paused. "I must speak my heart. I do not want my woman to risk herself."

"Of course not. And that is probably why dream dancers do not marry."

"Women are to be protected," Frog insisted. Why did women, the bene-ficiaries of this principle, so often misunderstand it?

She made a clicking sound at him. "Hunters risk their lives to bring us fresh meat. Is it so strange that your women risk theirs?"

Frog thought on this. It seemed very different to him. "Yes, strange. You risk soul more than flesh. It is not right. I was always taught that men risked their lives so that women would be safe."

"You think women do not risk their lives bringing new hunters, new mothers into the people?" she asked.

"Yes," Frog said. "But that is different."

She slid her small, warm hands over his. He wanted to take her away now, and love her, but did not ask. He could feel that she was sharing something of great importance to her, something she had never said before. "No, my love. It is not. We all die for what we love. A man's enemies attack from without. A woman's from within."

"From within?"

She turned her face away, momentarily unable to respond. Then she whispered her reply. "The Mk*tk were inside me, again and again." Her haunted voice broke. "They *hurt* me, do you understand? A man's seed dies if it does not take root. Does Mk*tk seed die?"

Frog felt numb, unable to absorb the words just spoken. "Do you know? Does anyone?" Her words confused him. "What are you saying?"

"Perhaps it lives within me, like a worm. Perhaps it waits. Perhaps this is not your child growing within me. In my dreams, I *see* it. It frightens me."

When he pressed his hand against her belly, she flinched away. "It is *my* child," he said.

"Would you swear by Father Mountain?" Her smile soured. "How could you? You don't even believe."

For a time they merely faced each other, neither finding the right words.

"I do not believe that your body, which has clasped me so many times, holds anything but love for our people. If there was anything in you that hated us, I would know."

"Can you be so certain?"

"Yes," he said. "I can."

Chapter Fifteen

After the dream dancers sang the new sun to life, after a mushy, flavorless breakfast of yam and crushed nuts, Frog was ready to lead the Ibandi farther north. They would cross the river and try to reach the wavering nut-colored foothills on the horizon. He had raised his hand to call Snake, when the straggly brush at the far side of the camp exploded. A lean-ribbed black boar burst through, an arrow flagging from its side. *God Mountain! Meat!* Uncle Snake and Leopard Eye galloped in after it.

The hog veered away from them, scampering through the camp, its stubby brown legs knocking up pockets of dust. Children were swept out of the way by their mothers and fathers and siblings. "Watch the tusks!" Leopard Eye screamed.

Foam flecked its jowls. Its ribs jutted from its muscular sides as it tossed this way and that, seeking escape. At every turn, a spear point threatened.

The people cheered as it headed into the river. "It's ours!" Leopard Paw said.

But then, at the very moment it reached the river, the water's surface burst. A black shadow lunged out of the depths, all teeth and scales and sudden death.

Snake screamed in sudden panic as the crocodile's jaws clamped onto the hog's front leg. Squealing, the boar tried to pull back. The reptile's tail lashed, dragging the boar into the river.

"No!" Frog screamed. They could not lose the meat like this! While the crocodile waddled backward, dragging its prey into the shallows, the Leopard twins stabbed and hacked and speared the crocodile. Its tail thrashed, and Leopard Paw flew through the air, thumping into the mud paces away. But in that instant, Leopard Eye drove his spear directly into its eye. In an instant the reptile lashed itself into an agonized knot. Its teeth unhooked from the boar's bleeding leg, and the crocodile tried to flee. But within moments three and then five more hunters plunged into the water, foaming it red as they stabbed both crocodile and pig.

The hunters splashed and stabbed and clubbed, knee-deep in foaming red water. Ribs were broken and skin scraped, but—thank Father Mountain! . . . none were bitten and none killed.

The hunters hauled the gashed, twitching carcasses from the water. They slapped one another on the back and strutted, each bragging that he had come closest to the fearsome claws and jaws and tusks.

In the end it was a good day: both predator and prey contributed to the Ibandi cook fires. The crocodile was a great find. Everything about it would be used: teeth and claws and durable skin, as well as good stringy meat and a tasty liver.

Frog had had crocodile liver once before. The memory made his mouth water.

"It is a sign," Snake said, and sighed with pleasure. "We have not been forgotten."

"It is terrible," T'Cori said.

"We survive another day," Frog said, watching as the men chopped crocodile and boar into pieces, hacking at the joints with their stone knives.

"Not that," T'Cori said. "It is the ending itself that seems terrible." She shuddered and turned away from him.

"What is it?" Frog asked.

"I remember," T'Cori said. "Things I haven't thought of in moons."

"What things?"

"I was thinking of my sister Fawn," T'Cori said. "I told you she was taken by a crocodile. I saw it happen."

He watched her face. Right before his eyes she seemed to become younger and more vulnerable. "It must have burnt your eyes," Frog said.

"Yes. There was something oddly beautiful, as well. It freed my *num*. Made my mind work better and gave me the idea of running away. That I could go in the river. That either I would escape or drown or be eaten . . . and it would be over."

"You no longer cared to live?" Frog said.

She came closer and whispered. I felt that my seventh eye, the one thing I was given to protect . . ." Her voice had grown shrill, and she calmed herself with a palpable effort. "I felt it had been stolen from me," she said.

"Every night this happened. I prayed that if I was pregnant, it would not be a monster. And if it was, I prayed I would die before it could crawl out of my womb."

Her hands caressed her swollen belly. Perhaps two moons until she gave birth now. Not long. "I always thought that when it was Stillshadow's time, I would feel strong," she said. "When I thought of having my children, I thought I would feel stronger. That my baby's *num* would feed my *jowk*. But these things did not happen."

He folded T'Cori into his arms and searched his mind for words. There was nothing he could find that was strong enough, deep enough, healing enough. So he merely held her, as their people butchered their kills, and the blood flowed into the river where, so recently, their children had splashed in play.

Chapter Sixteen

The Ibandi had walked north for moons, farther than any kinsman had ever traveled.

When at last they turned westward, for days they saw no animal tracks at all, and then, turning back south, found themselves following the herds once again. Heading back toward the mountains of their birth. Sky Woman had spoken of a new home, so they did not dream of returning to their bomas but to the west of Great Sky and Great Earth, there were said to be fine hunting grounds. If only those stories were true.

So the same great migration of the teeming herds called to them. Moons and moons they traveled, to the brink of exhaustion and despair—but not over that brink.

Not yet.

Three moons south of Frog and T'Cori, and three days south of Great Sky . . .

Sparks fled into the night sky, dying in the darkness. Four hulking figures crouched around a crackling, ragged fire, staring into its dancing light.

"God Blood watches us," said Flat-Nose. "He knows our strength and courage and smells shit in the guts we spilled. Know that he is pleased."

Bone Knife grinned. "What we did to those few weaklings, we could do to all their bomas."

"We do not know how many there are. We must learn." Flat-Nose said.

"But they killed so many of us before," Broken Sharp Tooth said.

"Did you not see that their men were gone?" Flat-Nose snarled, angered by his hunter's weakness. "That we killed them at will and took their women?" He slammed his fist upon the ground. "God Blood screams for vengeance. He says our time is coming." His eyes blazed. "No. I lie. He says our time has *come*."

All the rest of the night they sang their death songs. They had been good sons and brothers and fathers. If they could live the rest of their days from their balls, at the moment of death they would feel in their flesh not the fangs of wolves or jackals but those of God Blood Himself.

Then they would be part of His flesh. His teeth would be theirs, for all time, ravaging all of creation.

After the pain came the power.

Chapter Seventeen

Great Sky's slopes were choked with thornbushes and vine-thronged trees, and rich with four-legged game. Only as the slopes steepened did the vegetation thin, and only as the mountain rose so high that the land below seem peopled by ants did the mountain breezes cool. Finally, the thickly seeded slopes yielded to desert and from there to the only snows to be found anywhere in their world.

At the very top, the eruption had torn chunks away, melting the white cap and flattening the peak.

But before one reached such rarefied heights, in Great Sky's forests could be found the finest hunting beneath Father Mountain's sky.

Five Ibandi stalked Great Sky's lower slopes. Three were from the cardinal bomas: Moon Runner and Sun Runner from Earth, Fast Tortoise from Wind. The fourth was Boar Tracks, the last surviving hunt chief. The fifth was Rock Climber, his brother.

"How goes the hunt?" Fast Tortoise asked.

"I will not climb these slopes again," muttered Sun Runner.

"You saw the ghost?"

Sun Runner nodded fervently. "Yes, just for a moment. I am sure it was one of the dead hunt chiefs. I tell you, they return from heaven!"

Boar Tracks bristled. He was a tall, handsome hunter who had lived five hands of summers. He was the last of the chiefs, alive only because he had not been on Great Sky the night the mountain died.

Did the death of the mountain mean the death of their god? There was no one left to answer. Boar Tracks wished he could still consult with the elder hunt chiefs. With any hunt chiefs at all. He had never felt so alone.

Now he'd had word that Rock boma had been destroyed. Signs of Mk*tk raiders—so their loss in the Mk*tk wars had not been a permanent wall, merely slowing their progress. What now? If the dead had been seen on Great Sky, might it mean that the hunt chiefs would return to them?

"Why can he not come to us? Why would he hide in the shadows if he is one of ours? I say he is beast-man." The beast-men were people, he supposed. Not Ibandi, not Mk*tk, not even bhan. Barely more than monkeys, in his thinking, they lived in the sacred caves on Great Earth. Surely, the "ghost" was nothing more than such a wretched creature, far from home.

Sun Runner and his son Moon Runner were both fleshy men of great strength and skill. Scarred in battle and the hunt, their support of Boar Tracks would be critical to his future plans. There was no one left to lead the Ibandi. Surely, they needed Boar Tracks. Sun Runner tended to agree with him but was not yet convinced of his right to leadership. Well, a brisk session in the wrestling circle would cure *that.* "Perhaps the dead lose their way?"

"We hunt," Moon Hunter said. "I would meet this ghost for myself."

"Where did you see him?" Boar asked.

"It was near the big rock, where the water runs," Sun Runner said.

"Then that is where we will go."

Timing breathing to footsteps, the men hiked up the mountain. Green sprouts on every trough of the avalanche-plowed earth proclaimed that the eruption's damage had begun to heal. Blasted trees still lay scattered like toys discarded by an angry, infant god.

Boar Tracks lowered his cupped hands into the stream. He set one foot against a mossy log and splashed his face, wiping down the salt to discourage mosquitoes. He'd searched all morning and had yet to see anything remotely resembling a ghost. What would a ghost track look like? Until he knew, he would look for footprints, bruised leaves, broken twigs, scat . . . anything that might assist in his search.

Everywhere, the mountain's death throes burned his eyes: frozen rivers of mud, splintered trees, boulders and crushed brush funneled into a tumbled confusion. Frog and Sky Woman had seen all this while the mud still steamed and the demons roamed freely. Boar Tracks had not made that climb. Every night, before he slept, he asked himself if he had been a coward not to.

No. He had been right. Frog had returned from the mountain babbling that the gods wished the Ibandi to abandon their home. Someone needed to lead the Ibandi to their future. Frog and Sky Woman had fled. Boar Tracks would stand.

"What happened here?" Boar asked.

Moon Runner shrugged. "Is this where the gods died?"

"Died?" Boar asked.

"I do not know much, but it looks like death to me."

"Look," Rock Climber said.

There, partially hidden beneath a slurry of dried mud and a covering of morning frost, gaped a cave mouth as high as a man's waist. It looked as if an enormous rodent had dug away at the left corner, so that a tunnel led down through the debris.

Single file, they crawled through the narrow hole into the darkness and damp.

Boar Tracks wrapped moss around a dry stick and struck fire, fanning it into full flame. When he stood, a pale red tide washed the adobe walls. "The kiva," Boar Tracks murmured. "I was just a boy when first I came here. And after that there were many, many ceremonies. . . ."

"I lost my foreskin here." Moon Runner held up his torch. "But I never came again. There was nothing in all the world I wanted so much as to be a hunt chief. I was not chosen."

"I was chosen," Boar said. "At the time, I thought it a great thing." No regret or resentment tainted his voice. Sadness, perhaps. "Now, they are all dead."

Boar held a torch up to the walls. "It looks as if someone clawed this out with his hands." The flickering light revealed scraps of fruit, a gnawed skunk hide, some rat tails, a handful of charred sticks. "Someone has eaten, slept here."

"Who?" Moon Runner asked. "Beast-men?"

Boar shrugged, trying to act unconcerned, but the back of his neck burned.

They crawled back out and spent a quarter examining the rest of the site. Most hunt chiefs' corpses had been unearthed by now, but from time to time hunters discovered another screaming skeleton.

No bones this time, but Moon Runner dropped and traced his finger in a heel-shaped imprint. "A man."

"Ibandi?" Rock Climber asked.

Sun Runner knelt beside his son. Half a heel mark and three shallow toe indentions. "Who can say?"

Mk*tk? No, too small. But Boar Tracks knew he was looking at the print of an adult male. This much he could say but, like Sun Runner, could not go further to say if it was Ibandi, bhan or one of the outlying tribes. Why couldn't he tell? He was certain his dead brothers would have known at once.

But then, he had never been the best of them. Since the mountain died, he seemed to have lost whatever special *num* he might have once possessed.

Beside him, Rock Climber gasped. Boar Tracks spun to see a bone-thin figure approaching through a stand of young bamboo. From head to toe, his brown skin was smeared white with ash.

"A ghost?" the hunt chief asked. The ash-covered man stared at them.

Fear. Boar Tracks clenched his belly, seized control of his breathing. *Breathe like a brave man, feel like a brave man,* Cloud Stalker had sworn. "Do I know you?" Boar Tracks asked, and gave his name.

"And I am Sun Runner," the gray-hair beside him said.

The ash-covered figure seemed dazed. "I . . ." He shook his head.

With every breath, the ghost's ribs poked through his skin, so that he resembled nothing so much as a mud-covered skeleton. He held out one scalded, trembling hand. "Food," he said.

They offered the ghost a handful of dried antelope. He ate ravenously, then emptied their water gourds. Moon Runner handed him a piece of dried yam. As the others gathered around him, mystified, the stranger satisfied his appetite.

"Are you a hunt chief?" Moon Runner ventured.

Boar Tracks tensed. The hunt chiefs were dead. *He* was the last. What was this creature?

The ash man shrugged. "I do not know."

"Did you battle with demons? Did the dead water rise and suck your strength?"

The ash man's eyes glittered. "Yes," he mumbled. "I think I did."

"This is a great day," Rock Climber said, "a great, great day. A master hunter has returned from the dead!"

The ash man squatted, face buried in his hands, as if desperately pondering their words. Then he looked up. "I was!" he screamed. "I was in hell! I saw the dead animals dancing in their bones. They tried to catch me, but I was too fast!" Slowly at first, and then with increasing speed, he began to speak.

"Father Mountain told me to fight the demons," the ash man said. "I am a son of the mountain. When asked, I fought!" He danced and whirled and mimed hunting and fighting. Stiffly at first and then with growing fluidity he crouched and pounced and thrust.

"And what happened then?" Sun Runner asked.

"And when I won," the ash man said, "our mighty god brought me back to the world, back so I might speak His words."

Moon Runner jumped to his feet and raised his arms to the sky. "Behold the miracle!" he crowed. "He has come to lead us."

The ash man's eyes glittered. "Say this again."

"I said that you were sent by Father Mountain to lead us."

The ash man's stained teeth gleamed.

On the mountain that night, swaddled in skins and with a full belly for the first time in his strange and splintered memory, the ash man dreamed:

He saw his people frightened, scattered, crying for answers no man could offer. So seven were chosen to ask questions of Father Mountain Himself. The climb was an endless nightmare of fatigue and terror. Two had perished, a medicine girl and a hunter. Another hunter had gone lame and been left behind.

Frog and the nameless girl and the ash man had stood atop the damaged summit and felt the icy breath of Father Mountain. The nameless one said that Father Mountain demanded their people flee the Mk*tk, find new homes.

He himself had heard nothing.

They descended, exhausted and disoriented, and it came to him that the nameless girl must die. It was the only answer! The witch said that the Ibandi should run rather than fight. His fool of a brother refused to kill her. Fire Ant attempted to slay the witch, knowing that if she died, Frog would fall in line.

Instead of helping, a bewitched Frog smashed a rock into his head. The ash man saw the rock coming, tumbling through the air, swelling as it approached. He could have moved. Should have moved, but could not, somehow entranced by the spin.

Pain. Blackness. The next thing he knew, he was on his knees. At that moment, as if his senses had been heightened by pain, he glimpsed the witch's fire. It was . . . beautiful. A bright blue at the edge, a shimmering cloud of creeping flame with fist-sized shadows floating within.

Still, all night he had hunted for the two of them. But before he could lay hands upon the witch he plunged through the ice into a clay tube boiling with steam. He could not see, could not think. Could do nothing but scream.

The pain drove him out of his mind. When he awakened, the steam was gone.

Blistered, groaning, he crawled out.

He remembered little of what next occurred.

For moons he wandered half crazed, eating whatever carrion he could scavenge or half-rotted tubers he could claw from the earth. His blisters finally healed, and he was able to sleep an entire night without waking with his own screams in his ears. He was a wild two-legged living on the mountain, wandering with no thought of returning to the lowlands. Why would the dead return to the land of the living?

For certainly, this was what it was to be dead. Wasn't it? He was so alone. If all men who died went to Father Mountain, where were they? Where are the others? Why was he so alone?

He remembered finding a stack of rocks, and he knew there was something within it that was important to him. What was it about these rocks? Drawn with charcoal, the symbols for "hawk" and "shadow." Slowly, the pieces came back to him. The importance was . . .

Was . . .

This was not merely a stack of rocks. It was the marker for a grave. But whose grave? And why did he care? In a hell so vast and lonely that one dead man could not find another, of what importance was a single grave?

Hawk Shadow.

That was *the name. But what did it mean? What and who was that name?*

Brother.

Hawk Shadow was his brother.

He tumbled aside the rocks, finally revealing a torn and worm-eaten corpse.

He took the moldering skull in his hands and pulled. "Live. Up! Join me. Come with me and we will hunt again together."

The neck loosened in his hand. The stench of rotted flesh filled his nose.

"Run with me, Brother. Wrestle with me . . ." His voice broke.

The head came free in his hands. He stared at his brother's face, then pushed it back into the earth.

Alone in hell, he cried.

Ash man awoke.

Moon Runner crouched beside him. "Were you in the dream world?"

"Yes," the ash man said. "The dream world. Am I alive?"

"Unless we are also dead," the hunter said. "Our people will be so happy to see you."

The ash man was still a bit numb. He curled back up, sucking the knuckles of his right hand.

"Frog," he whispered.

"You know Frog Hopping?" Moon asked.

"Know him?" the ash man said. "I taught him to walk. Frog is my brother. My name," he said, "is Fire Ant."

Chapter Eighteen

The man who had once been Fire Ant was walked a day southeast to Fire boma, where he had spent his youth.

It seemed to him that the wall between the world of men and dreams, even the wall between the living and the dead, had thinned.

It was all strange and a bit dizzying. Wherever he went, children touched him, men and women embraced him. After, they whispered of the wildfire burning in his eye or how his flesh had nearly melted away. But they said these things only to each other, never to him. There was something about Fire Ant, something strange that had happened to him upon the mountain. Something that attracted and repelled his cousins.

His rescuers escorted Ant to the healing hut and set him upon a bed of grass. As the women slathered his flesh in healing herbs, a Fire hunter named Brave Buffalo crawled trembling to his side. "I tell you this, Fire Ant, because you returned from the mountain. Yesterday I saw a terrible thing."

Fire Ant rolled onto his side. "What?" Brave Buffalo. Did he know this man? All memories from before Fire Ant's death seemed to dissolve when he tried to fetch them, like clutching water.

"I was traveling in the south and came upon Rock boma. Its walls were burnt and broken. Most were dead. Five squatted in the ashes, drinking their tears."

"What happened there?" Fire Ant asked.

"I am not sure," Buffalo said. "But Mk*tk, I think. They attack our bomas. They make our hunters run."

"What can we do?" Boar Tracks asked. "They are too strong."

"None are so strong as he who returns from death," Sun Runner proclaimed. "Bone is stronger than muscle."

"We are blessed!" Moon Runner crowed. "No one can stand before us! The Mk*tk will tremble, for when they come against us again, we will be led by a man who cannot die." He dropped his voice to a superstitious whisper. "He is already dead!"

"Perhaps we do not wait," Fire Ant said.

"What do you mean?" Brave Buffalo asked. "We should run away, like Frog?"

"No!" Ant said fiercely. "I mean that we must make the Mk*tk fear *us*. We go to them. Kill them in their huts, not crouch and hope they have forgotten us."

"What are you saying?" Brave Buffalo asked.

"I am saying that the time for cool blood—for running and hiding—is past. I say that I came to you from Father Mountain and that he expects us to fight with courage."

Swayed by his passion, the others listened. "We must gather the people," Moon Runner said.

"Soon the people come together," Fire Ant said. "I will speak with them face to face. And then they will know."

All day, Far Sigh had walked with her mother and father. They had awakened her before dawn. In all her nine summers, she had never seen them so excited. Mama and Papa lived in a boma east of Wind, and the first runners had reached them just after midnight.

Not even waiting for breakfast, they walked.

Far Sigh was excited, too. They had told of a man come back from the dead, returned from heaven. All year, she had barely seen a smile on her father's face. Papa's brother had died fighting the Mk*tk. Papa sometimes awakened screaming in the night, so that Mother was forced to stroke his forehead and sing him to sleep.

At times, Far Sigh sang to him as well, her young voice blending with her mother's, trying to take Papa up into sleep.

By the next afternoon the first folk from Earth, Wind, and Water bomas gathered in the shade of the sacred Life Tree, the giant baobab that had shaded the Ibandi since Great Mother sang the first sun to life.

They had brought children with them, too. She didn't often see boys from other bomas and relished the opportunity. One day one of them would be her husband. She wondered who it might be. Mama had said that the first day she met Papa he had won a match in the wrestling circle. She gave him a handful of berries. Even as he ate them gratefully, she knew he was hers.

And Mama had been no older than Far Sigh!

The Life Tree shaded first two, then ten, then hands of tens of Ibandi. From around the Circle they had come, bringing all their precious hopes. Papa said that Fire Ant had new bones and could carry all their hopes upon them.

Far Sigh thought this to be a very wonderful thing.

"Can it be true?" a big-nosed Wind tribesman asked.

"We have all heard the stories," answered a woman holding a baby in each arm.

The Earth clansman who spoke next had narrow, nervous eyes. "What if the Mk*tk attack?"

"Since Great Mother first birthed the world," said a Wind woman with bone-pierced ears, "we have all come here every spring. We have danced in the Life Tree's shadow. We have never been attacked. No one would dare." Despite her words, she seemed to Far Sigh as nervous as any of the others.

"Wait!" the narrow-eyed man said, arm outstretched. "He comes!"

Far Sigh turned to follow his pointing finger.

Three men were walking from the direction of Great Sky, the man in the middle trudging as if he were half asleep. His hair was dusted white and so were the edges of his face.

Most of the adults around Far Sigh turned their heads away, as if afraid to meet his eyes. Their voices fell silent.

When Fire Ant had walked on ahead of them, the Earth tribesman whispered to the Wind woman: "His leg . . . he does not limp. I thought he had been injured."

She replied with a true believer's fervor, "New bones."

Fire Ant took his place beneath Life Tree's jagged canopy. He paused, waiting until their whispers stopped, then raised his arms. "I climbed the mountain! Not you . . . or you . . . or any of you did this thing. You remember what Frog Hopping said to you. I climbed. I died, and lived with the *jowk* and the hunt chiefs." He inhaled deeply, as if intoxicated by the air itself. "My brother returned to you, but I remained with Father Mountain, where I saw things no man may speak of."

The people whispered and stirred. "You seem a man . . ." a woman said.

Fire Ant turned his gaze upon her, and she backed away without another word.

"When I close my eyes I see the burning lake," he said, his voice a dreamy slur. "If you doubt, come with me. We will climb Great Sky together. Then, if you survive the wolves and demons and the freezing fire, you may ask the dead if I speak truth."

No one said a word. His voice sent chills from Far Sigh's toes to her fingers. Her little heart beat so quickly she thought she might die. This was the most wonderful thing she had ever seen. A man returned from the dead!

What had he seen? Had he spoken to Father Mountain? Would he kiss her head?

Around her, no one spoke. Their eyes were like Papa's when he sat up screaming in the night. Far Sigh knew they were afraid, but what was there to fear? This was a spirit come to guide them.

And so Far Sigh was the first to speak. "I will follow you!" she called. The adults around her shook themselves, as if she had stirred them from slumber. Then they laughed and cheered.

Little Far Sigh jumped up and down with joy. To see such a thing! And to be the first to speak! It was almost more wonderful than her small soaring heart could bear.

"I will follow him!" Moon Runner said.

"He has my spear!" his father, Sun Runner, said.

One at a time, at first a few and then by hands, they stood and cheered until the mountains rang with their call.

Some of the dream dancers had left with Stillshadow, but most had either remained or returned over the last moons. Five of the young dream dancers approached with caution and reverence. Slender deerskin flaps covered their breasts and genitals; their hair woven into tight curls, fixed with mud and bone splinters into glyphs representing their names and totems.

"We have awaited a sign." Water Song, the youngest of them said, then knelt before Fire Ant.

Boar Tracks had watched the fuss over Fire Ant for days, had held his tongue, but anger and resentment had swelled until he could no longer contain himself. "I have watched you eat and sleep and shit," Boar Tracks said. "I say you are a man."

"A man?" Fire Ant said. His nostrils widened and his eyes narrowed "A man may be beaten. A *man* may be killed." Fire Ant leaned close. Smelled him. "You are Boar Tracks, the last of your kind, the last hunt chief walking this world. I spoke to your brothers while I was with Father Mountain. Do you know what they said?"

Boar Tracks's mouth opened and closed without producing sound. His sense of shame warred with his anger.

"They told me there is a reason you are the last. They say that you *ran*," Fire Ant said, "that you ran from the Mk*tk like a little girl, piss dribbling down your legs as you fled. While the rest of us fought and bled for the Circle, you shook your ass at them and ran. They said you were not with them on the mountain when the terrible thing happened, because Father Mountain does not want cowards in heaven."

Boar Tracks growled and narrowed his eyes. Fear and anger wrestled. Anger won. "No man speaks to me so."

"I speak as I please, but I am no man," Fire Ant said. "You can spill the blood of a man or stop his breath. Come to me. Test my spear."

Boar Tracks had the strange and unsettling sense that he had danced too close to a consuming fire. "Spear? N-no," he stammered, tongue suddenly thick in his mouth. "If you wish to wrestle in the circle . . ."

"No!" Fire Ant screamed. "That was for another time. This is a time for Ibandi to be more than hunters! You doubt Father Mountain? And you doubt my dream—that our people can be more than great? We can be more than men have ever dared. But first, weaklings like *you* must bleed. Hear me. I have already died. Today, you go where I have already been."

Boar Tracks flinched, as if something sharp had nicked his gut. "No . . ."

Fire Ant was all bones. Boar Tracks knew himself to be strong and fast, a fine young hunt chief in his prime. But there was something, perhaps in Ant's *num*-field, that scratched at his nerves.

"Come," Ant taunted. "Taste my spear."

The world seemed to hold its breath as three men soberly paced off a wrestling circle and marked the perimeter with eight stones.

Fire Ant and Boar Tracks stepped in, each holding his spear tightly. As if preparing to face a charging buffalo, they lowered the fire-hardened tips. For several breaths neither of them moved, then Boar Tracks slid to the side and began to circle Fire Ant, who matched him step for step. Unnerved he may have been, but Boar found a rhythm that calmed his breathing, and he began to relax.

He stabbed.

Fire Ant leaned to the side and slashed within a hair of Boar's ribs. Boar felt as if he were a crane fighting a snake. His opponent had become a creature of pure motion, a wall of flickering spear. There was no opening. There was no hesitation. When Boar Tracks paused for a single instant, instead of retreating Ant *lunged*.

Sudden, blinding pain stole sight and thought and the very world itself as Ant twisted to one side and thrust the point of his spear into Boar's mouth and through the back of his head.

His teeth snapped down on the shaft in helpless reflex. He crumbled to the ground, all *num* fled.

• • •

Far Sigh could not blink or speak or even move. She knew that her father did not want her to see what she had just seen, but no one had shielded her eyes. All were fixed on the spirit man who had just done a great and terrible thing. Blood splashed everywhere, as if the great Boar Tracks was but a slain zebra.

Her mind spun. She wanted to scream, to hide, felt an awful urge to pee, but she could not look away. Father Mountain had filled the sky with black blood. And now, this man . . .

She pulled at her mother's hand. "Is he a god, Mama?"

Far Sigh's mother's eyes were as big as wattle nuts. "Ibandi do not kill Ibandi."

Fire Ant wrenched the spear free and spread his arms wide, crossed his fists and thumped them against his chest. Blood drops flew from the crimsoned shaft.

"Fire Ant is no ordinary man! He will not fail you."

"What of Stillshadow?" Papa asked. "What of Sky Woman?"

Far Sigh was still frozen in place, watching Boar Tracks's hands twitch, as if she were mired in a dream. No one moved toward him as the ground beneath his broken mouth slurred into red mud.

"Sky Woman?" Fire Ant asked. "Who is this Sky Woman?"

"What Stillshadow called the nameless one."

The man-god blinked like a chameleon squatting on a flat rock. "What Father Mountain tells a woman, Fire Ant cannot say. He told Fire Ant to fight!

"Come with me. You have hunted zebra and antelope and pig. There is more. I will teach you to be hunters of men."

Far Sigh jumped into the air, screaming and lifted on the screams of her people. And around her, Mama and Papa and all the others jumped and yelled and cried.

They had lost a hunt chief. The very last hunt chief. But in Boar Tracks's place was something even more precious: a messenger from their god Himself.

Twin fires cast their living light upon the bloodied wrestling circle. Fire Ant watched the flames carefully. His brother Frog had spoken of seeing faces in the fire. Could he, now that he was reborn?

Nothing.

In his childhood, Fire Ant had almost been burned alive of fever. What he now felt reminded him of that sensation: swollen, weightless, the world as glimpsed through a dust storm. Only instead of weakness, he felt stronger than he ever had. The *jowk* flowed within him. His *num* was more powerful than any man's or Mk*tk's.

Perhaps his traitor brother saw faces, but Ant saw truth. And the men who now swore to follow him saw the same truth: they must fight for their homes.

Blood boiling with excitement, Fire Ant realized he knew the way to do it.

"I know," he said later that night, "how to put the fear into them."

"How?" Moon Runner asked. "The Mk*tk know no fear or love, no mercy. They are not human!"

Fire Ant slammed his bloody spear on the ground. Although Boar's corpse had been dragged away, the others could not take their eyes from the gore-smeared wrestling circle. "No! They are very human. When we outnumbered them, we slew them as readily as they killed us. I will show you. We must not merely defend our home from their attack. We must go to them, to their land, and strike at them."

"I say they are human," Rock Climber agreed. Ant thought Climber would be a good fighter if he allowed the *jowk* to flow through him, as it ran through his own new bones. "Human. And men want revenge. We must never forget that. The days to come hold nothing but terror and blood. *Blood.* We slaughter them, they slaughter us. Where is the end?"

"You speak like an old woman. We sweep the earth of them. Kill them. Kill their pups. Kill their women. *Then* they know us. Then they know what it means to challenge Father Mountain's children."

"How can you say such things?" Rock Climber asked.

Fire Ant leaned close to him, gazing into the firelight reflected in Climber's eyes. "I speak as one already dead. You speak as one soon to be."

Rock Climber lowered his head. "I meant no offense."

"Then listen more than you speak."

Without taking his eyes from the ground, the man backed away, humbled and frightened.

Fire Ant threw his shoulders back. "Will you follow me, or do I fight the Mk*tk alone?"

One at a time, two hands of hunters stood.

As anyone could see, Great Earth was smaller than Great Sky. But the dancers believed that, beneath the ground, Great Mother's home was actually the larger.

Fire Ant and his ten hunters climbed trails until they found the terraced cluster of huts and sacred fire circles that were home to the dream dancers. Although six had originally traveled north with Stillshadow and Sky Woman, all but two, Sing Sun and Wind Willow, had returned to Great Earth.

"Tell me everything you know," he said to Wind Willow, the eldest of the remaining dancers. She was tall and thin. Ant thought she had the saddest eyes he had ever seen.

"After Frog Hopping rescued Sky Woman from the Mk*tk," Wind Willow said, "she told us all she could remember about her journey. She made this."

She led him to Stillshadow's sitting stone. It was as high as a man's shoulders, but smaller stones to the right made a ladder so that the old woman could climb without assistance. Its base was scrawled with drawings of sun and sky and men and beasts. And on one side, etched into the stone itself, was a map.

Ant traced his fingers across the drawings, feeling their power. Yes. These women were holy. Whoever had made such unspeakably beautiful drawings had been blessed by the gods. He felt their power, even now. "When my brother Frog returned with the girl, he told you all he knew."

Wind Willow nodded. "If our stolen sisters have not moved, it might be possible to find them. Sky Woman said that Dove and Sister Quiet Water remained with the monsters. If you could bring either of them home, it would be a miracle."

"And what if I found both?"

"Both?" Her eyes sparkled with awe. She looked at him in a new way, as if considering for the first time that he might be more than just a man. "If you could bring them home . . . To do such a thing, you will have to be very lucky and very clever . . . or beloved of Father Mountain."

"He wants me to bring your sisters Dove and Quiet Water back to the Circle," he said. "Now . . . tell me all you know."

Fire Ant listened to the dream dancers as they told of Sky Woman's journey. Everything she had said to them came now to him.

For men running and walking swiftly, the Mk*tk were only three or four days south. When he had learned all he needed, Ant gathered his two hands of men, descended from the mountain and walked south.

Chapter Nineteen

A drifting mountain of gray clouds masked the full moon. Within its pale shadows, the Mk*tk mothers and grandmothers roasted venison and yams for their men and children. Flat-Nose watched the others eat without tasting the flesh himself. He wanted hunger in his gut, gnawing like a rat.

Flat-Nose needed to speak to them, and he liked to do this when they were fed and he was hungry. Hunger was good. Hunger led to anger, which led to the killing fever.

"Your time has come," Flat-Nose said to the young Mk*tk males clustered at his feet. "God Blood put the strength in your balls. You need but call to him. He calls to you in your enemy's gut. Free God Blood to run in the earth, and you make the world strong. Make *yourself* strong. Your blood. Your enemy's blood and shit on your spear. All are good. Kill to free God Blood."

A young boy, his hair cropped at the sides so that it stood like a thin ridge of stones, jumped to his feet. "I am Wood Knife! Son of Pierce Bone. You are so strong. I will be strong, too." The boy seemed ready to piss on himself, so pleased he was just to sit with the men.

Flat-Nose did not let the pleasure he felt touch his face. "You will be strong and brave," he said. "Your uncles taught me to kill. All were great men, good killers. I promise: you will make God Blood smile."

He cuffed the boy affectionately. Wood Knife yelped, but his eyes glowed with pride.

* * *

"I am tired," Flat-Nose said, lying back on his grass mat. The thatch ceiling above him was an irritant. He wanted to be out under the sky, making his kill. But it was better to start off tomorrow, after resting. Flat-Nose hated to admit it, but he was not the spry young buck he had been ten summers past. In those days, it felt as if he could run and hunt and fight and hump from dawn to dusk, one moon to the next.

He flexed his left hand, staring at the stumps of his lost fingers, feeling numbness where once had flowed power. Sometimes, it felt as if the fingers were still there.

Ghost fingers.

He shut those thoughts away: there was still more than enough left of him to give God Blood His greatest feast.

His first wife, Hip Thorn, bowed her head. "Yes, husband. Let me feed you."

He grunted approval. "I will have food and then sex and then sleep." He turned to his third wife, short and skinny, kneeling in the shadows. "You will sex me," he said.

"Yes, husband," Dove replied, her Ibandi accent scraping at his ears.

For many moons now, Dove had lived with her Mk*tk captors in one of their scattered, extended family groups. Their clusters tended to be raggedly protected by strength of spears rather than the circled thornbushes to which she was accustomed.

As Flat-Nose's third wife and a prize of war, Dove was a slave of some privilege. Her sister Quiet Water was held by a family a half-day distant, composed of three brothers mated to seven females. While not a wife, Water was used sexually by all three men and beaten by the women for the slightest offense.

This morning seemed no different from the others: awaken before dawn, prepare food and wait until her man had eaten before satisfying her own growling belly. But the endless routine was interrupted when Quiet Water appeared in the boma doorway following two of the hulking brothers who shared her. Come to join Flat-Nose, no doubt.

They had seen each other few times in the last moons. Quiet Water was Dove's height, but had always had a placid, peaceful nature that reflected her name. Now Quiet seemed no longer a living thing. Her eyes were like cold stones. "Dove," Quiet Water said, "I have not seen you since Fish moon. I wish I did not see you now. It would be better for you to be dead."

Dove shook her head, feeling nothing but pity for her sister. "You do not change. If you do not, you will die soon. Remember Fawn Blossom?" she asked. "Can you still see T'Cori's face? Our sisters could not change." Fawn Blossom had perished in a crocodile's jaws. Their nameless sister had killed a Mk*tk hunter and then jumped into the same river, had screamed as she was swept away across the waterfall. What had happened to her? Dove did not know and could not allow herself to ask that question. To such questions, there were no comforting answers.

"What would you have me do?" Quiet Water asked.

"Give in to them," Dove said. "Since I did, Flat-Nose has not hurt me. I gather, cook, sex and sleep. Life is not bad."

She gazed out toward the northern horizon. Somewhere lost in the misty distance was Great Earth. In former years, the sight had gladdened her. Now, her heart was a stone.

"How can you say this?" Quiet Water whispered.

"What else am I to say? Our men did not rescue me. They did not save you. Where are they?" She raised her hands and shrugged. "Where is Father Mountain? I have learned something," she said, "a great truth. Would you hear it?"

Quiet Water said nothing. Dove leaned close. "God Blood's hate is stronger than Great Mother's love."

If Dove had brandished a knife, Quiet Water could not have retreated more rapidly. "Blasphemy! And a lie. Our men hurt them," she said. "You saw it. Not all returned, and the ones who did missed fingers and arms and eyes. I could smell it. Our men scared them."

"That is your own stink you smell. The Ibandi are not 'my men.'" Dove said. "The Mk*tk fear nothing."

"What are you saying?"

"That Flat-Nose is my man," Dove said defiantly. "And he is the strongest man in all the world. He could kill three Ibandi. Four."

Quiet Water paused, as if listening to the rush of blood in her ears. Then she wrapped her arms around Dove.

After a stiff hesitation, Dove returned the embrace. "I thought you would be angry. Why do you hold me?" Dove asked.

"Because there is a last time for everything," Water whispered. "Her bones still walk above the ground, but the sister I loved is dead."

Then, having no other words to speak, Quiet Water turned her back and walked away.

•   •   •

By the fifth day, Fire Ant had led his two hands of hunters deeply into Mk*tk territory. Now, every shadow had teeth. Their courage was dulled, no longer the sharp blade it had been while safe within the Circle. Then, the raid had seemed a splendid adventure. Now, they crept like mice at night and slept during the day. On the eighth night after leaving Great Earth, they spied the campfire of a Mk*tk hunting party and skirted it with great care.

On the ninth day, they edged up a rise and peered down on a cluster of ragged huts around an untidy central fire pit.

They watched as the Mk*tk males cuffed their wives and children affectionately, then marched off single file.

Not a war party, Fire Ant reckoned. *They hunt four-legged, not two.*

Concealed behind brush and the ridge itself, they scouted and whispered until the day was gone, and their plans were made. "Kill the women and grandfathers!" Fire Ant said. "Kill the children, if they interfere."

"Children?" Moon Runner asked. His fleshy face, his voice, everything about him seemed repulsed.

Ant hawked and spit in the direction of Great Sky. "Maggots make flies," he replied.

The first wide-boned Mk*tk woman, caught crawling from her lean-to, barely had time to scream before Fire Ant clubbed her down.

A Mk*tk girl, wearing a thin leather strap to pull back her thorny bush of hair, stood behind a boy with the same flat nose and broad ugly face. The boy ran up to Ant screaming gibberish.

Fire Ant was never quite certain of what happened next.

Did he thrust? Simply raise his spear? Did the boy run onto the fire-hardened tip to suicide, or had Ant meant to slay him?

All he knew for certain was that his arm had moved, the spear was red, and the thick-boned brat lay groaning. His lifeblood streamed out across the earth.

For a moment the sight of the dying boy froze Fire Ant in place. Then he wrenched himself away and joined his men as they ran howling through the camp, their spear tips red.

After the screams of the women and old ones had died to sobs, a hand of hot-eyed Mk*tk children panted, even as they were trapped against a thorn-bush. They hissed and spit at him, betraying not the slightest trace of fear. What spirit! For a brief moment he almost admired them. They were like cornered lion cubs!

"Where are our women!" Ant called out.

Young Sparrow Flies howled in triumph. "We have found Sister Quiet Water!"

When she was brought before Ant, the dream dancer fell to her knees, clutching her savior's thigh.

He rubbed her hair affectionately. She was an Ibandi holy woman, and he, Fire Ant, had saved her. A rush of blood in his ears and chest told him that Father Mountain was well pleased with His son. "Where is Dove?" he asked.

"She is dead," Quiet Water said, all flesh stripped from her voice. "My sister is dead."

"What of the children?" Moon Runner asked, panting.

Ant's hand tensed on his spear. Why not . . . ? a voice whispered. They stared back at him. One of them sniffled, eyes red, but they did not beg, or cry. Splendid.

Kill them, a voice in his head whispered. *They are beasts.*

But another, softer voice said: *What beasts have the courage of hunters? They are but children.*

For many breaths the two voices warred within him. Then at last he decided. "There has been blood enough," Ant said. "Tie them. Burn the huts. We go."

Flat-Nose smelled death before he saw it: the night wind carried the scent of blood for half a day's walk.

He and his men poked through the ashes of their homes, their faces turned to stone. The boma's bamboo wall was half burned, the huts smashed, and the bodies of their wives and elders scattered and torn.

He himself freed the children but did not allow his heart to feel joy as they cried and gripped his legs in gratitude. No softness. None.

A search for survivors yielded two females. Sobbing, they claimed that a few more might have escaped into the brush.

After searching the ruins, the hunters sat in a circle, crouching so close that their knees touched, saying nothing until their leader chose to speak. Flat-Nose squatted and then sat, his hands gripping his knees. A dull wind stirred the curls of burnt wood.

Flat-Nose clawed at the dirt slowly, gazing into it as another man might have studied the night sky, seeking answers or counting stars. He gouged out a handful of dirt and let it run slowly between his heavy, scarred fingers. "What do we do? We burn the bodies. Unite the clans. Find the one who killed my brother's son." His brother Notch-Ear had been killed by the Ibandi woman who had escaped over the stream. "We burst God Blood's belly."

"How?" A young hunter named Stone Hand asked.

Flat-Nose set his knuckles on the ground, grinding them against the pebbles as might a bull gorilla. "I tell you what we do. We sharpen our knives on their bones. We stick our spears up their asses." His eyes were banked coals. "They die. All of them. None may live. We drink the last drop of their blood. War to the marrow!"

And all the night, he sang his death song, composing new and terrible verses to an already crimson saga.

Chapter Twenty

While it had taken nine days to find the Mk*tk, it took only five days to return to Water boma, where the reception was joyous and the celebration mighty. Fire Ant's ten hunters gyrated around the twin fires, hooting their courage and skill to Father Mountain's countless eyes, until their legs burned and their sweat dried.

They laughed and boasted, intertwining their arms with those of the young women, pairing off into the tall grass for a hunter's reward.

Sparrow Flies moved closer to the fire, desperate for its warmth. Waves of cold shivered his arms and legs. "What happens to the *num* of the ones we killed?" he asked Fire Ant.

"It flows to their god," Fire Ant said.

Sparrow stared at the red crust on his spear. When he closed his eyes, his lids pulsed. Tonight, when he slept, his dreams would drown in blood. "To the *jowk*?"

"I do not know things of this kind," Ant said.

"Is our *jowk* the same as theirs?"

"They were not Ibandi," Ant said.

"No. Not Ibandi. But I think that they were men."

Fire Ant shrugged. "They did not treat ours like men."

"Is that the measure?" Sparrow asked, a frown creasing his narrow face. "Do we now allow others to say what we are?"

Fire Ant stared straight ahead. "I dream of the dead world. I do not see Mk*tk there. They may have *num*. Perhaps *jowk*. But they are not men."

Sparrow heard something dreadful in the darkness, a wavering blend of hyena and human voices. He gripped his spear more tightly, grinding grit into his palm. "Something moved beyond the firelight."

Ant stood, forcing calm into his voice. "We are ready."

Then, as if mocking their courage, an odd sound rose from the darkness beyond the fire: inhuman voices mimicking a human chant. A pause, then . . . sounds of confusion. Men and women screaming in anguish, followed by a hot, wet silence.

Sparrow moistened his lips, trembling. Something *final* had happened out in the thorny dark. To the hunters who had gone off with their women. To the women who had rewarded their men.

The chant began once again. Sparrow could not understand a single word. The sound swelled. "What are they? What do they want?"

"They want us," Old Wise Eagle said. "They know we killed their women."

"Silence," Fire Ant demanded.

Sister Quiet Water appeared behind him, her soft small hand against his arm. "They attack from one direction, driving their enemy. They do not surround," she said.

"So?"

"So let me take the women and children, as many as I can, and escape through the back wall."

Fire Ant considered, then nodded. "Yes," he said, "as many as you can."

"I think we die," Wise Eagle said as she left them.

"All men die," Ant said, "but some return."

They gazed at him, overcome with sudden hope.

"Truth?" Sparrow asked.

Fire Ant seemed to change, grow, his aspect swollen with the weight of his intent. "It is true!" he screamed. "If you fight, if you throw your life onto your enemy's spears, protect your women and children, Father Mountain will see. And He told me that the hunter who makes Him proud might, if he wishes, return to hold his woman and children once again. To again hunt the zebra and feel the wind on his face."

"Do you hear?" Sparrow's heart warmed, caught desperate fire. He stamped his spear into the dirt. "If we have heart, we hunt again!"

Some whooped and slapped each other, but Wise Eagle's face was dour. "Soon, we will all be silent."

"What do they want?" Sparrow asked again.

"What would *you* want if they had done what we did?"

That nightmarish gobbling sound chased the sparks up into the night. Far away, but closer now. Sparrow could see nothing save shadows and stars.

Fire Ant screamed, "Show yourselves!" His eyes were wide, almost as if he felt fear. Why? What did a man already dead have to fear from life?

A brief rustle in the shadows, and then they heard a sharp sound, a call. The shadows separated into hulking, manlike forms.

"In His name," Sparrow whispered.

"Silence!" Fire Ant roared.

"We will soon be atop the mountain." Rock Climber's thick chest gleamed. He stank of fear sweat. "Father Mountain, see us. Return us to our families." His eyes went wide. "What if our families do not live? To what do we return?"

"Stand strong!"

Then the clutching darkness vomited Mk*tk.

They charged like one horns, sudden and unstoppable. Without hesitation or fear they flew through the open gap in the boma wall, crashing through the huts and hurling speared bodies into the men's fire.

There in the narrow shadows, Sparrow fought for his life. A Mk*tk came for him. He retreated a step, then turned with a sob and met the charge. His spear met flesh, but he was still hurled backward into the walls of the healing hut. Sticks and straw burst before the shock, their splinters stabbing him in the back and sides.

Groaning, he rolled up and tried to stand, dizzy and half blinded by a torn scalp.

He blinked away a doubled world and stared out through the hole in the wall. *Fire and blood.*

Those were the only words that rang in his mind.

Although there were three Ibandi for every one of their brutish foes, they were hard put not to stab one another in the dark, and their enemies used their confusion and uncertainty against them.

There was no mercy or hesitation. There was only screaming, and slaughter.

Fire and blood.

"Back! Back!" Fire Ant screamed. Although he and the men at his side had managed to kill two of the monsters, it was easy to see that his people were breaking.

In the moonlight, blood ran black, and before long all who survived were slick with it.

Fire Ant knew that he must take bold action, or all was lost. If he could only show his people that they were great, that they were beloved in Father

Mountain's eyes, they might stand up to these beasts, who killed from darkness, and finally be free.

And then his chance appeared. The largest Mk*tk appeared before him, an elephant with the first two fingers missing from his left hand. His scarred tree trunk of a chest heaved with kill fever.

The monster charged him, seeking to overwhelm with sheer power, only to be nicked again and again by Fire Ant's spear point.

Ho! In a fog as thick and cloying as honey, Ant watched his spear move, almost as if it possessed its own mind. He drew a line of blood from the giant's side, then barely evaded a backhand swipe of a bloody spear that might have crushed his ribs.

He was Fire Ant! He wounded his enemy at the belly and just above the knee, and began singing a little tune to himself, timing his thrusts to his song.

Then, to his surprise the giant stepped back, smearing at the blood with his fingers. Ant had never seen a Mk*tk pause once the killing had begun. Something odd sizzled in the hooded eyes.

Curiosity. Without question, the giant was puzzling through something. Until that moment, Ant had not been certain these creatures thought at all.

Then with insane speed the monster lunged directly at Fire Ant's spear tip. At the very last moment he twisted aside, scoring along Ant's upper ribs.

Two of Ant's men hurled themselves between their chief and the monster. As they struggled with their foe, Ant rubbed his hands along his wound and stared at the blood on his hand.

Something strange boiled through his veins, emotions Ant thought buried with his first body. Could that be . . . fear? But how could a dead man feel such a thing?

"We die!" Rock Climber wailed.

"Stand! Stand!" Fire Ant backed away from the giant Mk*tk, confused by his own confusion. The monster killed one Ibandi, then another took his place. They tumbled out of sight into the shadows, lost in the howling confusion. "We kill them here or die!"

The night's darkness beckoned. A lone thought fluttered through his mind, brief and bleak as a dying butterfly. *What have I done?*

"They seek our softness," he called. "They would kill the women and children!"

Despite his quavering knees, Wise Eagle sneered at Ant. "As we sought theirs. *You* did this! We trusted you, and you brought us death! We die. Our children die."

Fire Ant balled his hand and struck the hunter to the ground. But even as Eagle fell, Ant's own mind echoed the words.

Wise Eagle rose from the dirt, spitting blood. He held his spear high, squinting into the darkness. Eagle opened his mouth, but before he could say a word the air in front of him blurred. A spear buried itself in his belly, driving him off his feet and back against the boma wall. His hands clutched at the shaft, staring at it as if wondering how such a curious thing had come to be.

Fire Ant smelled blood and shit, and his own stomach rolled.

Eagle's woman snatched her round-bellied son from the ground and screamed, "Run!"

The boy had seen no more than seven summers. He fled only a hand of steps before he was clubbed down like an antelope, then hacked to death in the shadows.

There were fewer battles now, only slaughter. The Ibandi no longer out-numbered their attackers. The unequal contest had become no contest at all.

The shadows were distorted by thick-limbed spearmen hunched over a splintered boma's whimpering survivors. Watery screams peaked and troughed with the sigh of knife against skin. And then, finally, even that yielded to the wet whisper of flesh torn from bone.

Desperation lent Fire Ant strength and speed. He deflected a spear and slashed back to open a Mk*tk throat. Dying, his enemy crashed against him, driving him against the wall. The monster punched the side of Ant's head, then collapsed. Groaning and blood blinded, Ant sank to the ground.

The Mk*tk dragged him away. A Mk*tk child, now recognized by the leather strap tied around her bushy hair, pointed at him, jabbering to the adults.

So. A man could not outrun his sins, after all.

Fire Ant wandered between the worlds of dream and flesh. The world of flesh was hard. His hands were tied. Spears jabbed into his ribs, just enough to draw blood and force him back to his feet and walking.

For two days he and five other captured hunters walked. They were al-lowed to lie down at night, but sleep seldom came. Not since the first days on the mountain had he known such marrow-deep fatigue. A hunter named Great Crane lost the strength in his legs and was butchered there in the sand. Although they prepared the corpse for cooking, flaying flesh from bone, they ate not a bite, leaving the meat for scavengers. Fire Ant's dazed mind refused to make sense of it.

Finally they reached a gully wherein camped a hand of Mk*tk families, each with a brooding male, two or three females, and a hand of hairy children.

And to his amazement, one of the women who approached him was not

Mk*tk at all but an Ibandi. His misty memory dredged up her name: *Dove.* She was the girl they had failed to save in the earlier raid. Hadn't Quiet Water said Dove was dead?

The hulking Mk*tk leader's face was a mask of crisscrossed scars, his nose was broken and only a thumb and two fingers remained on his left hand. He pressed his face close. He reeked with a thick, wet buffalo stink. His mouth moved, and he made noises.

Dove translated. "He is Flat-Nose. He wants to know what are you."

"You are a dream dancer," an astonished Fire Ant said. "What are you doing?"

"Living," she said. Although her mouth moved, her face was leeched of emotion.

"But you are a dream dancer," he said again. Confusion spun his mind.

"I was," she replied, "but you did not come for me. Now I am Flat-Nose's third wife." Flat-Nose growled and clicked. "He asks if you are a kind of monkey. He said you fight like a man but kill women and children. He does not understand."

"He killed ours," Fire Ant replied.

She translated. Flat-Nose grunted.

"He says that Ibandi are not men. That killing such weaklings is less than killing four-legged."

Fire Ant's mind reeled. "You are his wife now? You are a mountain daughter! How can your mouth shape such words?"

Without expression, she spoke, and Flat-Nose answered.

"He said that he fucks any animal he wants. Ibandi killed his brother and his brother's son, and for ending his brother's line, you will suffer."

Fire Ant could barely force his mind to think. "I am beloved of Father Mountain!" he said. "Free me!"

Dove translated.

Flat-Nose spit into Ant's face. Then he spoke again.

"What did he say?" Ant said, dismayed by the weakness in his voice.

Dove translated. "He says 'You are worth killing slowly. I will make you a gift for God Blood.' "

Staked to the ground, Fire Ant sat on rocks and gravel, legs straight in front of him, his heels a bare step away from the central fire. Sitting beside him, Sparrow tugged at the leather straps binding his arms, crying.

Sun Runner had been staked to an acacia tree. As he screamed, the Mk*tk women used glass knives to slice skin from his right leg. After exposing a wound, the Mk*tk women slathered on some salve that smelled like fresh-cut cactus.

The bleeding slowed. In time, Sun's anguished cries died to a whimper. Then the women began again, slicing a new strip.

It seemed to go on forever, until Fire Ant was certain that if he lived ten hands of lifetimes, his ears would never be free of Crane's screams.

Surely, these were not men but evil *jowk*.

"Fire Ant!" Sparrow cried. "You are with me. I am not afraid."

"Do not fear. I am at your side." Fire Ant could speak the words, but his voice was no longer steady.

Sparrow panted. Just a boy, really. Brave, and strong, but he had not even undergone his manhood ritual. He should have, but there had been no hunt chiefs to take him up the mountain. "Tell me about the next world."

When Fire Ant searched his mind, his memories melted like spiderwebs in the spring rain. "It is cold. . . ."

"Like night on high ground?"

"Only more. Cold that makes your teeth clatter together. Cold that makes your bones ache and then go numb. Cold that burns like fire."

Sparrow closed his eyes as if for the last time. He had begun to shake, and although he bit his lip until it bled, could not stop.

Dove approached, her head down. She was shorn of her breast flaps, nipples exposed to skies and eyes. She shuffled just ahead of two giant males. "Prepare yourselves," she said.

Sparrow searched her face. "What will they do?"

"They will search for your *num*," she said. "You will scream. They will not stop until you are drained. I am sorry. You should not have come for me."

"We had to come," Sparrow said.

"No," she said. "You did not."

Sparrow licked his parched lips. Although the boy was trying to be brave, even from his distance, Ant could smell the piss.

Why did his stomach knot? Was he not the chosen one? Had he not returned from heaven? The worm of doubt had burrowed into his ear, whispering *no*.

He fought to ignore the doubt. He had done right. Had he not done what he must, in the process freeing a precious dream dancer from the hands of monsters? Certainly, he was beloved of their gods, if not himself divine.

If he prayed, perhaps Father Mountain would weave Sparrow and Ant new bones or return them to the *jowk*. And then, just as he had once before,

Fire Ant would lead his people to victory. He would bring Sparrow with him down the mountain. Death was not a cave. It was a path through sheltering trees, leading the faithful back to the light. One needed but believe.

The Mk*tk dragged Sparrow to the fire, laughing and howling as they did. Terror clawed inside Ant, and the wounds bled prayers: *Father Mountain. Give us* num *or return us to the* jowk. . . .

Over and over again he chanted it, and remembered the world above the divine clouds, the manner in which the cold . . .

The cold?

Hazily, he blinked away the confusion and tried to focus on what was happening over at the fire. All difficulty fled as the first scream sliced his ears.

There followed a dance of knives and fire and many, many blows. Mk*tk drums shivered the night air as their hideous females chanted in unison. The women, who had seemed so passive and small compared to the males, were most eager to tear flesh. They hunched around Sparrow's bound body, lifted him up and staked him to a tree by wrists and ankles.

And then, as Dove had warned them, with fire and knife they peeled and probed. They peered inside Sparrow, deaf to his cries. Then the Mk*tk women closed the flap of skin, covered it with mud, and began searching in another place.

On and on they went. Sparrow fought to hold Fire Ant's eyes. "Where is Father Mountain?" he screamed.

"He tests us!" Fire Ant howled in reply. "Do not despair."

As the night wore on, the Mk*tk males seemed to have become bored with their play. Some few still drummed, but most tottered off to their huts.

At last the drums fell quiet.

"What do you see?" Ant whispered to the boy. "Do you see the mountain? Do you see Great Mother?"

Sagging in his leather thongs, the boy managed to raise his head. When Sparrow opened his mouth, blood drooled out, his teeth broken. He managed to mumble a single despairing word. "Nothing," he whispered. "Nothing."

Hearing Sparrow's words, the shambling Mk*tk women approached him again, the oldest's shrunken breasts dangling like rotted fruit. In her own thick-bodied way she might once have been beautiful, with full round hips and smooth skin. But that was long ago. Now her skin sagged and her toothless mouth was a wrinkled, stinking hole.

She lifted Sparrow's chin and thrust her hand into his mouth. Ant saw the knife descend, and her arm work back and forth. Sparrow spasmed, and then went limp.

Dead? Alive? Ant could not tell, but hoped dead.

She hurled Sparrow's tongue onto the fire. As it sizzled she whispered something that he couldn't hear. A voice behind his eyes said, *It doesn't matter. You speak no Mk*tk and the witch Dove was not here to translate.* Whatever secrets, comforts or insults she might have offered fell on deaf ears. Sparrow was beyond hearing or understanding.

Fire Ant turned away. *This is a test.* Even now, Father Mountain was lifting Sparrow up to heaven. The body would go into the earth, and his flesh would flow from his body. That liquid meat would sink deep within the earth and flow up to the top of the mountain, where it would receive new bones. And then . . . and then . . .

He could not put a word to it, because his heart was frozen in sudden terror: the Mk*tk women were coming for him.

Ant strained and pulled against his bonds, all his memories of heaven suddenly dissolved. Their knives slashed the thongs binding Sparrow's hands. *Num*less, he sprawled upon the ground. Two males pulled Fire Ant up and lashed his wrists. With what little strength remained he fought, struggling also to remember that *there was nothing to be afraid of. He had already walked this path. There was nothing that they could do to him that the mountain had not already done. . . .*

The old woman shuffled to the fire, then from it extracted a brand as thick as his thumb. Chanting something that he could not understand she waved the flame back and forth before his face, then touched it to his right hand. He bit back a scream. She touched it to his left, and he lost control of his tongue, babbling sounds that made no sense, even to himself.

She burned the top of his right foot. And then his left.

My eyes, he thought. *She is touching my spirit eyes. She knows our ways . . . or else (even more unspeakable!) our ways are the same.*

She thrust the torch between his legs. Fire Ant shrieked, both in pain and anticipation of greater insult to come. But the brand he feared would burn and tear merely grazed.

She smiled at him. "No," she said, shocking Ant by producing a word in his own tongue. Then changing angles, she thrust the glowing brand into his right eye.

The world died.

The stick in her hand sizzled and popped in the wind-whipped flame. She smiled at Ant as if they two shared some great and intimate secret. He blinked his remaining eye. *What a terrible thing,* he thought, *for this demon to be my last sight in this world.*

Would Father Mountain gave him new eyes? Why did he hurt so much? He had been through this before, had *died* before. Why was it so difficult to remember his previous passage from life to death, from flesh to bone?

Why?

Ant looked down at Sparrow. The boy trembled. Silent but for the rasp of wet, labored breathing.

Sparrow seemed both to accuse and beckon. *You led me here. I followed you. Now, follow me . . .*

She brought the burning brand close and then closer . . . and then pulled it back. She yawned, exposing teeth rotted to rancid stumps, brown as her wrinkled face.

"Later," she said, again surprising him with another Ibandi word. "Soon."

The others giggled. For half the night, they had played with Sparrow's body. Too soon, the sun would be reborn. Torture was grueling work: they needed their sleep. Before the sun was directly overhead they would rise and have their day. Perhaps their children would pelt him with spit and shit all day long. Dance for him, deny him food and water. Tease him with the sight and scent of their loins. And then when night fell, the adults would finish what they had begun.

Pain washed over Ant like a rain-swollen river overrunning its banks. His mind had spun into the dream world, where the thorn walls preserving the flesh world shredded as if in a windstorm.

Tears streamed from his left eye, and he struggled to blink away the blur. To his numb surprise, he saw that a Mk*tk sitting by the fire seemed to have grown a stalk of some kind. *Something* was projecting from his neck. Without a sound, the guard slumped to the side.

Fire Ant struggled to make sense of it.

Then he felt hands upon him and a soft word in his ear. "Quiet," Moon Runner whispered.

Fire Ant felt the tears flowing from his good eye. Some of his hunters had survived and they had not forgotten him!

Moon Runner sawed at the rawhide cords binding Ant's wrists. If Ant leaned his head back over his shoulder, he could see two more hunters spiriting Sparrow away into the darkness.

And although at first he could not walk, as the blood returned to his legs Ant was able to run. The air was as thick as mud in his throat.

The world contracted to effort. He could run and run toward the north, and it was not until he had staggered on for almost a quarter that he heard the first angry howls.

The hunters led him along rocks and through streams, struggling to obscure footprints. They traveled northwest and then swung back north, aware that the Mk*tk had picked up their trail and were nearly in sight behind them.

The fugitives walked carefully around two hands of elephants, grazing like four-legged gray boulders. The big ears watched them mindfully, blowing warnings and moving between their young and the human invaders. The ground shook as they moved. *If only we were elephants, the Mk*tk would fear us,* Fire Ant found himself thinking. *If only . . .*

Even in his dazed state, Fire Ant's fractured and exhausted mind birthed a notion. "Hunting," he said. "Fire. Drive them."

They stared at him for a moment, then grasped his meaning. Moon Runner struck flint and iron to make sparks in a pinch of tinder, nurtured spark to flame and set the grass crackling. His brothers spread out and did the same and fanned their flames to greater life.

Father Mountain be praised! Within moments the wind rolled from a soft burr to a flurry of dust devils, as if the gods themselves had awakened to aid their children.

The funnels of smoke and flame whipped through the brush, spreading their hungry light.

Leaning against a tree and trying to steady his trembling legs, Fire Ant held his breath. Could such a ruse succeed?

By the time that the great long noses recognized the threat, the fire had eaten through a wide swath of brush, and the shouting humans drove the elephants south in a fire frenzied stampede.

The ground thundered as the elephants panicked and ran, crushing trees and brush before them. Through the dust and flame Ant glimpsed the Mk*tk. Their enemies had been too close behind them, far too close. Their pain-filled, panicked shouts gladdened his heart.

Long before the herd had slowed to a walk once again, the Ibandi were long gone.

Chapter Twenty-one

While the hunters dragged Sparrow on a sled of branches and leather straps, Ant walked most of the distance back to Fire boma. He remembered little of the next days. He did know that he and Sparrow were taken to Water boma's healing hut, walls rebuilt in straw and sticks, the roof still open to the stars.

Quiet Water handed Ant a water gourd, so that he was able to wet the dust from his throat. Young Sparrow was beyond such comforts.

His voice stilled, Sparrow's eyes pled for relief. The stench of pus and putrefying flesh thickened the air.

Fire Ant crawled to him. "What do you need?"

Sparrow's lips moved, but Ant heard only moist gasps.

The leather flap on the hut ruffled, and Quiet Water entered again, accompanied by one of her sisters.

"Help him," Ant said to her.

Face placid and without emotion, Quiet Water inspected Sparrow's wounds, then consulted with the other woman in whispers. "We have herbs for this," she said. The women whispered to each other again. He heard the whispered words "last gift" and "strangleweed."

"You can heal him?"

"We have herbs," Quiet Water said again. Their eyes contained an unspoken truth. "We can end his pain."

He swallowed hard. "I have heard such things." He knew that an elephant-trampled hunter from Wind boma had been eased to the next world with such herbs.

"Leave," the medicine woman said. "The rest is ours."

"Treat him gently," Fire Ant said, crawling backward to exit the hut. "To life's very end, he was brave."

Once outside, he lurched upright and stumbled out of the boma, down to Fire River, and vomited. On hands and knees, he watched bile and bubbles of half-melted food float away in the current. His head pulsed.

Nothing made sense. Nothing was real. The world was woven of threads, and the threads were made of nothing at all.

His dead eye socket pulsed, pushing black blood back into his brain. Tears streamed from the corner of Ant's single living eye.

Ant could not sleep. All through the nights, he thought only of the terrible thing that had happened and what he had done to cause it. What had gone wrong? Was he cursed by the mountain?

He did not know and had no one to ask. If only Stillshadow had not abandoned them, things might have been very different. Perhaps he was not a ghost after all. In that, he may have been mistaken. But he was not wrong about the Ibandi's need to be strong. He was not.

Why then, did he seem woven of nothing but agony made flesh? He rocked back and forth, cradling his head. "What happened?" he moaned again and again. "What happened?"

"I lost my father," Moon Runner said. It might be days before Runner ran again. He still limped, favoring his wounds. "That is all."

The world was a blur. Fire Ant blinked his good left eye. "It is too late. Word spreads to the other bomas. The people flee into the grass and up into the mountains. We are broken: the Ibandi are no more. Father Mountain! What did I do wrong?"

He held his knees to his chest. He struggled in vain to summon his former strength and certainty. The men and women who believed in him were desperate for something he no longer seemed to possess.

"He sent you back to us," Moon Runner said, "surely not to see us die. There had to be a purpose to my father's death."

"The mountain's shadow no longer shelters us," Rock Climber said. "If only the great dancer were still here."

Ant closed his eyes, and in that darkness dreamed of what he must do. From that void the *jowk* whispered to him:

Find Stillshadow . . .

"What do we do?" Moon Runner asked.

Now at last Fire Ant sprang to life. "We find Stillshadow. We bring her back."

"But she followed Sky Woman. Perhaps she will not return."

Fire Ant was certain. "She will come. I will bring her. No matter where they are, no matter how far. If she lives, I will find her."

"She is with your brother," Rock Climber said.

Always Frog. Always, I knew I would see you again. Always.

When the others turned away, he whispered the next words: "And you, nameless witch. You have done this. All this. Your heart. My knife. Soon."

Chapter Twenty-two

Fire Ant gathered two hands of hunters, and set out for the plains and mountains north of Great Sky, a single song in their minds: *Find the refugees. Bring back Stillshadow.*

On the fifth day, humans were silhouetted against the horizon. They bristled as the strangers drew closer, then relaxed when it became clear that the approaching men and women were Ibandi.

The leader was a bald man with rainbows of keloid scar tissue above his brows. Ant remembered him as Zebra Shadow, youngest brother of Water boma's former leader, Water Chant. He and Ant had gone walkabout in the same year. They had hunted together many times since then.

"Zebra!" Ant called. "Hold!"

"Fire Ant!" Zebra called. Ant's old hunting companion dropped to the ground, trembling with fear and wonderment. "Sky Woman told us you died on the mountain!"

"Yes . . . yes I did," Fire Ant said. His men watched him carefully. He wondered if they could see beneath his skin, perhaps even read his *num*-field as did the dream dancers. When he closed his left eye, the dead right socket pulsed red-black, like a cricket chirping in the night. Could they see its heartbeat?

He continued, "But Great Sky had plans for me. Things for me to do in this world. I am not yet finished."

"We are returning to the Circle," Zebra said. "The way is too hard."

Fire Ant nodded. "Is the old woman still alive?"

No need to ask who Ant meant. "She is very weak. Blind. I think she may be mad."

"Mad?" Fire Ant asked. "How did it happen?"

"She sang the sun to life and was so taken with its beauty that she did not look away. Her face-eyes dimmed. Now, she speaks to the *jowk* all night." His face lightened for a moment. "But Sky Woman saved her. She is a mighty dream dancer."

Fire Ant's eye narrowed. "She is not the blessed one. Sky Woman did not give us names. She did not dance at our births, did not teach us the sacred songs. She was not Cloud Stalker's mate. Sky Woman is not worthy. We must bring Stillshadow back or lose our lives and lands."

"We see the same truth," Zebra said.

"How long ago was this?" Ant asked.

"Less than a moon."

Fire Ant squatted, motioning for Zebra to come beside him. He pointed at the earth. "I swear by Father Mountain and Great Mother," he said. "Come with me, and we will return them to the Circle."

Chapter Twenty-three

South Wind boma was just three huts within a vine and bamboo circle, nestled between a creek bed and a stand of thorn trees. Dry most of the year, the creek now ran with water and blood.

On most days the children's play shrieks were the loudest sounds. Tonight, the young ones screamed, but their cries were not those of pleasure and discovery. Tonight, their parents screamed as well, with diminishing strength and increasing despair.

Flat-Nose listened with interest as Dove translated the families' groans. His third wife kept a thick face as she did her job, speaking as a creature without emotion, sensation or thought. She was learning to be a good female. In time, he might send his second wife to his youngest brother, High Step, and let Dove take her place.

When she was done, Flat-Nose told her to return south to the Mk*tk enclave with one of his hunters as protection. She cried and clung to him, begging to stay, to go with them, but he shook his head.

He cuffed her, bringing water to her eyes. Then he told his brother to take her back.

"But what if you need me?" She sobbed. "You cannot hear their tongue."

"I am done with talk," he said. "This next part is not for you."

Flat-Nose did not look back as they walked on. When he was almost over the next rise he turned, and saw her standing there with High Step. She was half a head shorter than Mk*tk women, narrower of shoulder, smaller in breast and thigh. Mk*tk women braided their hair in a single club worn down the back.

When first captured, Dove had hands of little braids all over her head. After some moons she had begun to unwind them, perhaps intending to wear her hair in the Mk*tk fashion. Flat-Nose had told her no. With her frail features and narrow cheekbones, the strong, blunt Mk*tk hairstyle would have made her look like a child, and Flat-Nose did not sex children.

Ibandi women were so small and weak. Perhaps they were spirits of some kind, and not human beings at all. When he was inside her, he found her slick softness pleasing. When he spent, he found that the emptiness within his loins was no less satisfying than with his own women.

So, perhaps Ibandi men were weaklings, but their women were . . .

Flat-Nose did not have a word for what they were, but the thought of them, the memory of their scent and skin, made his root swell.

She was a decent woman, who had recognized a true man the first time he entered her. She knew to make pleasing motions with her hips. In time she might bear his child, and then she would be a Mk*tk woman forever.

But it was time to put all thoughts save vengeance from his mind. This was his time. He would travel far and do mighty deeds. And the song that his sons would sing of him would take him past the terrible fangs and down into God Blood's mighty stomach for all time.

Chapter Twenty-four

Fire Ant walked north.

Hands of days behind him, Flat-Nose traveled north as well.

Frog, T'Cori and the Ibandi had cut west and now were headed back south, following Stillshadow's vision. Instead of increasing their margin of safety, now every day the distance between them and their enemies decreased. No one knew, or could have known.

But every step any of them took, no matter how fast or slow, now brought all closer together. . . .

Frog bit a chunk of the dried smoked zebra. He took his time chewing it, grinding the tough fibers into mush. They were low on fresh meat again, but to his relief, the travel south had brought slightly better hunting. Families of the striped four-legged grazed a few spear throws away, and a hunting party would set out tomorrow morning, after they had rested.

T'Cori walked at Frog's left as they followed the banks of a wide, rippling stream deep enough to hold crocodiles and muddy enough to conceal them. They were careful that the children didn't play too close.

He knew T'Cori was weary, but he was proud of the fact that she rarely showed it. The Leopard twins pulled their sled-bound mother, Stillshadow, behind them. Ten and five tens of Ibandi straggled along behind, low in spirits.

In former days, old Stillshadow could be counted upon to cajole or inspire. Now she barely seemed aware of where they were, or perhaps even of who she was. She could not see, but she cocked her head sideways as if to catch the stream's rushing voice.

Frog called for rest, then took the twins aside. "We must be careful," Frog said. "Spearmen! Hold your places."

"So," Leopard Eye asked, "this place is shallow enough for us to cross?"

"Yes," Frog said, "but I think the river has teeth. Be careful."

T'Cori stared. "You remember what I said happened to Fawn?"

"The crocodile. I remember," he said. "We will take care."

They decided not to ford the river there, and traveled on some time, pushing through fear and fatigue, until clearer waters promised safety. A quarter farther along, the stream joined its source river, and here the waters were not muddy. The hunters took their positions at the riverside. Frog watched carefully as his people sloshed to the opposite bank. He noted every shadow, every eddy. The fan of branches floating past . . . were those merely wood? Or did something with fangs and claws live within or beneath?

Either the predators were absent, or Father Mountain was kind enough to keep them sleeping. No children were lost that day.

Together the Ibandi crossed the plains, the grasslands. Up ridges and through mountain passes T'Cori marched, wheezing with each breath of thinning air.

Each new dawn, T'Cori felt the life within her stir more vigorously. On days when they struggled through the higher passes, between stands of yellow-green brush and fields of grass so spiky it cut through her leathered soles, every step seemed to leech more of her remaining strength . . . but thinking of the life within drove her on.

"I breathe and breathe," she groaned, "and still I taste no air."

"You are strong," Frog said.

"It feels as if we are on Great Sky again," T'Cori said. "Remember when even the fire did not warm us?"

"That was a bad time, but Great Sky is far away. We'll make it. Always."

Despite the depths of her fatigue, his faith wrung a smile from her. "Because of Frog?"

"No," he replied. "No. Because of Great Sky Woman. Look at their faces. They believe in *you,* not me. They follow *you,* not me."

T'Cori turned her head. Behind them, their people were tired and discouraged but still trudged onward toward an uncertain future. If possible they were even more fatigued and discouraged than she. "They . . . believe in me?"

"Yes, every one. I more than any other."

"Without you," she said, "I could never have climbed the mountain."

"Listen to me." His fingers gripped her shoulders. "It was not me. It was not 'us.' It was *you*. You asked me to climb with you. I believed in you and did a thing that I could not do. You say that we must travel north, and I believe you. Stillshadow says we should turn west and south, and every person here looks at you to see if we should believe. You are our strength, don't you see?"

He placed his hand on the curve of her belly. "You are *his* strength as well."

"*Hers*." She smiled. "And you are wrong. I am not my daughter's strength. She is mine."

Placing one foot before the other and then pushing as hard as he could, Frog hiked up the rise, refusing to listen to his aching legs. Young Bat Wing climbed on ahead, up a wall of hills that ran from east to west almost as far as the eye could see.

Perhaps they could go around this barrier, but Frog was too tired to think, too tired to do anything but keep going and hope that somewhere amid the twisted trees and thornbush there might be something to keep them going.

Around them, some of the more energetic boys and girls ran and laughed, somehow making a game of it all.

Bless them. Had he suddenly become old? Where had his youthful *num* gone? His legs were straw. As the way steepened the vegetation grew sparser still, rocks poking through the earth to form ridges almost like gray flower petals.

Gray, like his people's increasingly dusty faces. Like his hopes for the future.

As they crested the hill, the last light of day shone down upon them from the west. The sun was dying, taking with it his dreams. They needed a place to rest, hoped for flat ground to camp upon.

That last dying sunlight shone down upon a darkened valley. The ridge of mountains on the other side was, what? Half a day distant?

Within that shadowed half-day's circle moved clumps of greater darkness. To eyes rapidly adjusting to the night, those clumps separated like a dark fluid running down over a rock, revealing themselves to be . . . living things. *Herds.* Was he dreaming?

"Where are we?" Stillshadow mumbled thickly, stirring from her trance.

"I don't know, Old Mother," T'Cori said, "but I have never seen a place like this."

"I think . . ." Snake said, "I think I have heard of this place. We are only five days from Great Sky, but our hunters never come here."

"Shadow Valley," Stillshadow whispered. Frog's heart jumped. "Be very careful. It is said that *jowk* walk here. The legend is of wolves who walk like men." It was more words than the old woman had strung together in many days.

As they descended the northern wall, the dying sun set fire to a lake in the valley's southwest quadrant. Water aplenty! Wobble legged with awe, they picked their way down the slope. At first Frog thought his eyes had deceived him.

Tens of tens of tens of four-legged. Striped zebra eating side by side with wildebeest. Buffalo? Yes, a spear's throw from the zebra, a wide-horned black buffalo grazed, gazing almost directly at him.

"My belly thought never to see such herds again," Frog whispered.

"Has any man counted so high?" Bat Wing asked.

There was a strangeness here. The hills that had grown to block the horizon from east to west ringed this entire valley, a rise of steep mud-colored swellings dotted with small flat-topped trees and grasses so green Frog wondered if this place had its own clouds and rain, different from that on the outside.

"Look at the mountains. They are a great circle," Snake said, voice soft with wonder.

"We rest. Our people are exhausted. Serve the last of the meat," Frog said, feeling new *num* flowing up his spine. His fingers tingled. "And then . . ."

"Then what?" Excitement boiled Bat Wing's voice.

"Tomorrow we hunt!"

The children had journeyed far, but despite their fatigue, they were eager and excited to explore the valley's sloping wall. They could not sleep, and their twittering noise kept the hunters awake. "Dance them a story," Stillshadow commanded of T'Cori, and she thought awhile.

At first she thought to protest: she felt too tired to do anything but sleep.

But she was happy that Stillshadow was still rooted in this world enough to care. Her mentor was probably correct: a well-told tale would calm them.

T'Cori began to sway, and the people put down their burdens and came to watch as her voice and body wove scene and story together into a waking dream.

"A long time ago," she said, "there was another hill, and another hard climb . . ."

A young hunter had been climbing all day, and at last became tired and sleepy. He thought he would lie down for a while, having drained himself searching for game.

While he slept, a lion came seeking water in the midday heat. It saw the young man and thought to drag this nice piece of meat to the shade for a leisurely meal.

It grabbed the hunter's leg, and the pain awakened him. The hunter was very frightened! He knew that if he made a sound the lion would know he lived and would kill him at once.

The lion dragged the man over to a tree and thought to have a nice drink of water before its meal. It jammed the hunter's head between two roots and turned to go down to the lake.

At first the man tried to struggle, then went limp as the lion turned around. The lion had seen the movement from the corner of its eye, and suspected that the hunter still lived. It returned before the man could escape. It sniffed and growled, but the hunter didn't move. The lion licked the tears running down the man's cheeks, enjoying the salt.

A stick pricked the man's back, but he couldn't move.

Convinced that the man was dead, the lion went down to the lake. When it did, the man sprang up and made his escape, twisting this way and that to confuse the trail.

When he returned to his village he told them that he had been almost killed and that they must wrap him in hartebeest skins so that when the lion came to seek him, he would not be found.

Because they loved him, they did this thing for him, wrapping him in hartebeest skins so that the lion would not find him.

Then the people went about their tasks, as if nothing had happened. The lion came and demanded that they give him the hunter. They refused, and it bit the throat of the closest hunter. They shot it with poisoned arrows, but although it screamed with pain, it would not die.

The village elders cried out that they must give the lion the young hunter

*that if they did this it would leave them alone. The people would not do this,
for they loved the hunter, who was their son. Many died as the lion raged
among them, seeking the hunter. They shot it with arrows and stabbed it, and
still it lived. It broke the huts to pieces, and they knew that it was no ordinary
lion. It was a* jowk *wearing a lion's skin.*

*And the young man knew that he could not let this thing happen any more.
He came out from under the hartebeest skin and went to the lion. The lion bit
the young man to death, even while the villagers were stabbing and shooting it.*

And only then did the lion die.

Frog did not watch the story: he had seen it hands of times before. Leopard
Eye was entranced, but Frog was watching the shadows.

For all his days, fire had fascinated Frog, and that interest had not decreased with time. After the others had wandered off to their sleeping
places, he placed more wood on the fire, and as it roared he took his spear
and fought the shadows. When they moved, he moved, thrusting and par-
rying until he lost the sense of being a two-legged, until his human mind
peeled away to reveal a beast of reflex and instinct.

Then, inspired, he pulled a piece of soft chalk from his pouch and drew
a Mk*tk outline on a slab of rock. He attacked the outline, watching the
shadow-play as he did. Again and again, tens of tens of strikes, each faster
than the one before.

Is this what the hunt chiefs had done? Was this how they had become
great? Was there any chance at all that if he wore his flesh to the bone, he
might discover some tiny fragment of their wisdom?

His fear mocked him. *It is not enough.* You *are not enough.*

But it would have to be enough. Stillshadow had called this placid valley
a place of *jowk.* By this she meant spirits who walked the earth. He did not
believe in spirits.

But monsters lived. There were monsters behind them. Monsters before
them. What choice to make? There was food here and water. Eventually,
hunters could not merely hunt. Certainly, the great hunt chiefs had understood this. The last year had taught Frog a frightful lesson: *Eventually,
hunters had to fight.*

He did not believe in spirits, but fire seemed to him a living thing. The
fire folk ate, they slept, they lived and died. Their sparks flew up to the
clouds. If there was magic in the world, it would be found in fire.

He fed the fire until it leapt up to lick at him. "Help me," he asked the
fire. "I want what you want: food and shelter and family. Help me."

The fire folk answered him with their dancing. Their shadows birthed enemies to pit against his speed and skill. And until his strong young body was slack with fatigue, he killed them again and again.

Frog awakened to see T'Cori sitting at the edge of their skins, gazing out across the valley.

"What is it, my love?"

"I was in the dream world," she said.

"What dream?"

"That I was you. And that I dreamed."

"You dreamed you were dreaming?" He scratched his head. "That is a strangeness."

"So many odd things," she said and nuzzled against him. They passed the night holding each other. Her scent was more dizzying than the magic water had been, and the living warmth of her belly pillowed his weary head.

Despite their lack of sleep, when the sun was finally born along the eastern mountains, neither was tired at all.

Chapter Twenty-five

Good hunting depended upon fortune, upon the elements of wind and fire serving them. For this, Frog trusted in luck. The others trusted in Great Sky's goodwill, in the songs and dances of the holy dreamers.

In the day's new light, it was easier to make a complete picture of their surroundings. The ridge of hills stretched off into the distance, arching around to make a bowl. The walls were rock tumbled but crowded with trees, more than they would have dreamed from the growth upon the outer wall.

The Ibandi had camped on a shelf of rock less than a quarter-way down the ridgetop. There, the families were crowded but not cramped.

As they ate their morning mush balls and jerky, the people gathered at the edge of the shelf and gazed down into the valley. Their stomachs rumbled and their mouths watered. Could anyone predict how long this bounty would last? Although the game below them seemed without end, this entire place was a miracle such as only existed in dreams. Mightn't the animals simply melt into the grass at any moment?

Mightn't Father Mountain be preparing the cruelest joke of all?

When Frog retreated from his thoughts, Snake was standing at the edge of the shelf, arms raised. When he saw Frog, Snake spoke with the strongest voice Frog had heard his uncle use for moons.

"When we hunt," Snake said, "we hunt as of old. We kill enough for all our people. Enough to dry the meat for hard times. Only then can we believe that what is here will last." Despite his words, the dead skin on the left side of his face crinkled as he smiled.

So they went down from the ridge and marched west, marveling at the kudu and fringe-eared oryx and impala. There, hiding just beneath the surface of a water hole, a hippopotamus twitched its ears, then sneezed a flume of water into the air.

"Could Stillshadow be right?" Frog asked. "Could her blind eyes see more than ours?"

"Shadow Valley," Snake said. "My father once told me that monsters dwelled here. Something more than beast-men. He said that my uncles fought great pale things, wolves that walked on two legs. And that we did not need this place: there was hunting elsewhere."

"Things have changed," Frog said. "Now we need it. We both know how stories grow," he said, and Snake winced. "I see no monsters," Frog said, "only the fattest, slowest giraffes."

"The unseen snake bites the deepest," Snake muttered.

And they looked. Monkeys swarmed up the trees, uncounted tens of flamingos stood on single legs, reflecting the newborn sunlight back in shimmering pink waves. The hunt chiefs may have told stories about Shadow Valley, but Snake knew better than most that legends and reality were not always the same.

They walked the grasslands at the foot of the hills, marveling at the streams and berry bushes and trees whose branches were laden with succulent fruit.

After a quarter day of walking they reached a cleft ten paces across, deep enough to walk into many tens of paces before narrowing. All agreed that this place would make a splendid trap. The fissure walls extended some hands of men high, but looked accessible from the top.

"Your eyes are open wide, Frog," said Uncle Snake, grinning. "Will this place be good?"

"I think so," he said. "I call this place Giraffe Kill, for the meat to come." They backed out of the fissure and looked back across the plain.

What had made this place? Surely, Father Mountain's mighty hands and no other's. It seemed to Frog that the grass was greener, lusher here than in the outer world. The sky above them was brighter, the clouds more crisply edged.

What was reality and what a dream?

Frog closed his eyes and inhaled deeply through his nose. The air even *smelled* better. Greener, crisper, cleaner.

He opened his eyes again. There, five spear throws distant, as placid as if they had never seen a lion or a man, grazed a hand of spotted long necks.

"It is too wonderful," said Leopard Eye. "What if there really are *jowk*? What if Mk*tk are here?"

"That is not the legend," Snake said. "My father said that the creatures were pale as grubs. The Mk*tk are as dark as we."

Frog's belly twisted. He had expected this question to arise, another reason he had spent so much time jabbing at shadows with his spear.

"There is more than enough for all here," he said. "If there are monsters here, and they try to drive us away, then we will see. There is enough here for many peoples."

"What if they are not people at all?"

"Then we will see."

They crept into position, then waited for the wind to shift. As it often did, in the morning hours the wind blew mostly from the north. By the time the sun died on the western horizon, the breeze came mostly from the east.

The hunters had surrounded a hand of giraffes, old gray furs and young colts. Frog and his people had busied themselves profitably, using bows and coals to create small fires in the dry grass.

Then, after a screaming, arm-waving signal from Uncle Snake, they fanned the fires.

While Bat Wing watched at his side, Frog set his ember to the dry grass. He blew and fanned and bent one stalk to the next. Bat Wing unrolled the zebra skin, and Frog shook it, making wind to drive the flame.

The fire folk roared to life, mating, bearing young, spreading rapidly.

By the time the first of the spotted long-necks smelled the smoke, they were half encircled.

Slowly at first, and then with increasing speed, the herd stumbled into a run, fleeing the smoke with their stiff, awkward gait. When they tried to break through the fires, the long-necks found a pair of hunters shouting and waving spears, driving them in the opposite direction.

Do not surround them. Always give the prey a path to escape. . . .

It was another thing he had learned from Uncle Snake. The panicky beasts galloped toward the little canyon. There they would be trapped, and the hunters, in pursuit, could pierce them with spears and arrows and rain rocks upon their heads from above. It was all to the good.

"Uncle," Bat Wing said, voice shot through with nervousness, "the fire is spreading too fast."

"Come quick!" Frog grabbed the boy's wrist and pulled.

In his excitement, Frog had allowed the flames to encircle them. The smoke wreathed his nostrils and crawled down his throat.

He wiped his watering eyes and squinted through the smoke. Fire crawled along the grass, chewing at the blades and curling smoke as it spread. The wind shifted and . . . *there!*

Not ten strides distant, a gap opened in the line of fire. Frog seized the boy and ran. Then as if the wind itself was an evil *jowk* it whipped into a frenzy, and the raging wall thickened. If he tried to leap it, he might stumble and perhaps be singed but survive.

But Bat Wing would never make it through at all.

His initial panic gave way, replaced by a cold, heavy feeling in the pit of his stomach.

Heat. Air that seared his lungs and blinded him.

Death.

His nose and throat burned as if he had inhaled fire. His heart drummed rabbit rhythm, speeding poison to every finger and toe.

Smoke, excitement, the clamor of the hunt . . . separately and together they had blinded him. So eager had he been to trap the giraffes that he had placed himself and the boy in peril.

So. You think you are smarter than other men? And that men are smarter than beasts?

Even giraffes know to run from fire, he thought. *You fool: this place is haunted after all. And soon another ghost will walk the plain. Would his flesh find its way up Great Sky?*

Up?

Smoke rises, he thought. *Fire climbs* up *a vine.* If he could stay close to the ground, perhaps he could spare them both a roasting.

Frog knelt and began to dig. "Dig with me!" he called to Bat Wing. The boy knelt, and they scraped with their hands, scrabbling until they'd clawed a trench in the earth. Frog slid down into it and covered his legs and chest with dirt.

"Get down!" he yelled to the paralyzed boy. Bat Wing climbed down next to him, and Frog pulled the zebra skin over them both.

As the fire tightened its grip, his heart thundered loud enough to drown thought. For a moment he dared to hope that it might veer away. Then the wind shifted again, bringing the heat right to them. Raw panic seized thought and worried it like a weasel with a rat. Every bit of him yammered to rise and run, to risk anything to get away. He forced himself to stay down, gasping as the air thinned and his skin scorched.

"Uncle! Mother!" The boy beside him coughed. "Your son is afraid. Help me!"

Then the smoke flooded his mind, and thought died.

By the time he awakened and crawled out from under the blackened zebra skin, the sun had set. Was he dead? No, he was breathing. Even more tellingly, he ached from hair to heel. Frog imagined that whatever death actually was, it was not likely to hurt quite so badly. Frog sat up in a field of blackened grass.

He smacked his hands together, woozily watching a cloud of ash dust fuzzing the air. His head wasn't working right. His eyes were blurry. Patches of skin on his face and shoulders and legs were singed, but he seemed astoundingly undamaged.

Bat Wing lay limp at his side. He rolled the boy's inert body over, and shook his shoulder. "Bat Wing!" he called. "Bat Wing! Wake up! You cannot be dead. It is Frog, your uncle, who calls you."

Bat Wing coughed. His eyes opened, crossed and then focused. Frog hugged the boy almost tight enough to choke him.

"Don't crush me." Bat Wing coughed, and they laughed together, rather shocked to find themselves alive.

At first so faint he doubted his ears, a chorus of human voices rippled through the night. Leaning upon each other, Frog and Bat Wing limped toward the canyon.

And there, they found the rest of their hunters. Despite the fact that two of the long-necks still thrashed their legs, the butchering had already begun. Some of the other Ibandi were already slicing away chunks of meat. To his weary amusement, Frog realized that the joy of the kill had been so great, no one had thought to look for him or Bat Wing.

And within moments, joining in the butchery, slippery with blood and intestines and breathing a cloud of hungry black gnats, he had almost forgotten his own toasting.

Chapter Twenty-six

That night, the Ibandi camp was a feasting glory. T'Cori and Sing Sun chanted and stamped and sang, performing their blessing ceremonies. The gods, if gods there were, seemed receptive to their entreaties. Frog wondered if such a miracle could actually be. Might they have found a home?

He and Leopard Eye had gathered branches and vines, constructing the camp's largest lean-to for Stillshadow, near an elephant-head-shaped rock half buried in the soil. T'Cori had led her mentor to the rock in the early morning hours. Blind and frail but blessedly agile, the old woman climbed up and sat cross-legged, staring out toward the camp as her people mended clothes, sharpened tools and prepared for their day. She had not yet called it her sitting stone, but that day could not be far off.

When Frog and the hunters returned from the valley floor, bowed beneath their bloody loads of giraffe ribs and legs, Stillshadow smiled even before the first glad cries of greeting rang in her ears.

While the meat sizzled on the twin campfires, she swayed back and forth to the rhythms of an invisible drummer. All in the camp felt their woes dissolving before the waves and eddies of that silent song.

T'Cori brought Stillshadow down from the rock and sat her near the fire to feed her. All were quiet and still until the chief dancer took the first bite. She set her teeth in it, and then pushed it away. "Later," the old woman said to T'Cori. "Bring it to me later, in my hut."

"The meat is good," T'Cori said.

"I knew it would be strong and sweet," Stillshadow said.

"It is right that we give thanks to Great Sky," T'Cori said. "We cannot see Him, but He sees us, blesses us, keeps us strong."

Frog laughed. "The night is His shadow."

He looked up at the clouds. There amid the billowings and shadings, he saw Hawk Shadow drawing a bow, aiming at a . . . rabbit? Yes, he could just make out the ears and tail. And there . . . the shape of a spiked cactus. So sad almost no one else could see the cloud world.

"Frog," Gazelle Tears said, "your son wants you."

"That is good," Frog said, "because I want my son."

She handed him a warm brown bundle of deerskin and wriggling arms and legs. Medicine Mouse gurgled and reached a chubby hand out to Frog, a broad and contented smile on his face.

"Perhaps," Frog's mother said, "you can teach him to see the faces."

Frog held his son. This was the only heaven he needed: his family, safe and near. T'Cori and Gazelle Tears. His sister, Little Brook, was on the far side of the women's fire with her own family, and his younger brother, Wasp, would probably marry soon.

This might be the place, he thought, *and this might be the time.* Shadow Valley had everything a man or an entire tribe could desire.

Gazelle Tears's face was sharp now, all cheekbones and chin. She had clipped her hair down to gray stubble, as grandmothers often did. It was a strangeness to Frog. Men and women started life as squalling infants, almost exactly alike. They diverged into different lives and patterns of dress as they reached adolescence. Boys with their loincloths, girls with their leather skirts. In adulthood they lived nearly separate lives, different tasks, different fires, different lodges. Then as elders, the circle completed itself, and they once again seemed almost identical. There was a wisdom and a shape to all of it that warmed him. "Mother, what kind of baby was I?"

"Like all others." Gazelle Tears smiled. "Wrinkled and ugly and beautiful."

"What do you best remember about me?"

She hesitated, searching her memory. "You'd had five summers," she said. "It was a cool evening. The east wind rattled the walls. We built the fires high that night. You were asleep when I laid my head down, but I awoke to find you gone." Her eyes widened. "So frightened I was! I thought that perhaps a jackal had wiggled under the wall and clamped his stinking teeth onto my son. I went out looking, and found you by the fire."

"What was I doing?"

" 'Making friends with the fire people.' " She cackled. "That is what you said. You said that you could talk to them."

Frog pressed his lips against his son's warm, smooth skin. His boy-child. His son. A boy to teach to walk. To talk. Perhaps to see faces in the fire. *Please, if there is anything out there to hear, let my son see the faces.*

For now there were two, Frog Hopping and Bat Wing. Let there be one more. Perhaps this thing, this strange sight, was like a fire. If only one man possessed it, it was a spark. Two, a flame flickering in the wind.

But three . . .

Three might grow into a blaze.

Curls of peppery steam wafted from the fist-sized chunk of giraffe meat T'Cori carried to Stillshadow. When she carried the mat of folded leaves into the lean-to, the old woman was curled on her side beneath a straw roof, muttering to the *jowk,* her gnarled face shrunken and withdrawn.

If she knelt, her head brushed the lean-to's straw roof. Still, it was wider than most, the ground draped with skins and scattered with Stillshadow's possessions: medicine bags, her ritual drum, a walking stick, bones for casting.

Sing Sun sat beside Stillshadow, busy scraping white fibrous fatty tissue from an ibyx hide with a flat rock. Beside her was a chunk of a young palm trunk the length of her forearm, already mostly hollowed.

A new drum?

T'Cori passed the meat beneath Stillshadow's nose, and after a few such passes her mentor took it.

She gnawed on it a bit, and then handed it back. "It hurts my teeth," Stillshadow said. "I did not want the others to see, but it is hard for me to chew now."

T'Cori understood. Without a word, she chewed the meat thoroughly, and then spit the gob into Stillshadow's palm, and repeated this process until Stillshadow emitted a low, contented belch.

T'Cori beamed with pride.

"Giraffe meat is good," her teacher said. "Did I tell you of my dream?"

"You have shared many dreams, Mother," T'Cori said.

"This one was of women with long, spotted necks."

"Did you see the valley?"

Stillshadow frowned. "I do not remember. But I saw a wall of fire."

"Ah," T'Cori said, brightening. "Frog was almost burned. That may be what you saw. But the long-necked women . . ." She chewed at the inside of her mouth. "Women . . . giraffes . . ." She shook her head. "Are we to be eaten?"

"If your men are good lovers, yes." Sing Sun cackled, and the three women dissolved into mirth.

It felt good, better than T'Cori had felt in many days, or even moons. "I need your help," she said to the old woman. "I need to know what to do now, to make this place our home."

For a time T'Cori thought that Stillshadow had wandered too far into the dream world, but then the old woman spoke. "The drum," she said. "We need to bless Sing Sun's drum."

"A drum," T'Cori said. "What songs would this drum need?"

"We will need to be wise and clever and swift in this new place. Here, we will need the rabbit song."

"Why that?"

"To be careful in a new place. Quick and clever—but not too brave," the old woman whispered. "Sometimes, caution is more important than courage. When the mountain died, we struggled to heal our people. I have thought of many things we did not try. And one of them is the rabbit song."

"You fear the gods have died?"

Stillshadow ignored the question. "I fear that we have traveled so far, and for so long, that we have broken our soul vines, that which connects us to the *jowk*. When I drum, my vine grows strong.

"The drumming is a way to find Great Mother within me. A way to speaking with Her. I must honor the tree *jowk* and the animal who gave her skin. The drum will teach us from the moment we sit down and touch it, speak to it, dance with it. My eggshell thickens and all my demons rise: I forget that tomorrow comes and want everything today. I want to believe that all that is wrong in the world is caused by others, not me. Never me. I am the great Stillshadow." Her mouth twisted in grim humor. "As a girl, I believed I could make something that could not be improved. But in my heart I feared that I could not be what my people needed me to be, that I could not fulfill my dream self. I feared that others might be better than me, and I hated them for it."

"Hate?" T'Cori asked, startled. "Mother, you feel such things?"

The old woman gave a brief, humorless bark of laughter. "Do you think that I did not hate when I heard what the Mk*tk did to you? That I did not fear, knowing that I must have been a very bad teacher?"

To that, T'Cori had no answer.

"I had every eye upon me. I could not be tired or angry or less than perfect. I could not be afraid. But all of us fear, my daughter. All creatures of flesh feel fear. But the children need to feel that there is someone too strong for fear to control."

T'Cori sat beside Sing Sun and ran her fingers along the palm trunk's grooved bark. Looked inside. The work of hollowing it out was half done, and she set herself to scraping out more of the wood pulp with a flat, sharp-edged rock. Time passed, and she lost herself in the light, pleasant trance induced by sacred work.

Sing Sun broke her trance. "Mother, are you sure this is the skin you wish?" She seemed to choose her next words carefully. "Did you . . . know it has a hole in it?"

"And you do not?" The old woman cackled. "Our holes make us what we are. Holes help you remember that only Great Mother can make a perfect thing. It keeps us from becoming proud.

"You will never find the perfect tree. And yet, all trees are perfect."

"How—" T'Cori caught herself and shook her head. "There is so much to learn. I will try to understand."

Stillshadow took the drum from T'Cori's hands. "We must open ourselves to the drum's spirit. Its spirit is the spirit of the deer or oryx or the tree, whatever flesh and bone the drum is made of." She set it between her knees, and began to slap. Her hands were a dancing blur. "When the drum moves your hands, you forget everything except the music and the sound. Great Mother's children are not spirits. Not gods. There are things we cannot do, must not even try.

"But to change anything, to do anything, to teach anything, I must go deeply inside myself. In the womb we hear the beat of our mother's heart. It is where we . . . and all rhythm . . . begin."

Although blind and seemingly near death, Stillshadow tapped and slapped a rhythm so rich and alive that the three of them swayed where they were seated. Magic! T'Cori watched the blinding-fast play of her hands, switching from flat to fingertips in a twinkling.

Now slow. Now quick. Now like water, and then fire and then the steady beat of the earth. With a flicker, it elevated into wind.

Stillshadow might have barely enough strength to walk, but her drumming humbled them all.

Now each hand moved at a different tempo. *Bah-bah-ba-bah!* "It was Cloud Stalker who mastered this," she said. "He taught me a bit, but there is a way of drumming that is a men's thing. I could never have drummed as he did. All the leaping and tumbling about! Hah!" She chuckled to herself, warmed by the memory.

"Great Mother gave us the drum. When men drum, they are rooting themselves, bringing the energy from their heads down into the earth. Drumming opens the feminine. When I drum, my soul vine roots into the ground. Drumming creates balance, and I am both grounded in Great Mother and connected to Father Mountain.

"The drum connects us to the truth of the *jowk,* the faceless face of all living things. We are one voice and we are all one. Fear disconnects us; drumming dissolves the fear."

Her hands fluttered. Now T'Cori no longer saw her wrinkled flesh, the wizened body ready to return to the earth. Stillshadow seemed wind, water, fire, *jowk* unfettered by flesh.

"A drum is passion. It burns at your touch. The drum seeks you, every bit as much as you seek the drum. If you make the drum with your whole *num,* the connection is there. Feel it tremble like the heart of a deer; hold the drum over your heart and direct the healing *num* toward the muscle that protects and holds your love.

"Each animal that gives its skin to the drum has its own medicine," she said. "Oryx medicine comes from the west. They are the thunder beings, wind *jowk,* water *jowk* and fire *jowk* dancing together. Oryx gives the stamina to stay the course and heal our hearts. It goes deep to our core, our guts, where we remember all we learned as children.

"Oryx helps us release tears, which heal and let us grieve our losses. Oryx helps us release to the world above Father Mountain."

Her words wove a trance. T'Cori felt her sense of time slipping away, the dream world slipping closer by the moment.

"But that would mean the void is closer to the hunt chiefs," her mentor's liquid voice continued. "Our hunters tear their flesh while hunting. How can you ask an animal to die for you if you are not willing to lay down your own life? The hunter hunts not only giraffe and antelope and pig." Her voice dropped to a rumble. "He hunts *death itself.* Not as an ending but as a new beginning. Drumming with oryx keeps us grounded in our *num*— our center, our power."

"And what of the deer?" Sing Sun asked. "My drum uses the skin of a deer."

"Deer medicine touches and heals our hearts—the medicine of the north: the red road and the path of the heart. When we are healing our heartbreaks, or opening the heart and learning to speak from the heart, drumming with deer is powerful medicine. Deer will open you to your heart's true dream.

"We make each drum with love, respect and prayer. We offer smoking herbs to the *jowk.* Our hunters bring us their kills. We strip the skins and scrape them. Then we look through all the hides and select only the finest for our drums."

"How do we make this special thing?" Sing Sun asked. "I never learned such wonder."

"All dream dancers and hunt chiefs make drums, and then the drums go out to the bomas. Each boma made its own drums, and some were wonderful, but always, those made by the dancers and chiefs were the best.

"I think this is a new time," Stillshadow said. "Call your sisters Flower and Morning Thunder. Call all who have will and heart. Now, from this day forward, every Ibandi woman must learn to dance."

Chapter Twenty-seven

On their third day, Frog and his uncle Snake went exploring along the valley floor, seeking better camping space. And a quarter-day's walk from their old site, Frog saw something that made him stop and stare.

Human tracks. Not Ibandi, though. The thick toes and broad forefoot were strange enough, but even more oddly, *wolf* tracks mingled with the human.

He knelt beside them. Sniffed them. Ran his fingers around the rim. His narrowed eyes scanned the trees and grass. Old hunters said their grandfathers had told tales of spirits in Shadow Valley.

He did not believe such stories, but what to make of this? Wolves that walked like men? Men that became wolves? "It is a new thing," he said.

"You and your 'new things,' " Snake said. But despite his mockery, his single good eye glittered. He crumbled a bit of mud from the man's tracks between his fingers. And then a bit from the wolf's. "I would say they were made the same day. But that doesn't mean they were made at the same *time*."

"No," Frog admitted, "it does not."

But his mind saw men with wolf legs, and wolves with men's feet. And his heart doubted what his mind thought it knew of the world.

Stillshadow dreamed. In that dream she hovered above the lake of living fire, the *jowk*. And that fire consumed the things and people she loved. They cried out to her as they were melted and created and melted again and again.

However many years the most benevolent gods might grant one of their human children, not enough time remained for her, or anyone, to fix the world. Because the Mk*tk had taken her, T'Cori now doubted her own magic. Sing Sun had never had much sight, and Blossom . . . poor Blossom had had none. The sisters she had traveled to join had little more.

The old ways were dying, the new ones not yet born.

What else was there? What could she do? This was a new place, where food was so plentiful their prey almost walked up to them and begged for death. What new rituals might it call forth?

A rounded valley, green when the grass outside its walls were said to be brown. Where water sparkled, while outside the streams ran muddy.

A place where men and wolves walked side by side.

The *jowk* called to her, promising rest after a lifetime of service. Cloud Stalker was there as well, or whatever the *jowk* might remember of her lover. She remembered him: his strength, his laughter, his moonlight caress. In her bones, she was his woman, his wife, even though he was dead. And she would continue so after her bones were in the ground.

But she could not go home to him until she knew her people were safe. Could not, and would not.

What to do? What to do?

She reached out across the web of soul vines connecting all sleeping two-legged . . . and came upon a knot of her children, the children of . . . Fire boma. Something had happened, and they had fled. She was not certain where they were. The dream world was a world of sensation, of emotion, not geography. But for the moment they seemed safe.

To her surprise, among them was Sister Quiet Water.

Ah. A deep well of pleasure rose in Stillshadow. A lost daughter whose *num*-field felt calm and content, with no shadow of violation or captivity.

This was a good thing, a great thing, a thing to gladden her old heart. And for the rest of the night, they danced the dream together.

Five days' walk southeast . . .

Halfway up Great Earth's tangled slopes, three hands of well-tended huts clustered on a series of flattened terraces. Before the new sun rose above the huts, Sister Quiet Water had already bundled her grass song mat on which she would kneel to sing the sun to life. Her medicine bag held her pellets of herbs and plant extracts.

So many strange turns her life had taken. Mother Stillshadow had taken her into the dream dancers when she had seen eight summers, and there she had thrived. Along with her sisters she had been captured by Mk*tk and endured horror and shame. But Ibandi hunters had rescued her and brought her home.

And now . . . Mother called to her.

She did not know where she was going, only that she had to walk. And that it would be far, farther than any dream dancer had ever traveled alone.

In most previous times, a hunt chief had accompanied a traveling dancer. But there were no more hunt chiefs. These were different days, a time to change the roles Great Mother and Father Mountain had established for men and women.

And despite whatever unknown dangers lay ahead, joy danced in her heart like sparks in a whirlwind.

Chapter Twenty-eight

Cross-legged and content, Bat Wing sat between the evening fires, enjoying the easy company of his mother and her friends as they laughed and gossiped. The night was crisp and clear, his chin tingled with the sticky juice of roasted gazelle haunch, and all was right with the world.

Then he caught a glimmer of something out of the corner of his eye, and turned to look beyond the shadows. At first the darkness yielded nothing, but he had a slow and growing certainty that he was being *watched*. He experienced the sensation as a creeping of the skin along his neck, an awareness that was like the *num* tremors that Great Sky Woman sometimes spoke of.

To the boy's shock, Uncle Frog had said he did not believe in such things. That he trusted only what he could touch and taste, see in the sky above him, feel in the earth below.

But what, then, was this strange certainty?

Might the fire children have something to say to him? Listening, he heard only the crackle of the branches.

No. Nothing.

"There is something in the shadows," Bat Wing said, and his mother, Butterfly, laughed.

"There is nothing in the shadows," she said. "This is another of your strange dreams."

"I am awake, Mother," the boy replied. "And there is something."

The boy walked away from the firelight. Yes, something lurked out here. The prickle at the base of his neck began to spread, as if he had rolled in poison vines. What was he doing? This was not his world. He barely knew this world at all. Back at Wind boma north of Great Sky, every stone had been his friend. He knew every lizard, every beetle and its kin, every cactus and sweet bush from root to leaf. But here?

"Hello?" Ten paces away, close to the ground, at first barely distinguishable from the play of light and shadow, was a pale, grublike hand, the shadowy suggestion of a human head. A spill of loose straggly hair, like dead grass, fell across its face.

Bat Wing ran for Frog and the men.

Frog had been smoking a pinch of sleep herb in his bone pipe, its pleasant trill intensifying the warmth radiating from Sky Woman's thigh, the satisfaction of a full belly and the companionship of fellow hunters. He felt more relaxed than in many, many moons.

Young Bat Wing came running to them with an expression of mingled excitement and anxiety.

He told them what he had seen. Curious but not alarmed, the five men, spears carried erect, ventured to the camp's edge.

"Come out," Leopard Paw said.

"Wait," Frog said. "There is a strangeness here." In all their years of trading and meeting with other tribes, only the Mk*tk had been disastrous. Even the Spider Face's people had simply warned them away. As a result, these strangers triggered caution but not panic.

T'Cori stepped forward. "What are you?" she said.

"Sky Woman says there are all kinds of *jowk* alive in the world," Bat Wing whispered. "Beneath rocks. Behind trees. Lurking in shadows. Perhaps this is one of those?"

Frog chuffed. No. No *jowk*. But was it a threat? That creeping of his skin indicated curiosity more than fear.

T'Cori held out a piece of yam the size of her palm.

A whimpering from behind the rock, and Frog lifted his torch. Then slowly, one chubby limb at a time emerged.

A child, perhaps eight summers in age. The first and most startling thing was that the child's skin was the color of a fish belly, sickly white. Had the child rolled in chalk?

"So ugly," Leopard Paw said.

Facial bones were broader and heavier than an Ibandi's child's face. Her hair hung limp as clusters of dead vine. Leopard Eye gripped his spear hard. "Mk*tk?"

"No," T'Cori said. "I knew Mk*tk children . . . they were not like her. She is much too pale. Paler even than beast-men."

The firelight reflected from her eyes as they might a cat's. She even made a mewling sound.

"She is hungry," T'Cori said.

"How do you know it is a girl?" Bat Wing asked. He himself was not even certain it was human. If it was a *jowk,* and he stared at it too long, mightn't it slip into his dreams tonight, eat his flesh and steal his skin? But Sky Woman surely knew more than he of such things, and she did not seem afraid.

Frog seemed to take his lead from her, so he did not show nervousness either.

Very well. He, Bat Wing, would not show fear either.

"I know," she replied.

"Where are her people?" Frog asked.

"I cannot say, but I know she is hungry." T'Cori took the chunk of yam to the edge of camp, to the firelight's wavering edge.

"Be careful," Frog cautioned.

She clucked at him. "You stay back, great hairy beast. Stay back."

"Nothing to fear," Snake said. "No one baits a snare with a child."

The pregnant Sky Woman knelt down, the piece of potato in her hand. In the wavering light of the twin fires, it seemed to Frog that the child's eyes were almost as pale as her skin.

"She cannot speak," Leopard Eye said. "She is not even bhan."

"She is a child," Sky Woman said, "and alone."

Frog glared at her.

"Well," Frog said, "if you're going to feed her, at least give her something she cannot find for herself."

He retreated to the men's fire and returned carrying a chunk of giraffe meat. With the edge of his glassy black knife he cut away a juicy strip and slid it onto a broad green leaf. The other men grinned at him. The Ibandi had traded with bhan and others for generations. The rules of hospitality were clear: a stranger was to be sheltered.

Any other rule would be death for all in an environment as unforgiving as the savannah.

Monsters such as the Mk*tk were the exception, not the rule.

Sky Woman's eyes closed. Her voice was as soothing as a sleep song. "I know what it is to be alone. If you cannot understand my words, hear my voice." She spoke as sweetly as if singing to Medicine Mouse.

"I am not your mother," Sky Woman whispered, "but I am all mothers.

You are not my child, but you are all children. Accept this food and fire, and I will stand between you and harm, as if you were my own. Hear my voice."

For an instant, their shared gaze wound together as tightly as strangler vines. Then Sky Woman put the food down and backed away.

After the child ate, she made a heap of grasses and vines, and curled up at the campfire's edge. The child stared at the little hutch where slept the blind but mighty Stillshadow.

There was no sound, no motion, no clue of her presence. Regardless, Stillshadow's voice rang out strongly. "Who is looking at me?" she called. "What is this child?"

"Sleep, Old Mother," Sky Woman replied.

"How does she *do* that?" Frog asked.

Sky Woman shook her head. "The *jowk* sees everything. She speaks to the *jowk*."

Sky Woman watched the child, her thoughts unknown even to herself. "We must protect her."

"It is not ours," Leopard Eye said.

Stillshadow spoke. "The wind blows, a leaf moves. Things happen, and things change. Light and shadow, sound and echo."

"What is this?" Frog asked.

Sky Woman raised her hand. "She says that we must treat this child as one of our own."

Leopard Eye remained unconvinced. "But who can say how her people would treat one of ours?"

"Yes. Who can say? Let us show the way. I say this child is bhan . . . but human. And that she is under our protection, as long as we have shelter to give."

Frog and T'Cori did not retire to their lean-to that night. Although it was cooler on the valley's rim than on the floor, their shared body heat and proximity to the twin fires kept them warm.

She had been unable to stem the excitement she felt building up inside her while watching the sleeping child.

"What is it?" Frog asked.

"I look at her, but see myself," she said. "Alone. Always I was alone, even surrounded by my sisters."

Frog scoffed as he carved bamboo slivers from the point of his spear. "Surely not true. None of us can live alone. It is not our nature." Earlier he had made a small fire, and let it burn out. The glowing coals were perfect, turning the spear point into a solid mass, more effective in the kill. He toasted it over the coals, watching for the tip to brown and little curls of pungent smoke to rise.

"Still." The night wind was warm, but T'Cori shivered as she considered the sleeping child. "That is the way it felt."

"I think her people are kind," he said. The spear was smoking a bit. He pulled it back, blew on it, and then began heating it again.

"How can you know this?"

"Because Great Mother makes most humans kind. And because she trusted us," he said. "Trust is learned, and easily broken. If her people had beaten or raped her, she would not have come to us so easily. Or if her people told her strangers are evil. Look how she rests. She smiles as she dreams."

"All children should sleep so," she said.

"We will protect her," Frog said.

"Yes," T'Cori said, "we will."

"Because you say so?"

"Yes. Because I say so." She laughed. But there was something there, a truth considered but unsaid, a new Life Tree's first green sprout.

They did not have long to wait for the next startling thing. The next morning, before the camp was fully awakened, before the child had stirred, three very strange males appeared at the camp's edge, accompanied by two equally strange females. They were pale as grubs, shorter and wider than Ibandi. When their lips pulled back, their teeth were square and blunt and impressively gapped. They wore loincloths and leather sandals with leather straps laced up their calves and thighs, and a sort of chest covering made of a zebra or deer skin with a hole for their heads. They carried spears at their sides, but upright, as hunters meeting hunters, not with tips low, as if confronting enemies.

They halted ten paces away, as if waiting for the Ibandi to say or do something.

All that made sense to Frog. The child's weak skin had prepared the Ibandi for such strangeness. What made him slap his own face was the impossible vision of three shaggy black wolves walking at their sides.

He remembered the odd footprints, the mingled imprints of men and animals. Those tracks had been the same depth in the same dried mud, suggesting that they had been made at the same time. But men might have been hunting wolves, mightn't they?

He knew now that all his clever reckoning had been in vain.

Male or female, two- or four-legged, all were silent. The child ran to them, braying in words he did not understand.

"What are they?" T'Cori asked.

Frog shrugged. "Never have I seen the like. Ugly. No color, like a cobra's belly. Surely they are the child's people."

Now there was movement: wolves padded back and forth around the strangers, keeping their distance from the Ibandi spearmen.

"Wolves!" T'Cori said. "Are these the wolf folk? Are those their . . . women?"

One of the strangers made grunting sounds deep in his throat and pointed. The child jabbered back, perhaps in monkey speak.

The pale ones took their child and left. The wolves walked behind the humans, crisscrossing as they paced back and forth until they were well down the slope and away to the east.

Chapter Twenty-nine

Two days southeast . . .

For a day and a half, Sister Quiet Water had walked without sleep, without rest, barely eating. When she needed to make water or defecate, she did. She occasionally paused to drink and fill her drinking gourd, but she gave her bodily needs no more care than that.

Her eyes were fixed on the western horizon. As of now, only a few dimly viewed trees broke the line. But soon, she hoped, she prayed. Soon.

"Mother," she said, placing one foot after the other. "You call. I come."

In the hutch where she lay in blindness and chaos, Stillshadow's mouth curled in a smile. It was good. Everything . . . was good. She could see everything, knew that good things were coming. And when they did come, Stillshadow, stretched so tightly over the abyss, would finally answer Cloud Stalker's call and be released from the flesh into the *jowk*.

She had known such things with Stalker. Truly, the *jowk* had gazed out at her through his eyes. Their soul vines had gripped each other, their fibers entangled. Soon, she would be with him again, and their love-play would rival that of Great Mother and Father Mountain.

They would make thunder!

She raised her voice, calling her spirit daughter, she who had earned the name Sky Woman.

She heard the sound of hands and knees shuffling across her hut's floor. Stillshadow sniffed the air. Yes, it was T'Cori.

"Yes, Mother?"

"Our men are hunting here, and the prey is strong. Frog almost died bringing us bounty. If our men take such risk, we must prepare for the day that they risk too much."

"What are you asking?" T'Cori's voice was so sweet. She would miss it. Stillshadow reminded herself that the girl was clever, with good instincts. She would have to phrase her request carefully.

"We need to prepare the last gift, in case one of our men is wounded too sorely," she said. She named a series of plants, including the one called strangleweed.

"Mother . . ." T'Cori's voice winced. The girl knew these plants. And knew that this formula would end a wounded hunter's woes, but they might also end those of an old medicine woman.

Stillshadow smiled. "Do not worry, my child," she said. "I promised to stay until I am no longer needed. All is well."

Stillshadow had never lied to the girl. Had never broken a promise. She would need every bit of that authority now.

Chapter Thirty

By the time the new day waned, T'Cori and Leopard Eye were a half day from the main camp, on a mission to gather strangleweed. The life within her seemed heavier with each new morning, but despite that burden, she was happy and surprisingly nimble of foot. It felt almost like returning to childhood, every step a dance, every gust of wind a song. This was what the dream dancers did, and it was comfortable returning to her accustomed role.

Frog had not been pleased by her plans to explore, so soon after their arrival. But it was not a man's decision to make. She was a dream dancer. Even more, she was Stillshadow's heir, and it was custom for the head dancer to travel alone for days at a time in the brush, trusting in her own skills and Great Mother Herself to keep her safe. A trip with only Leopard Eye was merely a step in that direction.

So much to learn and see! In the valley's center, near the largest watering hole stood a gigantic fig tree. Roots as thick as her body burst from the ground in a tangle. Its upper branches buzzed with bees. She had never seen such a tree, and thought it a great and sacred thing.

That morning, Leopard Eye had thrown a fist-sized rock with thrilling accuracy, braining a gray hare in mid-hop. He stuffed it into the leather sack she kept slung around her shoulders, and arched his eyebrows mischievously. "Supper!" he said.

This was a good place. So many birds, insects and plants to learn. And those strange pale-skinned people! Sheltering their child had been the first strong step toward friendship. The Mk*tk had been inhuman, killers who killed for no reason she could understand. The Spider Face's folk were merely defending their land and magic water. As sad and disappointing as that was, they had granted the hospitality of a night's rest.

Sharing was the way of the savannah peoples. And if these new pale strangers lived here . . . and knew that the Ibandi were protectors of children . . .

Was there not enough here for all to share?

Every fiber of her being said that it was good.

"Look!" T'Cori pointed at a red and white shrub only a hand's length high. "Another one. I have never seen anything like it. Birthweed keeps for many moons when dried. This is good, because at Great Earth it is so hard to find. But here, it seems to be *everywhere*!"

Leopard Eye nodded. "Sky Woman . . . we should think of making camp." He pointed to a trickling stream before them and then to the valley wall at their backs. "This place would serve better than most. It has water and some protection."

"Then it is good," she said.

He frowned. "In truth, I do not like being so far from the others. We do not know this valley well. Or, if we must travel so far, at least let us bring more guards for you. You are too precious to us, to our people. We see the same plants within a stone's throw of our people. Why take this chance?"

T'Cori clucked. "This is how your mother became who she is. She knew every plant. Some are for food. Some are for wounds, stopping bleeding. Some make magic smoke for visions."

He sniffed at a broken twig and shrugged. "If you say so. I can't eat it, and I can't make poison or medicine from it, so I don't know."

T'Cori smiled. "That's all right. That's why you have me. I will find the berries and plants, and you will carry them."

"Whatever you say."

Her grin was pure mischief. "Yes. And as long as you remember that, we will speak together well."

Leopard Eye bowed his head. "I knew you when you were just a little thing. Before you climbed the mountain."

"And how is it that you know me?"

He leaned on his spear. "Do you remember the Spring Gathering when we were twelve winters, when a boy kissed you and pushed you into the river?"

She furrowed her brows, struggling to retrieve the memory. It was a good one. "Ah . . . in fact, yes."

He puffed out his strong young chest, and slapped it with the flat of his right palm. "That was me. That was Leopard Eye. Paw dared me."

She was mystified. "Why me?"

"Well," Leopard Eye said, "we knew Stillshadow was our mother. And we knew you were special to her, but not to Blossom, our sister. Are you still angry?"

"No," T'Cori said, "but . . . don't do that again!"

Leopard Eye's smile was mischievous. "Which part? The push? Or the kiss?"

Her ears burned furiously. "Either. I'm the mountain's bride, remember?"

Leopard Eye nodded. "That stops others, but not Leopard Eye. After all, I came from Stillshadow's body. Even if I was not a hunt chief, I would still be her son. The mountain is not here. Always, I thought you beautiful. I still do. I would bring you meat," he said.

She gasped. Among her people, this was at the very least a proposition and perhaps even a proposal of marriage, if the woman in question were a bhan of little status.

Outrageous!

"No, Leopard. We will not speak of it." She paused. Then added, "But . . ."

"But what?"

"But I'd forgotten you pushed me in the river."

"But . . . you remembered the kiss?"

Suddenly shy, she nodded. "The first I ever had. I got pushed in the river a lot."

"While I live, no one will ever do it again."

When Leopard Eye stood straight, he was a half head taller than Frog. "You danced for me on Great Earth. Before that day I had never seen your breasts or your seventh eye. When you danced, you danced for no one but me. I fought, for you." He came closer. "That day you made me a promise. I ask only that you keep your pledge."

T'Cori forgot to breathe. "What . . . was promised?"

"Your body spoke to me. It said: '*If you are Ibandi, if you will fight for us, we will serve you.*' Do I speak truth?"

T'Cori stammered. "We . . . yes. It is true."

He squared his shoulders and straightened his spine. "I survived that battle. I claim what is mine."

"Father Mountain's child grows in my stomach," she said hesitantly.

He placed his hand on the smooth, warm curve of skin. "Let me wash him with my own seed," he whispered. His voice was a thief of thought.

Her *num* pooled in the pit of her stomach, then flew up like a raven, stealing all restraint with it. She groaned.

T'Cori searched for an objection in vain. Her heart betrayed her mind, or perhaps her sex betrayed both.

"There is only one thing I need to know," Leopard Eye said. "A hunter lives by his word. Does a dream dancer?"

T'Cori felt herself lose the center of her *num,* the warm, calm place from which she made her very best decisions. She had no need to delve more deeply. There was a part of her that thrilled to this fine young hunter's attentions. He had brought meat. His shoulders and back had been scarred in fighting for their lives and land.

It was not merely a matter of obligation. Despite the life growing within her, she welcomed his root. Her skin warmed, and her seventh eye softened in preparation for his touch. She longed to entwine her soul vine with his. Was she betraying Frog to feel so? To make sex for medicine was one thing, but wasn't this yearning something else?

Or had her eyes finally opened enough for her to be the dancer her people needed? One with the ability to connect with the *num,* with the living fire of the *jowk,* that it might join with a sick one's *jowk* to speed healing? Leopard set his spear aside and touched her shoulder. The sensation was like the tingle in the air after a strike of summer lightning.

The ocean of fire. The jowk. For the first time in months she felt her *num* flare, felt its threads reach out beyond her flesh, her soul vine entwine with this strong young hunter's.

T'Cori groaned, and her hips rotated in instinctual response. This was like the first bite of a cactus fruit: hot and ripe and almost too delicious to bear.

There by the stream where they had gathered seeds and roots, T'Cori craned her neck back so that her mouth was a breath away from his. His warm full lips caressed the side of her neck. His tongue traced its way along the line of her jaw, tasting her salt. Her fingers assumed a life of their own, caressing his thigh. Such a strong, fine thigh! So accustomed was she to Frog's legs that it was shocking to feel Leopard's more corded muscles. So strong was Leopard that Frog seemed almost feminine in comparison. The voice in the depths of her mind, the thing that cautioned her against yielding to her instincts, fell quiet. And the voice that begged her to take him within her body, that yearned to milk his root until he lost control and groaned and thrust against her and made his seed . . .

That urge strengthened, until it was a roar of wind, a clap of thunder. Until all thought vanished in her driving, urgent need.

Leopard's clever hands pushed her leather skirt aside and stroked the long, soft curves of her buttocks and legs. With gentle, irresistible strength he lifted her up and found a fallen tree trunk to brace her against.

Steady the breathing. Find the place within. Center. She babbled these things to herself, trying to keep this from being the personal satisfaction that her body now yearned for. She needed to calm herself, to protect her emotions. After all, she was Frog's woman. . . .

Leopard's hands caressed her intimately. She looked back over her shoulder to watch him lick the fingers of his right hand. He slid them slowly inside her. Probing, preparing. It was hardly necessary: she could not remember being any more ready than at this single burning moment.

· He pulled his fingers out and spit on his palms, moving his loincloth aside.

Fire surged within her as they joined. *Let me wash your child with my seed,* he had said. Together, they sought the rhythm older than all the days of men.

Side to side and in tightening spirals she pulsed her body. Her eyes were partially closed, so that light only impinged upon her mind in flashes. *A glimpse of a tree. A cloud. Women with long, spotted necks. Just a glimpse—*

A burning, a searing away of flesh and bone and nerve, leaving only the fire itself and not its fuel. *Thank you, Great Mother!* The Mk*tk had not stolen her *num.* Here it was, as strong as it had ever been. Perhaps even stronger. She was more than a woman of her tribe. More than a medicine woman. She was *all* women, in all of time, in all places. She felt herself falling into the long line of dream dancers, leading back to the first to crawl wet and blind from between Great Mother's earthen thighs to howl at the sky.

That cry built inside her before she heard it, before she knew that she was going to open her mouth and scream. Her egg was unraveling, the *jowk* flying away with her. No smallest part of Sky Woman was in control of this. No part of the Nameless One remained to guide.

She *was* that rush of *num.* She *was* that rush of sweet wind breaking from her throat, joining with the rising call from the man whose hips rolled against hers, whose root burned like fire within her seventh eye.

And when her voice reached its height his own call joined hers. She felt the spasm as he washed her child. There was a rising bubble, like a leaf on a whirlwind, a last awareness of self crying and sighing . . .

Yes. Yes. Yes . . .

And then . . . there was light.

T'Cori and Leopard lay on the ground together. Her vision seemed somehow both softer and clearer than it had before they had made love. Reeds swaying gently in the wind. Unseen birds cooed and whistled, at peace with themselves and each other. She nestled back against him. Gradually, she remembered her name and place in the order of things. The whisper of the water and wind and the steady beat of her heart reconnected her to the things of this world.

Leopard Eye was pressed so closely to her that she could feel his heartbeat against her back, feel it even as the soul vine dissolved, as his root shriveled again and slipped from her body.

Leopard Eye deposited a hand of brief, sweet kisses upon her shoulders. T'Cori felt small and precious and . . . content.

A slow crawl of thought, as she came back to herself. *Contentment.* How often had she felt such emotions? It seemed wondrous to experience such warmth and wonder with more than one person. Something seemed to awaken within her, a part of herself that could find happiness with this man. A part which knew that, in a different world, she would have felt blessed to be his woman.

Did that mean that she did not love Frog? No. It meant that Great Mother was kind, that Her gift of love sheltered Her children from life's pain and sorrow. And that gift was not given only once to each of Her children.

No, it was good. And if Leopard Eye was larger, stronger, different from Frog, Frog was different from anyone in the world. Anyone.

There were other men like Leopard Eye. There was only one Frog.

This was no betrayal. It was, however, a revelation. This was who she was, and had been born to be.

Leopard Eye's belly tightened against her. At first she thought that he was ready again. Did her promise, made so long ago in the shadow of war—she and her sisters swaying together atop Great Earth—did those dances obligate her to satisfy him a *second* time?

She smiled. How absurd. She needed no promise to please this strong, fine young hunter. Such a happy obligation. Pleasing him was pleasing herself. She pressed back against him, then was surprised to feel the flat of his hands against her shoulder blades. Those hands, so recently gentle, now seemed to have grown hard and calloused, almost as if they were suddenly attached to another man's arms.

"Shh . . ." he whispered into her ear. "Look."

Chapter Thirty-one

As slowly as if the very act of seeing might bring disaster, T'Cori raised her head and peered across the stream. Long rounded blades of yellow knife grass obscured much of her vision. However, if she focused her eyes carefully, there in the midst of the grass burned two fearsome eyes the color of a smoke-wreathed sun.

Lion.

She understood instantly. She and Leopard Eye were hunted and alone, a half day from any possible help.

Leopard Eye whispered in her ear. "There are at least two." His finger pointed ahead and to their right. She saw nothing but a field of yellow green, but she knew his hunter's eyes were sharper than her own. "They wish to trap us between them. That is the reason the first has not moved."

"What do we do?"

"Act quickly. Or die."

He took his spear up with his left hand, took hold of her shoulder with his right, and pulled her backward through the field. Swollen belly rubbing on the ground, she edged toward the rock wall behind them. If they could reach the rocks, and climb high enough, they would be safe. Could she manage it? With Leopard Eye's help, perhaps. Otherwise, she and Frog's unborn child were lost. Once, she had been a great climber, had snatched the garland from the top of the Life Tree at the Spring Gathering. Today might test whatever remained of those skills.

The fear drained her strength, made her suddenly sleepy and at the same time weightless, as if she were already in a dream.

The lion rose from the grass, and stepped toward them. No mane. Female, hunting for the pride. A scream clawed its way up T'Cori's throat. The possibility that their new home in the valley and the new life within her might be torn away was almost enough to crack her egg.

Leopard Eye sensed her thoughts. "Don't think, don't feel," he said. "There is no time. This is a hunting pair. One in front to hold us—the other will come from the side or the rear."

"What are we going to do?"

"Run," he said. "And climb. And fight." The muscles in his shoulders hunched. She knew the resolve behind the words. Leopard Eye would delay them. She would run and try to climb. In the end, it would not matter: both of them would die.

"When I say, stand slowly," he said. He clutched his spear, his left hand tensed upon it. His fingers left her shoulder, and she stood. The wind stank of hot, raw meat.

Then the wind, and everything else in the world, seemed to stop.

A second lion was to their right, only two tens of paces away. No mane: female. The cat was as long as Leopard was tall. Quiet as death it crouched, attending their every motion. Its eyes gnawed at T'Cori's heart.

Somehow, Leopard Eye matched its *num*. In an instant, her gentle, urgent lover was transformed into a beast, another animal on the savannah, as wild and terrible as either of the great cats. His long face was drawn, the muscle at the corner of his jaw tensed into a knot. But below his shoulders he was loose, relaxed, as if preparing to dance rather than fight for his life. His body spoke a language any predator could understand: *I am not easy prey.*

Leopard Eye lowered his spear tip, maneuvering to remain between her and the lions. They were watching now, curious, perhaps. Were the cats wondering what these creatures were? Had they seen men before? Enough to hate or fear them or consider them a likely meal?

Her throat felt choked with thorns. Her belly felt as if she had swallowed rocks. The world darkened and spun.

Back. Back. Leopard Eye and T'Cori were moving toward the rise of the vertical rock shelf. If they had tried to move toward the open grass, she doubted that the cats would have allowed it. But back toward the rock . . . the lions doubtless thought that T'Cori and Leopard were trapping themselves.

"*Hiyah!*" Leopard thrust at the cats with his blackened spear tip. They blinked hard but did not retreat.

Then the smaller female rose and stepped into the stream. It stopped, lifted its paw and examined it with apparent distaste, but the prospect of fresh meat propelled it forward, up to its belly. *Splash, splash, splash.* And then up and out. Droplets of moisture hovered in the air before settling like motes of dust. A rainbow, one swiftly born, and just as swiftly dead.

Its eyes never left them.

"Run," Leopard said. And holding her belly with her left hand, T'Cori did.

As she did, the lioness on the right charged. Leopard placed himself between the lioness and the dream dancer. The spear point jabbed at its eyes, so that it had to swerve. That was the last T'Cori saw as she ran with all the speed she could manage, ten paces to the wall. She searched for handholds and footholds, scrambling up as *something* hit the ground just behind her. Something brushed against her foot. She looked down and saw a female lion, with a white scar bisecting her face, leap up to claw at her as she climbed. Swift, sharp pain raked T'Cori's leg, then the cat was falling back to the ground.

One speckled gray stone projected far enough from the wall that she was able to set her heel firmly. Pain in her calf made her gasp, but by then she was stable and used that moment to glance down.

Below her Leopard Eye crouched with his spear held at the ready. She screamed at him, *"Climb!"* But she knew that he could not hear her: all his attention was on the blood-crazed beasts coming at him from either side. Leopard had backed against a boulder. With his rear protected, he was trying to keep the lions at a distance. The right side of his face bore three gashes, side by side, one laying the cheekbone bare. Gore spattered his leg and arm. The lions were gaining greater and greater confidence and no longer seemed so hesitant to attack.

The long, powerful muscles in the larger female's hind legs bunched as it leaped. Leopard went under the lion, bracing his spear against the ground so that the tip slid into its belly. It screeched, then fell to the side, hind legs scrabbling at the dreadful stalk.

But at the same moment, the white-scarred lioness attacked, trapping Leopard on the ground. The back of its head obscured Leopard's throat and chest.

If ever T'Cori had wished to close her eyes, this was the moment. She could not. His eyes stared up at her, body contorted.

She heard a sharp wet sound, like a piece of green fruit crushed underfoot.

T'Cori fought to summon calm. Then, despite her fear, she exhaled and breathed it to him. "Peace, hunter," she whispered.

His eyes, fixed to hers, relaxed. His lips, which had so recently brushed her flesh, parted as if he were trying to say something to her. Did he see her? Know her?

Blood drenched the sand. The screams of dying man and mortally wounded lion drowned T'Cori's own cries.

She pressed against the rock wall, shuddering, the afternoon's hot wind suddenly cold. Her belly pushed her back onto her toes, made it impossible to crawl into the rock, to ask the earth itself to accept her body as it had when she climbed as a child.

Above her, the rock face leaned outward. There was no path for a direct ascent. She could perhaps scuttle over to her right, where outcroppings of rock and plants offered some grasp for hand or foot.

A third lion had joined the two below, a thick tawny mane proclaiming its gender. The female who had taken the spear to the belly paid no attention to the others, or to anything at all save its own ghastly wounds. The male seemed to be looking up at T'Cori, almost as if it wanted to speak. Did the lions of Shadow Valley have language? Did they transform into humans, or was it only the wolves who worked such wonders?

T'Cori had seen so many strange things in the last year. One more would hardly have raised an eyebrow. But here and now, if she was so foolish as to allow herself to become distracted, she would lose her grip on the wall and plummet to the waiting fangs below.

The male clamped hold of poor Leopard's leg and began to tear.

T'Cori closed her eyes, both to shield herself from the fearsome sight and to connect more deeply with the divine. "Great Mother," she whispered, "guide your son to the Mountain." How strange and precious those words, especially considering that one misstep or misplaced hand . . . a single error . . . and her next prayer would be for a swift death.

T'Cori gripped the rocks carefully, and then reached out with her right foot to find purchase. She had to seal her mind away, not frighten herself by looking below. There might be three lions, or hands of hands of lions. It didn't make any difference: either way, if she fell, she was meat. Her unborn child was meat. All she could do was find one stone after another, try to reach what seemed to be a rock shelf, one just far enough away to tease her.

Could she make it? She stretched her leg out as far as possible, clawing at the rock with one hand. But for her swollen womb, she could have found the balance, made her way to the shelf, and safety.

A few handholds to the right, and there were different choices of grip. She could get up a bit, and then up again. Then she slipped, unable to muffle a scream as her fingernails splintered along the rock. As her face slid past a jutting root, she snapped at it with her teeth. The shock wrenched her head side-ways. T'Cori scrabbled for new handholds, and to her amazement managed to work around the belly bulk and find purchase for her toes. For a few moments she dangled there, trying to slow her breathing, then chanced a glance downward.

Four lions below her now: two eating, one dying, the last following her with its baleful yellow eyes.

T'Cori managed to lever herself over to the rock shelf. There, she lay curled on her side, struggling not to panic. What now? She could not go down. Neither could she go up. The shelf grew narrower before it rounded the wall and perhaps terminated there. Could she wait here? How long would it be before anyone came looking for her? A day? And a night? A quarter-day's run to cross the valley before anyone could even begin a search.

How would it feel to lie up on this ledge, exposed to an alien sky? The ledge sloped steeply away beneath her. If she fell asleep, mightn't she roll over and fall?

The only thing to do was to keep moving. She could either find a way down, away from the lions, or a place secure enough that she could wait there, build a fire and sleep.

The tribe's hunters could track her. But when? Dream dancers and their guardians often spent days searching for herbs. If she did not take her fate into her own hands . . .

T'Cori closed her eyes and prayed to Great Mother, seeking advice, permission, direction. Something. Anything.

The encroaching darkness offered no answers, and that in and of itself grieved her. Had she sinned in taking personal pleasure from Leopard Eye? No, women gave pleasure by feeling it themselves. There was no sin. . . .

Was there? No. Not for a dream dancer. But what of one who had been unable to protect that great gift to which she had been entrusted?

T'Cori shut her fears and guilt away, and continued to crawl.

Throughout the day, she edged along the wall, moving up or down when-ever she could. Twice she was forced to backtrack, move up, edge along an even narrower ledge, and then drop back down.

An outcropping of brownish-white roots wormed half out of the rock, dangling downward from a tree growing from the cliff above her head.

Had she any choice but to climb? Her left arm and shoulder ached.

T'Cori found some purchase for her right foot, and shifted her weight, balancing the strain to allow her left side to rest.

Looking back over her shoulder she tried to find her people's camp. Across a forest of flat-topped trees and a scattering of glistening water holes, a winding snake of a stream and clustering herds of zebra and giraffe, she could see the opposite valley wall . . . but no human beings.

She choked back a sob, furious that she had wasted energy on hope.

When the right leg was beginning to throb, she looked back down below her. Three lions now watched her. Leopard's body was no longer in view. Had they dragged it away? She didn't know, knew only that she had to save herself. If she could not, then his sacrifice would have been for nothing.

If she had been a weakling, if she was not vital to the tribe, would he have left her to die? Would Leopard have saved himself by making the climb that now challenged her?

The very thought drained the power from her limbs. *No.* He had died because he believed Sky Woman to be his tribe's salvation. She had no right to question that. To doubt herself was to steal the *num* from his sacrifice.

She was as rested as she was going to be. It was time to climb again.

Not too many moons ago, she could have done this with ease. The girl she had been had felt so little fear. That younger girl had been so strong and confident. Did that youngster still live anywhere within the woman?

Her heavy belly dragged at her, fatigued her arms, but could it lift her spirit? Was there fire within her body that called out for protection, that reminded her that her life no longer belonged to her, if ever it truly had?

She traced her fingers along a root's gnarled surface, then tensed her fingers and pulled. T'Cori wormed her toes into a crevice, and pushed.

The root tore into her hands as the rock bit at her feet, but she found that it could hold her weight.

As a younger girl, she had been able to visualize her belly fibers knotting into a rope stronger than her bones. But she no longer seemed able to find that same tenseness, felt that even if she had been able to achieve it, it might not be healthy for the child slumbering within her.

So she had to use her arms and her legs. Her belly, the center of her body, was just being hauled along like a soft, giant water gourd.

A pull with the arms, then a push with the legs. Then rest, followed by another effort. If she needed strength or motivation all she needed to do was look down. The lions gazed up with those same famished expressions, as if the splendid muscle gracing Leopard Eye's beautiful body had been insufficient to satisfy them.

She grimaced. Even thinking about the hunter who had sacrificed his life for her brought weakness to limbs that desperately needed strength.

T'Cori stopped looking down.

A step. Another step. And then one more. Pulling with arms and back, pushing with legs. She fought to breathe without tensing or cramping her stomach. Blood oozed from her torn fingernails. With the back of one grimy hand she wiped the tears from her face and went on. There was only this choice: climb, or find her dying place.

T'Cori didn't know how long she struggled upward, but as she did she found that she was touching the same current of *jowk* she had discovered when climbing Great Sky. It was a place that could accept pain, even death, but not failure.

This time there were no sacred visions to sustain her, no hope of meeting her gods at the end of the trail. There was only an edge, visible far above her, and hope that if she reached it there might be a resting place. Hand over hand and feet scrabbling for a hold she pulled herself up the root. T'Cori had to focus as if performing a ceremony. For her, now, there was no previous action. And nothing in the world to do afterward.

But somehow, one step at a time, she kept going. Finally T'Cori realized that she was pulling against the tree itself, and she managed to heave her legs up over the edge, panting as the dizziness and fatigue she had so long suppressed finally landed upon her with all the weight of Great Earth itself.

Once she had recovered her senses, T'Cori explored the little wide space to which she had ascended. The ground was sparsely grassed, very rocky and thorny. The bluff was more than a ledge, tens of paces wide.

The sun had begun to sink toward the horizon. Soon it would die. In the morning, its sun would be sung to new life by the dream dancers.

Had time passed so swiftly? There might be a way down or away from her spot here, high above the ground, but while she thought she could see across the valley's bowl to the Ibandi camp, they might as well have been in another world altogether.

That was not her greatest concern. Right now, she had to make herself shelter. On their first night on the valley rim, the breezes might as well have swept down from Great Sky. *Cold.* Unless she made shelter, this would be a brutal, unforgiving night.

T'Cori searched until she found a nook in the rock wall behind her that looked as if it might provide cover for the night.

Excused from many tasks normally performed by Ibandi women, dream dancers were taught to make minor repairs on their huts but not to construct them.

During her time among the Mk*tk she had learned many things. And during the days she and Frog had fled from Mk*tk lands toward Great Sky, she had learned more.

Never again, she had sworn to herself, would she be at a loss to provide for her body's needs. Among the other things she had taught herself was the making of a simple lean-to: just bare branches draped with leafier ones, slanted against the rock.

Using branches and vines as her basic frame, she jammed the branches into the rocks and bent them to create a little place for herself. Next came vines to hold them into place. A trickle of water ran along the rocks to the right of her nest, and she moistened clay to patch the gaps.

To her wan delight, the work went more swiftly than she had initially feared. In the end, the fruit of her labors resembled a wasp's nest.

When she crawled inside her little home, her stomach might have been empty, but her heart was full.

She opened her pouch and extracted the limp body of the gray hare Leopard had slain. Her protector had given it to her to keep. She slipped it back into the pouch, thinking that she would eat it . . . tomorrow. She was not hungry now, even though she knew she should be.

Odd how something as simple as creating a bit of shelter helped to balance her grief. It made no sense: every four-legged was born knowing how to shelter itself. Why her pride? Why could that selfish sensation in any way compensate for the loss of Leopard Eye?

What do I do now? T'Cori asked herself. *Where do I go? How do I get home? Frog . . . come for me.*

Chapter Thirty-two

Only after the last strains of morning prayers faded and Sing Sun and her trainees returned to their hutches, did Frog Hopping approach Stillshadow. One never interrupted the birthing of a new sun. Why upset his people, many of whom believed a terrible catastrophe would result? Frog personally suspected that nothing at all would happen if the dream dancers were disrupted in their morning prayers. He suspected that the same ball of fire was not reborn but rather circled the sky every day. Heresy, perhaps, but possibly a larger truth.

More from respect than fear, he waited until the songs were complete, then went to T'Cori's mentor.

"I am worried," Frog said. "Sky Woman should have returned by now."

The old blind woman nodded her head. "I had a dream last night, and it told me bad news would come." She extended her hand. He pulled her upright as gently as he could, alarmed at the weight she had lost in the last moon. She seemed little more than a breath of wind. "We will gather hunters and find my daughter and my son."

T'Cori's father, Water Chant; Leopard Eye's twin, Paw, and the boy Bat Wing immediately volunteered to go. Uncle Snake joined them as well, and together with Stillshadow they set off across the valley.

All they had to do was pick out the right set of footprints . . . and barely a quarter later, they found the marks of a sandaled man and a barefooted woman. Their quarry had paused near a poison-grub plant.

Even among the small group he had put together, Frog was not the greatest tracker. That honor belonged to Uncle Snake, who sank to one knee and studied the depressions. "They paused here," he said. "Picked berries. See this." He pointed out the very recent bendings and breakings of the branches. Sap had oozed and sealed the twigs, but frayed ends remained just a little damp to the touch.

"And then . . . they headed farther west." Pointing. "Southwest."

Now, the trail was not difficult to follow. It seemed that Leopard Eye and T'Cori had paused many times to pick or study. A blood-smeared rock suggested that they had killed something. A single brown hair wedged into a crack suggested a rabbit. Along the way they had evidently found berries and grub nests, and dug roots. It seemed to Frog that T'Cori and Leopard Eye had done well.

As they approached a stream, though, a lump rose in his throat. Where the tracks stopped, the bent and broken grass told its own story. His mind saw every painful detail, including the place where T'Cori and Leopard Eye had lain down together.

Clearly, T'Cori had been on her hands and knees, with a man—presumably Leopard Eye—kneeling behind her.

Leopard Paw and Uncle Snake grinned at each other, trying not to reveal their amusement. He knew what they were thinking: that T'Cori and Leopard Eye had not returned because they were pleasurably occupied, and come sundown or dawn tomorrow, would return to the camp concealing secret smiles.

Frog bore down hard on his emotions. Was his unease mere jealousy? If so, that was wrongheaded, unworthy for one bonded to a medicine woman. A dream dancer's sexuality was a gift to the tribe's worthy hunters, to be shared at her discretion. No man owned her.

"No," Stillshadow said, levering herself up off the sled. She bent to smell the soil, then brushed her fingers against reeds, her blind eyes blinking rapidly without producing tears.

"Something happened here," she said. "You were not wrong to come." The old woman knelt at the water's edge, scooped up and tasted a palmful of water.

She sniffed the air. "Lion."

No sooner had she said this than Leopard Paw called out. "Tracks!" he said, examining a heel print crested by four short, splayed toes.

Stillshadow sniffed the wind. "Help me up."

Together they walked through the reeds and rushes, coming to the place the hunters had discovered additional tracks. Near the rock wall Frog found a tangled mass of feline and human footprints. Near them lay an abandoned, gore-smeared spear. The soil was thick with blood and grooved with drag marks.

Smirks disappeared. Uncle Snake knelt and examined the footprints more carefully.

"Leopard Eye," Snake said. "And Sky Woman." He hung his head. "They died here."

Leopard Paw bristled, gripping his spear as if he would crush it with his hands. His gaze burned into the grass, seeking a target for his rage.

Frog could not speak. Could not even breathe. Those simple words had dropped him down a crevasse and stolen his *num*. T'Cori dead? Their unborn child in a lion's belly? No. No.

Tears flooding his eyes, Frog dropped to his knees and began to wail.

Stillshadow hobbled up beside him, as slowly as if her bones were rotted bamboo. She crouched and stirred around in the dirt until she found something thick and gummy. She smeared it between her fingers, then lifted it to her nose and smelled it . . .

And then touched it to the tip of her tongue.

Ten paces away, half concealed in grass, sprawled a lion's disemboweled corpse. The hunters probed and prodded the body, lifted its head and haunches to peer beneath. "Leopard's spear," Water Chant said soberly, striding in from the brush, holding the bloodied stalk. "Truly, he was a great hunter."

"This is *his* blood," Stillshadow said, hands stirring around in the grass. "My son is dead." Leopard Paw helped her up and over to the new site. She went on hands and knees again, rubbed the gummy wet soil between her fingers. She sniffed. "The lion's," she said. "Sky Woman's blood did not spill here."

The hunters looked at one another, unable to conceal their skepticism. "Old Mother . . . you have no eyes. We know your heart is broken, but—"

"No!" she said, voice fiercely urgent. "My daughter is *not* here. Her blood is *not* here."

The world swam in tears. "What then?" Frog asked.

"It was true. It was strange. Her footprints led to the rock wall . . . and then nowhere." Uncle Snake scratched his thin beard and studied the wall. "A pregnant woman could not climb this," he said.

"You do not know my daughter," Stillshadow said. "We will continue to search." She gripped Frog's hand, nails piercing his flesh. "Yes? You will search for her?"

The rock wall was broken by ledges and vines and small, tough trees struggling to root into rock. Where in the world could she have gone? Unless Father Mountain had lifted her up unto his bosom, nowhere at all.

But Stillshadow said . . .

The old woman was blind now, maddened, almost crippled. She was no longer the fleshly spirit who had led her people though so many dark days. . . .

Or was she? If Frog quieted the voices of fear within him, he had to admit that Stillshadow radiated a strange and soothing calm. Certainty, perhaps. It was seductive: he wanted so much to believe that his dearest love and unborn child had not died in such horror.

"My brother could still live," Leopard Paw said. Hope was alive in his eyes, if not his heart.

Stillshadow shook her head. "His heart is still," she said. "Father Mountain has taken another hunter."

Leopard Paw turned his head away from them and said nothing.

Frog's inner eye saw the struggle itself, could see it as clearly as he could see T'Cori and Leopard sexing by the stream. He sighed. What was he to think? T'Cori had given herself to Leopard Eye, as was her right and perhaps even responsibility. What had happened later was simple tragedy.

"Come," he said. "Let us search."

As sure-footed as a lizard, Bat Wing wiggled up the rock wall, shouting back down to them "Broken roots!"

"What else?" Frog called up.

"It looks like someone crawled along the rock here. I think it was Sky Woman!" He seemed so excited that Frog allowed himself to hope.

It took awhile to find another way up the mountainside, but Frog remained with Stillshadow as Leopard Paw and Snake climbed, and then shouted instructions back down.

Then he left Stillshadow with Water Chant, and began his own ascent.

Chapter Thirty-three

T'Cori fell asleep watching the sun paint the sky blue, and awoke again as it stood almost directly overhead. She noted that the earlier trickle of water had ceased, and she sighed. Her mouth prickled with a sour, dry taste she vanquished by licking dew from shaded rocks.

The instant one hunger had declined, it was time to satisfy another. Leopard Eye's hare was still in her pouch, but she decided to scavenge as long as she could, saving it for an emergency.

Some roots she recognized and knew to be edible. Those she was uncertain of, she broke off a piece the size of her fingernail and tucked it between teeth and gums. She would leave it there for a quarter, to see if her gums itched. Her body might react with soreness, swelling, a sense of sickness. In that case, she would eat no more. She had to keep moving but remain aware of the sensation in her mouth. If her spit still tasted good in a while, and if her cheek and tongue were not sore, then if she encountered another such bush later, she would consider it safe to eat.

She froze as a purple lizard poked its head out of a crack. Willing herself to disappear, to become part of the rock, she remained perfectly still, until it crawled within arms' reach. T'Cori snatched it up, dashing its brains against a rock. Grinning, she ate it, bones and all, save the tiny sharp claws. Its head she crunched with her teeth like a nut filled with juicy meat.

A little later, she was lucky enough to find a mass of grubs in the shadow of a rotting tree trunk. These she ate one at a time, crunching through legs and carapaces with relish, savoring their sweet, pulpy flesh.

Hunger temporarily sated, she examined her surroundings more fully.

The wide spot in the rocks was linked to a narrower path skirting the mountainside. She edged along it for some ways before it narrowed to the point that she had to stop again.

The valley floor was far below her, far enough to have dizzied most. Clouds cast shadows across it, shading the vast swathe of trees, twisting game trails and lush green elephant grass. She could imagine letting go, kicking away from the rock wall with her legs, plunging down and down to a swifter, more merciful end than any she might find beneath a lion's claws.

And then . . . an angry growl behind her. She whipped around to see the white-scarred lioness approaching from behind her, no more than ten long paces distant. Her thighs tensed as she fought a sudden, almost irresistible impulse to urinate.

So. There *was* another way to the ledge.

T'Cori backed up, clambered up a series of rocks and then pitted herself against a vertical wall, climbing twice her height before reaching an overhang she could not challenge.

If the lioness waited below, eventually T'Cori would weaken and fall.

Why postpone the inevitable? Why not just admit that Great Mother had decided it was time for her daughter to come home? Why not return her bones to the earth and dance on the mountaintop? Why?

Because everything inside her told her to keep trying. Keep fighting.

Then she remembered Leopard Eye's rabbit. Her herb pouch came next to mind, packed with the strangleweed and other herbs to create the last gift, the death potion that eased a wounded hunter's passing. Praying to Great Mother, she stuffed the herbs down the dead rabbit's throat.

She hurled the carcass down to the ravening, yellow-eyed cat. The lioness sniffed, snapped it up in one bite, then kept jumping at the rock wall, seeking purchase for her claws.

Rising on a fierce surge of triumph, T'Cori climbed. All she needed to do now was survive, unless herbs enough to send ten hunters to Father Mountain were insufficient to kill a killer.

She braced herself against the rocks as the lioness roared and snapped at her, just out of reach. Her legs quivered, and her strained back ached. Agony flowed up her bruised and bloody fingers.

Then the lion's roar weakened. If the cat had been human, T'Cori would have said its voice sounded almost confused.

The cat's rear legs collapsed. It coughed, tried to spit twice, and made a hacking sound, as if its saliva was congealing. It slipped, stood again and seemed to wobble. Took a few halting steps, and turned in a circle, as if trying to bite its own tail. And then, one leg at a time, the strength left its legs and it fell to its right side, exposing pale skin and teats swollen from recent nursing. Under other circumstances, T'Cori might have felt a flash of guilt.

Her mouth twisted into a triumphant snarl. T'Cori knew the signs of strangleweed: unbuffered by special herbs the weed was a swift, painful toxin. The lioness would strangle painfully to death, choking on thickened saliva and a closing throat.

Relief, and a fierce vicious joy rushed through T'Cori, refreshing as a dip in shaded water.

If the lioness had reached her ledge, did that mean there was a way down from above? She made her heart a stone and edged past the dying cat. It pawed at her weakly, then forgot the human and concentrated on its own struggle for breath.

Where had the predator come from? How had it reached the shelf?

And then T'Cori glimpsed a narrow path, as wide as her arm was long, jutting out from the cliff beneath an overhanging shelf of reddish rock low enough that she would have to crouch. She decided to crawl. Oddly, crouching on her hands and knees steadied her nerves, and, after a few nervous breaths, she was able to stand again.

Could she go up? Yes, if she retreated a hand of paces. T'Cori was able to grip enough rocks and roots to pull herself up to a wider path along the rock. There, finally, she was able to walk again.

This path came out in a wider, flatter place, and she stopped, surprised by what lay before her on the ground.

A rough circle of stones, set around a heap of crumbled ashes. She knelt, feeling the flakes. They were cold. The circle was less disciplined than those made by Ibandi men. Looser somehow. And yet . . . it did not resemble Mk*tk fire stones, either. Whoever and whatever had left this, belonged to neither group.

Perhaps the blunt-faced folk who had come for the child?

Which led to another possibility. Unless the people who had left this had climbed up from the valley floor, there had to be a way down from the top, and she intended to find it.

For the next quarter, T'Cori walked paths and climbed rocks until she neared the ridgetop. Looking down, she could see a switchback trail along the valley wall, leading down toward a much-more-inviting-looking mass of trees and grass and shrubs. Her heart lighter, she picked her way back down. From time to time she found berries, and once a kind of small orange fruit she had never seen. She did not dare eat it, but saved one, planning to tuck a portion against her cheek later.

Almost halfway down the slope, she froze. *Something was wrong.* Was it the wind? For a moment the breeze shifted, and she caught a sour, meaty scent.

Lion.

Where? Was it merely lion spoor or the cats themselves? Hunkering down behind a bush, she watched silently for a time.

Nothing.

Alert now, she descended with greater care.

Then she saw them. Two. Three. Were these the same that had killed Leopard Eye? How could they have tracked her up a rock wall?

Her *scent.* She had caught theirs. How foolish of her to doubt they would detect hers in turn.

Her fears had been justified. By sexing Leopard, she had somehow transgressed against Great Mother. Forces infinitely larger than human strength and will were in play. Great Mother. Father Mountain. The *jowk* must have decided that this was her time.

The three lions were clambering up the rocks, barely a spear's throw away. T'Cori backed up, trying to stay far enough ahead of them that they might not see her.

An angry growl behind her. There down the switchback crouched one of the big cats, tail lashing back and forth in anticipation. In that instant, their eyes meeting, predator and prey knew each other. There was no question now, and the lions were running up the switchback, one of them trying to climb directly up the side, sliding back down with a howl, skidding halfway down the slope before slamming into a boulder. It shook itself with a kind of injured dignity, glaring up at her.

Lack of food and water, the fatigue and fear all crashed down upon her at once. T'Cori's arms and legs felt limp and devoid of strength. An exhausting series of pulls and clumsy clamberings finally brought her over a boulder as high as her waist, leading to a flat grassy knoll. The young medicine woman was quivering and spent.

T'Cori did not doubt that if she tried to climb that way, the cats would catch up with her. What, then? What could she do?

Attempt a direct ascent of the rock wall above her? The footholds here were not as good, and she could only get a man's height from the ground before her escape route dead-ended. Immediately to her right, roots sprouted from the cliff face. No matter how she strained, they were out of her reach.

To the left a rock jutted from the face, but no matter how she extended her foot or tried to twist and turn, she failed even to touch it. This was as far as she was going.

Could she climb back down?

Too late. Up over the lip, no more than ten paces distant, scrambled two lions. Once on the knoll they froze, their yellow gazes locked upon her. Then one slow step at a time, they slunk forward.

Thought was slipping away, something beyond fear rearing itself in her heart: *surrender.*

She had seen this thing before back at the Circle in the days before the Mk*tk. While on a medicine walk she and her hunt chief guides had come upon a hyena stalking a wounded deer, and waited until the drama was complete. Still alive, the deer hung limply in the hyena's jaws, as if the leaf-eater feared that hope or struggle or any attempt to preserve life would merely prolong its agony. She had witnessed the surrender in its body, the limpness. *Kill me,* it seemed to say. *But don't hurt me. . . .*

A sense of that reality wound through a hunter's prayers, asking that an animal's *jowk* return to the burning lake, surrendering the fleshly shell so that a worthy hunter might provide his family with meat.

Deep within the pit of her stomach a sour, quiet warmth whispered: *give up . . .*

She climbed as high as she could, looking down at the lions as they searched for a way to reach her. The killers leapt after her, the only sounds the heavy thump of their bodies against rock and their low-throated growls.

Hunger, raw and hot, radiated from them like heat from desert sand. Leopard Eye had not satisfied them but had perhaps answered the question of whether or not these two-legged creatures were proper flesh.

Poor Leopard Eye. No: poor T'Cori! If she could not find an answer, she would be joining him soon.

Farther to her right a brown tangle of roots burst from the rock. T'Cori strove to work her way over there, but weak, slippery fingers betrayed her. Balance vanished in an instant, and only a desperate lunge for the roots prevented her from toppling over backward. Ten paces away the lioness licked its lips, already tasting the fresh meat.

Then she heard another noise. A hooting call, not quite an animal sound. Not Mk*tk, certainly, but she was certain that no Ibandi throat had ever made such a sound.

And despite the unfamiliarity, her pulse quickened. When she managed to turn her head to look, what she saw gave her pause.

There were four of the pale, squat males who had fetched the strange

child. Their jaws were wide and brows low. They were so heavily muscled
that they might have been sun-bleached Mk*tk. They were shorter than the
average Mk*tk, but from their proud bearing and well-fed frames, she reckoned them mighty hunters.

Each carried a bamboo spear. The weapons had stone heads lashed to the
tips, more complex than the simple spears favored by Ibandi hunters. They
wielded them as if the stalks grew from their bones.

The tallest motioned for her to remain still, and then lowered their
weapons to advance on the lions.

One of the three cats ran at the odd pale strangers, thundering its rage,
coming up short as the spear points lowered to threaten its face. Another of
the men lowered his weapon to address the big cat's belly.

The lions paced side to side in frustration, but every time they made any
approach to the men at all, two or three of the spearmen faced it. One tried
to disregard the flaked-rock spear points and come at the men from the side,
and was gouged for his trouble. Not a mortal injury, but meat-eaters cannot
afford damage that might limit their agility or speed.

The men were slower than Ibandi, but their width of shoulder and hip,
the thickness of waist proclaimed them stronger. They seemed heavy, perhaps even clumsy compared to the great hunt chiefs, but they moved in harmony one with another, as if a single mind controlled a pair of them. It was
a dance such as she had never seen before. A lion dance.

Jabbed and shouted at, the cats backed down the mountain, snarling
their frustration. One of the men watched them, keeping his spear at the
ready, while the others motioned for T'Cori to descend.

Despite their superficial resemblance to Mk*tk, T'Cori felt no fear. Their
eyes were yellow-blue and light brown, the limp hair on their heads a dirty
yellowish hue as well. Their teeth were broad, strong and flat.

The largest of them held his hand out to T'Cori, and as she took it she
recognized him: He was the gap-toothed giant that the girl-child had run
to. Her father? Uncle? Perhaps merely the leader of these strange folk and
therefore someone the girl knew would protect her?

She did not know. But her heart sang and said, *You are safe.*

And she believed it.

He grunted at her. The men surrounded her. Then, together, they descended the valley wall.

Chapter Thirty-four

Frog and his hunters had climbed up and down the wall, seeking a sign. A torn root here, an overturned stone there . . . T'Cori had made no attempt to conceal her passage. When at last they found a proper switchback, Frog sent Leopard Paw down to fetch Water Chant and Stillshadow. Together they dragged the old woman's sled up the steep grade. As the shadows shortened and then lengthened again the rescuers scouted and searched, until they lost the trail halfway up the valley wall.

Now they stood on a shelf of rock and dirt edged with scrappy yellowish bushes, with no idea what to do next.

"There was so much blood back by the stream," Leopard Paw said, voice dull. "So much. Perhaps . . ."

"No," the old woman said, her voice disturbingly certain. "She still breathes."

How could she say such a thing when Frog's own eyes told him there was no sign, except that which proclaimed his woman dead?

And then . . .

Uncle Snake pointed out at the dusty horizon, almost directly into the sun, now near setting along the valley's western rim.

Shimmering against the dying sun were four, no, *five* human figures. Was this, at last, the final battle he had so long feared?

Mk*tk?

He pushed Bat Wing behind him. Shoulder to shoulder, the four Ibandi hunters readied their spears. If their blood enemies had found them . . . well, perhaps all they could do was sell their lives dearly.

Frog squinted, finally able to make out three wolf forms. They were near the humans but not attacking them, nor being attacked *by* them.

"It is the strange ones," Snake whispered. His white-speckled beard trembled as he spoke. "The foundling's people."

Water Chant shaded his eyes, muttering under his breath as he peered out.

What did they want? Could they know something? Frog tensed: could they have harmed T'Cori? Were they masters of lions, as well as wolves?

There was someone *with* the male figures. It took only a moment to recognize it as an Ibandi female, heavy with child. And only another moment for his gladdened heart to realize it was his mate.

Spears held tip high, the Ibandi walked to meet the strangers. The strangers were as pale as the grubs that burned to death when exposed to the sun. They walked two on either side of T'Cori.

She looked exhausted and bruised, her fingers streaked with blood, her lips swollen and her braided hair clotted with dust.

But she was *alive.*

Frog began to run toward them. The men walking beside her looked at T'Cori as if to note her reaction before stopping and allowing her to walk on ahead, until Frog and T'Cori stood staring into each other's eyes. They linked hands and leaned toward each other until their foreheads touched.

Frog lived in a world of solid things, not spirits. And had lost the last of his hopes of another world atop Great Sky. But . . . now he felt as if the sun had emerged from behind a storm cloud. He felt contentment so deep, it was almost frightening. Was this all that it took to make him happy? For the woman he loved to hold his hand? To once again gaze into her eyes?

He laid his palm against the soft warm swell of her belly. Frog imagined that he could feel the life within. His child. *Their* child.

He slipped his arm around her, then looked up at the others.

"Our friends have returned," he said.

"They saved me from the lions." Her smile vanished. "They were too late to help poor Leopard Eye, but their spears saved my life."

Frog stepped toward them, stopped a hand of steps away. He touched his chest. "Frog Hopping," he said.

The second largest of the newcomers seemed to Frog to be the headman. The largest of them hovered at the headman's right elbow. Their eyes were the girl-child's shade of light blue. His nose was shaped like hers, broad and wide nostriled. His teeth were strong, square and gapped in front.

Family?

"Thal," said the leader.

"Frog," said Frog. He swept his arm, indicating the search party. "Ibandi," he said.

The newcomer's thick pale brows arched. "Vokka," he said.

The revel ranged from one end of the Ibandi camp to the other, and lasted until first light. Two of the Vokka males thumped awkwardly about, waving their arms and screaming to the sky in a shaggy dance with the Ibandi hunters. Soon after their return, another Vokka male had arrived, escorting several females. Frog noted that these females were not the subservient and docile sort favored by the bestial Mk*tk. Much of the time it seemed they were the ones giving the males direction. Men held children, and he saw one of them serve food to his woman.

So. Unlike Mk*tk these folk knew their women were human. Vokka and Ibandi were not so foreign after all.

Since T'Cori had appeared, Stillshadow had held her hand in a death grip. Held her, perhaps fearing that without touch, she could never believe that her daughter had returned.

Frog watched without speaking. He put fire to the herbs stuffed in his bone pipe, and took one deep, satisfied puff after another. The world, he decided, was a very good place.

Stillshadow's ancient cheeks tightened with a smile, and her blind eyes wept.

"My daughter has returned," she said. "Neither famine nor fire could take the joy from my heart." She suddenly looked up at the sky. "Oh! I should not say such things. The gods love troubles. It is why they gave their children so many of them. Still, this is a happy day."

Another commotion at the fire's edge, and suddenly six more Vokka appeared, including the girl-child they had sheltered mere nights ago. She was clean and washed, her pale eyes bright. Frog guessed that the woman walking behind her was a loving mother or perhaps an aunt. Their loincloths were rougher than those of the Ibandi, not of beaten deer leather but of lion hide.

Beside them trotted another of the gray wolves. It was a bit smaller, paler than the wolves known to the Ibandi. Its snout was blunter as well. It watched them warily, remaining close to the Vokka.

Uncle Snake appeared behind Frog. "What manner of two-legged are these?" he asked. "I do not understand them at all. We save their child, and they do not speak or come to make friends. Now, suddenly, they are everywhere and cannot get enough of us. And what of the wolves? In what world do two- and four-legged walk together?"

"This world, it seems." Frog and one of the wolves had locked eyes, and Frog refused to be the first one to turn away. Foolish, perhaps, to play such games with a four-legged, but then perhaps he was a fool. He would not lose a contest to a wolf. He was a man!

He blinked, suddenly laughing at the oddness of the thought, and realized that he had lost. The wolf's tongue lolled out, flickered back, and it turned away.

"I think I know," T'Cori said. "We saved their child, which put them in our debt. What they did was wait until they could do a service in return."

Still muttering to herself, Stillshadow hobbled forward, knelt and drew a crescent moon symbol on the ground with her finger. This was followed by a child symbol: an oval head, stick of a body, and short arms and legs. The Vokka woman commenced to do the same, and soon the ground was covered with scrawls. T'Cori and Stillshadow pointed and spoke. The Vokka jabbered in response.

"What are you doing?" Frog asked.

"It is our medicine," T'Cori answered, new confidence lightening her voice. "Every year at Spring Gathering, bhan arrive from horizons away. Not all speak well. It is our place to learn their speech and teach them ours. The *jowk* tongue is beyond words: symbols for woman, man, life, death, moon, sun. They are shared by many, perhaps by all. This is what women do: when *jowk* wears a man's skin, it loves to fight. In a woman's, *jowk* craves a joining. It is up to women to find the symbols we share."

After a long day of dancing and scrawling and sharing, Frog and T'Cori reclined on zebra skins. Beneath a sky that seemed so clear it was almost as if he was seeing it for the first time, Frog's mind could no longer restrain his heart. "When I thought I had lost you," he said, "I died. My heart did not want to beat. T'Cori, kill me now."

"What?"

Frog withdrew his knife from its sheath and placed its point against his breast. "Push it. End my pain. Or take me as your man."

Dry lightning ripped the sky above them, blistering the clouds. Holding his eyes without blinking she wrapped her hands around the knife and pushed until a trickle of blood flowed down over his nipple. Thunder rolled across the plain, and she smiled as if she welcomed it as a holy sign.

She placed his hand on her swollen belly. "Fool. We *are* a family. But I cannot be your wife." She turned away from him. "Leopard Eye washed my child, and now Leopard Eye is dead. I do not wish you to die."

"T'Cori," Frog said, "I sexed with Fawn Blossom, and she was taken. She died. When we were together after you ran from the Mk*tk, you asked if I would sex with you, and I said no. That was why."

"Because you thought that sexing Fawn might have caused her death?"

"Why not? You say that because you and Leopard Eye sexed, he died."

He pulled her more tightly to him. "There was no sin. That is *my* child inside you. I can smell it. *My* child. And I would wish no man dead for washing my child."

She gazed down into the valley's bowl. He could taste the teeming gazelle and giraffe and zebra . . . the smell and feel of it all dizzied him.

"It is like a dream," she said.

"You hold my child in your belly. *My* child. Not Father Mountain's. It is time I claimed you. Is it not best for a child to know his father?"

"His father might be a god."

"No!" Frog crushed her painfully tight. "I gave you that seed. *My* seed. My son. And no one, man or god, will stand between me and my son."

Her eyes flew wide. "You speak sin!"

He was prepared to do far more than that. All the terror he had controlled for the entire day suddenly exploded into rage against the gods she believed in, gods that had been willing to have their priestess devoured alive.

How could he make her understand? It was *men* who had saved her, not gods. "Sin?" he said. "Then let the wind whistle in my hollow bones. For you I climbed to the top of the world. I stood with you against my brother, and so he died. For you, I walked ten tens of horizons. You are my woman, and you will make me your man."

She tried to match his stare, and finally quailed, leaning the top of her head against his chest. "Frog," she said. "Frog. Once, I wanted nothing in the world more than to be yours. I wanted to taste your breath in my mouth, feel your skin so close I knew not where mine stopped and yours began. I was shown that those dreams were wrong."

"They were never wrong."

"They were never right," she replied.

"We can *make* them right. You and I. In this new world, where men walk with wolves, *we* say what is right and what is not. These are *all* our children, even the graybeards. You and I climbed the mountain." He spoke as if the idea amazed him still.

T'Cori shook her head. "Frog, Great Sky *let* us climb Him. And then allowed us to return to our people. For our own purposes? No. For His."

"I don't understand," Frog said.

"No, you don't. Once I hoped that you would see the world I see, but you do not. Perhaps cannot. As I do not see the faces in the clouds. We were given different eyes. Trust me," she said. "I see what He wants."

And this thought, at last, made him pause. "What does He want?"

"He wants His children to live," she said. "And grow. To find new places. To love and have children."

"Does He want us to be together?"

"Yes," she said. "I think He does."

Frog grinned. Gazelle Tears, Flamingo and Ember would dance to hear the words he now wished to speak, to know the emotions bursting in his heart. "Then He is a good god." Frog grinned. "And I will love Him again."

ChapterThirty-five

For many days, Fire Ant and his men had run north seeking signs of Frog. Now, at last, the signs had grown clearer.

Here at the riverbank the ground was cracked and dry, the easier for Fire Ant to read the footprints and the double tracks of Stillshadow's sled. This was a very good thing: if they were still carrying the head dream dancer, then it stood to reason that she was still alive.

His people had crossed here, and from the growth of brush he reckoned no more than two moons before. He and his men were closer. The hunters were closing the gap on the prey.

Ten men could travel faster than tens of families, with their old women and children to slow them down. That knowledge gave him confidence, and he pushed onward.

Ten days south . . .

Flat-Nose sheltered himself in the shade of a bushy-topped live-long tree, relishing the smell of blood and shit from the Ibandi hunter they had nailed to its trunk.

They would get no answers from the dying man. He had been gutting a freshly killed zebra when they had come upon him. The weakling had run like a woman and then fought like a girl.

Dove was not with them, so there had been no way to translate his groveling answers. Flat-Nose needed none, merely anticipated the pleasure of cooking and eating the striped kill before the Ibandi's bleeding, dying eyes.

Flat-Nose had the tracks of his true prey, could pick them out of countless others. He would find the man who had ended his brother's line. Soon, Flat-Nose would find the monkey and peel him.

Three double hands of his clan traveled with him, battle scarred and ready to sing their death songs. None had a goal greater than spilling their enemies' guts. Then they would probe the steaming mass of their innards for answers. The greater the foe, the more powerful the magic.

These Ibandi were powerful enemies. The men seemed almost like women, but they had had enough fire in their blood to enter Mk*tk territory and kill their children. There was something pure in that, and their response was just as pure.

Flat-Nose stood in the shade of the man they had spiked to the tree. Their enemy was traveling north, or had been, moons ago. But Flat-Nose smelled the wind and caught a whiff of something blowing from the west. A stench of weaklings. Flat-Nose thought his enemy was following the herds. According to his people's stories, the herds traveled north and then swept back south.

That meant that if he went toward the setting sun, he could cut moons off their pursuit. Catch the Ibandi.

Kill them.

All.

Chapter Thirty-six

Most of their shared campground was quiet now, but Frog sat by the fire, watching the camp's outer edge, where a few Vokka lay curled on their sides, sleeping. As he watched, a wolf padded in from the darkness to sleep next to the tall gap-toothed man named Thal.

"Look. Another wolf," Snake whispered as a gray-muzzled beast padded in from the shadows. "Let's watch, and see if it melts into a man."

Frog said nothing. If he remained awake and alert, would he be rewarded with such a miraculous sight?

"Wolves," Snake whispered in Frog's ear. "How can you stand to rest so close to them? With their fangs so close to your only child? Wolves killed your brother."

"Time kills us all. I do not hate time."

"You are the strangest man in the world," Snake said.

"Are they really wolves?" Frog asked. "Are the Vokka really men?"

"Yes, I think them men."

"See that the Vokka trust them with their children."

"Then," Snake whispered, "the Vokka are ugly fools."

Uncle Snake rolled over to his own space, and was soon snoring. Frog lay down, and kept one eye open as long as he could. He did not know when he fell asleep, but he did know that, so far as he could see that night, no wolves transformed into men.

• • •

Clumsily at first, but gaining grace with every passing day, Ibandi and Vokka began a dance older than either people. They shared tubers and nuts and ways of constructing huts. They compared ways of dancing, sharpening knives and splinting broken bones. T'Cori found the Vokka hard on the eyes but human, kind and, she thought, good.

Ibandi and Vokka men fell at once into competition with one another. Who could jump highest? Run fastest or longest? The Vokka had the edge in raw physical power, but T'Cori found them a little slow to grasp nuance.

But if males came to know each other by test, women accomplished the same thing by sharing.

The leader's soft-eyed woman was called Kiya. Kiya was apparently the aunt—or older sister—of the rescued child, whose name was Rushing River. Thal, whose name meant "Tall One," was either father or uncle.

Kiya was heavy with child, but still spry and strong enough to caper with the others, and encouraged T'Cori to join them.

For a moon following T'Cori's flight from the lions the two expectant mothers had shared a nightly dance, the others clapping and cheering to their odd meld of skill and clumsiness. Then one night, their good fortune ended.

The drums had pounded, the twin fires leaped and roared. The very stars above shimmered in time with their calls. Suddenly, Kiya clutched her belly and fell to the side, her legs glistening wet in the firelight. T'Cori caught her before her head struck the ground, both crying out as if they shared a single heart.

Kiya's kin helped her onto a grass mat and began the business of bringing a new child into the world. T'Cori sat with her, holding Kiya's thick strong hand, rocking back and forth and saying what few words of comfort and reassurance she knew in Vokka.

Their efforts were of no use. The baby was born backward and bluish, the cord wrapped around her neck. Dead.

Blood smeared Kiya's legs, muddied the mat beneath her.

T'Cori watched, forgotten, as the dead child was bundled and put to the side, and the Vokka women fussed over their sister.

From their efforts T'Cori realized that the Vokka knew nothing of stop-bleed, the flowers that could slow the seepage. She still had a handful of the crumbly dried purple blossoms in the medicine bag slung around her shoulders. Within a quarter she had brewed the potion, adding other herbs to make it stronger.

She brought the brew to Kiya and her sisters, and made sign for her friend to taste it. The woman was feverish by now, too delirious to decide. But her sisters had danced with T'Cori. They looked at her belly and reckoned one mother unlikely to poison another.

Kiya sipped the potion from its ostrich egg cup, and by nightfall, she bled no more. Kiya had lost her child, but Kiya's husband, Thal, Tall One, had not lost his mate. And that was, at least, something good.

T'Cori did not understand the Vokka, but friends need love more than understanding.

As men stalked the valley for food, the women hunted for the things that would make this their new home, searched together for the wood to construct drums, for a great ceremony of beginnings.

Night after night, T'Cori, Gazelle Tears and Stillshadow sat with the Vokka women, seeking the bits of the *jowk* tongue embedded in the human language. Through dance and drawing and hand symbol and sand painting, they sought the words and concepts both shared: "Food" and "water." "Birth" and "death."

They drummed, danced and mimed their tales of hunting and fighting and traveling. The Vokka drum rhythms were primitive, bland, slow. Within their two beats the Ibandi found five.

Uncle Snake and Leopard Paw tried to teach the Vokka their own rhythms, but found them slow in uptake, heavy footed and easily frustrated. These new bhan were good friends but hardly family.

Chapter Thirty-seven

T'Cori had spent the early hours searing breakfast mush balls in last night's coals. Each was the size of a child's fist, crisp brown on the outside, grainy orange within. More important, they were delicious.

As the morning shadows retreated, she glanced up at the eastern edge of the ridge and shaded her eyes and saw a single stick-thin figure staring down upon them all.

It waved. T'Cori waved back as the stick figure clambered down toward them. At first T'Cori merely wondered who this person was. Then something in the walk, the angle of the head seemed . . . familiar.

Impossible. It could not be.

Could it?

T'Cori pushed herself up and walked east. Disbelieving, she climbed up the slope, touching each rock and bush to assure herself that this was no dream.

A miracle of miracles. Dehydrated, exhausted, half starved, the stick figure collapsed, then rose again.

T'Cori climbed as quickly as she could and embraced Sister Quiet Water.

"How did you find us?" she whispered into Quiet Water's warm, braided, dusty hair.

"How could I be anywhere else?" Her sister sobbed. "You filled my dreams."

For a long time they cried together. When T'Cori looked up, Frog and Leopard Paw were beside her. "Who?" Frog asked, confused.

"It is Quiet Water." T'Cori sobbed, wiping the tears from her eyes.

They came down from the ridge, gathering tribesmen as they went, until they were flooded by children and fathers and mothers, all excited by the dancer's arrival even if they had no idea exactly who she was.

By the time Sister Quiet Water crawled into Stillshadow's hut, the great one was already awake and sitting erect.

For a time they did not speak, just sat opposite each other, breathing in rhythm. Then Quiet Water leaned forward and kissed the dry-leaf skin of Stillshadow's forehead.

"It is good to see my daughter," the old woman said. A wan smile warmed her face. She turned to T'Cori. "You needn't have gone so far, and through so much, to feed the strangleweed to a lion. You needn't have feared I would kill myself. I think that Great Mother will take me when she is ready."

In every spare moment, from dawn till dusk and later by firelight, Frog practiced with his spear. But he was no longer alone. Now ten Ibandi lined up to practice with him. They thrust, twisted and danced bravely at the chalked Mk*tk silhouettes.

"What are they doing?" Stillshadow asked.

"What do you hear?"

"Sticks clattering against stone. But it is not what I hear. It's what I *see*." Her blind eyes opened wider. "Their *num* flares. Threads form vines. The color is not green or blue but red, like fire blossoms. I see anger and fear."

"They're practicing, Mother. I cannot see their *num* as clearly as you but think that you are right. I think Frog is afraid."

Her mentor nodded. "Some things in this world are worthy of fear. Something crouches in my darkness, something to do with—" she closed her milky eyes "—lions." She turned to T'Cori. "Was there something about the Vokka and the lions? Something you should tell Frog?"

T'Cori closed her eyes. Within that divine darkness she watched the glowing *num*-threads spin off her body out into an umbilical connecting her to the coming years. Her body was a hollow gourd, filled with light. The soul vine whispered of courage and cowardice, purpose and ability. When all those *jowk* walked toward the same horizon, it was a magical thing.

T'Cori thought about that, and dreamed. The next day she went to Frog, telling him of the way the Vokka had fought the lions.

And that very night, he went to their new friends, asking that they show him their hunting ways.

The lion dance was a three-man ritual, with one man playing the part of the cat. The other two practiced staying in time and distance with each other so that no matter how the lion attacked, their weapons were perfectly poised to strike. They moved like mated eagles, turning and diving in harmony.

For days Stillshadow listened to the sound of the men thrusting and dancing, until finally she shook her head.

"What is it, Old Mother?" Quiet Water asked at last.

"The stick sound has no *music*," she said. "I know little of hunting, but something of dance and drum. There is something that the hunt chiefs had that the Vokka lack. That Frog and Snake lack. There is no *music* in their step. Teach them," she said. "Teach them our dances."

"Our *dances*?" T'Cori said, shocked. "But hunting is a man's thing. . . ."

"Once, it was," Stillshadow said. "Once, Cloud Stalker held the men's secrets, as I did those of the women. But that time has passed. Teach them what you know."

And obeying, T'Cori had tried to teach, and the men struggled to learn.

Stillshadow listened to the clatter of sticks and did not hear what she wanted. The men stumbled over their feet and crashed into one another and banged one another with sticks. And inevitably, they grew frustrated that they could not learn in days what it had taken years for dream dancers to master.

"I have an idea," T'Cori said. "What works for women might work for men. Here in the valley are the makings of dance tea. I have seen the mushrooms, the leaves, and . . . even a bit of strangleweed."

Stillshadow laughed. "But just a bit," she said. "Just a spice of death. Enough to crack their egg."

The next day the women—with many guards and an eye for lions—picked the spices and herbs and even the spotted mushrooms necessary to make the dance tea.

The brew stank, and it tasted even worse than it smelled. At first Frog thought that it had no power. Then after a time he realized his feet were numb, as if he was floating a fist's width above the ground. The air pulsed as if he were floating within a living heart. As the dream dancers moved around him, they left glowing pathways in the air, and he had but to move within those paths, like walking in tall grass behind an elephant.

Never had he felt the *num* so clearly. He danced with both hunters and dancers. All night they gyrated. When they lifted the spears again, it was as if the weapons moved by themselves. The women taught them the dance moves, and they crouched and leapt until their sweat dried and it was long past dawn.

And it was good.

And so as days passed, they taught and shared the ways of men and women, the ways of Vokka and Ibandi. T'Cori gave everything she had to every dance up until the time that, half a moon before anyone would have expected it, she felt a warm slickness upon her thighs, and knew that her water had broken.

Frog's sister, Little Brook, and T'Cori broke water upon the same day, which many considered a sign of very good luck indeed.

Usually, Ibandi women gave birth surrounded by their closest female family. Bhan often birthed alone, day or night, whether or not the bush was dangerous with lions or the spirits of the dead.

Often a bhan woman would not even say that she was about to give birth, unless it was her first child, in which case her mother or aunt might help her.

But whether surrounded by family or alone, it was both Ibandi and bhan custom that a woman might clench her teeth or let the tears flow, but never cry out or show her pain. A test of womanhood, perhaps a preparation for times when an enemy or predator might lurk near a hiding woman in the throes of childbirth.

Stillshadow offered up her own shelter as a birthing hut large enough for five to sit in comfort. Despite its generous length and breadth, with two women sitting with legs wide, and four more clustered to help, it was hot and dank.

Little Brook clutched T'Cori's hand until her nails sank through brown skin to draw red blood. When the pains became very strong and very close together, T'Cori's sisters and Frog's mother, Gazelle Tears, prepared a bed of grass for them and helped them stand so that they could crouch over the twin beds.

Little Brook gave birth first, moaning and biting her hand so that the blood ran but never screaming. Her son emerged into the world onto his bed of grass, and after the cord was sawed off, he was cleaned and placed in her arms to suckle.

T'Cori watched as Gazelle Tears gathered the stained grass and tissue, and carried them out of the hut. She would find a place in the brush and bury them, marking the spot with a cairn so that no hunter would step upon it and lose his power to hunt.

Then T'Cori's body clenched like a fist, driving all thought from her mind.

The muscles deep within her danced in a rhythm older than thought. Although she made little sound, inside her head she screamed. It felt as if her body was tearing itself apart, and she clutched at Sing Sun's arm until her sister's flesh tore.

"Push!" they whispered to her, and she bore down as strongly as she could. "Push!" they said again, mopping the sweat from her brow. And then . . .

She heard a cry, a newborn cry, the sweetest sound she had heard in her life. At that moment, she could have died, and been happy to do so.

"A girl," Sing Sun said.

"Give me my child," T'Cori said, and the baby was given to her. T'Cori gazed into her daughter's eyes, which stared blindly out into the world . . .

And then . . .

They fixed upon her mother's face. She cried, howled, announcing her birth to the world.

Chapter Thirty-eight

When the Ibandi first laid eyes upon the towering, thick-rooted fig tree in the valley's center, its branches already buzzed with tiny, winged life. To celebrate the first births in Shadow Valley, the men decided to raid it for honey.

Like hunting, honey gathering was men's work. The lowest hive was located in a branch higher than ten men standing on each other's shoulders. Both Vokka and Ibandi had been stung upon even casual approach.

This, Frog thought, *was a good thing.* Stinging bees always guarded the best honey!

Gathering the sweet, sticky stuff was a painful pursuit, but the rewards were well worth it. A hand of volunteers from each group, Ibandi and Vokka, offered to brave the stingers.

At dusk, ten men crept to the tree and boosted one another up the trunk. The Vokka were slightly better climbers, and Tall One was the first to reach the fist-wide crevice in the tree trunk. Within that darkness hung the chosen cluster of pale combs. They looked like rows of huge grubs nestled together side to side.

Tall One gestured to Frog, and Frog climbed up beside him, carrying a leather pouch of embers and green grass. Together they blew on it until the sparks flared, wafting smoke into the crevice. Frog winced as a bee stung him on the cheek and another on the hand.

God Mountain, that hurt!

But those were the only stings, and after a time the bees grew sleepy and uninterested. With two swift slices the Vokka cut the hive open, pulled out sections of honeycomb and threw them down.

The tribesmen on the ground caught the chunks with their hands wrapped in broad palm leaves. They ran off, slapping at the waking bees. If they could get away before the bees recovered from the smoke, all would be well. But otherwise, it was going to be a long and very painful day.

The groggy insects were everywhere, clinging to the comb, sticking to their skin, but the thieves were away in time: a few welts on arms and legs could not diminish the sweetness of victory.

The brew of honey and herbs was delicious and potent, thinning the wall between the dream and human worlds. The Vokka smoked and danced with them until dawn, welcoming the new children into a new home, beneath a new sky.

T'Cori held their new child to one breast, and Medicine Mouse to her other. Her milk had descended and she was happy to nurse her children at last. Frog stretched his arms around the three of them. Perhaps they could not have the marriage ceremony, but he would have life with her, here in Shadow Valley. He would gladly step into the circle with anyone, man or giant, who denied that T'Cori was his woman or that this was his family.

The Vokka were so different: strange in custom, broad-faced and bleached-bone ugly. Frog heard all his people saying these things, but he also realized that the Vokka probably thought similar things of them.

Soon, Frog hoped, would come a naming ceremony. With luck, Stillshadow would decide to remain in this world long enough to give T'Cori's newborn girl a name. But that was for her to decide, not Frog or any other man.

He was very tired, and glad for the time to stare up at the dark clouds. He wondered if the Vokka could see things that the Ibandi could not. They knew different things . . . and if the Ibandi seemed to learn the Vokka ways faster than the Vokka learned the Ibandi's, still, perhaps . . .

He pointed up into the sky. "Cloud," he said. "Face."

Tall One frowned. "Cloud. Face? Where face?"

Frog sighed. Then again, perhaps not. Not like him, not like Ibandi, not like Mk*tk. The Vokka might almost have been monkeys, the way they never seemed to tire of grooming each other. Or of entertaining their fellows with mimed stories of hunting and screwing and spirits of the dead, falling over and rolling on the ground in fits of laughter as long as the fire threw sparks into the night sky.

Tall One loved to dance, and that night walked on all fours, miming great size and strength, pretending to have twin tusks and a long, agile nose.

When he had finished, Tall One knelt to draw in the dust. T'Cori watched carefully, and then translated. "He says that this dance was taught him by his granduncle, who learned it from his. He says that our elephants are naked, and theirs were much larger and covered with hair."

What a thought! The Ibandi had a great good laugh at that. The Vokka were wonderful liars, indeed!

As the days passed, Frog struggled to think more deeply. What if Still-shadow was right? Could vital knowledge have been lost when the hunt chiefs died on Great Sky? Would it even be possible to find those knowings once again?

Late on one lazy day, when the Vokka were sharing gathered fruit with their camp, Frog tried to communicate his concern to them. "You have taught us many things, and we would share with you in return. We have mixed the men's and women's magic, and found it good. You have been good friends, and we wish to share what we have found with you."

His expression uninterested, Tall One danced his answer, and T'Cori struggled in translation. "No. We have no need to learn these things."

Stillshadow was seated on her new sitting stone. He had thought her to be off in her own world, but she responded. "I have seen you practice with spears for the hunt."

When T'Cori translated, Tall One snorted in disbelief, and danced. "Seen? You are a blind woman. What can you see?"

"Only my face-eyes have dimmed," Stillshadow replied. "I see more now than I ever did. You are very brave, and all of you have been hurt many times."

The hunter shrugged his scarred, sun-burnt shoulders. "It is our place in the world."

Stillshadow continued. "We can teach you new things. Ways to catch flesh without so many wounds. Ways to turn plants into allies, poisons to bring the giraffe to their knees, offering their throats to your knife. We have medicines to heal your bones."

The Vokka hunter huffed. "We have our own medicines."

"You say your grandfather's fathers came here, from many horizons to the north," T'Cori said. "But all Ibandi fathers, since the beginning, have lived in this land. What we have learned, we remember. Many of your ways work well here, or you would not live. But others, not so well I think."

Tall One's expression remained flat and unreadable. "What do you want?"

T'Cori did not answer him directly. "I share my healing arts, everything I know."

The hunter watched her eyes, knowing that there were many things unsaid. Still, he nodded. He danced. And from time to time he paused to draw in the dust, as the Vokka women struggled to interpret Ibandi words.

T'Cori translated for Frog. "He says there may be good in this. He fights for his women and children, because it is what he must do. He says they are our friends. But he and his people need nothing from us. If he takes from us, he must give in return. He says that this is the only reason anyone ever gives anything. They give so that later, they can take."

T'Cori looked to Stillshadow. "Mother? You have heard. What do you say?"

Stillshadow blinked, as if her eyes were irritated by the warm dry wind ruffling the grass. "The Vokka are our friends, as much as they can be. But if trouble comes, we must help ourselves."

"How can we," T'Cori asked, "when so much was lost to us?"

The old blind woman was silent for so long that Frog began to study her chest, just to be certain she had not finally surrendered the *jowk*. Then she spoke. "We must go back to the beginning. What the hunt chiefs knew is buried with them. But Cloud Stalker and I were together most of our days. Whatever I taught you was touched by him, as what he taught the chiefs was touched by me. Share what we do know. T'Cori, teach the dances to your man. Somewhere at the core of them is what they need. It is in the dance. I know it. I feel it. At the core of all is nothing. And the nothing becomes something because of dance. That," she said, "is all there is."

Chapter Thirty-nine

When hunting with the Vokka, Frog noted their amazement that the Ibandi threw their spears. The Vokka, in contrast, were expert stalkers, capable of sneaking within stabbing range of a buffalo. Despite the thickness of their bodies, they moved almost as silently as shadows.

And the wolves! The Vokka's four-legged companions did not hunt the way humans did: they ran their prey down, nipping at the ankles and legs of zebra or impala until the terrified and exhausted creature stumbled and fell. Then, the wolves were upon it in a killing frenzy. When they killed, they actually shared with the men. When a man speared or wounded an animal, the wolves dragged it down and ripped out its throat. When their squat, pale, human companions came close, the wolves went into an odd kind of semitrance, growling deep in their throats but not snapping as the Vokka carved the prey into pieces.

However, if an Ibandi came near, those deep-throated growls grew more menacing. Their eyes grew brighter. Thus far, no Ibandi had come within biting distance of a Vokka wolf. No one wished to be the first to test those teeth.

Ibandi and Vokka hunted for food and for sport, and sometimes their new friends came to the Ibandi camp just to amuse themselves with Quiet Water or T'Cori's efforts at translation. It was on one of the hunting expeditions that Frog discovered a familiar bush: dark green stems, little red flowers, as broad as it was tall.

"Look at the poison-grub bush," Frog said.

"Poi-*sen*," said Tall One.

"The juice goes on the spear," Frog said. "The spear kills with a scratch."

Quiet Water translated haltingly. The Vokka men struck their spears angrily on the ground.

"What are they saying?" Frog asked, curiosity fully stirred.

"They say that this is cowardly. That with such things, any woman could kill an elephant."

Frog's face went hot. "Cowardly? Because I wish to feed my family, I have no heart?" He hawked, thinking to spit into the dust at their feet, and then changed his mind and walked away. "Tell them what I said," he called over his shoulder.

When he returned to the camp, he told Stillshadow what had happened. He had to repeat it three times before she seemed aware that he was standing in front of her. She raised her wrinkled hand. "No, Frog! Listen to me. They have their own ways. You say they have many scars. How do they justify those wounds, their broken bones, except by believing their gods demand that they pay such a price? What we offer them will take time."

"How do you see so much with only five eyes?"

The old woman smiled. "How do you see so little with seven?"

From that point forward, a women's circle, combining the ways of Ibandi and Vokka, met almost every night

When Stillshadow roused herself from trance and sang with them or for them, her voice and fragile dance held them rapt. "We are the ones who bring the men into this world."

The Vokka woman called Old Young spoke in word and sign and symbol. "Eight have I brought through my body. The last almost killed me." She slapped her knee. "But I am here! And he is tall and strong."

Stillshadow nodded. "We lose our teeth bringing them into the world."

T'Cori and Sing Sun scrambled to translate back and forth.

"A tooth for every child!" Old Young said.

"Men see the things," T'Cori said, dancing and gesturing as she did. Sing Sun drew glyphs in the dirt to clarify. At times, T'Cori had to pause, find new ways to say the things she needed to say. It made for painfully slow communication, but their speed increased a little every day.

She continued. "But men miss the web *between* things. It is our place to see these, as we see the past and the days to come."

"We are women," Old Young said. "We hold the world together."

Ember sighed. "It is the way of women to be lonely. I miss my Fire Ant."

"You have knowledge, as we have," Stillshadow said. "I say that the men can wrestle and run and test one another, but we, as women, know how to share."

Old Young was adamant. "Men are always boys. As women we must lead them." Her voice was strong if rough. Her dance was halting, but its very torpor contained a measure of clarity.

Stillshadow lifted her hand. "Let this smoke seal our friendship."

She reached into the leather pouch at her side and extracted a handful of herbs, which she threw onto the fire. The women breathed deeply, growing dizzy and light-headed as the cloud enveloped them.

"It is good." Old Young said. "This is how it was when the world was young.

" 'Once, all the children of earth were one people, but the men fought among themselves. "I am the greatest hunter" one would say. And another would say, "Yes! But I am the greatest runner!" And on and on, until the gods wearied of their boasting and divided the people and separated them.' "

Stillshadow agreed.

" 'Women do not do this. All are proud of their own children, but they say, "See how beautiful your girl is!" "See how fast your boy runs!" '

" 'We take pride in these things that men cannot understand,' " the Vokka woman said.

Neither the women nor the men saw the shadow watching in the darkness.

Moving stealthily at first, it crawled back up over the valley ridge. As it blended into the shadows on the far side of the ridge it stood and ran, until it joined ten others.

"What did you see?" Moon Runner asked.

"They are there," Fire Ant replied.

"Did you see the dancers?"

"Yes," Ant said, "young and old."

"Why do we wait?" Moon Runner asked.

"Because there was something else. Like Mk*tk. But not Mk*tk."

"What are you saying?"

Ant shook his head. "There were strangers, not like people I have ever seen. Wide. Pale, with straight hair."

"So . . . what do we do?"

"Whatever it is, we do it tomorrow," he said, and rolled over onto his back, folding his fingers beneath his head. "My head hurts," he said. "Tonight, we sleep. Tomorrow . . ."

"Tomorrow?" Moon Runner asked.

"Tomorrow," he said, "perhaps we kill."

Chapter Forty

The day began like any other, with a new sun sung to life and Frog's countless thrusts against a now pockmarked baobab tree trunk.

By the time he was finished, the morning meal was prepared, and Frog sat with his family and enjoyed his first food of the day. No more mush balls and jerky! This was fresh dates and juicy roasted boar. It was clean water from sparkling springs. It was the promise of life to come.

A deep sense of contentment welled up within him, like a morning glory embracing the sun. This, then, was what he had lacked for all these moons.

Even to himself he had dared not confess such a wonderful emotion, for fear that it might be taken from him, and the pain of loss would be greater than never feeling joy at all.

Then his eyes focused on the valley wall behind them, and he could not breathe. Ten-and-one men were approaching. Not Mk*tk, thank the mountain: Ten-and-one new *Ibandi* hunters. New spears for the hunt!

Then he saw the last face among them. Burned and scarred on the right side of his face, but still known at once.

"Fire Ant," Frog whispered.

The thunder of his heart drowned out all sound. Rooted in place, unable to run, Frog watched his brother's lips move, unable to hear a single word.

"My brother," Ant mouthed silently, "have you no food for a ghost?"

Frog searched for words and found none. He felt as if his head were filled with the hard, cold water atop Great Sky.

Fire Ant stepped toward him, his handsome face scarred and burned, the right eye torn from its socket as if he were Uncle Snake's younger twin.

Frog could not believe his eyes. Certainly, this could not be true. Not be *real.* Only when he felt Ant's chest against his own did he really think he was not dreaming.

"It is a gift from Great Mother!" the women called, and fell to their knees, wailing and pulling their hair.

"Father Mountain sends a sign!" the men cried, and thumped their spears against the ground. Whooping and calling and dancing and crying, they brought meat and water and fruit for the walking miracle men.

Frog's ears buzzed, without producing voices. His people gathered around, watching Frog's ghost brother eat. Every bite, every chew, every step or word was proclaimed a miracle, the greatest wonder that they had ever seen. For had not Frog told them all, time and again, that his brother had died atop Great Sky?

Ant's face brought it all back in a thunderclap: the terrible climb, the death of Scorpion and Small Raven. The ascent to the summit. There, he and Ant had seen nothing . . . and T'Cori had seen Everything. Her insistence that Father Mountain wanted his people to leave the shadow enraged Ant, and for the first time in their lives, the two brothers had reached a branching path: Frog needed to protect her, Ant needed to kill her. The decision had torn Frog's heart to pieces. Only fear of the Mk*tk had driven the terror and shame of those days from his mind.

But Ant had not died. Here he was, eating and laughing and very much alive. And if Ant's burn scars and empty eye gave him a fearsome aspect, he was still a living man, and that was a wonder almost beyond imagining.

For months, Frog had told the story of Ant's "heroic" death. And if Ant now appeared, then he was a walking miracle.

For Frog would not lie . . . would he?

Ant belched, thumped his fists against his chest and spread his arms wide. "I am here, Brother! Great Father Mountain set me free."

Frog rubbed his eyes. "It is not possible. I dream."

"Brother!" Fire Ant said. "I told you upon the mountain that you would see me again." The corners of his mouth turned upward, baring his teeth. "Don't you remember?"

Frog's followers looked from one to the other, as if uncertain what to think.

"Yes," Frog admitted. Speaking that word felt like pulling fish bones up his throat. "I remember."

Fire Ant grinned. "Will you welcome your brother?"

Frog felt like a mouse cornered by a fox. "Welcome to the boma," he said. "Meat and water are yours if they are ours to give."

Ant's grin was a hunting cat's. "So generous of you. To offer what you have to give. Believe me, I will remember the meat you share. As I remember all things that happen . . . or have happened between us."

He leaned closer to Frog and whispered: "*As I twist the knife.*"

Chapter Forty-one

Clutching her hands to prevent them from trembling, T'Cori approached the rocks where Frog and Fire Ant sat talking, surrounded by hands of awestruck Ibandi. She prayed that her naked fear would not shiver her voice.

Ant spit, spattering a dung beetle as it rolled a bit of caracal scat into a ball. "Ah. *There* is the woman. I remember her, upon the mountain. Do you remember?"

Frog leapt to his feet, standing between them, eyes darting back and forth, panicked.

T'Cori fought to keep her eyes on Ant's face, but time and again they flickered to the knife he shifted idly from hand to hand. Her vision clouded: for a moment, the air around Ant boiled red and black, like a mixture of blood and mud melting into a pond.

Great Mother, now *you give me my sight?*

"Yes," T'Cori said. "Yes. Do not speak as if I am not here."

Now Fire Ant rose to his feet. "I need not speak at all if it ends now, in this moment."

Although four hands of Ibandi stood or crouched about, only half of them Fire Ant's men, not one moved to her defense. They were transfixed by the spectacle of blood conflict between two such mighty beings: the woman beloved of Father Mountain and a man returned from the dead.

T'Cori stepped back, eyes wide, raising her hands to fend off a lethal blow.

But as his hand twisted back for the strike, a withered voice said: "Stop, unless you would kill us both."

Fire Ant glared at Stillshadow, as the ancient woman hobbled toward them, leaning on Uncle Snake and Gazelle Tears. Little Wasp walked beside her, his face filled with wonder. Gazelle Tears cried openly.

Ant chewed at the inside of his cheek as if he had just discovered something tasty tucked into its folds. Then he nodded and sat back down, his good left eye crinkling with ugly humor.

"All of you leave," Stillshadow said. "Only family remain. My children need to speak privately."

Wasp ran to his older brother, wrapping his arms around his waist. "You were gone!" he said. "You were dead."

Ant smoothed Wasp's unruly hair. "I came back for you," he said. He squatted down until he was at Wasp's level.

"What happened to your eye?" Wasp squeaked, his own eyes opening wide.

"The Mk*tk," he said. "I took their lives, they took my eye. It was a fair trade." He kissed his younger brother's forehead, lingering for a moment, then kissed him again. "Go. Play. The adults must speak."

"But you will find me, later?"

"I promise," Ant said.

When Wasp was gone, Ant turned to his mother, Gazelle Tears.

"Son," she said, and leaned her forehead against his chest. He held her. "You are dead . . . but feel warm. I do not understand."

"Neither do I," he said, voice soft. "Perhaps if we are loved enough, we can return. Your heart was always the strongest thing in my world."

The water ran from her eyes, and she held him tightly. Then she held him at arm's length. "There are many things I do not understand," she said, and looked from Ant to Frog to T'Cori and back again. "I feel it in the air. I ask one favor."

"Ask," he said.

"Let this day be a happy one. Tomorrow always comes. But this day. For your mother?"

"If I can," he whispered.

"I go now," she said. "This is not my place." She gripped his hand. "One day," she repeated, and left them.

When Gazelle Tears had gone, Stillshadow squatted down. "Speak."

"I would speak first," Snake said.

"You may," Stillshadow replied.

Snake crouched down, balancing on his heels. "I raised you, Fire Ant, and it was my pride to see you surpass me as a hunter and a man."

Ant's face did not soften, but T'Cori saw his eyes grow moist, as if flooded by unfamiliar memories.

"Whatever happened upon the mountain, know that I love you. Your brother loves you. And that Sky Woman has done everything she could to take care of us."

Ant looked at Stillshadow's eyes, and his mouth twisted bitterly. "I can see how well—"

"Do not *dare*," the old woman said. "Do not credit or blame my daughter for a matter between me and Great Mother. Do not dare." Her words carried a mighty weight, and Ant was silent.

"Have you more to say?" she asked Snake. Frog's father and uncle shook his head.

"Then you should speak, Ant."

"Yes, Old Mother. I will speak," Ant said respectfully, then turned to T'Cori. "You are here. And I am here. And our people are lost. You are the one we trusted."

"No, Ant." T'Cori was surprised to find the strength to challenge him. "I have listened to your men speak. You came down the mountain, and lied about what happened to you there. You told them you died fighting demons and then returned from the dead."

"Not *my* lies, girl. I stand on my *brother's* lies," he snarled. "*Your* lies. Do not forget."

"Yes," she said. "We told them so that those who loved you would not be shamed."

He blinked. "So?"

"So," she replied. "Why did you tell *your* lies, Ant?"

"I didn't know they were lies," he said. His voice had strength, but she detected a bit of doubt. Perhaps . . . of shame?

"Ant!" a woman's scream. He turned in time to see Ember running toward him all a-jiggle.

Ant stood, face slack as if he had forgotten he had a wife. He glanced from Stillshadow to Frog and back to Ember again, and now at last some of the heaviness seemed to fall from him as he took his lost wife in his arms. They embraced, and then he stepped back half a pace, gripping her hair and holding her cheeks steady to study her. In return she held the side of his face, and shook it side to side, laughing and crying. She gazed into his dead eye and blinked back tears. A single tear welled as she leaned forward and kissed his scars.

"I . . ." he said, suddenly uncertain. "We speak more, later."

"I'm sure we will," T'Cori said.

And she watched as Ember led Ant to her hut.

* * *

What is love? Ant wondered. *What is life?* For so long he had felt nothing but frustration, shame and rage. His heart had held no room even to remember the woman he had once loved, or the child she might have borne him. But when he met his unnamed child for the first time, the sight and smell of his son nearly burst Ant's aching heart with joy.

Here. Here is life.

She sat kneeling as he held his child, so that Ant looked from wife to son and back again, the smell of both stirring something long dead in his heart's war-scarred depths.

It felt like *home.*

Life and love.

She had borne him his first son, a new life to carry his blood. Then that night, when the camp grew quiet, she drew him to her and gave him the other. And when their urgent fire died down, she roused it again.

And then again.

When passion had fled, and she sobbed out her loneliness and gratitude that he had returned to her, for just a little while he could not remember his anger.

For just a little while.

Later that night, in the moon shadow of Stillshadow's new sitting stone and away from the sight of all save Sister Quiet Water, the old woman and the dead man shared words.

"Come," Stillshadow said. "Come, Ant. Sit with me."

"I am here, Old Mother," he said.

"This is a good place." She sighed. "A place where our people might thrive."

"That you would say such a thing . . . say that there is any place for us but in His shadow, troubles my heart."

She reached out toward him, found his hand. "There are many things we do not understand, Ant. I do not know why Father Mountain did not turn the Mk*tk away. I do not know, but I dreamed of a reason."

"What is that reason?" Ant asked.

"Perhaps He is luring the Mk*tk close. Then He will unleash His fury and kill them all."

For an instant, Fire Ant was swept away by her vision. "Might He do such a thing? Such a great, great thing?"

"You tell me," the old woman said. "After all, you are the one He sent back down the mountain. Tell me, Fire Ant . . . might Father Mountain have a plan for all this?"

"A plan for what?"

"The world. For men and Mk*tk. For Fire Ant." Stillshadow sighed. "I have little time left here, Ant. The *jowk* calls me. Cloud Stalker waits for me, pulls at me. I am losing the strength to say no." She tilted her face up at him. "Can I die, Ant? Can I leave my children, or will they tear each other to pieces as soon as my flesh cools?"

Fire Ant blinked. "Perhaps before," he said.

Stillshadow stared blindly at Fire Ant for many breaths. Then she tugged at Sister Quiet Water, who helped her up and led her silently away.

In the late morning, the warming air above Shadow Valley's ponds shimmered, swarmed with insects and birds, flavored the breeze with mint and grass. Standing alone at the edge of the camp, Frog breathed deeply, savoring, filling his senses, painfully aware that one of these mornings would be his last.

Perhaps this one.

He felt Fire Ant's presence before he saw him, like a wall of fire closing in. Now, though, even the earth would not shelter him.

"So much," his brother said, close behind him. "Herds, water, canyons. I can see it all, as if I stood atop Great Sky." He smiled. "Show me more."

Show me. Take me where the others cannot see, so that no one can stop what must be done. "Of course." Fear, shame, regret . . . all mingled until Frog could not tell one from the other. Until it no longer mattered.

Frog took Fire Ant for a walk up to the camp's edge. Almost as if he were merely strolling and enjoying his day, a watchful Leopard Paw wandered along behind, spear in hand.

Ant turned to Paw. "No. From here on, we go alone. Yes, Brother?"

"Yes," Frog agreed.

"Good," Ant said.

Below them, the cloud-shaded valley floor promised richness untold. Across the valley in every direction, mountain ridges formed boma walls.

Ant grinned. "So good to see you, Brother. I often wondered where you were. What you were doing. But this valley is even better than I could have dreamed."

"So . . ."

"So I still stab you, of course." Ant paused. "But perhaps I won't twist."

So. The food, the welcome, Ember's love, and Mother Stillshadow's heart had not cooled his anger. Could Ant ever forgive Frog's betrayal atop Great Sky?

Frog recounted his travels, struggling to remain calm.

"We hadn't had water in a day, and food had run out. This is what we found."

Within the vast green bowl of Shadow Valley grazed the largest zebra herd Frog had ever seen. But that was not all: almost as staggering were the mouth-watering clusters of wildebeest and eland, vast pink mantles of flamingos and frond-choked pools where great fleshy gray hippopotamuses lay submerged up to their nostrils.

Fire Ant sighed. "It is a great, great thing."

"It was more than I hoped for," Frog said. "We were almost done. And then this. Almost as if we were supposed to find this. And the only thing wrong was that my brothers were not here beside me." A pause. Then, "But then, no matter what, you would never have been beside me."

"No, Brother," Ant said. "Hawk Shadow might have stood here." Ant's good left eye looked at him carefully. The scarred right socket gaped. "Which of us did you love better?"

"Hawk," Frog said. "By a hair. When I thought you both dead, I cried."

"It is good that you speak the truth. A man should not go to Father Mountain with a lie on his lips."

"No." Frog could act. Could try to strike first. Could gather allies and banish Ant from the valley. But although his brother taunted him, Frog could feel that there was something more . . . almost as if Ant was looking for an excuse not to kill him. And if Frog could be very, very clever, he might give Ant just that thing.

"Perhaps," Ant said, "you do not have to die. You have found a good place. I will rest and eat and think. Then we will talk again."

"You would say this even if you meant to kill me."

"Yes," Ant said. "Of course I would."

And for the first time in many moons, the two brothers laughed together, just a bit.

"Sit with me before you go?" Frog said.

"Yes," Ant replied, and suited his action to his words.

"I understand your anger. And how you must hate me."

Fire Ant blinked in surprise. "Go on," he said.

"Things are good here," Frog said. "Our people are safe. The children are fed. There is water and food enough for our grandchildren and new friend-ships to explore."

Fire Ant shook his head in wonderment. "The Vokka are strange and ugly. What manner of men walk with wolves?"

"I do not understand them or their ways," Frog said. "But they are friends. And that is a precious thing in this world."

Another pause, as the wind whistled. "As are brothers," Fire Ant said.

The wind cooling Frog's cheeks was the one that had carried the spring butterflies when they were children. "Is there no way you can ever forgive me?"

Ant's laugh was ugly. "If you had been the one who fell into fire, you would not ask."

"Whatever I may have done, or not done, I never thought to hurt you. You want me to fear you, Fire Ant? All right. I fear you. What now?"

Fire Ant looked at him carefully, finding no answer.

"What, Brother?" Frog said. He slapped his own chest with both palms. "Here I am. We are alone. Why not end it now? Kill me, and say anything you want about how I died."

Ant was genuinely curious. "Why do you want to die?"

"I do not," Frog said. "But I would rather die than fear my own blood."

Ant searched his brother's face for lies. "So."

"So. What do we do now? When will you decide?"

"Soon, Frog. Soon."

"I ask one favor."

"Ask."

Frog forced his breathing to deepen and calm. "If you will not kill me now, let this one day, just one day, be as once it was. I would remember your smiles, your hugs, your laughter and love, and give you mine. Just one day. Then tomorrow, if you must, do as you will. But I would return to the mountain with that memory. Do me this favor."

Ant pursed his lips. "Why? Why should I do this?"

"There is only one reason: because Fire Ant wishes it. You did not want it to be this way. You did not wish this pain between us. It is not close to your heart. But if it is what you need to do, no one can sway you from your path. But we are still brothers."

"Still brothers," Ant said. The corners of his generous mouth curled up in a smile. "You do not die this day. Come, Brother."

He slid his knife from its sheath.

"Ant?" Frog's stomach clenched. Was he as ready to die as he had tried to sound?

Frog's older brother opened his arms. "Come to the brother you say you love and trust. I have made you a promise."

Frog watched his face, then walked to his arms. Surprised at first, Fire Ant returned the embrace. The blade did not bite.

"No matter what you think," Frog whispered against his brother's neck, "I love you, Ant. Watch over my children when I am dead."

Ant said nothing in reply.

That day, Fire Ant watched Frog and the others practicing the lion dance, sets of two men pitted against the chalked Mk*tk outlines. He marveled at the strangeness of women teaching men to dance, and dancing with them with sticks. Men and women dancing together? With weapons in hand? Had the world gone mad?

Finally overwhelmed by curiosity, he queried Sister Quiet Water. "What is this?"

The young woman was breathing hard, but went into a kind of rapid low-belly pant and swiftly regained composure. "Vokka lion fighting saved Sky Woman," she said. "The dream dancers have a drumbeat that makes it even better. We are working to join these things."

Ant shook his head and wagged his finger at Frog. "You and your 'new things.'" He laughed. "The world is good enough as it is!"

"You fought the Mk*tk," Frog said. "If we fight them again, would you not want a new thing?"

Fire Ant thought again on what had been said and done in the last year. He would indeed want something new if ever again he faced the Mk*tk. "Let me see," Ant said, and took one of the sticks.

Ant learned that it was true, that Frog and one of his men were able to jab him, no matter which way he turned.

He would run after one of them, only to be thumped in the ribs by the other. He would turn to defend himself to the left, only to be stabbed from behind by the one on the right. It was frustrating and not a little frightening. In the end, he considered it a very good trick indeed.

"That—" Ant said, wiping the sweat from his face "—is a new thing." And for the second time since his return from the dead, he smiled.

Chapter Forty-two

Fatigue had turned her feet to stone. T'Cori bedded down that night before her mate returned to their hut. She awakened near midnight, feeling him tossing restlessly beside her.

"My heart?" she asked.

"I cannot sleep," Frog said. "I know that he waits. I know that he will kill you. He may kill me as well. If I become certain it will come to that, I will have to try to kill him. Until I am certain, there is nothing I can do."

"Nothing?" T'Cori asked.

"Nothing but wait."

And realizing the truth of that made it hard for her to sleep. She had assumed that somehow Frog, or Stillshadow, would find a way to weave their hearts together. That in the face of their new home's wealth and beauty, Fire Ant's anger would wither.

Doubt had begun to replace hope, and doubt made sleep impossible.

Exhausted, the dancer sat up before the stars closed their eyes. She crawled out of their hutch without awakening children or mate. The air was crisp and clean and cold enough to raise bumps on her skin. She treasured this time. When she closed her eyes, she could almost hear and see her sisters back at Great Earth gathering, singing, weaving the new day. The ancient prayers came swiftly to her tongue, and she sang the new sun to life.

Her task complete, T'Cori busied herself with breakfast, served it to Frog and nursed her children. She cuddled and cooed to them, and then turned both over to her sisters and went to find Stillshadow. The old woman was at the rock chosen as her new sitting stone. She sat with her spine as straight as a spear, staring blindly out at the western horizon.

Every day her mentor's skin seemed a bit more ashen, although every night Sing Sun rubbed her body with a salve made from cactus juice and gazelle fat. Every day a little more flesh melted from Stillshadow's bones, until at times, when the sun was just *so*, it seemed to shine *through* rather than around her.

"Mother?"

Stillshadow's head did not move. "My child?"

"I fear what Fire Ant might do."

Stillshadow's dead eyes blinked. "What happened atop the mountain? What is it that moves him?"

"I heard the voice of Great Mother. Of Father Mountain, saying that the Ibandi had to leave the shadow."

"The others could not hear?" Stillshadow said.

"No, they could not," T'Cori said. "You trained me well."

"There is more. Men and women see different things. And because of that men will always fear us, just a bit."

"What should Frog do?" T'Cori asked.

"You ask the wrong question. For you, he cut the cord binding brother to brother. For you. Because he believes in you. Be worthy of that trust, girl." She leaned close, and when she spoke, her voice was like a knife scraped across stone. "You have no right to be weak. Your false face will kill us all."

T'Cori's hands fluttered helplessly. "What do I do?"

Stillshadow sighed and hung her head. "No Ibandi man can stand against Fire Ant. I see it in his *num*."

"Then there is no hope."

"I said, no *Ibandi* man." She paused. "No Ibandi *man*."

At first, T'Cori could but stare, void of comprehension. Then she found words. "The . . . Vokka? Their men will not interfere."

"Then you must speak with their women," Stillshadow said.

Frog had spent the morning watching the children wrestle and sing and dance and read sign. At the point when the sun was at its highest, Uncle Snake came to him.

Snake thrust the tip of his spear into the dirt and waited until Frog called rest. "Look, children!" Frog said to the young ones. "Great Snake is watching! You must work hard, harder, hardest! If you would make your elders proud, you must work until your aching muscles fall off the bone."

"Yes, Frog!" the young ones said, and raised their spears to Snake. "We will try!"

When they went off to find shade and water, Frog came to him and embraced his uncle. "They need practice," Frog said, "but I think that we make progress." He stepped back and looked at his uncle's scarred face more carefully. "Something troubles you," he said. "What is it?"

In a low steady voice Snake said, "I love you, nephew, but when Fire Ant returns to the Circle, I wish to go with him."

Frog blinked. "I don't understand. There is so much here, Uncle." Snake's face did not change, and Frog felt as if the bottom of his stomach was dropping free. "Uncle," Frog said, "I need you."

"Why?" Snake asked. "What do you need from me? I have no advice to give. Son, you are wiser than I ever was. I have no courage to offer. If ever I dreamed I was brave, the climb on Great Sky awakened me." A bitter smile curled the right side of his mouth. "You don't need me. You need a great man who climbed mountains and slew wolves."

"Uncle . . ."

"I know the lies you told. I believe when you say that they were told only for the good . . . but I was on the mountain. I climbed until my mind and heart failed. And now, my hero's deeds make our children strong. They look up to me, and want to be like me, and I know in my heart that that is the last thing that any of them should want. I know what *really* happened to your brother."

"What are you saying?" Frog asked.

"I'm saying that I see how the stories begin. They come from someplace inside you, someplace that has never seen the real world." Snake said "I am not that! I am flesh and blood. A hunter but no hero. You should have let me be shunned, Frog. Now I *have* nothing, *am* nothing save a story."

Frog swept his arm across the valley. "There is meat and water and fruit and game. Everything that we need for ten lifetimes."

Snake spit and turned his face away. "There is more to life than meat and water. We must have our god as well. I do not believe He is here. We must believe in something, if we cannot believe in ourselves. I am too old to have neither," Snake said. "I want to die in the shadow. I want to go home."

Chapter Forty-three

Every day, Frog brought his brother extra meat. He invited Ant on hunts and drew him into the dance circle. They had smoked and laughed and sung together, but always, Ant had kept a little distance. Never had he spoken the words that Frog craved: *I forgive you.* And as he had always known it would, the day Frog dreaded finally came.

Ten dawns after his arrival Ant came to Frog just as he and a hand of men were beginning their morning spear thrusts. The sun had not yet been born.

"Frog," Ant said, "I wish a boon of you."

"Of me?" Frog said.

"I would run against you," Ant said.

"You wish to run me where the others cannot see and then slay me." He paused to consider. "It is a good plan: you can leave me where the lions and hyenas can find the meat."

"No," Fire Ant said. "We run as hunters."

Frog peered into his brother's face and suddenly understood. The empty right eye, the scars marring his beauty, twisting the lips that had kissed him so often . . . he seemed a ghost of the man he knew. "I see. You hope to win the tribe."

"It is our way," Ant said.

"What of you and me?"

Ant's face was neutral. "We decide that later."

"Where? Across the valley floor?" Down the slope, the tea bush chaparral and flowering cactus gave way to grasses, and that to acacia and date palms, and glistening streams and ponds surrounded by lazy herds of buffalo and flocks of pink-backed pelicans. The morning clouds shaded the grasses, so beautiful. His eyes thirsted for the sight. So strange, how easy it was to take such wonder for granted.

"No," Ant said. "This valley is a good place, a home for our people. It might be best not to poison it with our . . . sweat."

Don't you mean blood, Brother?

Frog studied Ant for a long time and then nodded. "I cannot say no. *My people!*"

The other men began to gather around. If he asked, they would defend him. But that would cripple what little authority he had. That would destroy the myth of Ant, the man who had returned from the dead. Which would mean that Frog was a liar.

And that might begin the end of everything. The decision was simple. "We run together," Frog said, and raised his voice. "Fire Ant challenges me."

T'Cori abandoned her morning meal and went to find Frog. Her beloved was at the edge of camp. He lay facedown on the ground, tensed his gut and raised his hips, scooting his knees forward then allowing his body to ripple forward. One segment of his spine curled forward at a time, like cracking a whip. He twisted and turned to his limit, then relaxed a bit and went in the other direction. Frog rolled back over one shoulder and then another, then braced himself against a tree, raised his hips high and pushed his heels back against the ground.

So many times she had held Frog. So many times the strength and agility in his body had saved her life. So many times she had bathed it, soothed his wounds, kneaded his muscles, wrapped her legs around his hips to pull him more deeply into her.

No matter how she fought for control, tears welled in her eyes.

When Frog stopped, his fine young body gleamed with sweat. He smiled at her, but there was no real warmth or hope in it, only resignation.

"Frog," she whispered, trying to remain strong for him, "can you win?"

"I don't know," he replied. Honest to the end, her Frog. "He hurt his leg, and that may be enough. But I think it won't be. Could he have come all this way if the leg was weak? He does not limp." Had Father Mountain actually given him new bones? Could Frog be so certain Ant had not died on the mountain?

"Why does that matter?"

"Because," Frog said, "if he limped, if he thought his legs weak, he would have found another way. I think his leg is strong. I think I lose today, and die tomorrow."

Oh, Frog. How could I have ever dreamed that there could have been another man for me? You, only you, see life as it is. Or see me, at all. Without you, I walk my life alone. "No matter what happens," T'Cori said, "I am your woman. Your children and I love you. Will always love you."

He rested his forehead against hers, brushing their lips together. "As I love you. It is time."

Fire Ant and Frog walked up the ridge, standing on the flattened top just as the sun was sung to life on their right, out to the east. The dream dancers and their ancient song rang in Frog's ears. He glanced at his brother. Would Fire Ant hear the magic in their song? Certainly, no matter what had happened between them, Fire Ant remembered what they had been to each other. Certainly their shared and precious childhood still lived in his brother's dreams.

Surely he would hear the voices and be swayed. He glanced over at his brother, hoping to see a smile or any flicker of softness on the beloved face.

Nothing. Only hard purpose lived in the eye that had once loved him. Frog's heart cooled. He knew in that moment that his single hope was no hope at all.

"It is time," Ant said, and Frog nodded.

Side by side, they trotted down the slope to the plain north of Shadow Valley, allowing their pace to accelerate naturally as the footing improved, until they were running comfortably side by side.

On other days, the thought of running with his beloved brother would have seemed a wonderful dream. But this . . .

"Do you see the tree?" Ant pointed at a horn-pod tree standing alone on the northern horizon.

"We run around and back?" Frog asked.

Ant nodded.

And with those words, talk ended. The brothers ran. At the beginning, each merely grooved their pace, not trying to best each other. This was the time for each to take the other's measure. Ant's stride seemed natural and strong, his shoulders relaxed, the rhythm of hip and heel a hunter's song. Soon, they began to speed until the breath burned in their throats. Hyena running, *hun-huh-huh*, forcing each stride to push a little air out of their lungs.

Ant increased his pace, and Frog increased his in turn, drawing slightly ahead of his brother. Was this where he wanted to be? In front, where his back might tempt Ant's knife? Even now, could Ant's hand be rising for the death stroke?

Frog turned his head to the right, intending to look back over his shoulder for a glimpse . . . when he saw something odd against the horizon, and skidded to a halt.

"Stop, Brother," he said and then hunched down.

Fire Ant took several more steps, then stopped and walked back. "What is it?" He panted. "Do you yield the tribe?"

"Look," Frog said, and pointed east.

At the horizon's edge, silhouetted below the sun, five squat figures lumbered westward. He would not have seen them if the light had not been just *so.* He would have recognized that gait at twice the distance.

Mk*tk.

Frog heard his brother's sudden intake of breath. The two of them turned and ran back south, grateful for the sheltering shadows.

By the time they had climbed back over Shadow Valley's ridge, their throats burned and their sides ached. Frog felt as if every nightmare that had plagued him for a year and more had suddenly collided, exploded like Great Sky's peak, spewing a vast pale cloud of raw, blinding terror.

"The Mk*tk come!" Frog screamed. The tribe was gathered across the slope, hands of hands of them scraping hides, curing meat, sharpening and repairing spears, building huts. When his calls echoed from the rocks, they put down their tasks and tools and gathered around him.

"Why? Why do they follow us here?" Ember asked, staring at Fire Ant as she said it. Ant couldn't meet her eyes. *She knew.*

"I killed their women," Ant said. "Their children."

"Their . . . children?" Ember whispered, holding her own babe tightly to her breast. "How could you do such a thing?"

Fire Ant's mouth worked, but he spoke no words.

Frog screamed into that void. "Brothers and sisters! The day we feared has come. Today we must fight or die!"

T'Cori gathered the women and children together and guided them to the center of a circle surrounded by hunters, even as the baboons had once protected their own softness. So many lives. So many children. Would all be lost? Was there no way at all to survive this?

Most hunters stood between their women and the ridge above. Mk*tk could swarm down from the top far quicker than they could cross the valley floor. How long would they be able to resist the onslaught? T'Cori's breath would not come. Ember came to her, bringing her unnamed child.

"I will keep Medicine Mouse with me," Ember said, "but the new child . . ." She looked away. "If it goes wrong, it may be best for you to name her and send her home."

Yes. Any name at all would be better than none. With a name, Great Mother would know her daughter and welcome her. With a name, Father Mountain might spare a set of bones for the child, that T'Cori might hold her girl again, in the next world.

Perhaps.

Oh, Mother, that it had come to this.

Would their enemy find them? Was it at all possible that those Mk*tk hunters had come upon them merely by accident?

And . . . how many were there?

The wind shifted, carrying with it a song such as Frog had never heard. No Ibandi throat had ever wailed so. The voices were deeper, stronger, less musical, more like toneless chants than music.

"Death song," Sister Quiet Water said.

"What is that?" Uncle Snake asked her.

She spit eastward, toward Great Sky. "It is what they do when they wish to die killing their enemies. When they think that there is nothing that they wish so much as to die killing. How many hunters do we have?"

"Four tens old enough to fight."

"Not enough," Frog said, and rubbed his hand over his face. He tried to think of another answer, and failed.

Another thought crossed his mind. He wanted to banish it, but could not, and the more he thought about it the more certain he became.

He had to either recruit the Vokka to his cause or else give their new friends the chance to flee.

Her unnamed, newborn infant girl suckling at her breast, T'Cori followed Frog and Leopard Paw to the base of the valley's eastern rim. Every small pull of the precious mouth against her nipple was like the tug of life itself.

Beneath a sheltering of palm trees, some hands of hands of their thick-faced, slow-moving friends were encamped. At first Kiya welcomed her with a gap-toothed smile and open arms. Then her husband saw Frog's face.

"I come to you for help," Frog said.

One hand clutching her infant to her breast, T'Cori translated Frog's words with gestures and dancing hips. She slipped into a trance, floating up above her body, watching her own actions.

Once, upon the mountain, she had stood on ice above a lake of fire. That was where and what she was now: a woman standing above a lake of burning emotion, feeling only ice.

But the mouth against her breast. Urgent. So alive. She tried to fly above the fear, and the small brown lips brought her back.

"Over the last moons we have shared much," Tall One said when Frog had finished. "Hunted together. Birthed each other's children. What do you wish of us?"

"Help us against our enemies," Frog said.

Tall One seemed more curious than startled. "How many of them are there?"

"We do not know."

"When do they come?"

"Now," Frog said.

Tall One's odd, pale eyes seemed to pierce Frog's skin, to see his heart. T'Cori knew that Frog was afraid. Could Tall One see it? He spoke, and her heart fell.

She translated the Vokka's words for Frog. "He says that our enemies are not his. Why should their sons and fathers die for us?"

"We have no right to ask you to bleed with us," Frog said, voice flat with defeat. "You have been good friends. Stay away from us. From everything that is about to happen. Live."

Her heart broke as she translated. Hope itself had fled. Why had they not remained in the shadow? Better to die there, for their bones to rest in familiar earth, than to travel so far, in a terrible unclosed circle, and die in a strange place.

But if there was no hope for her, perhaps one good thing could come from all of this.

She blinked back her tears. "Your wife lost a child," she said, and cradled her infant in her arms. She kissed the sleeping girl's brow. "I would give her mine, to replace the one lost." To lose a child was almost beyond bearing. But to keep her girl only to cause her death . . . that would be beyond endurance.

Silently, she begged Kiya to agree. While another part of her begged her to refuse. Even a few more moments. Even if it cost both their lives . . .

"What did you say?" Frog asked.

She felt something collapse within her. "I asked her to take our child." She expected anger, hurt, bluster.

Instead, he softly said: "We should have brought Medicine Mouse as well."

Kiya looked at her husband. Tall One's expression remained unchanged as he gave his head the slightest of nods. Kiya stepped forward, and took the baby.

T'Cori made a single strangled cry and turned, walking away into the shadows, Frog and Leopard Paw at her side, broken heart flooded with joy and pain.

Chapter Forty-four

Just before dawn, their lookouts gave a brief cry of alarm, followed by screams of shock and pain.

"*Mk*tk!*"

Frog had slept lightly, his spear jammed against his ribs. He grabbed it and leapt to his feet.

The dusk sky had cast deep, dark shadows, and Frog could see little. The men threw wood on the fire, seeking to increase the light. The sight nearly made him wish for darkness once again: there in the shadows and amid the low fires, three hands of Mk*tk prowled the camp, killing all they could. Man-shaped shadows already hunched and crouched among them, cracking skulls and breaking limbs

"Lion dance!" he screamed. Swiftly, their men paired in the manner they had practiced for the last moon. The women and children ran to the center of a loose circle, surrounding the twin campfires, as the men faced out into the darkness.

"There!" Leopard Paw called. Almost as quickly as the alarm was spoken, a snarling Mk*tk charged out of the night.

Instead of clambering forward and attacking the Mk*tk as individuals, giving their opponents the chance to slaughter a man and move to the next, each Mk*tk found himself confronted by a pair.

As they had practiced, Frog and Leopard Paw fought side by side, Frog to the left and Paw to the right. Jabbing and thrusting, Frog drew a slash in response, while Paw thrust up into the exposed armpit.

The Mk*tk roared and turned as if swatting an offending fly, while Frog slashed at the tendons behind his right knee. Another roar, but this one of confusion, as they drew the Mk*tk's attack back and forth between them, until he buckled.

Snarling, Paw drove his spear into the bunched muscle beneath the Mk*tk's ribs, then wrenched it out with a cry of triumph.

Without pausing to celebrate, they turned to help their fellows, only to find that the Mk*tk were retreating.

Fire Ant was blooded along the left side of his chest, but his spear was red halfway through. "That . . . is not like them," Frog's brother said. "The last time, when they came for me, they attack and attack, and kill and kill. This time we kill two, and they run. I have never seen them withdraw."

"No," Frog said. "After our first battle, south of Great Earth, they ran. There were three of us for every one of them, and they learned we could kill them."

"How many of them are there?" Snake asked. "Do we have enough?"

"I do not know," Frog said. "I would give anything to know." In truth he knew that that was one question to which they were likely to receive an answer.

Out beyond the valley's rim, Flat-Nose squatted, waiting to hear what his men had to say. He had hunched like this since dusk, staring off into the desert. It was now near midnight.

"What happened?" he said. "How many of them are there?"

"Ten tens, I think," Brave Tortoise said. "Many old ones and children. We have more fighters. And each of ours is worth a hand of theirs."

Flat-Nose gave a short, somber laugh. "They are stronger than we thought," he said. "I have woven my death song. I see it in my dreams: I end here. I sing it for you. Whoever lives, sing it to my children, that they might sing it. That God Blood might be pleased and take me into His belly."

He sang them the song, and they listened, that they might sing it to Flat-Nose's many children. And they marveled at its beauty and at the simplicity of the request he made of God Blood:

To die killing.
To kill, dying.

That was all. And for the children of God Blood, that was enough.

Chapter Forty-five

Fire Ant sat on a round, flat rock near the crackling fire. His people huddled in family knots, waiting for the end.

Stillshadow lay above him on her new sitting stone. Sleeping? Awake? Dying? He didn't know. But his dreams had been . . . troubling. He saw the death of everything he loved, everything he knew, and for the first time, truly understood what he had done.

Fire Ant bowed his head, and cried.

His mother, Gazelle Tears, and his wife, Ember. His sister. His brother. Now all would die. Because of what he had done.

Because of him. He had led their greatest enemies directly to the heart of their greatest hope.

He cried.

"Hear me, Brother," Ant said, after his tears had dried.

"What would you say now?" Frog said. "What words? I know you hate me. I know you wish my death. I suppose that your own life is a small price to pay for such a sight."

Ant set his chin strongly, but his voice betrayed his grief. "Hear me, please, Brother," he said. "I look out at your children. My nephew and niece. All that is left of us. And now I see I have been a fool."

Frog doubted the evidence of his ears. "A fool?"

Ant nodded. "This is my doing. All. I never hated you. I hated Sky Woman, and wished you to step aside. My people will die, because I wanted the Circle. Because I believed I was more than a man. I know now I was wrong. I am a man. A foolish, foolish man. Now my mother and sister and you . . . all will die. And I am the cause."

Although a cool wind stirred the leaves, Frog doubted if that was the cause of his brother's trembling. "Brother . . ." Frog said.

Ant held up his hand, shushing Frog. "I heard them sing of me. Watched the women dance my death. I was the one who returned from the mountain! Returned from the dead! I knew that my grandchildren's grandchildren would remember my name."

"Brother . . ." Frog repeated. He had never seen pain like this on Ant's face. Not when Ant had lost his wrestling match with brother Hawk. Not even when faced with betrayal by Frog. This was something different, like a man standing on the branch of a falling tree.

"A man must face the truth of what he has done," Ant said. "I am many things, but I am a man." He gripped Frog's hand hard enough to hurt. "You never were false. I was so surprised that you lied about what happened on the mountain. Why?"

"Many love you. It would have hurt them to hear the truth." He paused. "It would have hurt me most of all."

Fire Ant released his grip. "You could have led our people. You should have had that chance."

Frog could say nothing.

"I look at you . . . and your woman. Great Sky Woman. And I see something I have never seen."

"What is that?"

"I think . . . I see what Stillshadow and Cloud Stalker must have been, when they were young. I never understood the way you think. You led us to a new home and proved the myths a lie. You are the best and wisest among us. And Sky Woman?" He shook his head. "I never understood the dream dancers. And now I know that it does not matter if I understand. And that, I know too late."

"Not too late," Frog said, clasping his brother's shoulders. "Just in time."

Chapter Forty-six

To Frog, it seemed that most of the tribe had fallen into a kind of sleep-walking grief, keening and moaning around their cookfires, saying good-bye to one another as if already convinced Father Mountain had demanded their bones.

His uncle Snake sat with a knot of other hunters around the central fire, the orange-red light lapping at their faces, the shadows flattening their expressions into pictographs, fragments of genuine human emotion.

"I have thought," Frog said, sitting beside him. "There may be something we can do. We can run and hide. Or stand and fight."

"Is there something else?" Uncle Snake asked.

"We can trap them. As we trapped the giraffes."

"In the same way?"

"And in the same place." Frog squatted, drawing a circle and a curve with his fingertip. "Here along the western wall is the canyon," he said. "If we flee, but we leave a trail, we could trap them *here*"—he touched the ground—"and could have the high ground if our men were *here*."

Snake peered at the scratching and shook his head. "They are not long-necks. We can't use fire to drive them."

"No. We will have to *draw* them," Frog said.

"With what bait?" asked Leopard Paw.

"Living bait. Some of us will have to wait there."

"They will think ambush," Snake said. "They will never believe it."

"They must," Frog said, slamming his fist onto the ground. "They have to. What else—"

"They will believe," T'Cori said, "if we bait the trap with the one thing that they would never expect."

He stared at her, at first uncertain of her meaning. Then he understood. "You cannot mean . . ."

"Listen to me," she urged. "The thought did not come to me until you spoke of giraffes. Stillshadow dreamed of women with long, spotted necks. And now I know what it meant."

"What are you saying?" Frog's mind spun. What insanity was this? This was no time to speak of dreams!

"That the only bait that would work would be something no Mk*tk would ever expect. And there are only two things of this kind: women and children. We will not use children," she said.

Of course not children. But if not children, then . . .

Then . . .

Father Mountain. No.

He thought to protest, but the stone in her eyes left no room for argument or doubt about her intent. They had lost a hand of men in the first skirmish. Including Fire Ant's men, they had four tens of hunters who could fight. Not enough.

"Any who did this thing . . . would not survive," Ant said.

T'Cori shrugged. "What matter? What matter the risk? If we do not act, we die. This way, some of us may live."

Frog narrowed his eyes. No. No. No matter his trust of T'Cori, he could not even contemplate such a possibility. At the very best, it was insanity. "You know that the Mk*tk would look at a man, or men, and know it was a trap."

"But women . . ." T'Cori said.

Sister Quiet Water made a keening sound, her eyes so hot they looked like glowing rocks. She rocked back and forth, arms wrapped around her knees. "Please. Give me the chance," she whispered. "I would kill them all.

"Every night," Sister Quiet Water went on, "I prayed Father Mountain would send someone. Or that I would find death, as Fawn Blossom and the nameless one did—" she paused. "As I thought T'Cori had. There was no end to my pain. Then I find that T'Cori was sent strength to save herself. That, and a rescuer in Frog."

"And He sent Fire Ant, for you," Frog said.

"Too late, Frog," Quiet Water said. Her face softened when her eyes met Ant. "Sweet Fire Ant. You tried, didn't you? And look what happened. So it is too late for me. I don't know where that girl went. But if I could not live as I wished, perhaps I can die as I choose."

"My heart cools," Frog said. "I have no words for you. I have been to the mountaintop, seen the gods." He shook his head in amazement. "But never have I seen courage such as yours. If we can find another way, I ask you to find the strength to live. But if we cannot . . . I gratefully accept your sacrifice."

"Better to die saving one's people," Fire Ant said, and seemed to Frog to be more . . . more *Ant* than Frog had seen since before their days upon the mountain.

Chapter Forty-seven

At the west end of Shadow Valley was the narrow canyon they called Giraffe Kill. It was wide at the mouth and in the middle narrowed sharply before opening once again. There, they would make their stand.

There, surrounded by sun-bleached bones, the two hands of Ibandi who had volunteered to be living bait spent their last moments together. Several were young women: T'Cori and her sisters, Morning Thunder and Flower, and a few others. Some were old and tired. Tired of running, tired of fear. If their bodies could make good bait, so be it.

And six were the best fighters that Frog had trained, Leopard Paw among them.

Snake had chosen to stay as well, and nothing Frog said could dissuade him.

Young Bat Wing begged to join them, but Frog held the boy, hugging him close. "Medicine Mouse will join you," he whispered. "Be a brother to him. Grow strong. Teach him to hunt."

Bat Wing sniffled and nodded his head. Frog ruffled his hair and pushed him away, swatted his bottom and waved as, crying, Bat sought safety.

Frog took T'Cori and Medicine Mouse to a private spot near the rear of the defile, past the place where the rock walls narrowed and almost touched, before they widened again. Mouse suckled happily, and then fell asleep. Frog and T'Cori placed him on a grass mat, and then sat together, sighing.

"I have dreamed," T'Cori said.

"What were these dreams?" Frog asked.

"I dreamed that our new child was safe with the Vokka. And that we were spirits . . ."

"No dream," he said. "Tomorrow's truth."

"Hush, my love. What comes will come. I dreamed that Great Sky welcomed us and Medicine Mouse forgave us."

"I would be with my son," Frog said. "But I would wish that he grows tall, has a chance to hunt and love before his bones return to the earth."

"We cannot control such things," she said, and leaned her head against his shoulder. "But if we die, would it not be best to be welcomed home?"

Welcomed home. There was no home. No heaven. Nothing but death. But he would not say such things now. There was no longer any point to it. Wasn't a comforting lie better than a cruel and hopeless truth?

Stillshadow had said it once: *Who is more wretched than he who knows no gods, yet dreams of demons.*

"A good dream." He paused. He did not want to say the next thing, but the certainty of his own approaching death weakened him. "T'Cori. On the mountain . . . I did not see Father Mountain. In fact, I saw nothing but dead water. But . . . I heard voices, and one of them may have been my father. I don't know."

"I saw. I felt. It was all there, my love. I carry those visions still."

"They speak to you still?" Frog asked.

"Still."

"Did you see my father?"

"I saw things," T'Cori said. "*Jowk,* woven into egg cocoons. One may have been Baobab."

"Did he say anything about me? To you? Did he give you anything to tell me?"

He heard the fear in his voice. With all his certainty that the world contained nothing save rock and flesh and fang, he knew that he was asking her to lie to him. Her soft brown eyes were filled with nothing but love, nothing but caring. And nothing but truth. Especially at such a time, no dream dancer could speak a lie.

"I do not know," she said, and brushed her lips against his. "But tonight, as I sleep, perhaps He will come to me."

"Perhaps," Frog said, "we go to Him, instead."

"Frog," she whispered, "do not think of death. Even if this is our last night, let us think instead of life." He pulled her into his arms.

Hunters had carefully broadened the trail from the rim ledge to Giraffe Kill, while wiping away the trail the rest of the tribe, those who had not elected to be bait, had left escaping toward the south. If their efforts were insufficient, the Mk*tk would follow the wrong tracks, find their women and children, root them out and slay them all.

But for now there was little to do save wait and hope.

And perhaps to love for the last time.

"Life," they whispered into each others' mouths. Were there tastes that were beyond taste? Smells that were beyond smell?

This was not the last time. It was the first, and perhaps the only time. Her skin was not merely smooth, it felt like grazing his fingers along the surface of a warm pool. When his lips touched hers she clutched the back of his head, pulling his mouth down on hers as she never had before, as he had never known before.

Her tongue was fire, darting into his mouth, probing against his teeth, her eyes opened so wide and urgently that he felt he was falling into them.

T'Cori's hands were everywhere, pulling at him, her nails scraping against his skin, raking, pain and pleasure mingling so that each became the other. His mind spun.

Then her hands slipped to his loincloth, and had grasped the thickness beneath. His own hands were moving now, sliding up her thighs, pushing aside the deerskin flap, until he found the moist folds at the juncture of her legs.

His tongue pushed hers back into her mouth, and she sucked at it, desperation driving away all emotion save the urge to join, to be one, to dissolve all distinctions between them until their flesh burned away and all that remained was the *jowk*.

Sex was the heat of burning.

Male and female was a lie. *Jowk* was the truth.

They joined.

Her moist flesh moved against him, pulsed, rolled, squeezed him and then released. On the outside she was calm, they were unmoving, but within her body she was taking him where he had never been. He groaned, beginning to tremble.

"Make a fist at the bottom of your root," she whispered in his ear. And he did, and the sense of imminent release retreated. Again and again she took him to the edge, and then coaxed him to drive his seed back.

On and on she went, until the world retreated and all consciousness contracted to a single point of light, and then her mouth was on his again, her tongue soft, not urgent, upon his.

His world died in fire and was reborn.

There was a time without time, when he did not know what was Frog and what was not-Frog. And then slowly, he came back to her.

Remembered his name, and her name, and where he was. For a moment, he had glimpsed something . . . different. Something beyond flesh. Just a glimpse, given to him by his woman.

And he marveled. When he regained his breath, Frog whispered: "You . . . never showed me that before."

"Shh," she said. "It was a secret for the hunt chiefs."

"I am no hunt chief," he said.

"Who is to say?" she said, and they laughed together, and then held each other and whispered until his body told him it was ready once again.

And when at last they fell asleep holding each other, he thought that if he died on the morrow, it would be a small price to pay for a night such as this.

Within Shadow Valley lived an entire world of contrasts: swamp, desert, trees, arid ground, grasses and cactus. Flat ground at the bottom, sharply rising green-choked walls around the edges. Sun and shade, each in abundance.

Tall One liked a drier campground than did the Ibandi. The brown folk loved the dense green, while the Vokka preferred the ground beneath and around their huts to be burnt grass and wood flakes. Vokka huts had sharper, more pointed roofs than the rounded roofs of the Ibandi. They tended to build their huts where the ground felt right, rather than according to some strange pattern the Ibandi carried in their heads.

Tall One sat on a log between the two largest huts, sharpening his favorite knife with a flat stone. Across from him his wife, Kiya, whose name meant "Changing Seasons," held Sky Woman's unnamed brown daughter. She rocked back and forth, keening.

She rose, and came to him, holding the child tight in her arms. "She took my milk," Kiya said. "My breasts no longer ache."

"That is good," Tall One said, without looking up.

"Sky Woman gave me a great gift," she said.

His broad, flat face did not change. "You should not have taken the baby," Tall One said.

"Then I will take her back," Kiya said, stepping toward the east.

Her husband glared at her, then looked more carefully at the infant. The child was strange, with tangled hair and shadow skin. Then again, it had all the fingers and toes, and was full of squalling life. "She will die if you do."

Kiya stood still, child held tightly in her arms, as if daring her husband to say more.

Tall One's mother extended her hand to Kiya's, who pulled her upright. The old woman's spine was twisted by seasons. Her toothless mouth gaped, but she could still see and still speak. Once, Tall One remembered, she had been beautiful.

"I gave birth to you, my son. I know you grieved when you lost your child. I saw your pleasure when Sky Woman gave you hers. And I say that you owe a debt."

Tall One glared and turned his back, gazing out across the valley. This was not his fight. His grandfather had told him stories of the journey south, how wanderlust had led his people to travel on and on, over generations. Of their hardships and glorious victories.

Tall One was a peaceable man. He liked these Ibandi. In all his family songs, there had been nothing quite like these brown-skinned folk. Had they not sheltered his niece, Vokka and Ibandi might have bled over these hunting grounds. But . . .

He was confused. His obligation was to protect his own.

But who exactly *were* "his own"?

As turn the seasons, the falling of night and the coming of dawn, all things destined come in their time. And in Shadow Valley, the time had come for good-byes.

Frog kissed the soft, warm skin above Medicine Mouse's eyes, then gave his boy to Ember. He watched Fire Ant embrace her and his children, and stood with his brother as two hunters took her away.

He watched his mother and Uncle Snake hold each other, fingers playing with each other's hair. Last night, he knew that Snake had taken Gazelle into the shadows and loved her as they had not in many moons. He knew this because, despite her sadness, this morning Gazelle walked like a girl again.

Snake rubbed his grizzled cheek against hers, then sent her with the children and old ones to a place of hiding on the valley's south side.

No matter what happened next, this was a good day.

Frog sat crouching in the sand near a heap of bones, shaving slivers off the point of his spear. "You did not have to come," Frog said to his uncle as Snake watched his wife disappear into the grass.

"Yes," he said. "I did."

"This will be hard."

"Everything in life is hard." Snake took his hand. "Frog, I died on the mountain. Everything I thought I was, I was not. Did I ever really live at all?"

"Sky Woman says this—" he waved his hand at the valley "—all this is a dream of a dream," Frog said. "That when we sleep, we are more awake than when we walk." Frog rubbed his temples with his palms. "It makes my head hurt."

"If I do not try to become the hero they think me to be, it is worse than death. Can you understand?"

"Uncle . . . perhaps none of us are ever really known."

"Frog," Snake said, "give me this one thing. I have lived too long without pride. Perhaps one day you . . . and your sons . . . will see *my* face in the clouds."

Chapter Forty-eight

Flat-Nose ran down the valley wall, following sign. His clumsy prey had attempted to hide their tracks, but their efforts were in vain. Soon, he would show them. He would show them for days.

They had no chance of escape, now or ever. He and his men trotted across the valley floor, amazed by the health and number of the herds. Now *this* was a hunting place! Surely, his people could kill the Ibandi and move here and live like godlings until the end of days. Food! Water! Fat, lazy animals to hunt and, only days to the east, weaklings to kill.

Life was good.

The grass here was withered and black. Lightning fire? Something cautioned him to slow, but the tracks led into a narrow canyon, and he didn't want his enemies to get too far ahead of him.

There! Around the corner of one of the bruise-colored bushes appeared one of the fragile Ibandi women. Her head jerked at the sight of him. She screamed and then ducked her head back into the crevice. The weaklings were trapped! Flat-Nose would slaughter their men and take their women. His mouth watered, contemplating many happy moons of their pleasing slickness against his root.

Three tens of Mk*tk fighters entered the defile. Was there another way out? Could the valley wall break here, and their prey already be fleeing back out onto the savannah? Of little matter. By dusk, their guts would steam on the sand.

By the time the Mk*tk had gone two tens of paces, he saw enough to guess that the cleft dead-ended far up ahead. Sobs echoed from beyond the rocks, and he knew them trapped. His blood burned, boiled, until his vision narrowed into a tunnel. *Soon. Soon.* Ibandi blood would slick his spear.

The walls narrowed further. The ground was littered with half-bleached, well-picked skeletons. Bones of the spotted long-necks. Someone had done great killing here. Even for these weaklings, hunting had been good! He hoped that some of that spirit would be left to resist. Where was the sport in slaughter without a struggle? Without the opportunity to watch your enemy's courage dissolve into terror? To steal a man's spirit was far more satisfying than merely tearing his flesh.

The mud-colored rock walls narrowed again. The first worms of doubt gnawed at his gut. Where were his prey?

And then . . . *there* they were. Just beyond a tangle of yellow-green brush he spied four women, hiding under a rock shelf. Before them crouched a knot of their pitiful males. Hiding with their women! What manner of filth were these?

Flat-Nose felt disgust. He had hoped for a battle to thrill God Blood, and then this! He wouldn't wipe his ass with such weaklings.

Best to end this and get on with the pleasurable business of seeding their women. He waved his men forward.

Anger and disgust warred with a grudging admiration. The monkeys hadn't been entirely stupid in choosing a place to make their last stand. *Good.* He would break their pitiful defense, and even if Flat-Nose had no hope of a decent death here, he might get a thrilling wound.

Howling, the Mk*tk raced forward. After five hands of paces the walls narrowed. Flat-Nose could see that beyond the narrow space, the walls widened again.

Flat-Nose smiled. No, they weren't stupid at all. This fight might be a good one. God Blood would enjoy it.

Just before the Mk*tk reached the narrow gap, the Ibandi stepped back and braced themselves and the Mk*tk crashed against a forest of spears. Blood and screams sprayed the air. Two Mk*tk made it through, but two of Flat-Nose's cousins were speared through throat and groin, and those behind them tripped over their bodies.

There was the monkey! The coward who had escaped torture. He stood beside a smaller man, and Flat-Nose went at him.

He lashed his spear at the small man to move him out of the way, and the weakling ran to the side. Good. Flat-Nose turned to the one-eyed Ibandi and jabbed—

And roared as one-eye flinched to the side, body moving faster than his mind, twisting away from a spear thrust. The smaller man had danced out and in, in the instant Flat-Nose's attention had wavered.

Before he could move, Flat-Nose was forced to the side as the eager young ones behind him pushed through, and by the time he spun and forced his way back to the gap, he saw his two men beyond the gap speared by six Ibandi without landing a single blow in their own defense.

But every time they tried to work through, spears bristled in their faces. The gap was so narrow that only two of their fighters could attack at a time, but on the far side, four of the Ibandi filth poked spears at them.

They were not strong or fast. But Flat-Nose stabbed at one, and as he did, a spear from the other jabbed up into his armpit. He barely managed to get his arm down in time, and even his slight deflecting turn nearly exposed his armpit to a stab from the right. Blocking it gave the other monkeys a chance to slash his cheek. He backed away, blinking and wiping blood out of his eyes.

As well as any man could be in such a horrible place and time, Frog was happy. To his right was Fire Ant. To his left, Uncle Snake. For the first time in their lives, they fought side by side by side.

The Mk*tk were packed tightly here as they tried to force their way through the spot where the walls narrowed. Ibandi spears drove them back. And those spears were not only sharp and well positioned but some were also dipped in the juice of the poison grub and the red-jawed fire beetle mixed with the gray, sour-smelling bark of the stinger bush. This place belonged to the Ibandi. If the Mk*tk wanted it, they would have to take it.

Snake and Leopard Paw worked as a team, drawing a Mk*tk in, stabbing with poisoned spears. It was not honorable. It was not a thing ordinarily done to men. But the Ibandi were not a people of war, and they had no traditions for times such as this.

They had run as far and as fast as they could, and the Mk*tk had followed them. The attackers did not deserve to be treated as men. So, for the first time in Ibandi history, the poison used on animals was used on men.

A single scratch was death.

Snake fought with courage and with the speed of the hunt chief he had once dreamed of becoming, the hero he had dreamed of being since childhood.

Here, where the walls closed in, Frog fought with the men of his family, bleeding, panting, sweating.

Some part of his mind said: *This, this melding of mind and heart, this human dance of fang and flesh . . . It is good.*

Something within him bared its teeth and howled.

Frog. Snake. Ant.

Together.

First, the trap. Then, the poison. Then . . .

Death from above.

Flat-Nose's frustration took flame when the first rock fell.

He glanced up, and barely avoided a crushed skull as a stone crashed down from the top of the canyon, hammering against his shoulder.

God Blood! That *hurt*. A weaker man would have been crippled. Now he saw the truth: most of the Ibandi were above him. He would slaughter them, every one. First, he would see the blood of those on the ground. If he could get close enough to the weaklings, he would be safe from the monkeys above. They hadn't the heart to endanger their own!

But when he again tried to work his way through the narrow gap, Flat-Nose had to step over his brothers' bodies. Some were dead from terrible wounds. Burn them all! The Ibandi spears were in his face again.

The Ibandi had speared four of his men to death, and rocks had crippled or killed two more. Several men rolled on the ground, dazed and in pain, although to Flat-Nose their wounds seemed slight.

Furious, he managed to stab two of the Ibandi, but by now the falling rocks had become a landslide, an avalanche. The Mk*tk had to either push their way through the gap or retreat.

This was wrong! Next to him, his cousin Strong Spear's head swayed to the side as a jagged chunk of stone ripped a flap of his scalp away. For a moment Strong Spear stood blinking tears of blood, then he crumpled to the ground.

"Back!" Flat-Nose screamed. Spears now, falling like bamboo rain.

The Mk*tk ran back, dodging rocks as they went. The cliffs seemed to be feathered with Ibandi, who hurled rocks and cast spears with maddening accuracy.

They would retreat, regroup, and then—

What in the name of God Blood?

There, guarding the entrance to the defile, were the strangest creatures Flat-Nose had ever seen. They walked like men, but their flesh was as pale as bone. While short, they were broader than Ibandi, almost as muscular as Flat-Nose's people.

But as odd as that was, there was worse. *Magic?* Wolves, or things that looked like wolves, snarled at their sides, foam dripping from their muzzles.

For a moment, awe froze Flat-Nose. He barely reacted when one of the pale men lunged like a flea jumping from a hot rock, his spear catching Stone Hand squarely in the chest.

The wolves leaped forward. When his men tried to spear them, they moved away as if they knew what the Mk*tk would do next. If they allowed themselves to be distracted by the wolves for even a moment, the arrows and rocks struck. And if they ignored the wolves, their thighs and ankles were savaged.

Rocks. Arrows. Spears. Wolves. He could not think. Desperately needed a moment to think.

The line of pale, short men stood firm. When the Mk*tk tried to rush the Ibandi, they were driven back. When he tried to retreat, the wolves and the short men attacked from the rear.

And through it all, death rained from above.

Then a rumbling from above them, and a nightmare rain of stone fell in the middle of his men, crushing them. The air filled with dust that blinded and sent his men into coughing fits. Those trapped in the middle were pounded to the ground, arms and legs and skulls splintered.

Up at the top, barely glimpsed through the dust, howling Ibandi. Hunters. Old ones. Women. Even children. Throwing and pushing stones.

Head whirling, hacking up stone dust and half blinded, Flat-Nose screamed, "Fight for God—"

And was trying to work his way forward, attempting to break through the line of wolves and short men, when night fell like a stone.

Chapter Forty-nine

When Frog, Fire Ant, T'Cori and Sister Quiet Water emerged from the back of Giraffe Kill, the sight greeting them was a thing of nightmare. Seven Ibandi sprawled dead, stabbed and broken. T'Cori's father, Water Chant, was slain, speared through the throat. Uncle Snake's left arm was badly gashed, but a thong tied above the wound seemed to have staunched the blood.

No one spoke as they climbed over the fallen rocks. Snake coughed. Around Frog, others hacked up rock dust.

Arms and legs protruded from beneath the stones. Frog counted ten Mk*tk, then another five, and another and another.

A few had escaped the rocks only to be speared or torn by the wolves. Three were still alive, thrashing weakly as the Vokka sawed their throats open.

T'Cori ran to them as they faced the last Mk*tk, a wounded giant with two fingers missing from his left hand. Despite his wounds the Mk*tk had put his back against the rock wall, keeping them at bay with wide swipes of his heavy spear.

A stone-faced Fire Ant used his sling, and the giant slumped to his knees, bleeding from his forehead. The Vokka held his arms and lifted him so that the wolves had access to his throat.

T'Cori leapt up. "No!" she screamed. "He is their leader, Flat-Nose, and he is mine!"

Sister Quiet Water had appeared behind her, seemingly from nowhere at all. She could not take her eyes off the helpless Mk*tk. She said nothing, just staggered to him and stood over him, looking down as if staring into an abyss. No one spoke. No one moved.

A chunk of rock the size of Flat-Nose's head lay half buried in the ground. She stooped and wrapped her arms around it, tugging without effect.

Now, finally, she turned to T'Cori and spoke. "Help me," she said.

T'Cori looked at Frog, who shrugged. This made sense. No one had more right to end this Mk*tk than the two dancers.

A handful of gravel rolled down the embankment above them. Frog shaded his eyes against the sun to see two hunters carrying Stillshadow down to the valley floor. They waited silently until she arrived. The old dream dancer rolled onto her side and then managed to push herself up on one elbow.

She gargled something none of them could hear, then gathered herself, cleared her throat and began again. She raised her hands. "Are my daughters alive?"

"We are here, Mother," T'Cori said.

"We live, Mother," Quiet Water said.

"Would you kill him? Would you rid yourself of demons?" the old woman asked.

"Yes," T'Cori said. She sounded as if she'd swallowed a coal.

"He is the one who ripped you from your place?"

T'Cori swallowed loudly enough for Frog to hear. "Yes," she said.

"You would take your *num* back from him?"

"Yes," T'Cori said again, unable to tear her eyes from the unconscious Mk*tk.

"You would have your children, and their children, be safe for ten tens of generations?"

T'Cori did not answer. No answer was necessary.

"Then," Stillshadow said, "you cannot kill a helpless man. He is no hunter now. Now, he is nothing more than an animal. To take your power back, you must defeat a human being. You must take him as he took you."

T'Cori's shoulders sagged. She stared at Stillshadow in disbelief. "It is not possible."

Then the hunters helped Stillshadow sit upright, and to them she seemed as weightless as an armload of dead leaves. Only her eyes burned with life.

T'Cori sucked in a chestful of air. The tip of her pink tongue moistened her lips, and she gazed at Flat-Nose hungrily.

Beside her, Quiet Water made a low, hungry sound.

"Mother," T'Cori said, "give me dream tea. I will remember the lion dances. I can do this."

"Please, Stillshadow," Sister Quiet Water pled. "Help us. We need dance tea. Make our feet swift."

Stillshadow shook her ancient head. "No. The teacher plants are strong. But if you think your strength comes from them, you lie to yourself. Strength must come from within *you*." She slapped her hands against her lower stomach. "You are not mere flesh and bone. You are that from which flesh and bone is spun. At the very most, teacher plants can point the way to the *jowk*. If you are to do this thing, you must do it from your womb." She touched her seventh eye. "For this generation, and the generations to come. Are you willing to try?"

T'Cori's gaze would have melted rock. The corners of her mouth lifted, but Frog would never have called her expression a smile.

Frog helped drag the helpless Flat-Nose to a weeping wattle tree, binding him upright to its twisted, swaybacked trunk. When the Mk*tk finally awoke, his arms and legs were lashed far apart. He struggled. Frog had personally tied those bonds tight enough to cut the skin. Given time, his hands would die from lack of blood.

He hoped they had time.

Flat-Nose struggled against the leather thongs until his shoulder wound oozed and his torn scalp bled. Flat-Nose thrashed and screamed, and then, at last, only panted and glared at them.

His eyes locked with Frog's. *I would kill you,* they promised. *And I will, given any chance at all.*

"We'll never know," Frog said to him. He did not know what Stillshadow had in mind, but he was quite certain that it did not include giving this monster a chance to kill any more Ibandi. Ever.

The women formed a circle and began to drum.

As the sun peaked and fell, T'Cori and Quiet Water danced. Stillshadow sat upright, refusing to allow anyone to help or support her as she sang endlessly of rocks and earth, of birth and death, the changing of seasons and the creation of all things.

T'Cori and Quiet Water twirled and stamped. The men brought their drums and slapped palms against the membranes. The hollow, booming calls echoed against the valley walls.

Their Vokka friends joined as well, their voices and simple hollow-log drums calling rhythm with the others.

Frog danced in place, feeling the drumbeats burning through him, taking him into the song itself. He tried to feel his way to its heart. What was this song? What was this ceremony? He didn't know, but he felt his thoughts sucked away like bubbles into a whirlpool.

In a strange way, even the screams of the lashed Mk*tk captive blended into the same song, until the members of three tribes filled Shadow Valley's bowl with their screams and calls and music.

And in the middle of it were the two dancing women. Exhausted, Frog and the other male dancers fell to the side, but T'Cori and Quiet Water danced on, as if guided by something beyond their own strength and will.

Dizzy and sick with fatigue, Frog feared for his mate.

Surely this, on top of everything else that had happened, was too much. Surely . . .

But as T'Cori staggered, and almost fell, something was happening. As her body grew weaker, Stillshadow, even without sight, seemed to sense every misstep. When T'Cori fell to her knees, dripping sweat into the sand, Stillshadow's voice rose with scorn, driving her student upright once again.

When Quiet Water vomited in exhaustion, Stillshadow mocked her weakness, commanded her to stand once again.

As the sky darkened and the infinite eyes of Father Mountain and Great Mother opened in the sky above them, T'Cori seemed to molt, shedding her human aspect.

This was not the woman that he loved. Quiet Water was not the kind healer they had known. It was as if the two women were empty shells and now something very different was emerging from within.

If he believed in such things, Frog would have said he was peering *through* their flesh into the living fire within.

The Vokka wolves howled along to the drumbeats, as if recognizing T'Cori and Quiet Water as their own.

And all the time Flat-Nose watched them, his arms suspended above him. As T'Cori gained strength where there should have been none, as Quiet Water lost her air of injured desperation and became a woman of fire, something grew in Flat-Nose's face, something that Frog had never seen before.

Could the wrinkle between the hooded eyes be *fear*?

What did the old woman see? In her blindness, did her inner vision ignore the flesh? And if so, what did she see in T'Cori's *num*-field? In Quiet Water's?

In Flat-Nose's?

Just past midnight, without any signal, the drummers ceased to play and the singers silenced their voices. The two women, eyes dilated and sweat dried, stood panting, staring blindly into the darkness. Their hands were crooked like claws.

"Cut him down," Stillshadow said. "Give him his spear."

"No!" Frog shook himself out of his own trance, unable to believe what he had just heard. He had supposed that T'Cori might stab a bound Mk*tk in some bloody ritual of vengeance. Freed, even an unarmed Mk*tk would be an insane risk. But *armed*? Before he could leap to her defense, three Ibandi jumped upon him, threw him to the ground and held him there.

T'Cori turned, and her eyes met his with an impact like a blow beneath his heart. For an instant, he saw something else in her . . . or she *was* something else. His eyes had betrayed him, were telling his mind something impossible. He could not see her body, just her head, her head grown as large as her body had been, almost as if it had been carved from a boulder.

He blinked, and she was once again the woman he loved.

"Give Flat-Nose his spear," she said. The voice from his woman's lips seemed not her own. It seemed . . .

It could not be, but it seemed . . .

He looked over at Stillshadow, who sat staring at T'Cori, lips curled into a small, dry smile as they moved continuously, saying things that no one in this world could hear.

Fire Ant sawed the leather thongs on Flat-Nose's right arm. The Mk*tk snarled as his wrist came free, and Ant dared not loosen his left. Nor did he need to: Flat-Nose ripped the left thong free, and then those on his ankles. He flexed his left hand, pausing to stare at the stumps of his missing fingers.

Ant threw his spear into the soil at the Mk*tk's feet. Flat-Nose stared at it, slow to comprehend. Then he wrenched it from the ground. Frog recoiled from the sound, struggled again against the hands pressing him into the ground.

Hot, stinging tears flowed into the soil beneath his face. He blinked until his vision cleared. If this was the death of love, he wished to burn the vision into his soul.

He longed to know what hell was, because when he rose, he was going to kill Stillshadow. If that was not enough to damn his soul, he could not imagine what was.

The air seemed to crackle, as if it was on fire.

The Mk*tk watched in confusion as T'Cori and Quiet Water grasped a spear, and advanced upon him. Incredulous, his mouth hanging half open dumbly, he watched. Not until Quiet Water drew blood from his ribs was he even able to move.

T'Cori watched her body without controlling it. She felt as if that physical shell was a child's plaything, controlled by some force she had never really known. Something that had always known her.

Flat-Nose was stronger, faster, more skilled, more savage than any Ibandi male. And it did not matter.

She felt no fear, only a kind of hazed curiosity, as if she viewed everything through smoke, while her body went its own way.

How strange.

She saw Flat-Nose's arm stab and sweep at Quiet Water in a blur that looked a bit like what happened if she stared at the sun and then closed her eyes, watching the orange disk against the blackness.

Real-unreal.

Blink.

The slashing swipe had not happened yet. She moved before he did, but her spear reached him as his motion commenced, exposing his armpit.

She saw him lash that spear back toward her, saw Quiet Water respond, dancing, dancing. Lunging.

She blinked.

No. It had not happened yet. Her body ducked as a slashing blow cleft the air above her head. Flat-Nose roared with pain.

Quiet Water's spear had struck home.

Flat-Nose stepped back, rubbed his left hand against his ribs, and then stared at it. His blood felt sticky as he smeared it between his fingers. He had seen his blood before, many times. Why was this time different?

He had felt fear before. All men did. It was a natural thing. But what he felt now was very different. Fear and *shame.* He could not die like this. Not like *this.*

These were *women.* Just women. This could not be happening. Their spears were not poisoned, but his limbs felt as if they were filled with stones.

Anger could kill fear. This he had always known. This he had learned from his father and grandfather, almost before he could walk.

He found the anger and let it consume him.

Screaming, he sprang at them.

It was a nightmare. No matter how swiftly he moved, he could not touch them. It was like trying to spear smoke. It was not that they were so fast . . . the women simply *were not there* when he struck. If he focused his attention upon one, the other stabbed. If he turned, in the moment his attention flickered, the other spear was in his thigh or ribs or gouging his neck.

He swung and kicked. The women were like willows, bending and twisting out of the way. They nicked his tendons.

His right heel bled. His shoulder was gashed almost to the bone.

Throwing caution to the winds he charged the smaller woman, the one who had killed his brother and jumped into the river. He would destroy her, even if the other one stabbed him in the back. He could survive a wound from one of these women. Then, with only one enemy to defeat, he could turn all his rage upon her.

Even if she killed him from behind, such a coward's blow would not diminish him in the eyes of the mighty God Blood.

But the small one melted away in front of him. When he charged, she knelt, bracing the butt of her weapon upon the ground, the point threatened his groin.

Screaming frustration, he skidded on his heels and blocked it, but even before his arm swept down hers was rising, as if she had known what he was going to do even before he did it, stabbing him so deeply in the upper arm that as he reared back, it wrenched the spear from her hand.

Desperate now, Flat-Nose pulled her spear out of his flesh. Blood pulsed from the wound. His hand was numb. He opened and closed it, but it had no strength.

Pain!

The larger one had just smashed a stone into the back of his head, and was ducking even as he spun to strike.

Pain!

The small one had a new spear, and his right leg, speared three times now, was finally buckling.

Another stone, this one to the side of his head, and he staggered, the night exploding with stars that burned like suns.

He groaned, turning toward the larger woman, and the smaller one smashed the other side of his head. Suddenly, he no longer possessed the strength even to raise his arms.

No! This could not be happening! It could not. It—

Chapter Fifty

Flat-Nose lay bleeding, exhausted, his scalp torn and matted with blood. He groaned, but could not rise.

Frog could not believe his eyes.

Fire Ant stood motionless beside him, staring at T'Cori as if she were the face of Great Mother.

And perhaps, Frog told himself, *just perhaps she actually was.*

Stillshadow reached out to the hunters at her sides. They pulled her erect. She hobbled to the prostrate Flat-Nose.

"Hold him," she said. Despite his wounds and fatigue, as they laid hands upon the defeated Mk*tk his body convulsed violently. It took four of them to hold his limbs. Stillshadow pulled his loincloth aside and extended her other hand.

"Knife," she said.

Without hesitation, Leopard Paw handed her his blade. Her arm swept down, and Flat-Nose screamed.

Frog turned his head.

When he looked back, Stillshadow was handing T'Cori a small chunk of bloody meat. T'Cori stood hugging her sister, both completely exhausted. "For your medicine bag," she said. "Dry it. Keep it, always. His power is now yours."

Then she handed another chunk to Quiet Water. "For yours."

"Fire," she said to Uncle Snake. He handed her a burning branch. She thrust it between Flat-Nose's legs. As he writhed, in a cold flat voice she said, "so you will not bleed to death."

He thrashed and snapped at her as she took his right eye, and the tendons of his right wrist, once again searing the flesh with fire.

"Translate for me," she said to Quiet Water, after the shrieks had died to groans. "Tell him I do this not because it gives me pleasure, but because it is the only language the Mk*tk understand. Tell him to return to his people. Tell him that our women can now kill his men. Tell him that if they ever return to our lands, we will kill them all and burn their bones. Tell him!"

Although barely able to stand, Quiet Water spoke in a guttural, barking voice. Flat-Nose's head lolled to the side, coughing blood. Frog wondered if he had bitten his tongue.

Then the four hunters released Flat-Nose, who crawled a hand of paces, then staggered to his feet. He looked back at them, his single eye vast and dark, then disappeared into the shadows.

When Frog turned to speak to Stillshadow, she had collapsed. The old woman's blind eyes stared up into the night clouds, "Cloud Stalker . . ." she whispered. "I come."

T'Cori and Sister Quiet Water knelt and cradled Stillshadow's gray head between them. She said nothing more but smiled up at them. For a moment Frog swore that her dead eyes focused on the dream dancers.

Just for a moment . . .

Stillshadow balanced above the burning ocean, the jowk. *It churned, containing all forms and no form. Within it, she saw everything she had ever known and loved that had passed on, as well as everything that would ever be born.*

It gaped for her, and she felt a flash of fear, uncertainty. No. It was not her time. . . .

Then, out of the chaos, a face she knew.

A face she loved.

"Cloud Stalker," she whispered.

His arms opened for her, and after a moment's hesitation, she returned the embrace.

The jowk, *she thought, there being a final time for all things. The Kori. Nothing.*

Everything.

Chapter Fifty-one

Drifting fingers of acrid smoke clutched at Frog's nose, at the valley walls. After the Mk*tk corpses were burned in bonfires, their bones would be scattered. *God Mountain would not want them,* he thought.

The Ibandi buried their own dead in the valley floor, that their flesh might run into the earth and their spirits flow to Great Sky, where, Sky Woman said, Father Mountain would give them new bones.

Fire Ant had died in Giraffe Kill. He and his brother, dead in Shadow Valley. Dead securing their new home for their tribe's children and children's children. The Vokka sprinkled his grave with flower petals.

Stillshadow was burned upon her sitting stone, that her spirit might rise to Father Mountain more swiftly. Then her bones were buried. Father Mountain and Great Mother would give the holy one new bones, strong bones, that she might dance with them, and Cloud Stalker, until the end of days.

The Vokka had lost two of their own and one wolf. Both two- and four-legged were buried amid somber songs and the graves heaped with fragrant flower clusters. The Ibandi stood respectfully behind them, humming along to the songs and swaying in rhythm to their dance. Only the dream dancers understood the words, but the emotions needed no translation.

After the sad singing ended, the Vokka whooped and began to dance. For folk such as these strange pale ones, sadness was not meant to last. Death begat new life. The night was only the hiding place of a new and better day.

They urged and cajoled the Ibandi into dancing with them, until the journey up to the campground was a moving celebration. Fire Ant and Uncle Snake remained behind with Frog. "They bled for us," Snake said. "To save us, they lost two of their own."

"These are not friends," Ant said. "They are family now, or I do not understand the word." He examined his uncle's wounded left arm, torn by a Mk*tk spear. Muscle had been severed but not tendons. He doubted Snake would hunt again, but that was not a bad thing: it was time for Uncle Snake to teach the young ones, make spears and join the elder's council.

"Uncle," Frog said, "you are a hero, or I do not understand that word either."

Snake's eyes filled and spilled as Gazelle Tears pressed herself against his back, wrapping her arms around his waist. He leaned back, resting his neck against the top of her head. "You have always been the smartest of us, Frog. What a son I have." He grasped Ant's shoulder. "What *sons* I have."

Snake and Gazelle Tears left Ant and Frog together. Frog finally seemed to realize that his brother was staring at him, and had been for some time.

"What?" he asked.

"I just realized that I never knew you, Frog."

Frog said nothing.

Ant heard the wind whistling high through the branches and smelled the smoke from the distant bonfires. So much death, in the service of life. He found the strength to smile. "I would like to spend the rest of my life undoing that mistake."

"Long life to us both," Frog replied.

They danced that day, and into the night. Shared meat and honey and song and touch, one with another. The Ibandi children came close to the wolves, who let them feel their fur and, rather than biting, gave them licks and playful nudges.

And the next morning, two wolves stayed in the Ibandi camp, and from that time on, Ibandi and Vokka moved back and forth between the camps as if they were family.

As Fire Ant had said. As in time, they became.

At dusk on the second day following their great victory, T'Cori and Quiet Water stood before a roaring fire and addressed the tribe.

"We have been blessed to live. The Mk*tk who chased us are dead. The one who lives carries our message: *Our women are not prey. We are not prey.*"

Quiet Water stalked the circle, a cold and terrible smile twisting her lips. "I shattered his egg," she said. "His body is mine."

They spoke of many things that night, weaving a picture of the future they could have here in the valley, if only they kept heart. Fire Ant's men pledged to remain. No one spoke of abandoning their new home, only questioning where in the vast valley they might best build their first boma.

The singing and dancing and speaking continued until the children were asleep on their parents' laps and it was time to put them to bed.

T'Cori's sisters kissed her. "I dreamed of knowing Great Sky Woman," Morning Thunder said. "I never hoped to stand with my sister."

"We have many days to stand and dance and dream together," T'Cori said to Thunder and Flower. The three women hugged, then her sisters returned to their families.

As the others drifted away, Kiya brought T'Cori the infant that the dream dancer had borne in her body and given away for safekeeping.

"We gave her a name," Kiya signed and said, "we call her Naya. Friend."

"A good name," T'Cori said and touched the child. No tears. No sign of sorrow. A gift is a gift. *You are not just a mother. You are chief dream dancer. Dream dancers give their children away. Their bodies, and the fruits of their bodies, belong only to Great Mother.*

But she knew in her heart she was lying.

Kiya's face crinkled in a smile. She spoke and gestured. "I wonder . . ."

"Yes?"

"It might be good for a child to have two mothers. To have two people. We named her, so she is ours. I think you would like to raise your daughter. I think that this would be a good thing."

And so saying, handed the squirming bundle to T'Cori.

The dancer could not keep the tears from her eyes. "Now I owe you," she said.

"In time," Kiya said, "I am sure you will find a way to pay."

Chapter Fifty-two

That night, for the first time in almost three days, T'Cori slept.

Her dreams were not her own. She felt like a spider in the middle of a web that reached from horizon to horizon and beyond.

All the dream dancers who lived, or had ever lived, were part of that web, like jeweled dew in the moonlight.

These were not *her* dreams. They were Stillshadow's. They were the dreams of every chief dancer. Vaguely, she could sense that there were other women, from other tribes, clustered just out of her sight. The world was larger than she had ever thought, and smaller.

She dreamed that she saw the future of her people, and it was one of peace and prosperity. And knew in her bones that this was no dream but a glimpse of the world they had earned by faith and courage.

There . . . *there*. She raced along the web until she found a familiar face, voice . . . until she found a place where the *jowk* took human form as someone she knew well, Wind Willow.

Her sister dream dancer Willow was sleeping, dreaming in her hut on Great Earth. Waiting.

Sister Willow, T'Cori said. *All is well. Tell the people. Tell them to come to Shadow Valley. If their hunting is poor, if they wish new sights, and to meet new friends . . .*

Tell them the Circle has grown.

• • •

When Frog awoke the next morning, he felt a deep and fulfilling contentment. His brother was his brother again. His family was whole and safe,
T'Cori at his side with Medicine Mouse and Naya nursing at her breasts. It
was difficult even to imagine hunger or thirst in a place such as this.

And he knew that his fear, and constant obsessive training, had birthed
something that had never existed before. A meld of hunt and dance, male
and female, life and death. Men and women who were not just hunters or
dancers . . . capable of waging war without losing their hearts.

Warriors.

That was what he had created.

It was a new thing. A good thing. He sighed, a deep, thorough sigh.

The happiest sigh of his life.

"Good morning, my love," he said.

"Good morning, my life," she replied, and kissed him.

"I have been thinking of Great Sky and Great Earth," he said finally. "We
need to—"

"It is done," she said.

"What do you mean? The people need to know—"

"They know," she said. "Everything is safe."

"We need to teach them—"

She smiled. "It is done."

He gazed into her wide, placid eyes, and . . . the voices of fear within him
faded. Died. It was the strangest thing. It was a new thing.

"Yes," Frog said. "Then . . . it is good?"

"Yes. Everything is good. Everything is perfect."

Frog did not understand. "You lost your mother," he said.

"I never had a mother," T'Cori replied.

He stared at her, uncertain. "Stillshadow," he said. "She was your mother.
Your teacher."

T'Cori shook her head. "Stillshadow was not my mother. She was not
my teacher."

"Then . . . what was she?"

Within their shadowed hut, her eyes were focused on something far
away, beyond the valley walls. Beyond Great Sky and Great Earth. Beyond
Frog and Mouse and Naya and the things of this world. "She was me."

Was it his imagination, or did her eyes seem a bit darker than they had
just a moon ago?

If Ant and Snake could find healing, what of Frog? What wound was
there for him to close? Only one, the one torn in his soul by the emptiness

atop Great Sky. He now knew the meaning of that emptiness. And that if his curse was to be the only one to see it, it was his responsibility to fill it or walk his life in a shadow deep enough to devour thought and hope and happiness.

Only one thing could fill a void so deep and terrifying.

He took his woman into his arms and, feeling her heartbeat against his own, knew he had made the right choice.

"What is it, Frog?" she said. "Something just changed in you. I see it in your *num*."

He laughed, aflame with a joy bright enough to banish any darkness. "I do not know if I believe in *num*. Or *jowk* or gods," he said at last. "But I believe in you."

Afterword

Six years of research have gone into the tale of the Ibandi, contained in the two books *Great Sky Woman* and *Shadow Valley*.

Before I go any further, I would like to thank the three most important women in the project's life: my wonderful editor Betsy Mitchell, who set everything in motion, guided with a light hand and ensured I always had the necessary time and resources. There is no one better in your field, as either an editor or a human being.

To Eleanor Woods, my agent, who has been with me from the beginning. How incredible it is that my first professional contact still has a guiding presence in my life.

And my wife, Tananarive Due. Meeting you was the completion of one entire act in the story of my life, and the beginning of another. Every day has been filled with wonders and miracles. But even if I didn't believe in such things, I would believe in you.

That research involved travel to most of the locations in this story but extended to books such as *Specimens of Bushman Folklore* collected by W. H. I. Bleek and L. C. Lloyd, *Africa's Great Rift Valley* by Nigel Pavitt and *When the Drummers Were Women* by Layne Redmond.

I would like to thank Harley Reagan, Diane Nightbird and the facilitators of the 2002 Aura Perception Analysis workshop in Phoenix, Arizona.

Jon Wagner, Ph.D., professor of anthropology at Knox College, and his wife, Jan Lundeen, of Carl Sandburg College, were incredibly gracious to provide opinions and information for this project. They warned me often of the degree to which I bent anthropological data to a novelist's needs: any transgressions are solely my responsibility. Hopefully, while many rules were bent, none were actually broken beyond repair.

Extinct Humans by Ian Tattersall and Jeffrey H. Schwartz was a phenomenal resource. Could Neanderthals have traveled as far as central Africa? The experts I consulted with opined that, while there is no evidence they did, it is certainly within the realm of possibility. A fantasist can ask nothing more. At any rate, it was certainly fun, and I hope that readers will indulge the presence of the Vokka, strangers far from their homeland.

I have to mention *Nisa, the Life and Words of a !Kung Woman* by Marjorie Shostak, and *Kalahari Hunter-Gatherers,* edited by Richard B. Lee and Irven DeVore. While the Ibandi have greater levels of social organization than most hunter-gatherers of the time, by combining selectively chosen practices of the Koi-San peoples, I was able to create an amalgam who, I hope, would not have been entirely alien to their Upper Paleolithic ancestors. The works of Professor Barbara J. King and Professor Brian M. Fagan, teachers of biological anthropology and the history of ancient civilizations, were extraordinary sources during the germination and structuring of both books. In fact, their Teaching Company lectures set the foundation for my research.

The real Shadow Valley is the Ngorongoro volcanic crater in Tanzania, arguably the finest wildlife preserve in the world, the place where my daughter, Nicki, and I were charged by an elephant, that had been provoked by a crazed tourist.

I confess to using both dramatic and documentary film to tweak memory and imagination. These works include the Imax film *Africa, the Serengeti,* 1980's unique and hysterical *The Gods Must Be Crazy* (whose hero, Kalahari bushman and wonderful natural actor N!xau, died in 2003), Howard Hawks's amazing *Hatari!* (if you haven't seen the giraffe hunt sequence, you must. I doubt anything like it will ever be done again), and countless hours of the National Geographic Channel.

Again, thanks to Gebra Tilda and Djusto, the Chagga tribesmen who shepherded me in Tanzania, and Buck Tilly, station manager for Thomson Safaris, whose facilities and expertise I would recommend without reservation.

One and all: this couldn't have happened without you.

Glendora, California
August 1, 2008
www.lifewrite.com

About the Author

STEVEN BARNES is a prolific author and scriptwriter who has been nominated for Hugo, Cable Ace, and Endeavor awards. His work for television includes episodes of *The Twilight Zone, Outer Limits, Stargate, SG-1,* and *Andromeda.* A lifelong student of human performance technologies, he holds black belts in judo and karate, has lectured at the Smithsonian, has an instructor certificate in Circular Strength Training, and is a trained hypnotherapist. He lives in Los Angeles with his wife, novelist Tananarive Due.

About the Type

This book was set in Garamond, a typeface originally designed by the Parisian typecutter Claude Garamond (1480–1561). This version of Garamond was modeled on a 1592 specimen sheet from the Egenolff-Berner foundry, which was produced from types assumed to have been brought to Frankfurt by the punchcutter Jacques Sabon.

Claude Garamond's distinguished romans and italics first appeared in *Opera Ciceronis* in 1543–44. The Garamond types are clear, open, and elegant.